UNTAMED HEARTS

"Easy on the Heart"

By Jodi Thomas, *USA Today* bestselling author of
When a Texan Gambles

Trying to rein in his three matchmaking sisters, cowboy
Cooper Adams finds the woman of his dreams where he least
expects it . . .

"Coming Home"

By Patricia Potter, *USA Today* bestselling author of *Cold Target*

A confiscated Texas ranch gives spinster Beth McGuire and
her carpetbagger father a second chance. Until the rightful
owner comes marching home, ready to claim his land—and
Beth's heart . . .

"Tombstone Tess"

By Emily Carmichael, national bestselling author of
Becoming Georgia

Tough-talking, hard-riding Tess McCabe is one of Arizona's
most ineligible females, but if she doesn't get hitched in six
months, she'll lose her ranch. She's got to rope herself a temporary husband—no romance required . . .

"Finding Home"

By Maureen McKade, author of *His Unexpected Wife*

It's been ten years since horse breaker Winston Taylor rode
out of Caitlin Brice's life. Yet he's the only man who can save
her stable's future—

D0032178

How To Lasso A Cowboy

Jodi Thomas
Patricia Potter
Emily Carmichael
Maureen McKade

JOVE BOOKS, NEW YORK

These are works of fiction. Names, characters, places, and incidents either are the product of the authors' imaginations or are used fictitiously, and any resemblance to actual persons living or dead, business establishments, events, or locales is entirely coincidental.

HOW TO LASSO A COWBOY

A Jove Book / published by arrangement with the authors

PRINTING HISTORY
Jove edition / June 2004

Collection copyright © 2004 by The Berkley Publishing Group.
"Easy on the Heart" copyright © 2004 by Jodi Koumalats.
"Coming Home" copyright © 2004 by Patricia Potter.
"Tombstone Tess" copyright © 2004 by Emily Krokosz.
"Finding Home" copyright © 2004 by Maureen Webster.
Excerpt from "A Texan's Luck" by Jodi Thomas copyright © 2004 by Jodi Koumalats.
Excerpt from "To Find You Again" by Maureen McKade copyright © 2004 by Maureen Webster.
Book design by Julie Rogers.

ISBN: 0-515-13771-5

A JOVE BOOK ®
Jove Books are published by The Berkley Publishing Group,
a division of Penguin Group (USA) Inc.,
375 Hudson Street, New York, New York 10014.
JOVE and the "J" design
are trademarks belonging to Penguin Group (USA) Inc.

PRINTED IN THE UNITED STATES OF AMERICA

10 9 8 7 6 5 4 3 2 1

Contents

Easy on the Heart

✪

JODI THOMAS

Chapter One

THUNDERCLOUDS HUNG LOW along the western sky, darkening Cooper Adams's mood even further than the rock bottom he had started the day with. He stared out the grimy window of the saloon, waiting for a stage he feared would arrive on time. He was blessed with the best stretch of freshwater rangeland in Texas, and cursed with three sisters whose mission seemed to be to make his life hell.

Downing the last of his drink, Cooper thought of his ranch hands pulling double duty with a dozen sick cattle in Echo Canyon, threats of flash flooding along the breaks, and rumors of rustlers. The last thing he needed was another visit from his old maid sisters.

He knew why they were coming. The three had finished raising him when their parents died before Cooper turned ten and next month he would be thirty without a wife. The fact he had more important things to worry about than finding a bride never crossed their minds. The army in petticoats would arrive to fight for Cooper as they had all his life, even if they had to battle him on their quest to make him happy and settled.

Happy. Cooper almost laughed at the word. For him there was no such place. What did it matter if he were wed or single? The world would not suddenly become peaceful, there would still be more work than hours of daylight, and nightmares would continue to rush through his dreams. All that mattered to him was the ranch, the new colt he'd bred from the Steeldust line, and selling enough cattle up north to make it through the winter.

In truth, Cooper favored the overall idea of marriage and family. It was women in general he disliked. They were chatty, confusing, helpless, and costly. Somewhere there had to be a woman with more redeeming qualities than irritating ones, but he had no time to look for her.

He poured himself another shot of whiskey, walked out on the saloon's porch, and watched the roots of his aversion to the fairer sex climb off the noon stage. His sisters, dusty but determined angels of matrimony. Three old maids who were worried about him.

He gulped the last of his drink and walked across the muddy street to the stage.

The sisters saw his bachelorhood as a curse and the death of the family name, yet they viewed their own single status as a blessing. After all, they had each other and enough inheritance to live comfortably in their small house in Dallas.

Cooper studied them as he neared, guessing that when they had been in their prime, no man got a word in between them to pop the question. Or maybe any suitor was frightened away with the possibility that he might have to take the whole batch if he proposed to one.

Smiling, Cooper watched the trio order the stage driver to hurry with the luggage lest they get wet in the downpour that was sure to come any minute. This was their fourth trip up from Dallas since spring and Cooper knew he would have them on his hands until the first good frost this time. Then, the bedding plants back home somehow upstaged any mission.

Cooper glanced at the clouds, wishing for an early winter. He might as well stop swearing under his breath and make the best of their visit. There was nothing he could do to stop them, short of moving to the Oklahoma Territory.

"Cooper!" Emma shouted when she spotted him moving toward them. "Oh, Cooper, we're here. We made it! Can you believe it? We're finally here."

He laughed to himself. Emma hadn't said anything that wasn't obvious to the rest of the world since she learned to talk. Somehow, she believed that if she did not tell everyone the sun was shining or it might rain no one else in the family would notice. She was a town crier in a village where everyone could see the clock.

"Welcome, Emma, how was your trip?" Cooper took her bag.

Before Emma could answer, Johanna heaved a small trunk toward Cooper without bothering to greet him. "Oh, don't ask Emma," Cooper's oldest sister shouted. "I don't think I can bear to relive one moment of this day."

"Hello, Johanna." Cooper shouldered her luggage. If a six-foot statue could come to life and wear a bonnet, he was sure she would look just like Johanna, all starch and glory. "The wagon is right over here. I'll have you home before the rain sets in."

She retrieved her hatbox and traveling Bible from the coach and marched to the surrey Cooper had bought a few years earlier for the sole purpose of hauling the three old maids.

"The ride from Dallas *was* horrible," Emma whispered, determined to tell her story. Though she looked much like Johanna, nothing about Emma was quite as polished. Not so tall, not so proper, not so proud in her bearing. "A man smoked right in front of Johanna without even bothering to ask if he could, then when we switched stages in Sherman, the driver seemed determined to hit every hole in the road." She shook her head, making her tiny wire glasses dance on her nose. "I thought Johanna would surely climb up beside him and instruct him on how to drive a team. Winnie could have done a better job with the stage, and we all know how Winnie drives."

Grinning, Cooper nodded. Winnie was the only sister who'd bothered to learn to drive a team and all she had gotten was criticism for her effort.

Cooper helped both Johanna and Emma into the buggy then turned back to fetch the youngest of the three, Winnie. If Johanna was a grand harbor statue, Emma her copy, then poor Winnie was only a tugboat circling round them both. She was short, broad in the beam, and forever whistling slightly as she hurried along out of breath.

He found her behind the stage surrounded by luggage. "Welcome, Winnie." He leaned down so he could see beneath the brim of her lopsided hat.

"Hello, Cooper Boy." She grinned, shyly patting his cheek as if he were still a child. "You're looking very handsome today."

"I hope all these aren't yours." He glanced around at the bags, trying not to let on that her pet name bothered him. He'd struggled for six years to carve a ranch out of this wild land and, before that, he'd fought the Yankees in a war he thought would never end. The name "Cooper Boy" didn't fit, but he could not bring himself to hurt Winnie's feelings by telling her so. He also figured any hint of being handsome had long been weathered from him by life's storms. His sandy-colored hair was already salted with gray at the temples and worry lines usually plowed across his forehead.

"Oh, no, only one bag is mine." Winnie continued her search. "At least, that's all I remember packing. Johanna said I should buy a new traveling bag, and I did just before we left. Now I can't remember just what it looked like. It was licorice black. No, cocoa gray. No, it might have been chocolate brown."

"Come on along, Winnie!" Emma scolded from the buggy. "We are waiting on you. It's sure to rain before we make it to Cooper's place. And once it rains, that road will be nothing more than a muddy lake."

Winnie lifted her dusty, purple skirt a few inches and hurriedly circled the luggage as if they were yard chickens and she could eventually catch one.

Grabbing what he thought looked to be the newest bag, Cooper held it up. "This one?"

"Yes." Winnie smiled. "That must be it. Brown. I remember now. It was walnut brown."

Cooper offered his arm and finally escorted his last sister to the surrey. He'd been drinking the hour he waited for the stage and now wished he had arrived even earlier at the saloon. There would be no more hard liquor in the house until his sisters departed. He wasn't a man given overly to spirits, but his sisters' visits usually went well when seen through a whiskey fog.

He maneuvered the horses past the flimsy buildings of Main Street with Johanna telling him how to drive, Emma commenting that Winnie was always the last to do everything, and Winnie attempting to open her new bag.

Twenty minutes later, when they arrived at the ranch house, the conversation hadn't changed and Winnie was still trying to get into her new luggage.

"Need some help?" he whispered as he guided her down from the surrey.

"No." She laughed. "I love a puzzle. The man who sold this to me told me the secret of opening it. I just seem to have forgotten."

Emma climbed off the bench making the same statement she always made when returning from town. "I'll never understand why they call that settlement Minnow Springs. There are no springs anywhere close to town and a minnow would die of thirst around here."

Cooper didn't bother to ask why his sisters had come. They invaded regularly, like a colony of ants, constantly on the march. He knew he'd have his answers soon enough.

When he sat down to supper, Johanna began her campaign as she opened her dinner prayer. "Dear Lord, thank you for allowing us to arrive safely on our mission to help our poor brother to find a mate."

"Amen." Winnie lifted her fork, then reconsidered when Johanna only opened one eye.

"And Lord," the oldest sister continued, "help us in our quest so that our brother will be fruitful and multiply."

"Amen," Winnie whispered again and managed to stab a piece of roast before Johanna continued.

"And thank you, Lord, for this meal. And bless it to our bodies *before* we eat it."

Winnie stopped chewing.

"Amen," Johanna said while Cooper fought down a laugh.

Winnie continued eating, but Johanna lifted her fork and paused, waiting until she had Cooper's full attention before speaking. "We've been talking, Cooper, dear, and have decided we've been wrong in our efforts to help you find a bride." She glanced at Emma and waited for her nod of agreement before continuing. "I had thought we could find a nice girl and introduce her to you and let nature take its course."

"But nature doesn't seem to be cooperating," Emma interjected. Raising an eyebrow at Cooper, she added, "In your case, nature seems more dead than alive. Don't you know one woman in these parts who is irresistible? Someone who makes your heart race? A girl you simply can't live without?"

"Don't get carried away, Emma," Johanna snapped. "I swear to goodness, sometimes you're as silly as Winnie. What we need here is a woman to be his partner in working the ranch. One with strong bones so she can have a large family. You sound like he is looking for someone to be the death of him."

Cooper thought of the unlucky women his sisters had managed to drag home so far. One who was too frightened to talk; one, still in her teens, who giggled every time Cooper looked her direction; and the final candidate, who swore she was only twenty-eight but looked twice that age. They were all quite easy to resist.

Before he could take a breath and hope that they'd given up their quest, Johanna destroyed any possibility.

"We decided we should launch a full campaign before it is too late and you are past your prime."

Emma agreed and added, "Once a man's past thirty, he begins to fall apart. Losing hair in spots, gaining it in others. Making strange sounds and talking about his youth like it was something to brag on."

Johanna interrupted her sister. "We have come up with a plan that cannot fail. I'll invite every unmarried woman in the county to a party. Then you can pick one and save time. You've a house and barn big enough to hold everyone. If it takes feeding them all to find you a bride, we're up to the task." Johanna raised her fork a few inches higher. "Your sisters will not let you down."

Emma wasn't following the call. She stared at the ceiling and added, "A ball would be nice. A grand ball with dancing and tea cakes." She glanced at Johanna, obviously trying to read her sister. "But maybe a country ball would have to do. An all-day event, with barbecue and square dancing," Emma added, coloring her vision. "Cooper will have plenty of opportunity in the course of an entire day to get to know the right young lady and won't feel like we're rushing him into anything. They could sit on the porch and watch the sunset and dance in one another's arms."

"I'll make my famous potato salad," Winnie said, finally joining in the conversation, "if I can remember the recipe." Emma might be moving through her dream night, but Winnie has stopped at the food table.

Emma looked over her glasses at her younger sister and frowned. "I hope so, Winnie. Are you aware that you are still wearing your traveling clothes? Johanna and I changed hours ago."

Winnie nodded, but made no explanation. After all, Emma wasn't really asking a question, only stating a fact.

Cooper didn't need to think the idea over. "No. I've no time for parties. I'm up to my ears in trouble out here and winter's coming on. Right now every rancher, including me, is rounding up cattle for one last drive north. There can be no country ball. Not at this time."

Looking at his sisters, he realized no one was listening to him. Emma and Johanna had already started a list of things they must do and Winnie was trying to remember her potato salad recipe while she ate. Between bites she mumbled ingredients.

"I said no!" He raised his voice. "It's impossible." He couldn't think about hosting a party or finding a wife right now. He had all he could handle running the ranch. They were crazy to think he'd find one of the local girls irresistible over barbecue and Winnie's potato salad. There wasn't a woman in the county he wanted to face over breakfast for the rest of his life and it was time they all came to terms with the fact.

Johanna stared at him as if she'd forgotten he was in the room. "Whatever you say, Cooper. After all, you are the man of this house, even if I happen to be almost fifteen years older than you and the three of us raised you as if you were our child from the day Mother and Father died and left you this land."

She went back to her list making. Cooper felt like he'd been sent to the corner. Standing, he walked to the door without commenting that this land had been worthless when he'd finally grown old enough to claim it and that the herd was sold the day after the funeral of their parents to buy the sisters a house in Dallas.

He would have no part of this insane country ball. Life was hard out here. No one had time for that sort of thing. The three sisters had gone too far.

Just as he crammed his hat low and grabbed the doorknob, Winnie's whisper caught his ear. "Anything's possible, Cooper Boy. Something can even happen when you've given up all hope. You turn around one day and suddenly someone you never suspected becomes irresistible." She giggled. "It could happen."

He hurried out the door not wanting to hear any more. Let them have their dreams and fantasies of balls. He'd seen enough of life to know the truth. There was nothing but hard work around the corner and no dances or wishing would make it any different.

Chapter Two

COOPER DID NOT return until long past when he knew his sisters would be in bed. Part of him felt guilty for destroying their dreams. He tossed his hat on the bench by the door and crossed to his desk in the center of what he called the great room, even though it was not as large or great as he'd planned.

His desk was his favorite place in the house, though. From its vantage point, he could see every room.

As he leaned into the give of his leather chair, he thought of the winter of '63 when he'd been ill with fever and heartsick after watching most of his friends die at Chattanooga. His sisters crossed half of Texas and most of Arkansas to reach him. They hounded the doctors at the field hospital until Cooper was released into their care. He was so weak he couldn't walk to the wagon, but they managed to carry him without asking for any help from the exhausted doctors.

Winnie drove. Johanna and Emma sat on either side of him in the back of the wagon. It had taken weeks to reach home and months before he recovered, but they never deserted him.

From his desk he could see down the hallway to the three doors that were his sisters' bedrooms. Four years ago he'd built the house over a dugout his parents had used. He'd planned three children's rooms, but now wondered if they would ever be used as such.

If his sisters wanted a party, maybe he could talk them into coming back over Christmas. Then there would be an excuse for one and it wouldn't look like he was the door prize at the box supper.

Cooper glanced down at a guest list on his desk that Johanna and Emma had already started. Beside each name he could think of at least one reason why he wouldn't want the unmarried daughter or sister as a wife. Men out here outnumbered women several times over and all that was left in most families were the ill-tempered and homely.

Wilson, the rancher south of Cooper, had two daughters of the right age, one with a full mustache, the other with beaver teeth big enough to down a tree within the hour. Smith, a farmer to Cooper's north, had a sister who never missed a chance to visit. The good thing about marrying her might be that her tongue was so sharp she would make any man forget it was cold outside. Her husband would work himself to death to keep from coming home every night. Then there was Miller's . . .

Cooper heard a sound and glanced up from the list. "Winnie?" he asked as his sister hurried toward the kitchen with a blanket wrapped around her shoulders.

She stopped as if she'd been caught while on a secret mission. "I . . . I was just getting your sewing kit," she said without looking at him. "I didn't mean to disturb you."

"That's all right," he said, watching her continue the journey.

A moment later, she reappeared, the cigar box he used as both a sewing and medicine kit in hand. "Cooper Boy," she whispered, as if she feared her sisters might hear her, "could you hitch the buggy for me first thing after breakfast? I could walk to town, but it'll be muddy. I seem to have forgotten a few things and need to make a quick trip."

"Do you want me to drive you?" Winnie wasn't known for turning the right direction and four miles was no short stroll. He would rather take the time to drive her than worry about her until she found her way home. "I need to pick up some lumber in the morning. If you don't mind riding in the work wagon, we could start early."

Winnie smiled. "Oh, no, I don't mind, but just tell the sisters I'm riding along with you. Don't mention my forgetting anything."

Cooper almost felt sorry for Winnie. It must be hard to live all your life with one perfect sister and one who reminded you of all your shortcomings. "You got a deal." He winked at her. "I'll drop you at Debord's General Store, load the lumber, then pick you up. We'll be back before they think to miss us."

"Deal." Winnie almost danced as she hurried away. "Good night. I have to go to bed now. I'm really quite tired." Her blanket blew behind her in full sail.

Cooper mumbled good night and began the paperwork he'd been putting off for a week. An hour later, when he lowered the wick on the lamp, he noticed the light under Winnie's door still shone.

Even so, just after breakfast she was all ready, dressed in her same purple traveling suit, when he pulled the wagon around.

"Certain you want to go?" he whispered. "We're sure to get caught in the rain today. Those clouds have been promising all week and so far all we manage to get are a few sprinkles."

Winnie giggled. "A little rain won't hurt me. Maybe I'll get lucky and shrink."

Neither Johanna nor Emma paid more than passing interest as Winnie climbed up beside Cooper and announced loudly that she was going along for the ride. Winnie was always the extra in the first few days after the sisters invaded Cooper's house. She was never given an assignment in the

cleaning that had to be done before Johanna could relax.
Winnie had always been the extra who was called to do one
task after another while the two generals organized.

But today, Cooper had the funniest feeling Winnie wasn't
running from work, but escaping on some grand adventure.
She talked of how pretty the day seemed even though thunderclouds looked like a mountain range to the west. And
she laughed at nothing as if she were in her teens and not a
woman of almost forty.

He let Winnie out at the general store and picked up the
wood he needed. Cooper took the opportunity to stop in for
one drink, hoping to give Winnie plenty of time to visit. To
his surprise, when he returned to the general store, Mrs.
Debord and her husband said they had not seen her.

Frustrated, Cooper walked out of Debord's General. He
didn't have time to waste looking for Winnie. His sisters
always visited with the Debords like they were old friends
when they came to Minnow Springs. And in truth he usually enjoyed listening to the town gossip on the ride home.
Why would Winnie say she needed things, then not even
bother going inside the store? If he didn't know better, he
would think she had a secret lover somewhere.

Cooper caught himself laughing out loud. Wouldn't that
be a kick to find out Winnie had a lover? If ever there was a
woman born to be the maiden aunt, Winnie fit the bill. Everyone loved her for her sweet, confusing ways, but no man
seemed likely to give her his name.

Cooper gazed along what little there was of the street
everyone called Main. Two saloons, a hotel, a carpenter/un-
dertaker shop, the stage and livery station, the telegraph office, and Woodburn's dilapidated mercantile. Winnie would
never go in one of the saloons. The hotel was not much better. She had no reason to see the undertaker; although sometimes Cooper felt his sisters' schemes might be the death of
him, they all three appeared to be in good health.

That left Woodburn's Mercantile or the stage line. He
headed toward the tiny store, guessing Winnie would have

no business with the stage line. Johanna always booked all reservations and carried the tickets for all three sisters when they traveled.

Few locals went into Woodburn's Mercantile. It was small and offered little choice compared to Debord's General. The front door was so plain anyone might miss it stuffed in between the hotel and the undertaker. Cooper noticed the wind had blown off the last three letters of his sign, making the business look even less prosperous.

Miles Woodburn was a Yankee who'd settled here after the war. Most of his business came from the cattle drives and settlers passing through. He took trade for foodstuffs so folks down on their luck usually found his door.

Winnie must have forgotten about Woodburn being from the North. Like most folks in the South, Cooper tried to put the hatred behind him, but it wasn't always easy. Woodburn's limp reminded Cooper, even before his clip northern accent greeted him, that a half dozen years ago they might have faced one another across a battlefield. Cooper's bullet could be the reason Woodburn limped or had a thin scar across his left cheek. Woodburn, and a thousand like him, were the reason Cooper walked the floor most nights, afraid to sleep. Afraid he would dream.

Cooper hurried across the street trying to forget memories that haunted him. He had been in Woodburn's place a few times when Debord was out of something he needed. Most of the merchandise was dusty on the shelf. Poor Winnie would never find what she was looking for in a place like that.

As he stepped onto the planked porch, he thought he saw Woodburn unloading a wagon at the side entrance, but Cooper pretended not to notice the man. They would nod at one another, but they weren't the "pass the time of day" kind of acquaintances.

When Cooper pushed the door open, he heard Winnie's musical giggle. It took a moment for his eyes to adjust to the store's shadowy light. Clothing hung from the rafters like floating ghosts and the smell of spices thickened the molasses air.

Winnie leaned over the counter helping a slender woman wrap purchases into one square of brown paper. She giggled again as items slipped from her grip.

"Maybe we should put it in two bundles." Winnie laughed.

"Maybe." The young woman answered without a hint of southern accent in her voice. "Or you can hold it closed and just bind everything else up with your hands."

Winnie finally noticed Cooper moving toward her. "Oh, Cooper. I'm sorry I'm late. You see, Mary and I were just wrapping the few things I bought."

Cooper met the young woman's stare. She was as plain as her name with blue-gray eyes. Stormy day eyes, he thought, deciding she must be Woodburn's sister. He'd heard folks talk about her, said she was a real bookworm, reading, instead of dusting, when the store wasn't busy.

"Morning, miss." Cooper removed his hat. There was no reason not to be polite, no matter whose sister she was. To be honest, he must have seen her before. The town was too little to miss anyone for long. But he couldn't remember her.

"Good morning," she answered. A hint of fear darkened her eyes as she studied him. "We could use some help, Mr. Adams," she finally said, "if you don't mind."

He wasn't surprised she knew his name, but the alarm he'd seen cross her gaze startled him. The woman had no reason to be afraid of him. He meant her no harm. Unfriendly to her brother, maybe, but no danger to her.

Cooper set his hat down and offered his support to holding the packages together. His large hands made easy work of the chore. Mary wrapped the string around tightly. When she leaned closer to him to tie the knot, a strange fragrance rattled through his senses. She smelled of fresh-baked bread and spices, and spring water and blankets warmed in front of an open fire.

The scent of her was nothing like he would've expected.

She was plain, washed away even more in her faded brown dress. Yet there was nothing false or bottled about the aroma in the air when she stood so close.

"I'm finished," she said a few inches from his ear. "You can let go now."

Cooper stood back, embarrassed that he'd leaned so close. He crammed his hat low on his head and picked up the purchase. "I'd say you forgot quite a few things." He teased Winnie as he nodded politely to Mary.

"You won't tell the sisters, will you? I'll never hear the end of it."

"I promise," he said without glancing back toward the girl. Winnie had always called Johanna and Emma "the sisters" as if they were a matching set of bookends.

When he turned to leave, Winnie stopped him, taking the bundle from his hands. "I did buy one more thing. Mary will show you while I say good-bye to Mr. Woodburn."

Cooper had no choice but to follow Mary to the back of the store as Winnie headed out the front.

"I hope my sister wasn't any trouble to you." He was searching for something to say. "Sometimes she can get to talking and . . ."

"She was no trouble," Mary told him. "She's a treasure."

Cooper tried to see the woman's face as she wound around counters and shelves. Surely she was kidding. He loved his sister dearly, but few others saw her charm.

As they passed into the crowded storage room, Cooper had to duck to keep from hitting rusting clutter hanging from the rafters. The place was a wreck, boxes, empty trunks, old furniture stacked, piled, and hanging everywhere, skeletons from a better day.

Mary stopped so suddenly, Cooper bumped into her. He gripped her shoulders in an effort to steady both himself and her.

"I'm sorry," he said against the back of her hair.

The smell of her surrounded him once more. That clean, fresh fragrance almost made him believe there was still a kindness in the world he once saw as a child. He'd take that aroma over any he'd ever smelled from a bottle, but he couldn't name exactly what it was.

Twisting suddenly from his grip, Mary backed away. Even in the shadows, he saw the fear in her eyes.

"I'm sorry, miss. I didn't mean to slam into you." Cooper felt as clumsy as a drunk staggering on the street. "I was looking up trying not to bump my head when you stopped."

She watched him for a moment as if considering screaming for help. Then, slowly, she took a deep breath and seemed to force herself to relax. "It's understandable. This room can be traitorous at times."

No smile softened her words.

He found himself studying her closely, wishing he understood her. There were secrets behind her cautious eyes. Secrets he wasn't sure he was brave enough to investigate. She'd been hurt by a man, sometime, someplace, and as the brother of three sisters, Cooper hated to think of any woman being harmed.

"Your sister's purchase." Mary pointed to a huge wooden rocker hanging from nails on the back wall. "I wasn't strong enough to lift it down."

Cooper evaluated the ugly chair. Too large, too old, too scarred to be of much use. "Are you sure Winnie bought this?" He felt like a fool for asking even before the words were out of his mouth.

Mary nodded. "She asked if we had a rocker and insisted on this one the minute she saw it. She said something about every woman should have a rocker sitting next to her hope chest."

Groaning, he reached for the chair. When he'd been a kid, he remembered his sisters having hope chests filled with what they called "someday items." Surely Winnie had given up on the idea of someday having her own home and family.

As he lifted the heavy oak from the wall, his hat tumbled. Cooper twisted trying to find a place on the floor to set the chair while he retrieved his hat. There was no room.

"I'll get it," Mary finally offered, squeezing past him and the chair.

When she leaned up and placed the hat back on his head, her body brushed against his arm. Cooper flinched like he'd been hit by a cannonball in the gut. Her nearness in the shadows was the most intimate feeling he had ever known. He wasn't some schoolboy who had never been close to a woman, but every part of his being reacted to her.

For one moment, totally by accident, they had connected. He felt as if, with her slight movement, she'd somehow brushed against his beating heart.

He forced himself to move, to follow her back to the front of the store and out the door. He was being foolish. Nothing had happened between them. They had touched by accident, nothing more. He wasn't even attracted to her. But for all his bravery, he couldn't force himself to look at Mary Woodburn.

Maybe she hadn't noticed a thing.

Maybe she was still as afraid of him as she had been earlier.

If he met her expressive eyes, he would know. She couldn't hide the truth any more than she could hide her fear.

One thought kept his gaze on the ground. What if, when they touched, she'd felt the slight shift in the earth he had? By magic, or witchcraft, or pure fantasy, what if they both had felt it? What if the shy little woman truly had touched his heart?

Chapter Three

MARY WOODBURN STOOD at the window of her brother's store and watched the tall cattleman maneuver his wagon down the muddy street. He seemed hard as leather, yet he'd worried about her when they bumped together. A kindness lay just beneath his weathered toughness; a kindness she'd guess might be there when she observed him moving about town.

"Best stop your dreaming, girl," her brother said when he noticed her staring. "He wouldn't give you the time of day, that one. Only reason he spoke to you now was because you were so nice to his sister."

"You don't know, Miles. Maybe he's different."

"If there's one thing I do know it's the men in these parts." Miles blocked her view of Cooper Adams. "They're a wild bunch, probably only half tame when the war called them and completely loco when they came home. The fellows out here are too wild to live in respectable towns. Murderers. Thieves. Rebels. And worse even than the Johnny

Rebs are the deserters who hid out in these parts refusing to fight." He mumbled the same things he had said for years. "I might hate the Rebs, but at least I can respect them. For all you know that Adams was one of the worst."

Mary didn't want to hear any more of her brother's never-ending lecture. "But Adams took good care of his sister just now. He was kind to her even though I could tell he was in a hurry."

Miles nodded. "That he did. I'll give him that much. A nice lady like that must be pained having such a mean brother."

"You don't know he's worthless or mean. Winnie says he's killing himself trying to run his ranch all alone without a wife to help him."

Miles frowned at her as if he felt truly sorry for her. "Mary, don't go making up some story in your head. There are no 'happy-ever-afters' out here. You know firsthand how mean these men can be."

Mary felt her face redden. She quickly backed into the corner so her brother wouldn't see how his words had hurt her.

"I'm sorry." He cleared his throat.

"I don't need reminding," she whispered.

"I know. I just don't want to see you hurt again."

She watched Miles limp toward the back of the store. He didn't mean to be cruel, he'd just hardened a long time ago.

Mary shoved a tear from her cheek. She was slowly mirroring him. Before long they'd be made of rock. The first two petrified humans to still be breathing.

Maybe Cooper Adams wasn't mean or even worthless, but she knew he was not for her. She didn't want to marry a rancher and look like she was fifty by the time she turned thirty. She had seen the settlers' women come in the mercantile with children hanging all over them while they traded their last family heirloom for a month's worth of groceries.

She'd been told there were only two kinds of women out here, wives and whores, but as long as she had her brother to live with she would be neither. She'd stay here hiding. Invisible.

Chapter Four

"SHE'S SURE NOT the girl for me," Cooper mumbled as he rode along the north border of his ranch toward the breaks. He had tried not to think of Mary Woodburn when he drove back from town with Winnie chatting at his side or while he'd unloaded the lumber. He tried, but he hadn't succeeded. He must have relived their short time together a hundred times during the night.

The memory of her touch was a way to help him through the night, nothing more. Anything was better than remembering the battles.

Now, this morning, no matter how many times he told himself he had more important things to think about, thoughts of her wormed their way into his mind. Blue-gray eyes lingered.

"She's as plain as this land. A mouse of a woman who probably fears every man who walks into that shamble of a store," he continued to argue, muttering to his horse. "The odd tingling I got when she brushed against me was probably more like that feeling folks get when they say someone just walked over their grave. More eerie than intimate. So what if she smells all clean and fresh? For all I know she just finished taking her monthly bath."

Cooper kicked his horse into a gallop. If he didn't stop talking to himself he would be as crazy as Winnie, buying furniture for a house she would never have. How did she figure to get that old rocker home on the stage?

All afternoon he pushed himself harder than usual as he helped his men move cattle away from the arroyo where flash flooding might happen this time of year. Most of the day he didn't think of anything but work. By midafternoon, the rain rolled in at full gale as the heavy clouds had promised. Now there was no *if* to trouble's calling, but only *when*.

Just after dark he returned to the house. His only comfort lay in the fact that he wouldn't have to face his sisters. They were like chickens, getting up and going to bed with the sun.

He climbed down from his horse in the stillness of the dry barn and smiled, knowing Winnie would have left his supper on the stove warming. After being cold all day, he'd end with a hot meal. He hoped he could stay awake long enough to enjoy it.

The feel of a barn always made him relax. When he'd been a boy with older sisters and a mother forever watching him, the barn had been his hideout. He loved the smell of hay and the way rain tinked against the roof. Air always drifted through the cracks in the walls letting him know he wasn't yet inside and completely safe. The low noises of the animals whispered a welcome. The creaking sounds of the walls made him think the barn itself was an aging giant stretching around him.

The side door thumped against the barn wall. Footsteps, muffled by yards of material, shuffled through the hay toward him.

"Cooper Adams!" Johanna's sharp voice sliced through his peace. "It is about time you got home."

He removed his hat, letting a spray of water circle him as he turned. "Evening, Johanna. What's wrong?" He'd been able to read her moods in the tone of her voice for twenty years. "Surely you weren't worried about me."

"Of course not." Johanna's features hardened. He'd insulted her by even asking. "You can take care of yourself. It's Winnie. She has disappeared completely. Doesn't have the sense God gave a goat, it seems."

Cooper's muscles tightened. "What do you mean, disappeared?"

Johanna looked like she was trying to communicate with the cow. "She has simply vanished off the face of this earth. Emma and I have been beside ourselves all afternoon. Lord help us through this trial."

"Slow down, Johanna." To his oldest sister everything fell into the category of "trial" or "blessing." "Just tell me what happened."

"When last we saw her Winnie was polishing that horrible chair she bought. When we called her an hour later for lunch, she wasn't there."

Cooper stormed toward the house. Maybe Emma could tell the facts. Johanna, for once, was making no sense. Winnie wasn't a child. She wouldn't just walk off.

"Did she take the wagon?" he said without slowing.

"No," Johanna shouted over the rain as she matched his stride. "I had your bunkhouse cook, Duly, check. No horse or wagon is missing. If she rode out of here she did so on a pig. Not that she isn't dumb enough to try it. I swear, the older she gets, the more absentminded she becomes. I only pray I live long enough to take care of her. It is my cross to bear in this life."

Cooper reached the porch, running across the wood without caring that his spurs might be scarring it.

"Winnie's missing." Emma stated the obvious as he stepped inside. "Gone. Disappeared. Lost." She paced like a toy wound too tightly, as she waved both arms, twin windmills blowing in circles accenting each word. "She's been acting stranger than usual ever since we got here. Everyone knows she walks for her constitution every day, but never far, never long."

Cooper tried to calm down his sisters. Johanna saw herself as a martyr and Emma followed suit as second in command. "She couldn't have just evaporated," he said. "Has she ever done this before?" The thought occurred to him that he didn't see them all that often. Maybe this was something she did on a regular basis.

"No," Emma answered. "She goes in her room sometimes and reads. And she goes for walks, but never long ones. I've told her fifteen minutes is all she needs of exercise each day to be regular as a clock. That's very important at our age."

Emma paced in front of the fireplace, putting pieces of an invisible puzzle together. "She must have been reading late last night because her eyes were red this morning. I've told her a hundred times not to read by lamplight or folks will think the color of her eyes is red and not blue."

"What was the last thing either of you said to her?" Cooper could guess. They said the same things to Winnie and somehow she managed never to listen.

Emma wrinkled up her forehead. "I said she must have had to search long and hard to find a dress as ugly as the one she bought while she was in town with you. I can hardly believe the Debords bought such a pattern."

"Did that upset her?" Cooper asked.

Emma shook her head. "I don't see why it would. Someone had to tell her, after all. Did you see the thing? The lines were out of date and the material looked like it was faded along one side."

Johanna stepped in front of Emma like a seasoned tag-teamer ready to take on the cause. "Did Winnie talk to anyone in town yesterday?"

"You think she's been kidnapped?" Emma whispered her fear. "Oh, my. She was taken wearing that terrible dress." Emma's face paled. "Maybe the Apaches got her. I've heard of such things. They come into the house all silent like and snatch the first woman they see. Take her back to their camp and make her one of their wives."

Cooper studied Emma carefully, trying to decide if she'd

been dropped on her head once too often as a child. "First, there are no Apaches in these parts and, second, it would take two or maybe three strong braves to *snatch* Winnie. Something tells me she wouldn't go quietly, so we can forget any possibility of her being taken against her will."

As the women made other guesses, he thought of Woodburn back in town. Winnie *had* left the store saying she planned to say farewell to the man, but when Cooper brought the chair out, she was already sitting in the wagon. Woodburn was strange, always silent, always keeping to himself, but Cooper could not connect him with this trouble. He wasn't even sure his sister had spoken to the man.

"The rain's finally stopped," Emma announced.

Cooper reached for a dry coat on the rack by the door. "Good, I'll start searching. I'll circle the house, then widen the search. Maybe she just went for a walk like you're always suggesting, Emma, and then decided to hole up somewhere until the rain ended. If so, she'll be home soon."

"Where would she *hole up?* This land is so flat a grasshopper would have trouble finding a dry spot to hide." Johanna stood so rigid her back might break if a breeze blew by. "Be logical, Cooper; we already have Winnie making no sense, we don't need you falling prey to a weak mind."

Cooper had no doubt her anger was directed toward him, for she'd obviously waited for him to come home with the answer and he had disappointed her. The one thing Johanna hated more than trouble was having to deal with it herself.

"Eat before you go." Emma hurried to the kitchen and brought his meal. "Ten minutes won't matter. You look dead on your feet. While you eat, Johanna and I will search the house and barn again. Maybe we'll find a clue. If she's been kidnapped, surely she won't be deflowered in the few minutes it takes you to eat a bite."

"Emma, don't even think of such a thing," Johanna snapped. "Talking about her constitution was bad enough and now this."

"All right, sister. Maybe our Winnie just went for a walk and got caught up in one of those flash floods Cooper is always worrying about. If it could wash away a cow, it could drown Winnie. She is probably floating down toward the Gulf by now."

Cooper raised an eyebrow. "That's right, Emma. Look on the bright side."

He downed a few bites of his meal while the sisters tried to think of other dire fates that might have happened to "poor Winnie," as she was now referred to.

When he finished, Cooper headed out to saddle a fresh horse. As he walked from the barn a few minutes later, he thought he heard a wagon.

Cooper waited in the shadows. If trouble was riding in, he would just as soon whoever approached not know he was watching.

The noise grew louder, drifting in the damp breeze. Mixed with the jingle of the harnesses was Winnie's laughter.

Cooper let out a long breath and waited. The buggy pulled into the light shining from the windows. He smiled.

It appeared the Apaches were bringing Winnie back.

Chapter Five

JOHANNA AND EMMA were on the porch when Woodburn pulled his rickety old buggy up to the house. Cooper could make out three people crammed into the shadows of the small carriage. He watched from the drizzling darkness as the Yankee climbed down and helped Winnie to the ground.

There was no mistaking Woodburn, even in the dark. Thin as a willow, favoring his right leg, his head bowed as if apologizing for stepping foot onto a man's land without permission. Cooper would have to search hard to find a reason to like the man.

"Thank you, Mr. Woodburn," Winnie said as he held her arm until she reached the solid first step.

The Yankee didn't seem to hear her as he turned and reached in the boot for a box.

Winnie rushed nervously onto the porch where her sisters stood, openmouthed and staring. "Mr. Woodburn, I'd like you to meet my sisters, Miss Johanna and Miss Emma."

Johanna recovered first. She folded her hands tightly in front of her and closed her mouth.

The store owner removed his hat and made a slight bow but Winnie gave him no opportunity to speak. "Mr. Woodburn was kind enough to give me a ride home from town. I waited, hoping the rain would stop, but when twilight came, he insisted."

Emma glared at the strange man, then addressed her youngest sister. "And how did you get *to* town, Winnie?"

Cooper moved closer. He wasn't sure he cared for the Yankee bringing his sister home, but he knew he didn't like the way Emma talked to Winnie, as though she were a child.

"I walked." Winnie giggled. "And had quite an adventure, I must say."

Emma planted her fists on her hips. "Everyone knows it's been cloudy and windy all day. Did I forget to mention that before you decided to go for a walk? You could have caught your death and no one would have even known where you'd gone off to. We were worried sick about you."

Johanna shifted in front of Emma, ending any planned lecture. She lifted her head and stared level into the stranger's eyes. "Please, Mr. Woodburn, won't you come inside?" Her words were far colder than the wet wind. "No matter what the weather, we are grateful you brought our sister home."

Woodburn hesitated. "It's late. I'll just set her box inside and be on my way." He tried to pass.

"Nonsense," Johanna stated with a glance behind her at a still angry Emma. "You'll stay for a cup of coffee, at the very least." She swept one arm as though opening an invisible door. "Winnie, please get your guest a cup before we send him back out in this damp air."

Winnie hurried inside. Woodburn had no choice but to trail behind. Southern hospitality would prevail even if it had to be forced on the guest.

Straightening their shoulders, Emma and Johanna followed like silent sergeants-at-arms.

Cooper realized no one noticed him standing in the

shadows, and Johanna must not have seen the third figure curled into the corner of the buggy. It would not have been like his proper sister to leave someone out of an invitation.

He let his spurs jingle as he neared the buggy. He didn't want to frighten Mary.

"Miss Woodburn?" he asked from several feet away. "Would you like to join the others?"

When he didn't go away, or say anything else, Mary finally leaned her head out from behind the tattered leather. "No, Mr. Adams."

Cooper smiled. At least she answered him. He took another step. "I'm sure the coffee is hot and, knowing my sisters, there are at least two desserts in the pie safe."

She didn't answer, so he guessed she must be at least thinking about the offer.

"Please"—he lifted his gloved hand to assist her—"we'd be honored to have you stay for a few minutes. After all, you may have saved Winnie's life."

Mary let her hand rest in his as she gathered her skirts and climbed from the folds of the buggy. "Nothing so heroic, Mr. Adams. She looked exhausted after walking to town. I talked her into staying for a late lunch and resting a while. Otherwise she would have been home before the rain started."

He watched Mary carefully, not knowing if she accepted his invitation because she wanted to be with the others, or because she was afraid of remaining in the dark with him. He could feel her hand tremble even through the leather of his glove.

Cooper paused at the first step. "Do you think you could call me Cooper? Mr. Adams seems too formal." He wished she'd raise her eyes to meet his. He felt like he was talking to the part in her hair.

"All right." She didn't offer to let him call her Mary.

He held the door for her and a moment later the kitchen chair. It seemed to him that she was being very careful not to accidentally touch him. She didn't look at him as she drank her coffee and ate a slice of Emma's buttermilk pie. He tried not to stare at her, or to act as if he cared one way or the other about her, but even when he talked to the others, he was aware of her every move.

There was something about Mary Woodburn. Not attraction, he told himself, but something. She was as plain as ever in a black dress with no hint of lace or frills. Her hair was pulled so tightly against her head it could have been painted on. If he shouted, she'd probably jump and run like a deer.

Her brother wasn't much more of a talker. Except for mentioning, when Emma related their trials by stage, that the stage line had left one of his bags in Sherman, Woodburn didn't say a word.

Cooper found himself wondering how Winnie and the Woodburns had made it through the ride out. Knowing his sister, their shyness would make her nervous and whenever Winnie was nervous she chattered on and on. He could almost see Woodburn pushing the horses faster and faster as they moved away from town.

Winnie's explanation about how she had to go to town to get a can of varnish for her rocker didn't make much sense. If she'd mentioned it to Cooper or Duly, the bunkhouse cook, he would have told her there was a gallon of varnish along with paint in the work shed.

Johanna, as always, was the perfect hostess, inquiring about the Woodburns' health and offering to pray that this ride in the damp air brought them no harm. Emma, for once, lost her tongue, but Cooper held no faith that it might be a permanent condition.

To Cooper's surprise, Winnie asked Woodburn to take a look at her chair and offer his advice on restoring it. He dabbed the corner of his mouth with a napkin and stood as if suddenly on an important mission.

Emma and Johanna followed, frowning as Winnie directed Woodburn to her bedroom and the rocker. Just before they reached the door Cooper heard Emma whisper, "Right into her bedroom. Can you believe it? I'll have to talk to her about this."

Cooper looked back at Mary, wondering what she thought of his two older sisters. She'd said Winnie was a treasure; who knows, maybe she liked the other two as well. He wanted to tell her they really were not so bad once you got to know them, but he wasn't sure he believed that himself.

He had to say something. He couldn't just stare at the poor creature pushing the crust of her pie around on her plate until the others returned. "Would you like more?" he finally managed to get out, thinking that of course she wouldn't like more, she had not finished half of what she'd been served.

"No, thank you."

"More coffee?"

"No."

That was it. There was nothing else to offer and he had no idea of what to say. He thought of volunteering one of his sisters—after all, he had an abundance—but he didn't know if she would get the joke. He knew nothing about this woman and he wasn't sure he wanted to. She looked to be in her mid-twenties and he had heard she liked to read.

Her hand shook slightly as she raised her cup then clanked it against the saucer when she lowered the china back in place.

"Mary." He waited for her to look at him.

Slowly, her stormy blue eyes met his. They appeared more blue than gray tonight, but no less frightened than before.

He said the first thing that came to mind. "You don't have to be afraid of me. I swear I mean you no harm."

She didn't have to say a word. He knew she didn't believe him. He racked his brain trying to think of why she would be so scared. He couldn't remember speaking directly to her before yesterday. The few times he had been in the store it had always been her brother, not her, who waited on him.

"Is it because I fought for the South?" Maybe something had happened in the war that still haunted her.

Mary shook her head.

"Is it because I'm a man? Are you afraid of men in general?"

Again her head moved with the same answer.

Folding his arms across his chest, Cooper leaned back in the chair trying to understand her. Silence thickened between them. Voices drifted from Winnie's bedroom, but Cooper couldn't make out what any of them were saying. So, he guessed they probably couldn't hear Mary and his conversation either. Assuming they were having one, of course.

Her silence wouldn't have bothered him if he'd just thought her shy. He'd often found shy folks good company. The air didn't always have to be charged with words. But Mary wasn't just timid. There was something else. She was truly frightened.

With a thud, he rocked the chair into place and stood. "I want to show you something," he said, then wished he had moved slower. "Don't be alarmed. I'm just going to my desk."

Moving briskly, he pulled open the bottom drawer and grabbed a book, then forced himself to walk back to her slowly. "During the war I tried to always carry a book in my pack. Sometimes I'd read it ten times before another came in the mail. More than once I traded with someone else doing the same."

He laid a tattered copy of *Great Expectations* beside her plate. "I could never trade off this one, though. It saved my life." He leaned lower, wishing she would look at him. "See the bullet hole. Went clean through the cover, but lucky for me it didn't make it into my back."

Mary's finger traced over the pit mark in the upper corner of the book.

"I never told my sisters about the shot. Didn't want to worry them." His hand rested a few inches away from hers, but he made no effort to touch her. Somehow by sharing his secret, he had offered his friendship. Now it was up to her.

"Have you read Dickens's book?"

"No," she answered. "But I'd like to."

He'd found the key, he thought. A bridge over the fear.

"I could loan you this book, but you have to promise to bring it back. It's kind of my good luck piece. No matter how hard things get around here, I can always pull this book out and remember how close I came to not making it back home."

She raised her head. A smile touched the corners of her mouth. "Thanks. I'd like to read it. I promise I'll be careful."

She didn't look so plain when she smiled, he thought. She might never be his friend, but at least she wouldn't cringe the next time she saw him.

Cooper heard his sisters returning. He sat back down in his chair and noticed Mary slip the book into her pocket. The book was obviously something neither of them planned to share with anyone else.

Chapter Six

WINNIE THANKED WOODBURN one last time from the porch. Her round head, topped with an equally round bun, bobbed up and down as she rattled on about the day. The Yankee, on the other hand, stood straight and tall as if at attention. Neither of them seemed to notice the wind whipping around them, but Mary huddled into her shawl and hurried toward the far side of the buggy.

Cooper hesitated a few seconds before offering to help Mary into the carriage. When she placed her hand in his this time, without his gloves, he felt the gentle warmth of her touch.

"Thanks again for your help." He wished he had the guts to ask her if she sensed the bond that shot between them when she was so close. He felt as though he walked through his life along a gallery of paintings and suddenly he'd discovered one had a heartbeat.

"Thank you." She brushed her free hand over the book. Her whisper carried on the wind. "For the loan."

"Maybe when I come to town again, we can talk about it. I'm not usually around folks who spend time reading." He didn't want it to sound like he was asking her to step out so he added, "If you have time between customers at the store, of course."

"All right." She smiled again, a little broader this time, then disappeared behind the leather of the buggy.

Cooper realized he held her hand too long, but he didn't want to let go. The warmth in her fingers made him wish he'd tried before now to be her friend. He couldn't think of anything to add, so he backed away, letting the breeze rob him of even the fragrance of her.

As he walked around Woodburn's old rig, he noticed his sisters had already stepped inside. Woodburn meticulously checked the lines of the reins. When Cooper passed by, the Yankee whispered, "Stay away from my sister, Adams. You're not welcome company."

The insult stung like a slap. "I could say the same thing to you," Cooper countered.

"I've not sought your sister out, sir." Woodburn's words were clipped, irritating in their truth.

"Nor I yours." Cooper wanted to know where the man stood. If he had an enemy, it was best to know it now. "My presence in your store has always been for business. Nothing more." How could the Yankee think that he might be courting Mary? All Cooper was trying to do was make her not jump with fear whenever she saw him.

Woodburn nodded once. "Then you're welcome as long as we understand one another."

"We understand one another." Cooper turned and stomped up the steps. He didn't go inside, but watched the moon glisten off the tattered buggy as it disappeared down the ribbon of road toward town. Anger rushed through his veins like a prairie fire in a draught. He wasn't some hotheaded youth who needed to be warned to stay away from his sister. Cooper had done nothing improper. Mary was in her midtwenties, an old maid by anyone's standard. Even if he had been courting, she could speak for herself. She didn't need a brother riding herd over her.

He smiled, realizing he'd been even more absurd than the shop owner suggesting there might be any hint of a flirtation between Woodburn and Winnie. She would be forty her next birthday. Even in her youth, Winnie had never been the kind to draw a man's eye.

By the time he went back in the house, the sisters had retired to their rooms, like birds nesting for the night. He poured himself the last of the coffee and sat down at his desk. He intended to work, but couldn't resist opening the bottom drawer. There, hidden away from the world, was his collection of books. Dickens, Poe, Thoreau, and a dozen others.

Not many, he thought, compared to the private libraries in homes back east, but more books than most had this far west. His parents had settled this land with one book, the Bible. They hadn't thought reading or writing very useful skills but Cooper's mother taught Johanna, then Johanna taught Emma, then Emma taught Winnie. Then of course, Winnie taught him.

Cooper grinned. His schooling was not only sparse, it had been filtered down to the point he should be surprised to recognize his own name.

He picked up Kingsley's *Westward Ho.* A year, maybe longer, had passed since he'd held a book in his hand, but the welcome feeling was still there, inviting him in, engaging him to stay. He told himself there was never enough time to read anymore, but he knew it was more than that. Cooper no longer believed in dreams. Somehow, one has to be able to dream to be lost in a story. And of late, just making it through each day had become his only goal.

Leaning back, with the book in his hand, Cooper looked around his home, really seeing it for the first time since he'd built it. After the war, when he came back to the ranch his father had homesteaded, he could not wait to increase the herd, build this house, and start a family. He had it all planned out, wanting to forget the fighting and the time he lost. He wanted to start living.

But the war wouldn't stay over. Everywhere, even on the frontier, there were reminders of the open wound that remained after the fighting stopped.

The battles returned when he tried to sleep. Sometimes he woke in the middle of the night and rushed to the washstand, trying desperately to rub away the smell of blood that still lingered on his hands. He would see a part of a uniform, blue or gray, and the bitterness he had lived with for two and a half long years stung his tongue once more. Turning from a boy to a man on the battlefields, he'd managed to survive, but a price was paid with nightmares.

Closing his eyes, Cooper swore he would never tell anyone about the ghosts that haunted him. They'd think him crazy, and he had too much responsibility to let that happen. He'd seen the ones ghosts had claimed in towns across the South, men who never came home in their minds. Men who wandered, still seeing battles, still crying for their lost brothers, still hearing bugles long silent.

Cooper gripped the book with a determined hold, refusing to reach for the bottle he kept in his right drawer. Tonight, he would read. He'd force himself into a story until exhaustion lulled him to sleep.

Somehow, knowing Mary was also reading made it easier. Cooper concentrated on each word, thinking that, if their paths crossed again, he'd give her this book also. If he did, he might need to remember the story so he could talk to her about it. Maybe one day they could visit without fear shimmering in her eyes.

"Follow the bridge," he mumbled to himself. The books were all he had that linked them. He was afraid to question why he needed this bond with a woman he hardly knew, for if he reflected too closely he might find the whole of him packed with loneliness.

Two hours melted away before he looked up. Laying the book down, he stretched, his muscles relaxing. Tonight he might be able to sleep.

As he stood, he noticed the thin slice of light beneath Winnie's door. On impulse, he crossed to her room and tapped, fearing she might have gone to sleep with the lamp still burning.

"Yes," she answered too quickly to have been asleep.

Cooper opened the door. "You all right?"

Winnie put down her sewing. "I'm fine. I was just doing some mending and got carried away." She lifted her watch pin from the nightstand. "I didn't realize it was so late. It's been such a delightful day, I guess I didn't want it to end."

Cooper smiled. Only Winnie would lose track of time while mending or think getting caught in the rain was delightful. "Well, good night." He started to close the door then paused. "Promise me the next time you need to go to town, you'll let Duly or me hitch up a wagon for you. One of us is usually around."

"I promise." She returned to her mending. "By the time I realized what a walk it was, I was already over halfway there. Thank goodness Miles could bring me home."

"Miles?"

"Mr. Woodburn." Winnie blushed.

"Yes, thank goodness for Miles." He closed the door before she saw his frown. He didn't like his sister calling the Yankee "Miles." He didn't like it one bit.

Three days passed with Winnie still talking about Mr. Woodburn, and every word stuck in Cooper's craw.

No one in town liked the man. Surely Winnie could see that. Oh, they might go in his store from time to time, mainly because he took trade for supplies. Most in the South were money poor, though rich in land and cattle. The cattle drives and settlers traveling through used him because he'd deliver out to their campsite. Debord gladly gave Woodburn that business. It wasn't practical to lose half a day's work delivering supplies then try to get back to town before some down-on-his-luck cowboy robbed him.

But with Winnie, it was Mr. Woodburn this and Mr. Woodburn that, like he only spouted universal truths. She must have repeated his every word at least ten times.

Cooper wondered how the man had had time to say so much in the course of one afternoon.

Johanna and Emma had long since grown bored with her chatter about the Woodburns and the chair she was redoing. They talked over her as if she were little more than a babbling child making noise in the corner.

Cooper couldn't bring himself to do that. After all, Winnie had been the one who taught him to read and write, and to imagine what might be in the world. She had played games with him when there were no children near his age and made dragons of the clouds in the lazy summer days before he became a man and gave up such things. So now he listened to her, again and again, without commenting.

At night he read, rediscovering how much he loved it, how much he missed it. As the days passed, he decided that the strange feeling he got when Mary touched him was nothing more than loneliness. No woman had been near him for quite a while. No respectable woman anyway. The girls at the saloon were always brushing up against him when he stopped by for a drink, but they were like cats purring and pawing. He'd long ago grown cold to their nearness. But Mary was different.

By the end of the week, the curiosity to see her climbed beyond his good sense of steering clear of her brother. He told himself it would be good for him to at least talk to a respectable girl. His sisters were making plans to invite every lady in the county to a party as soon as he gave in to a date. Maybe Mary would offer him a little practice at conversation.

After all, what harm could it do?

Chapter Seven

MARY LEANED OVER the counter, watching the movements of the Minnow Springs population. Though she knew most of the people, it was more the curiosity of viewing an ant bed, than any particular interest in one person. Or at least it had been until Cooper Adams rode in.

She knew his routine. He'd stop at the post office, tying his horse to the hitching post near the alley. Then he always walked down Main Street to the saloon. On the way, he took care of business, dropping into a few stores before having a drink. She guessed he must not be much of a drinker, for he never stayed long. Most times she would see him leave the saloon and cross over to the hotel for dinner. He always ate alone at the window seat.

She wasn't keeping up with him specifically, she reminded herself. She was just observing the comings and goings of the town. Why would one rancher deserve any more notice than another?

Yet there was something about the way he stared out into

the night from the hotel's dining room window that made her watch. It was almost as if he were looking for something or someone to materialize out of the darkness. There was a sadness about him that seemed older than his years. She imagined him wondering, as he ate and watched the night, if there were not more to life than the hard lonely life he'd chosen.

Mary had read the book he loaned her and hoped to have time for another reading before she returned it. But liking the book didn't parallel with liking him. She'd learned her lesson. Men were not always what they seemed.

Miles limped in with a box of apples. He set them down on the counter and asked, "That Adams I saw riding past?"

They both knew it was, so she didn't bother to answer.

"If he comes in here, I want you to go to the storage room, Mary, and let me wait on him."

"But—"

"I think I know best," Miles snapped in an angry tone that had long ago molded itself around his normal voice. "If Adams walks through that door, you'll go to the back and stay there until he leaves. I don't need any trouble."

Mary wanted to argue that Cooper might be different, but fear paralyzed her mind. She had stood up to her brother once and insisted a man had only wanted to talk and she'd been wrong. Now, even the slight jingling of spurs reminded her of how terrified she had been and of how nearly her brother had come to losing his life.

"Cooper Adams is heading this way." Miles broke into her thoughts. "I'll call you when he's gone."

Mary slipped into the shadows of the storage room as the mercantile door opened.

"Good evening." Miles's greeting was cold, formal as always. "How may I help you?"

Mary peered between the slits at the back of the shelving. She noticed Cooper glance around. She knew he looked for her. She wondered if he could feel her near, for she swore even with her eyes closed she would have known he was close by. Something about the man drew her, but she no longer trusted her instinct.

"Winnie sent a list of different size needles she needs. She said you had the best selection in town." Cooper handed Miles a scrap of paper. "She also asked that I pay her respects to your sister."

Miles took the sliver of paper and carefully examined it. "Mary is not available, but I'll pass the message along. It'll only take me a minute to wrap these for you. I'll circle them up with a strip of the new ribbon we just got in. Miss Winnie might like that."

Cooper stood in the middle of the store. He wore his hat low, shading his eyes from view, but Mary had the feeling he searched for something.

She touched the book tucked away in her pocket. Maybe he'd only come in for the novel and the reason he wanted to see her was to get it back. After all, he'd told her it was his good luck charm. The least she could do was walk out into the store and hand it to him. Nothing would happen. Not in broad daylight, in the middle of the store, with her brother right there.

Cooper shifted. She heard the jingle of his spurs and stilled.

"Will there be anything else?" Miles shoved the packet of needles across the counter.

"No, thank you." Cooper hesitated. "Don't forget to pass my sister's regards along."

"I'll remember." Miles folded his arms over his chest. "Good day."

Mary watched as Cooper walked out of the store.

"Good riddance." Miles's comment blended with the door's closing.

Mary moved from the shadows. "We don't have any reason to hate the man, Miles. He doesn't have any grudge against you."

"You can't trust these people, Mary. Any of them. They don't care about us, even if a few of them act like they do. I've told you that a thousand times. It will take a generation, maybe more, for the bitterness between North and South to die. Our moving here doesn't change that."

Mary nodded. They'd left Virginia with nothing six years ago. Miles's leg kept him from working most places and the few desk jobs he'd been qualified for had a hundred other veterans apply. Running the mercantile for their uncle seemed the only option. But by the time they got to Texas, their uncle Luther had died, leaving them the dilapidated remains of a once thriving business and no extra money to repair or restock. Slowly, Miles had built the business, hating every minute, trapped and resenting fate's twist. No one had offered to help him at first and he had not bothered to ask.

Miles's smile was sad when he added, "How about we close early tonight? I could take the empty apple crates and a load of supplies out to the Kiley place. You could read." He sounded like he truly wanted to make her feel better. "You know Mrs. Kiley will insist I bring home one of her pies. We could eat it with a late supper when I get back."

Mary smiled, silently agreeing to the truce. "Sounds like a good plan. I found an old reader in a chest you traded for the other day. I'll send it out to their youngest boy. Remind them he should be starting his lessons this year. Unless you want me to go along and talk to them?"

Miles shook his head. "With all the empty boxes I'll be carrying and the bad road, the wagon will rattle all the way. No use in both of us having to listen to that. But I'll be sure to pass along the advice and the book."

Mary put away items left on the counter as she talked. "I did promise I'd work with the Andrews children on math for a few hours tonight. Not one of them can add."

Mr. Andrews owned the livery and had a child every fall like clockwork. He couldn't pay Mary anything for her lessons, but loaned them a wagon or buggy anytime they were in need. "If I don't work fast, there will be more kids in that family than any of the Andrews can count."

Miles pulled down the paper blind over the door's glass. "I'd rather listen to the rattling of the boxes than those brats. You're not bringing them all in here, are you?"

"No. I've learned my lesson. Half a pound of candy

disappeared last time. We'll work in the loft over the livery tonight."

Two hours later Mary wished she'd gone with Miles. The Andrews kids might not be able to add, but they could all talk. In fact, none of them seemed to know how to stop. Her head pounded as she crossed the road and headed back to the apartment above the store.

It didn't matter which side of the street she walked, she had to pass a saloon either way. Mary kept her head down and hurried as fast as she dared along the poorly lit walkway.

She made it past the door of the saloon before she noticed two men sitting in the wicker chairs between the saloon's windows. Light shone on either side, but they were in shadow.

"Evenin', miss." One man stood as she neared. Tall and thin, his mustache hung below his jawline.

"Evenin', miss," the other echoed in a slurred voice. "Nice night for a walk." He tried to stand, but fell over the arm of the chair and almost tumbled off the porch. "Wanta join us?"

Fear contracted Mary's muscles. Her lungs refused to pull in air, her hands clutched the books she carried as if they somehow could hold her afloat. She heard the jingle of their spurs as the two cowboys moved on either side of her. Their shadows crossed over her, landing invisible blows, stirring terror into her blood.

"How about we walk you home, Miss Woodburn?" The first cowboy took her arm as her name rolled too freely off his tongue. "Whatta you say, Frank? We should walk the Yankee's sister home?"

She attempted to pull away. The music from the saloon door was so loud no one would hear her if she screamed. "No," she tried to say without sounding frightened. "I can make it home fine. I've only a short way."

"Yeah." Frank moved closer, almost falling into her as he tried to take her arm. His breath polluted the air with the smell of bad whiskey. "We'll walk you home, girl."

"N-no," Mary managed to say. "Leave me alone." She

fought to free her arm, but the tall cowboy held tightly. "I have to go. My brother is waiting for me."

Frank snickered. "No, he ain't. We seen him driving out of here with a load of apple crates." He snorted a laugh as if Mary were simply playing a game with him. "Only one place your brother would be taking them: Kiley's farm. He won't be back for an hour, maybe more."

The hold on her arm tightened as the other drunk leaned closer. "We'll have time to get to know one another real well by then. We heard tell you like getting to know cowboys."

"No!" Mary dropped the books and tried to free herself. "Leave me alone!"

As panic and fear strangled her, she heard the jingle of a third man's spurs coming up from behind her in quick, pounding strides.

Suddenly the thin cowboy turned loose her arm as he flew across the porch and hit against the saloon's wall with the thud of a ripe pumpkin. Frank stumbled away, mumbling that he wanted no part of a fight.

Mary felt his nearness even before the man behind her stepped into the light.

"Miss Woodburn, are you all right?"

He stood so close she could feel the warmth of his words against her cheek. She was so relieved to see Cooper Adams she almost hugged him. He bent and picked up the books she'd dropped. When he stood, he whispered, "Would you allow me to see you safely home?"

Shyly, she took his arm, unsure she trusted him, but knowing she didn't trust the two men watching them.

He placed his hand over her fingers as they rested on his sleeve. "It's all right, Mary," he added as soon as they were far enough away that the two drunks couldn't hear. "You're safe now."

They moved between the shadows of the stores, strolling as if they were no more than a courting couple out for a walk. She couldn't stop shaking and hated herself for being so weak. This was a country where bravery was highly valued and she must be proving herself the greatest coward in the state.

Cooper slowed to a stop. "Mary, are you really all right?"

"No." Panic still darted through her veins like tadpoles swimming in warm water. "I-I'm sorry." It made no sense. The unpleasantness with the cowboys was over. But she couldn't relax, her body wouldn't stop shaking.

At the steps between porches, Cooper faced her. He stood one stair below so that their eyes met. "Mary?" he asked as he opened his arms.

If he'd tried to hold her, if he'd made a move toward her, she would have run. But he didn't. He just stood there and waited.

Mary closed the space between them. Wrapping her arms around his neck, she let her entire body melt against him. Needing the comfort he offered. Wanting, for once, not to be afraid.

Cooper gently closed her into the circle of his arms. He held her tightly, protectively. "You're all right now, Mary," he whispered against her hair. "No one is going to hurt you."

The shaking stopped; she breathed. For the first time in years she relaxed, feeling shielded from all harm. This man she'd watched for so long, wondering what he thought, had somehow read her mind tonight and offered the one thing she needed, shelter from fear.

Cooper Adams, a man she hardly knew, took no advantage, made no improper move. He held her safe in his solid arms. The warmth of his body pressed into hers like a soothing, healing balm.

For a long while, she rested her head against his chest and listened to his heartbeat. Finally, he lifted her up as if she were no more than a sleeping child and carried her to the mercantile.

When he lowered her at the door, he touched his hat. "Good night, Miss Woodburn," he said formally as if they hadn't just held one another a moment before. "Will you be all right until your brother gets home?"

Mary nodded. She thought of asking him in but knew Miles would be furious if he came home and found Cooper Adams inside the store. "Thank you," she said as she unlocked the door.

"You're welcome." He stepped away without another word.

She climbed the stairs to the apartment. Once locked inside, she crossed to the window before she turned on any lights. There, across the street, hidden in shadows, she saw Cooper's outline leaning against a wall. He watched, waiting to make sure she was safe.

Mary smiled. She had her own private guardian angel.

An hour later when Miles pulled the wagon to the side entrance, she looked out the window again. As Miles climbed down from his wagon, she saw Cooper move away, unnoticed by anyone but her.

"Thank you," she whispered, wishing he could hear her.

He glanced up at her window as if he caught her words on the wind, then disappeared into the night.

Chapter Eight

COOPER COULDN'T GET Mary Woodburn out of his mind. The woman was a plague worse than yellow fever. For the next few days she managed to creep into his every thought. It was just a matter of time before he talked about her the way Winnie talked about Woodburn, relating every topic of conversation to him. His sister hardly knew the man, yet somehow he'd become her center.

Johanna and Emma convinced Cooper they needed to schedule the shindig before the weather turned cold. By the end of the week they had half his men doing odd jobs for them and running errands as though the cowhands were part of the social committee.

Cooper worked longer hours rounding up cattle for the season's last drive to market and trying to stay out of his sisters' way. After a day of branding, he returned just before sundown covered in mud. He brushed and fed his horse, then walked toward the house, musing that it would take more than one tub of bathwater to get him clean.

He'd almost reached the porch when he spotted Miles Woodburn's delivery wagon pulled up by the front gate. The man sat there as if unsure whether he wanted to come onto Cooper's land.

Removing his hat, Cooper waved the mercantile owner forward. Maybe Woodburn had had trouble on the road while making a delivery. Maybe he needed help. Not liking the man wouldn't keep Cooper from being neighborly.

Woodburn pulled the rig forward, but stopped short of the front porch, and well out of sight of anyone inside the house.

Cooper walked up to the side of the wagon, wishing Mary were here with her brother. "Evenin'," he said without smiling. "Having trouble, or is this a social call?" If Woodburn had stopped by to warn him to stay away from Mary one more time, Cooper might have to knock some sense into the man.

"It's not a social call. In fact, I'd just as soon your sisters not know I'm here." Woodburn appeared hesitant, uncertain.

"All right. What's on your mind?" Cooper wasn't sure why, but he had a feeling this wasn't about Mary. He would bet his best cutting horse Mary hadn't told her brother about the night he'd walked her home. Cooper wondered if she felt him against her the way he swore he still felt her body against his.

Woodburn climbed down from the rickety old wagon and faced Cooper. "I don't know how to say this other than straight out." He looked like he swallowed poison with each word. "I think your sister stole my luggage."

"What?" Of all the things Cooper thought might be on the Yankee's mind, this wasn't even on the list. "That's impossible." None of his sisters ever stole anything in their lives.

Woodburn seemed embarrassed to say more, which was all that kept Cooper from swinging at him. "The stage line only has one unclaimed bag and it's mostly filled with sewing notions. They keep saying it's the bag that I shipped from Sherman. I traveled by horseback from there the same day your sisters arrived by stage. I remember them climbing into the coach at Sherman as the driver tossed my bag up top and said he'd see me in Minnow Springs. All I can figure out is that one of them took my luggage and left her own unclaimed."

Cooper swore. "Impossible!"

"I thought so too, at first. My case was new, brown. The one at the station is black, but it looks brand new and made about the same as mine. Your sisters were the only ones who could have taken it unless it fell off the stage somewhere along the trail. That still wouldn't explain the extra unclaimed piece. If one of them took mine, why wouldn't she claim her own?"

"You've got some nerve, Woodburn, accusing one of them of such a thing," Cooper shouted as he remembered the morning Winnie arrived. She hadn't remembered the color of her bag, or how to get it open. She'd worn her traveling clothes until he'd taken her to town to shop. "My sisters are not thieves!" He yelled the words as if ordering them to be true.

Woodburn looked as miserable as Cooper felt. "Then why didn't they return my luggage? Theft is the only reason I can come up with and that doesn't make much sense since my bag only contained clothes and the journal I've kept since the war."

Cooper wanted to flatten Woodburn. The man had been asking for it for years. The way he talked, reminding everyone he was not a Southerner. The way he looked down on folks in town. The way he wormed his way into every conversation Cooper had with Winnie lately. Anyone would think she'd known him for years, knew his every thought, the way she talked about him.

Grabbing the front of Woodburn's jacket, Cooper pulled him forward as his right fist connected with Woodburn's jaw in a powerful pop.

The Yankee made no move to defend himself.

Cooper seized the other side of his jacket and hauled

Woodburn to within an inch of his nose. "No man insults my sisters."

He shoved the Yankee hard against the wagon and delivered a blow to his midsection. Just as his fist connected, Winnie's scream shattered the air.

"Stop!" She ran toward them. "Stop!"

Cooper backed away, letting Woodburn crumple to the ground like a broken toy. He held his arms open to Winnie, planning to assure her he was all right, the Yankee hadn't landed a single blow.

But Winnie ran right past him and knelt beside Woodburn. "Miles! Miles! Are you all right?"

Hooking his hand under Winnie's arm, Cooper tried to pull her to her feet. The shock of seeing her brother fighting must have pushed her over the edge. Woodburn was also trying to push the crazy woman away from him, but Winnie would have none of it. She felt Woodburn's face and patted on him as though trying to fluff a pillow, while she searched for any breaks or blood.

"Winnie." Cooper pulled harder, but lifting her was like trying to shovel quicksand. "You don't know what this is about. Stay out of it."

"No! You don't know." She leaned over the shop owner, wiping her tears off his lapel. "Miles won't fight you. He swore he would never lift a hand against another man after the war. He's never told anyone, not even his sister, but he'd let someone beat him to death before he fought again."

She continued patting on the man. Cooper stepped back, trying to clear his mind. He'd caught his sister's insanity. She worried over Woodburn and, in Cooper's opinion, Woodburn wasn't making near enough protest.

"Winnie? If he's never told anyone, how do you know?"

The Yankee slowly stood and helped Winnie to her feet. She didn't even come to his shoulder now so she had to content her smothering to dusting his jacket.

"She knows"—Woodburn stared at Cooper—"because she's read my journal." He let the words sink in before adding, ". . . that was in my bag."

Cooper looked at Winnie. She didn't have to say a word; he read the truth on her face. If she'd traveled with the James brothers, they would have never had a career long enough to fill a column, much less a dime novel.

Johanna's voice snapped orders from somewhere behind them. "Come inside, all of you. What would the neighbors think if we lived close enough for them to hear you? We will sort this problem out over coffee. I'm sure it is just a misunderstanding."

To his oldest sister, the War Between the States had been "just a misunderstanding." Why should Cooper be surprised Johanna viewed Winnie's theft and his beating an innocent man any differently?

They all sat down at the table while Winnie went to get the luggage she'd lifted the day she arrived. Cooper knew he was going to have to apologize to a man he didn't like. That fact bothered him more than the sudden revelation that his sister had sticky fingers.

Emma poured everyone a cup of coffee, but no one drank. "I knew something was amiss," she said to anyone at the table who would listen. "I just knew it. I have a feeling for these things, you know, always have."

Cooper felt like counting "one," for he knew Emma's statement would be repeated at least a hundred times.

Johanna excused herself, saying someone must attend to dinner. On her way to the kitchen, she paused to invite Mr. Woodburn to join them as if he were here on a social call and hadn't been being slugged by her brother only moments before.

When Woodburn declined, she smiled and said, "Maybe another time," before disappearing into the kitchen.

Johanna might be a ball of fire when fighting for the date of a party, but trouble was like dust to her way of thinking. It should be swept under the rug and never spoken about.

Winnie brought in the brown bag she'd carried home the day she arrived in Minnow Springs and handed it to Miles. "I mended all your clothes. Most were in need of a stitch or two."

Miles lifted a shirt from the bag. Winnie's fine stitches could barely be seen. "I've been wearing this shirt with the collar torn loose for some time." He nodded a silent thank-you to Winnie. "I should have replaced it, but the rip didn't show if I kept my jacket on. I try not to ask my sister to take care of me and my sewing skills are nonexistent."

He pulled his dress coat from the bag and ran his hand along all the buttons. "I thank you for this. It was no small task."

Winnie smiled. "I guessed that no one sewed for you. And the buttons were no problem; Cooper had ones on his dress coat he never uses." She glanced at Cooper daring him to argue. "I replaced all of your efforts so the stitches should hold as long as the material does. It took a few nights more time than I imagined it would, I'm afraid. I meant to get your things back to you as soon as possible."

She brushed her hand over the material as though it somehow partly belonged to her now. "I didn't mind the work, though. It was kind of like I had someone to do things for, if only for a while. I've never had that." She blinked away a tear bubbling in her eye.

"Why didn't you tell us, Winnie? How could you have simply kept his things?" Emma circled the table, a one-woman war party. "Sewing a gentleman's clothes as if he were your man and not some stranger. It beats all I've ever heard of."

Embarrassment warmed Winnie's round cheeks. "I'm sorry." She lowered her head. "I didn't mean any harm. I only wanted to pretend for a while."

Cooper felt so sorry for Winnie he wanted to hit Woodburn again. The Yankee didn't much look like he would mind. He must have hated like hell to ride all the way out here and accuse Winnie of stealing.

"How's your jaw?" Cooper wanted to say he was sorry, but the words clogged his throat.

Woodburn rubbed the side of his face and met Cooper's stare. "It'll be sore for a few days, but I'll live."

Apology issued. Apology accepted.

"Did you read his journal too?" Emma rounded the table again. "Winnie, you read a man's private thoughts? How could you? It's a crime, nothing but a crime. Why, you never even got so much as a letter from a man, and now you read a whole journal. It's a wonder someone doesn't lock you away for doing such a thing."

Winnie took a step backward, offering no defense.

Woodburn stood so fast coffee splashed from every cup on the table. "Mr. Adams," he said in almost a shout, "as the only male in this family, I feel it is only proper to address you about a matter."

No one breathed as Cooper stood. He wasn't sure what he would do if Woodburn suggested filing charges against Winnie. She'd already admitted her guilt, but Emma was the only person alive who'd think of locking Winnie up for mending someone's clothing.

Cooper closed his eyes and waited. Right or wrong, she was his sister and he'd fight any battle the Yankee lined out if he had to for her. "What do you suggest, Mr. Woodburn?"

"I suggest, Miss Winnie agreeing, of course, that you give me permission to call on your sister. My intentions are honorable, I assure you."

Winnie giggled in surprise.

Emma hit the floor in a dead faint.

Chapter Nine

COOPER FROWNED EVERY time he thought about the Yankee courting his sister, but he couldn't help smiling when he remembered the way Emma reacted to the news.

Woodburn and Mary came to dinner the following Sunday. Everyone silently agreed to allow Winnie and her caller the privacy of the porch for courting after the meal. Cooper still didn't like the man, but he did enjoy talking about books with Mary after the dishes had been cleared.

By the third Sunday their visits became a pattern that Cooper looked forward to. Mary's shy questions and comments on what she had read the week before made Cooper think. Johanna and Emma were always in the room, but lost interest quickly in any discussions. Mary, on the other hand, had a good mind. Her intelligence kept him reading late most nights. She might be plain, from her simple hairstyle to her drab clothes, but there was nothing ordinary about her logic.

Cooper wished he could talk to her of other things, but

knew the time was not right. He learned that she tutored several children in town. Every week, when she talked about her students and their lessons, he heard excitement in her voice. Her kind way made her a natural teacher.

When the conversation turned to the party his sisters were planning, Mary showed no interest. Finally, one Sunday when they walked out alone to view his newest colt, he asked if she planned to attend the dance. He wasn't surprised when she mumbled an excuse while giving most of her attention to the colt.

Cooper accidentally brushed her hand as he reached to pat the colt's head. To cover up the awkward moment, he said, "I call this one Future because I bred her special from a descendent of the famous Steeldust. The way I see it, she's the future of this ranch."

Mary asked a few questions about the horse, but she kept glancing back at the house as if wanting to return to the others. Or maybe, Cooper thought, not wanting to be alone with him.

Since the party was the topic of choice for his sisters, Mary usually remained silent around them, fading into the background, almost as invisible to them as she used to be to him.

Fear slowly ebbed from her eyes as the Sunday visits continued. Yet late one Monday afternoon when Cooper walked into the mercantile she glanced up and he saw terror flicker once more.

He didn't bother pretending not to notice. "What is it, Mary?" he asked, not caring that her brother might be within hearing distance. He felt they had become friends and guessed she enjoyed visiting with him as much as he did with her. It troubled him that he could still frighten her so easily.

Mary stared down at the ledger she'd been working on. "Nothing."

Removing his hat, Cooper leaned against the counter. "Yes, there is. I see it. What frightened you so when I walked in just now?"

She remained perfectly still as if waiting for him to disappear. When he didn't, she answered, "Your spurs. Or rather the sound they make. I heard them before I made out who you were."

Cooper bent over and pulled the silver and leather straps from his boots. He laid them on the counter. "Anything else?" He grinned. There were a hundred questions, but they'd wait. "Or should I just continue stripping?"

She smiled, the tension forgotten. "No, only the spurs."

Raising an eyebrow, Cooper waited.

"I won't tell you why." She lifted her chin an inch.

"I won't ask."

"Good." She let out a long-held breath. "How can I help you, Mr. Adams? My brother is not here." She rushed to add, "Though I expect him back at any moment."

"I could wait if you like."

"Oh, no. I'm sure I can fill your order. Then I have to lock up. It's almost time to close."

Cooper couldn't remember what he'd been planning to buy when he walked into the store five minutes before. It was some item he'd decided he needed on the way in to pick up the mail.

"Have dinner with me, Mary." The words were out before he realized he'd said his thoughts. Hurriedly, he added, "I want to discuss the book you loaned me a few weeks ago." His reasoning made no sense, he saw her yesterday, but she was kind enough not to notice.

When she met his gaze, they both knew the talk would not be of books tonight. Every time he saw her there were things both almost said. For just an hour he wanted to visit with her, just her. Not of books or his sisters and her brother, or the town.

"We'll walk down Main and eat by the window at the hotel, then I'll walk you right back here. You'll be safe, and your brother only has to look around to know where you are. I promise to have you back at your door by sundown."

To Cooper's surprise, Mary turned without answering and lifted her shawl from a peg.

He offered his arm. Of all the things he'd thought of telling her, the topics he had wanted to discuss, the questions he wondered about her life, Cooper did not say a word as they walked down the street.

After ordering two of the café's specials and coffee, they sat by the window as he'd promised, eating their meal in silence. He guessed they should be talking, but all he could think about was how good she smelled and how he enjoyed the comfort of her near. She was so different from any woman he'd ever met. She was the first female he'd ever thought of as a friend.

The sun's dying glow lit the street as they strolled back toward the store. Cooper decided that somewhere over the past six years of living alone he must have lost all ability to communicate. Unless he counted "Pass the gravy" or "Would you like some pie?" he hadn't thought of a thing to say to her. At this rate he would stand around all day at his sisters' big party and just stare at the eligible women from all over the county. He pictured them walking past him, gawking at him or, worse, pitying him as a fool. Picking a bride wasn't like bobbing for apples. At some point he would have to talk to the woman he planned to marry. What chance would he have if he could not even think of something to say to Mary?

"I've never been much of a talker," he said aloud.

"I guessed that." She tried to hide a smile.

He rested his hand over her fingers on his arm. "You don't mind the silence?"

As always, she was kind. "I don't mind."

"Then, we should be great friends?" He liked the idea. Friends didn't make him exactly a ladies' man, but at least it was a start.

"We are friends." She lifted the hem of her skirt as they stepped onto the porch in front of the mercantile. "Thank you for dinner."

"You're welcome." Cooper watched her unlock the store. "If you ever need me, Mary, you'll let me know." When she glanced back at him, he added, "That's what friends do. They watch out for one another."

"I promise. And you'll do the same?"

"Cross my heart." Cooper tipped his hat and walked away.

Mary stepped inside, humming softly. He'd done it again, she thought. He'd made her feel like she had her own private guardian angel. Someone watching over her. Someone caring.

She started into the dark corners of the cluttered store. Unwanted memories crept out to greet her, reminding her of another time. Even the glow of the sun had disappeared that night. The store had been quite like it was now. She came down from the apartment above to retrieve a book she'd forgotten and noticed the door standing open. Dirt blew in from the street, thickening the air. Before she could reach the lock, she heard the jingle of spurs and a moment later she was fighting for her life.

The attacker swore she asked for it as he pulled at her clothes. She had talked to a stranger that afternoon, even flirted a little. The cowhand had laughed as she screamed, accusing her of playing with him before he smothered her mouth with his and ended her cries.

Now, the fear from that night choked Mary.

She couldn't remember how many times she had broken free and screamed. Once, twice. Miles hurried down the stairs to help. But at the bottom step, he hesitated. He froze, without reacting, allowing the stranger's two friends to attack.

Mary glanced over at the counter, pushing the memories aside. Trying not to remember the way they had beat him without Miles ever landing a blow. He'd just stood there, like a man made of straw, while they'd took turns hitting him. If someone hadn't walked by the open door and shouted for help, Miles might have died and she didn't even want to think what might have happened to her.

Trying to remember to breathe, she fought the memory, forcing herself to look around the room, to see that there was no one in the shadows waiting.

Cooper's spurs reflected in the dying light, pulling her back to the present. He had taken them off and placed them on the counter without thinking her silly or asking questions. He'd done it simply because she had asked.

On impulse, she grabbed the spurs and ran out the door. She was halfway to the post office before she realized she wasn't running away from her fears this time, but to something. To him.

Cooper stood next to his horse, checking the saddle's straps. He decided he might ride into town again in a week or so and see if she'd go to dinner with him a second time. The food at the hotel wasn't nearly as fine as his sisters cooked but his ears sure enjoyed the rest.

The tapping sound of someone running across the boardwalk registered a moment before he glanced up. Mary ran off the end of the walk. Cooper raised his arms just in time to catch her in flight.

She held tightly as he swung her down beside him. He pulled her close, breathing in her nearness with deep hungry breaths.

The shadows of buildings hid them from prying eyes, but he wouldn't have cared if the entire town saw them. Cooper held her inside the circle of his arms, feeling her heart beat against his own, surprised at how glad he was to see her once more even though it had only been minutes since he had left her at her doorstep.

Slowly, she relaxed, but she didn't pull away.

"Are you all right?" he whispered into her hair, fearing that someone might have bothered her again.

"Yes." Her answer was muffled by a nervous laugh against his throat. "I just brought you the spurs you left. I was afraid . . ." She held tighter. "I was afraid I'd missed you."

Sliding his hand along her arm, he took them from her fingers. "It's all right," he said as he looped the spurs over the saddle horn. "I would have returned."

Stepping a few inches away, she remained close. "Would you do me a favor as a friend?"

"Of course." He patted her shoulder, liking that they were now good enough friends to touch. "Name it. I'm at your service."

"Would you mind terribly kissing me good night?"

Cooper didn't answer. He couldn't answer. How could he tell her that he wasn't sure he felt about her that way? She was his friend. He admired her intelligence. He enjoyed her company. He looked forward to seeing her. He even liked the way she smelled, but he didn't feel about her the way a man should about a woman he kissed.

He leaned forward and lightly brushed her cheek with his lips.

Mary vanished into the darkness as quickly as she'd appeared. Like a rush of wind, she was gone, leaving only the slight sound of an escaped sob behind.

It took Cooper a moment to realize what he'd done. Dear God, he hadn't meant to hurt her. She'd been asking for something else, something more.

He ran toward the store, but as he neared he saw Miles Woodburn unloading a wagon, limping back and forth. It was too late to talk to Mary. Too late to say he was sorry.

Chapter Ten

ANY HOPE COOPER had of finding time to apologize to Mary evaporated in the frantic days that followed. He'd agreed that the final cattle drive before winter would start from the natural corral on his land called Echo Canyon. As each rancher brought in his small herd, Cooper had to be there to help. For many of his neighbors the success of this drive would mean surviving the winter without having to go to Dallas to find work.

His sisters planned the country ball for the night before all the men had to leave so there would be enough dance partners for every single woman. The big day arrived on Saturday amid cloudy skies and high spirits. Ranchers and their families started pulling onto Cooper's land by mid-morning.

Though the Adams ranch was throwing the shindig, custom required no one come to call empty-handed. Cakes, pies, and cobblers were added to the sisters' desserts. Jellies, jams, and fresh breads were piled atop Cooper's desk. The

Williamses brought cider they had shipped from Tennessee.
The undertaker proudly displayed three bottles of peach wine
he had bought in the hill country when he'd gone after hard-
ware. And of course, the Kileys lugged in apples for everyone.

Unmarried daughters were presented, first to Cooper's
sisters, then to him. Thanks to an abundance of cowhands,
Cooper had no difficulty introducing each woman to eligible
men more than happy to monopolize her time.

Cooper spent his time hanging around the pit built to
roast half a beef. The heat and smoke kept the women away.
He was in no mood to be sociable. The fact that he'd hurt
Mary's feelings bothered him and the more time that passed,
the more awkward he felt about saying something to her.

Lunch consisted of sandwiches sliced from the first
brisket to be declared cooked and desserts. As the afternoon wore on, several of the families spread blankets out
in the loft and on the porches. Some were for visiting,
some for sleeping children. The slight nip in the air made
cuddling comfortable as couples paired off to get better
acquainted. As far as Cooper could see, no unmarried girl
wandered around looking for him with an expression that
said she might just die unless she became Mrs. Cooper
Adams. In fact, they all seemed pleased with their choices,
smiling up at some stammering cowhand with true love in
his eyes. It had never occurred to Cooper until today that
the ladies might consider him too old, or too hardened for
marrying. He'd been thinking he wanted the pick of the lit-
ter. Now the question seemed to be, Did the pick want him?

Several men stood around the cook fire, talking of
weather and the threat of rustlers; women bordered a quilt
frame. Cooper had no idea what they talked about. For a
man with three sisters he should know more about women.
Mary taught him different. He thought they were friends.
But before he could get at ease with the agreement, she ran
into his arms and asked him to kiss her.

He managed to figure one thing out in almost thirty
years. Women were nothing but trouble. He liked the idea

of being friends with her, but he had no right to be thinking about how good Mary felt next to him.

She had asked him a simple favor. "As a friend" she'd said, and without a word he had let her down. His peck of the cheek must have made her feel ugly and unwanted. No woman wanted to feel that way. He'd done what he thought a friend would want him to do and somehow it had all gone wrong.

"That's women for you," he swore under his breath. "Should've kept my distance."

Cooper glanced up and noticed his sister Winnie standing on the porch. He smiled to himself. She'd never had a gentleman caller. Now she ran around singing and blushing like a young girl. He wasn't sure if Woodburn asked to court her because he liked Winnie, or because the man simply didn't like the way everyone treated her. When Cooper checked on them one Sunday, Winnie had been talking away and Miles sat all straight and stiff as if waiting on his turn to get out of purgatory.

If Woodburn was just being nice, allowing Winnie her fellow for a while, Cooper still couldn't say he liked the man, but had to admit the Yankee irritated him less.

Cooper turned the slowly cooking beef and stared out at the boiling sky to the north. The color reminded him of Mary's eyes. Stormy weather blue. For all he knew, he was the first man she'd ever asked to kiss her. Maybe she figured no man would try. She asked a friend to let her know what it was like.

Cooper knew that even if he explained she wasn't homely, she wouldn't believe him. How could he say the words and be honest with both her and himself? She might never be a great beauty, but she was easy to look at. He should have told her that. She had pretty eyes, the kind a man could get lost in. And her voice was soft, like her words were meant only for him to hear. He should have said something. Maybe that would have helped.

By midafternoon, every man, woman, and child in the county tromped around his ranch, except Mary and her brother. Cooper told himself he didn't care, but every time he looked up, he saw Winnie watching the road. The Yankee and his sister might not want to come to the party, but they had no right to hurt Winnie.

The more Cooper thought about it, the madder he got. As shadows melted together and the three-piece band warmed up in the barn, rain blew in like an unwanted guest.

Cooper rushed with everyone else to move things inside. Every time he passed Winnie, he saw her worried expression and her gaze turned to the road. Finally, he grabbed a slicker, saddled a horse, and rode out toward town. If Woodburn wasn't bothering to show up, he would have some explaining to do.

Almost within sight of Minnow Springs, Cooper spotted the old borrowed buggy of Woodburn's leaning almost sideways, a back wheel propped against it. Miles stood alone in the muddy road, his jacket off, his sleeves rolled to the elbows.

Anger turned to worry inside Cooper. As he neared, he yelled, "Having trouble?"

Miles shoved his thinning hair off his face. "This time, I am."

As Cooper swung down from the saddle, Woodburn added, "I finally got the wheel patched enough so it should hold, but I can't lift the frame and roll it into place. Would you mind giving me a hand?" He chewed on the words a minute before he added, "You see, there's a party I promised to attend."

Cooper moved to the boot of the old buggy. Bracing his feet in four inches of mud, he lifted.

Miles maneuvered the wheel around the axis. "Thanks," he shouted over the rain as he stood.

"Where's Mary?" Cooper tried to make his question sound casual while he watched Miles roll muddy sleeves down over even dirtier arms.

"She walked back to town. With everyone already gone to your place, she decided she could get a wagon and be back faster than I could fix this wheel." Frustration deepened the lines on his scarred face. "With this leg, it's hard for me to walk on flat ground, much less in the mud. I talked her into coming along and now it looks like we may miss the party."

Cooper swung onto his saddle, realizing riding a horse must be impossible for Woodburn or he would have ridden bareback to the ranch and left the wagon by the road. "Go ahead. Winnie's worried about you. I'll head toward town until I find your sister, then I'll make sure she gets to the ranch safely."

Woodburn grumbled at the suggestion, but climbed inside the buggy.

Cooper lowered his hat and rode straight into the wind. He hoped Mary had made it to town before rain drenched her.

A deserted Main Street, dressed in thick gray fog, greeted him. Rain hung in the air, soaking him despite the oiled slicker. Cooper tried the Woodburns' store first, then realized Mary was probably at the livery.

There would be a slim selection of wagons left if the old buggy had been their best choice before. And she'd have to rig it herself, for the Andrews clan had been among the first to show up at the ball. By midafternoon Cooper had no doubt the children were instructed to eat their weight in food.

When he stepped into the livery, the sound of someone crying drifted around him seeming to come from no particular direction. For a moment, he thought it might be one of the Andrews kids who had been accidentally left behind.

He moved closer, hearing the jingle of his muddy spurs blend with the sobbing. Pausing, Cooper let his eyes adjust to the dim light.

Finally he spotted Mary, curled into a ball, arms hugging her knees, head down, hair wild around her shoulders. She was sitting in the back of a wagon that would have taken both a carpenter and a blacksmith a week to get in even fair shape to travel.

Cooper waited, knowing that if he took one step toward her the spurs would frighten her. "Evening, Miss Woodburn," he said slowly. "Nice day for a ride."

Mary's head shot up. Bright blue-gray eyes sparkled on a muddy face. When she spotted him in the doorway, she quickly shoved a tear, along with caked dirt, across her cheek.

Cooper couldn't help but laugh. "You look like a mud doll."

Mary grinned back. "You don't look much better."

He smoothed a layer of muck off his duster. "And I got all dressed up for the country ball."

"Me too. Miles said I had to go for Winnie's sake, but my efforts to dress were wasted. I fell twice running toward town, trying to beat the rain. I'd hoped to find a rig that might make it out of the barn, but I've failed. Miles is stuck out on the road, unable—"

"He's on his way to my ranch," Cooper interrupted. "I'm supposed to bring you along."

"I'm not going." She stared down at her clothes. "It's impossible."

"Then the party will come to you." Cooper took a step forward. "I don't care if I return or not. The whole thing is a hoax. After everyone stuffs themselves a few more times and dances a couple of rounds, they'll probably raffle me off to the highest bidder."

"Oh. You think you'll go for a good price?"

"Of course. If you don't count the undertaker, who owns his own business, I'm the most eligible bachelor in this part of the state." He laughed at his own lie. "I'm sure I'll go to the girl whose father can send the most acres along with his daughter's hand."

Helping Mary out of the wagon, he added, "You look mighty pretty, Miss Woodburn." To his surprise, he meant it. "Would you like to dance before I'm hog-tied and carted off to the altar?"

"I hate to turn a man down whose freedom is now counted in hours."

He pulled her into his arms before she could say more, holding her far closer than he would have dared to in public. With her feet barely touching the ground, they twirled around the hay-covered floor as though they were at a grand ball.

When he slowed the dance, he realized she was soaked and shivering. In one swing, he lifted her into his arms and carried her toward the door. "Do you trust me, Mary?"

"I think I finally do."

"Then, let's get you into some dry clothes and try dancing again on my barn floor with music playing. We'll both catch pneumonia if we stay in this drafty place much longer."

Before she questioned, he ran into the rain toward her store. By the time she unlocked the door they were both newly soaked.

Laughing for no reason other than it felt good, he followed her upstairs. Cooper hesitated only a moment when he reached the threshold.

She crossed into the darkness and returned a moment later to hand him a dry towel. "Come in by the fire. I'll change." She hurried across the room and disappeared behind a door.

Cooper stood in the center of the small apartment and scrubbed the water from his face. Then he stirred up the fire and looked around the room. Hundreds of books lined the walls and art, fine art, blanketed every inch of space left. He knew, without having to ask, that these were the few, final treasures of what once must have been a grand home. He'd always thought of Southerners coming home to only the crumbs left of their former lives. He never thought of Northerners losing everything in the war.

Slowly, he realized what a joke it must have been for him to loan her books. She probably grew up with a real library in her house.

He pulled off his duster and damp coat, hanging them over chairs to dry. Unlike the store, the apartment above was neat, orderly, with a once valuable rug adding a warmth that made the small place a home.

He saw what must be Miles's room across from Mary's closed door. Maps and charts covered the walls of his chamber. A cot was crammed into one corner, making room for a huge desk weighted with books and papers.

"Your brother studying something?" he yelled toward the closed door.

Mary's muffled answer returned, "He wants to write a book about the battles in the war. He's already written several articles that sold back east."

"And spent all the money on more books," Cooper guessed.

"I'm afraid so." Mary could barely be heard. "But it will all be worth it once he's published."

Cooper couldn't bring himself to invade Woodburn's private space. He never would have guessed the cold man would have such a secret.

Mary's door opened, shining more light into the room. Cooper turned and watched her move about.

"I'll put on some tea." Nervousness shook her words. "We can drink it while my hair dries." She crossed into the tiny square of a kitchen and poured water into a pot.

He couldn't take his eyes off of her. Against her robe, he could see the outline of her body and the grace in each movement. She didn't belong in faded dresses.

After she handed him a cup of tea, she pulled a stool close to the fire and began brushing her hair dry in the warm air.

Cooper had seen his sisters do the same thing a thousand times, but as Mary dried her long chestnut mane, he couldn't stop staring.

"I'll only take a few minutes," she apologized when she looked up.

"Take a lifetime," he whispered. "It's beautiful to watch."

Mary laughed. "If we're to be friends, Mr. Adams, you can't tease me. I'm fully aware that I'm plain. Miles says when we save enough money we can go back east and I'll become a schoolmarm. He says I have the look of one already."

"You could teach school here," he said more to himself than her as he moved to the chair behind her stool.

She went back to pulling the brush through her hair.

"Mary, why'd you ask me to kiss you the other night?" he inquired after several minutes of silence.

"I don't know." She didn't look at him. "Maybe I just wanted to know how it felt."

"My kiss or any kiss?"

"Yours." She stared into the embers. "I was kissed once and didn't like it. I thought that if you kissed me then I wouldn't think of it as being something ugly."

She rose to her feet. "The rain sounds like it may have stopped. I should change."

He stood, blocking her path. "Do you think I could try again? On the kiss, I mean."

She stared at him-with her wonderful, expressive eyes. He saw a question, but no fear. They'd finally gotten beyond her fright.

"No." She shook her head, letting her curls tumble around her shoulders. "It is kind of you to ask, but . . ."

"I'm not being kind." He swept a strand away from her cheek. "I'm being honest. There is nothing I'd like more than to kiss you right now."

He leaned down and brushed his lips against her cheek as he had almost a week ago. When she didn't retreat, he cupped her chin with his fingers.

His mouth swept over hers, forever erasing the bruising kiss she'd once endured. Mary had read about such a kiss. She'd dreamed about it, but she never thought anyone would kiss her so. She closed her eyes, trying to remember every detail.

"More?" he whispered across her lips.

"More," she answered and rested her hand on his shoulder to steady herself.

This time, he leaned closer, his warm lips caressing her throat before he ventured to her mouth. She couldn't hold back the sigh that escaped as he found her lips once more. Never, not for one minute in her life, had she ever felt beautiful, but she felt so now.

A sensation of being cherished washed over her, filling the very depth of her soul. Her lifetime would now be measured in the before and after of this one moment. She'd never be the same. In the twilight hours she would think of this and at dawn, just before she awoke, she'd remember the way Cooper Adams tasted on her lips.

"More." She repeated her request when he moved once again to her throat. "More, please."

His words tickled her ear. "You only have to ask once, Mary."

His arm curled around her back, pulling her close. He tried to keep it light, as he guessed a woman would want her first kiss to be. But when she came so willingly to him and he felt the length of her pressing against him, he deepened the kiss.

Heaven had stepped into his arms. The warmth of her, the fresh, rainwater smell of her surrounded him. How could he not have known she had been so near for years?

Her body fit against him perfectly. She was gentle, soft spoken, intelligent. In her arms his worries faded. The taste of her left him longing for more. The beauty in her could not be measured in just a pretty face. She had a beauty that settled against his heart.

As her arms circled his neck and her fingers crossed into his hair, he lifted her off the floor and opened her mouth with his tongue. He knew he was bold. She was a woman who needed to be treated tenderly. But he was starving for the taste of her.

She jerked in surprise.

He moved his hand along her back, calming any fears as he brought passion to her simple request for a kiss. If she had pulled away, he would have stopped, no matter how much he'd have hated to. But even in her shock, she clung to him.

One step at a time, he taught her. Kissing her deeply. Lovingly moving his fingers over her body. Letting her know the magic that happens when the senses overload with pleasure.

Her heart beat wildly against his and he knew she wanted his touch as dearly as he needed to feel her near. Her hand fumbled with the sash of her robe a moment before the heavy wool parted and her body, clad only in undergarments, pressed against him once more.

She gulped for breath as she leaned her head back. His kisses explored her throat. His mouth covered where her pulse pounded as his hand moved up to brush over her breast.

So great a pleasure exploded in her senses, she would have fallen had he not held her. His tongue journeyed along her throat until his kisses reached the bottom of her ear, making her forget to breathe. His thumb slid across the tip of her breast, caressing her until she ached for more. The taste of him was paradise. The smell that was only him filled the air around her. They were suddenly floating in a river without shores, without boundaries, and her only thought was that she wanted more.

She craved all there was of this lovemaking she'd known nothing of before today. Before Cooper.

Pushing him an inch away Mary tried to remember how to speak. She had to tell him of the wonder he'd helped her discover. He had to know what a gift he'd given her with his touch.

But before she could say anything, he whispered, "Dear God, Mary. . . . I'm sorry."

Chapter Eleven

COOPER STEPPED OUT into the night air while he waited for Mary to finish dressing. He wished the rain still pounded. Hell, he thought, he wished lightning would strike him right now. Maybe if he got a strong enough jolt he would be knocked senseless and feel better.

Nothing could make him feel worse.

"I'm ready," Mary whispered from behind him as she stepped out, then turned to lock the store door.

He glanced around. Back in her plain dress, with her hair pulled tightly in a knot, little remained of the passionate woman who'd been in his arms minutes before. He couldn't tell if she had been crying—she refused to look up at him. He wouldn't blame her. If she had not pushed away from him when she did he might have made love to her. He had never been so out of control, so mindless, in his life.

Cooper pulled his horse close to the porch and waited. He didn't want to even guess what she thought of him right now. She probably wondered what kind of friend offers a kiss and then starts undressing her.

"Can you help me up?" she asked in little more than a whisper.

Awkwardly, Cooper placed his hands around her waist and lifted her onto the saddle. He tried not to think about how she had felt earlier, but he wasn't sure he would ever forget the fullness of her breast in his hand with only a layer of cotton between them. She hadn't said a word since he apologized and from the way she stiffened when he touched her, Mary was doing her best to forget he still breathed on the same planet.

He thought of walking home and letting her ride alone, but that would only serve to make him a bigger fool. In this mud it would take him an hour or more and they would probably get rained on again.

Attempting not to touch her, he slipped his boot in the stirrup and swung up behind her. When his body wrapped around her, she stiffened once more.

"Are you all right?"

"I'm fine." The lie frosted the night air. "I'd just like to get to the party. My brother will be worried about me."

Cooper gripped the reins in front of her, trying not to notice that his arm rested just above her waist. Her nearness would probably drive him mad before they traveled a mile. He kicked his horse into action. For a moment, they bumped together, both making every effort not to touch the other.

Finally, he wrapped his free arm around her and pulled her against his chest.

She made no protest as he held her securely in his embrace. He wouldn't have been surprised if she'd fought him. By now, everything about the woman he held was a surprise to him.

Their bodies moved in unison, but they were halfway to his ranch before she relaxed and rested her head against his shoulder. His hold on her remained constant, secure.

When they were within sight of the ranch, Cooper slowed.

He couldn't go back to the party without clearing the air between them. He didn't want her hating him. "Mary, there is something we've got to get straight. I didn't mean for what happened between us to happen. You've got to believe I never meant to hurt you."

She twisted within his arms until her words whispered against his ear. "What happened between us, happened *between* us, not *to* me; and you didn't hurt me until you said you were sorry."

They were so close to the house he was afraid someone might hear him so he didn't answer her.

As he lifted her down from the saddle she added, "But don't worry, it will never happen between us again. So you can stop apologizing. In fact it might be better if we simply never spoke to one another again." She shoved a tear off her cheek with an angry movement.

Mary vanished into the house before he had time to think of an answer. Women. He was right about them. Mary might not be as chatty as most, but she made up for it by being helpless and confusing. This time she had not even bothered to say thank you for his riding into town to get her. And he had no idea what she was talking about when she said "between" and not "to."

He walked toward the barn thinking all the people enjoying the party had better eat up because there wasn't going to be another bride-finding ball. He never planned to marry.

Chapter Twelve

THE ORANGE GLOW of twilight was the unofficial time for the dance to start, but Cooper's sisters insisted on waiting until he returned to the ranch. As he tied his horse on the corral fence, the three musicians stopped warming up and played the opening strings to the Virginia Reel.

Johanna stood on the porch and yelled loud enough for anyone within five miles to hear that it was time to move inside the barn.

Emma organized a chain of ladies to pass all remaining desserts to the tables set up along the fringes of the dance floor. Quilts were hung from the loft, hiding the stalls and along the rafters to block wind. Color rainbowed the interior, adding a feeling of warmth to the old shelter, while the aroma of hot cider melted through the air.

Mary stayed in the kitchen cutting pies with a silver pie server Johanna insisted she use. She wanted no part of this dance, or of Cooper Adams. But Winnie pulled her out, insisting she had to watch Miles dance.

"He doesn't," Mary tried to tell her as they hurried toward the barn. "He can't."

Winnie didn't bother to argue.

Ten minutes later, Mary stood just out of the circle of light glowing from lanterns above and watched as her brother took Winnie's hand. They walked to the center. Music played. Miles bowed as if he were dressed in formal clothes and Winnie in a ball gown. Winnie placed her hand in his and they began to waltz.

Everyone watched as they danced alone in the center of the dirt floor. His step was awkward. Winnie's short, round body and his lean frame didn't match at all. But no one in the room noticed, for Winnie smiled up at the scarred face of Miles Woodburn as though he were the most handsome man in the state, and he looked down at her with eyes that told everyone that she was beautiful.

Slowly, others joined the waltz. They circled around the strange couple. Mary lost sight of her brother. For a while she stood in the shadows, fighting tears and trying to remember how long it had been since she'd seen Miles smile. Years ago she decided he had forgotten how.

As the music changed and folks sought other partners, Mary sank into the darkness between quilt curtains, wishing, as she often did, that she could become invisible. All these years she thought her brother had been the sad one, the lonely one, and she'd been the one who stayed with him. She was the rock and he was the one who suffered from all they'd lost. The possibility that she might have been the sibling who couldn't have survived alone clouded her mind.

An hour into the dance, a group of cowhands from the Rocking R arrived, accompanied by several men she'd never seen. They must have started drinking while cleaning up for the party, for they entered loud and the atmosphere shifted subtly from that of a ball to a dance hall.

The rough newcomers reminded her of mustangs. Restless, untamed. She guessed they had been hired to help with the cattle drive leaving at dawn. She noticed the county marshal had quit dancing and watched the crowd.

Mary curled deeper into the shadows. She wished she were home reading and away from these men she'd never seen before. Their manners belonged on the trail, not in polite company.

Lost in her thoughts, she didn't notice people moving about her. She closed her eyes and tried to remember what it had felt like to dance with Cooper in the Andrewses' livery. She tried to pinpoint the moment she realized she loved him. Maybe it was when he kissed her, or when he handed her his treasured book, or maybe it was before they ever spoke. Something about him drew her, long before he knew her name. She liked the way he tipped his hat to the ladies when he walked down Main Street and the way he always patted his horse at the post office as if thanking the animal. She'd watched him for years, wishing she were brave enough to talk to him.

Not that it mattered, she told herself. They would never talk again, or even be friends now. Her pride would not allow it. Not after he said he was sorry for kissing her.

The murmur of a man's raspy voice drifted into Mary's thoughts.

"Another half hour, that should be about right."

Mary didn't breathe. Someone stood only a foot away from her, but hadn't seen her in the darkness. She pushed against the thick pole that stretched to the roof, wishing she could disappear into the wood. A quilt above her head blew in the evening breeze, playing hide-and-seek with her in the shadows.

"We'll give everyone a chance to enjoy the dance, drink a little too much, get tired," the low voice whispered again. "Then, when the shouting starts, they'll react without thinking."

A youthful voice answered back. "I don't know about this plan. If you ask me, we should do some more pondering before we act. After tomorrow, most of Adams's men will be gone. I figure, then the three of us can take him if he catches us."

Mary guessed the second man must still be in his teens

for his voice hadn't completely changed. He sounded frightened.

"Don't chicken out on me now. You want that horse, don't you? In an hour we'll have every man in this county running after rustlers. All we have to do is walk away with that Steeldust colt of Adams's. He'll never know what happened. He'll just come back from chasing a lie and the little horse will be gone, vanished into thin air."

"But what about the women?" The boy's voice cracked again. "Them old maid sisters of his don't exactly look helpless. Hell, half the women here can probably handle a gun better than me."

"Don't worry about them," the man with gravel in his tone answered. "Once the men leave, the women will head into the house. They'll be so busy talking they won't even hear us. And if one of them does wander out of the house, Len will take care of her with his knife."

The second voice climbed higher. "Now, wait a minute, I ain't for no killin' of women. I thought we were just here for the colt, nothing more. I know you don't like Adams 'cause he fired you, but that ain't no reason to hurt the womenfolk."

"Don't worry. Women never wander out on their own. They only travel in herds."

"Well, just in case, tell Len to say he's supposed to move the colt if one of them comes out. That way it won't cause no suspicion. I don't mind killin' Adams if he gets in the way, but I don't want to start leaving too many bodies or the next thing I know, the Rangers will be looking for me the way they're looking for you."

"You go tell Len. He's out by the corral waiting." With a mixture of anger and authority the older man left no doubt that he was the leader. "I want to watch the dancing."

Mary heard them moving behind her. The tinkling of their spurs soured the music's rhythm. She waited, hoping one of them would step into the light, but there were too many people. One, or both, could easily blend into the crowd.

She circled between the groups of people, eager to spot the face that would match the young southern voice. But most of the cowhands looked the same. Tall, lean, tanned by the sun. The lively music and laughter intermingled voices. She hoped to catch a few words that sounded like one of the men she'd overheard.

She didn't notice Cooper standing beside her until he spoke.

"Would you dance with me, Mary, if I promised not to talk to you?" His face was guarded, void of all expression. She couldn't be sure if he looked worried, or angry, or if he was simply playing host.

Dancing was the last thing she wanted to do, but she had to tell him what she'd heard. Even if it was some kind of joke the boys were playing, Cooper had a right to be warned. Only they hadn't sounded like they were joking.

Mary faced him and slowly raised her hand. "You promise not to say a word?"

"Cross my heart, darlin'," he answered. The hint of a smile fought its way across his face as his hand reached for hers. The worry lines along his forehead relaxed.

"Good, because I've something I have to tell you." Mary couldn't read him. He gripped her fingers as if he had been looking for her for hours and didn't plan to let her go anytime soon, but his eyes held an uncertainty. "It . . ."

"It can wait," he whispered against her cheek as he pulled her onto the floor.

His arm felt solid around her waist, but he didn't pull her as close as he had when they'd danced in the livery. His fingers caressed hers as he swung her in time to the music. For a man who claimed to hate dances and told his sisters he saw no need for a ball, Cooper managed to keep in step. At first, Mary thought of nothing but trying to stay up with him without making a fool of herself. She wasn't about to tell him she had never truly danced, but she feared it was apparent, for she could not seem to follow him or the music.

When she tromped across his boots for the fourth time, he leaned close and whispered, "Why don't you just stand on them, darlin'. At least then I'll know where you are."

Mary felt her face blush all the way to her hairline. She

fought to pull away, but he held her as they continued to try to follow the music.

Anger boiled inside her. She was trying to help him but he guided her into the center of the room, a place she never wanted to be. Mary fired out the first thing that came to her mind. "Stop calling me darling!"

He pulled her far too close to be considered proper. "I'm not even talking to you." He brushed her ear with his lips as he spoke. "Relax. Dance with me, Mary. Just like you did before when no one was watching."

"I don't want to dance," she answered, aware that people stared at them. "I need to talk to you."

"I thought we were never speaking again."

"Shut up and listen." Mary decided Cooper would drive a mute woman to scream. Her own meek ways were fading fast in frustration.

He laughed again, loud enough that several couples turned to face them. "You're sure getting bossy, Mary, my dear."

Releasing all but her hand, he walked to the side of the musicians' stand. The tune was too loud for conversation. Mary didn't want to shout. Without a word, she tugged at his arm and pulled him into the back of the barn.

He made no protest as they slipped between the patchwork blankets and melted into the blackness of one of the horse stalls. Mary slowed and gripped his arm tighter. The place had been swept clean, but the smell of hay and horses still lingered.

As she crossed the darkness, he moved closer, letting her know he was right beside her. The warmth of his body comforted and excited her at the same time. When she touched the smooth wood at the back of the stall, she turned to face him. "Cooper, I have to—"

"I know, I lied." His hands moved up her arms and into her hair. "I'll never be sorry for kissing you," he said, a moment before his mouth found hers. His kiss was hard and hungry, as though he'd been starving.

Mary opened her mouth to protest and the kiss deepened.

He leaned closer, pushing her against the back of the stall. Her mind told her this was insane, there was information he must know. He might even be in danger. But pleasure stampeded over reason.

Wrapping her arms around his neck, she returned his kiss.

He took the advance with a low moan and welcomed her along the length of him. They moved, like old lovers, in perfect harmony to this dance.

Her hair tumbled free. His hand spread into the dark curls, lost in the softness as he drank deep of the taste of her. Quiet, shy, plain little Mary had somehow become the woman he knew he couldn't live without. Even in the darkness, with the music playing and people laughing only a few feet away, Cooper couldn't bring himself to stop. From the moment he'd helped her off the horse and she slipped from his arms, all he'd been able to think about was her. He'd gone half mad trying to look for her without being obvious. About the time he decided she must have left the party and walked back to town, she appeared.

She rushed to him, saying she needed to talk, pulling him into the shadows. He forgot all the words he'd planned to say to her. Now he couldn't get close enough to her. It didn't matter if they talked, as long as they held one another. He planned to take a lifetime to convince her how he felt; right now all he wanted to do was show her.

She thawed as he touched her.

Hesitantly, he brushed his fingers over her breast and caught her reaction against his lips. She moved so that his hand caressed her once more.

Pure pleasure bolted through his blood. He closed his fingers around her, feeling the soft mound through thin cotton. Her dress might be drab and ordinary, but there was nothing short of perfection in his hand.

Widening his fingers, he moved his hands slowly along her sides as he kissed her, loving the way she swayed against him when he cupped her round bottom.

He wanted to undress her. To make love to her. He didn't

care if the entire county saw them. But he would wait. For now, just holding her would have to be enough.

His arms closed around her and he straightened, lifting her off the ground. She was his as surely as if they'd said the words. He had finally found his mate. Whether he bedded her this night, or waited a year, didn't matter. She was his other half, and he was hers.

He pulled an inch away and whispered, "Marry me, Mary."

Before she could answer, shouts exploded from the other side of the quilts. The music stopped. Everyone spoke at once. Cooper circled his arm around her shoulder as they ran toward the light.

"Rustlers!" someone yelled beyond the dancers. "They're driving the herd out of Echo Canyon. Hurry!"

The women cried out and scrambled for their children. The men moved in a mass toward the barn door and their horses.

"Let's ride!" one man shouted. "We'll catch them this time!"

"Get my rifle from the wagon. I'll give them a fair trial before I shoot every last one of them."

"Hurry, men! We don't want any to get away."

Cooper almost dragged Mary along, for she held with a death grip on his arm. They crossed with the others to the corral, where the horses seemed to catch the excitement.

"You can't go!" She pulled at his arm, realizing for the first time how much stronger he was than her.

He barely heard her above the crowd. "I have to. A year's work depends on those cattle." He tried to be gentle. "Don't worry. I'll be back in a few hours."

Her grip didn't loosen. "You can't go! I heard men talking. . . ."

Cooper pulled from her as Duly brought up his horse. The midnight mare pranced between them. "Stay with my sisters!" he yelled as he swung onto the saddle.

"Don't go!" She had no time to explain. "Your future is in danger. Don't go!" Mary wasn't sure if he heard her last words. Everyone shouted as the men rode off toward Echo Canyon.

Once the men left, the women and children stood outside the barn and listened until they no longer heard the sound of hooves pounding. For a few minutes all was silent. Too silent.

Johanna's voice rang like a lone bell. "Come along. Let's go inside. We've nothing to do but make coffee and wait."

Everyone seemed to agree. They gathered children and moved inside the house. Mary glanced around in panic, wishing she had a horse. Maybe she could catch up with the men. If she tried harder, she could make him understand.

But even the old nags had been untied from the wagons and ridden bareback by men in a hurry. Nothing remained in the corral except a dozen young colts shooed off into the corners.

Mary hurried to the fence. One of them had to be the Steeldust colt the strangers planned to take. But which one? She tried to remember what the colt had looked like the day Cooper showed him to her, but she'd been paying more attention to his hand touching hers than to the horse.

She couldn't watch them all. It was so dark she wasn't sure she could even see several of the animals. And even if she did keep her eye on the colt, how would she be able to stop men from taking it?

Glancing back at the house, she noticed Miles standing alone in the shadows beside the porch. She knew why he was there. He wouldn't go in with the women. He couldn't ride with the men.

Mary ran to her brother. As she pulled him toward the corral, she tried to remember all she'd heard. They had to somehow protect the colt. But the enemy had no face and she knew few details.

Miles listened to her ramblings, but she could see it in his face as clearly as if he'd said the words, *What can I do? What help would I be?*

When words finally came all he said was, "Go in with the women, Mary."

"I'm staying," she said as he took a step toward the house.

He shifted, waiting for her to come to her senses. "You're going back to the house," Miles ordered, as he always did.

"No," she answered just as strongly. "Not this time. It is my fault Cooper wasn't warned about the trick. I should have told him."

"But what if you run into the rustlers? What then, Mary? You said there were three. You don't even have a weapon."

Her brother knew her for the coward she was. Afraid of the dark. Afraid of the sound of spurs. Afraid of almost every man in the state. What did she think she could do against three men?

"Come back with me," Miles asked again.

"No," she answered. "I have to try."

Even in the darkness she could see it in his eyes. He would no longer play the parent role in her life, she would never again be the child. "All right." He moved toward her. "Then I'll stay also."

Mary knew they were still no match for three armed men, but she was glad Miles stayed.

"Evenin'," came a low voice from the shadows. Spurs jingled as a man stepped into the faint light coming from the barn door. "So, we meet again."

It had been almost a year, but Mary knew the stranger's voice. She'd heard it last in the darkness of the store.

She couldn't breathe as the man moved closer. The feel of his hands gripping her arms, his hot words shouted in her face, the smell of whiskey, all flooded her mind. He had been so polite, so nice that afternoon, but in the shadows, anger twisted his words.

"Adams will be back in a few minutes with his men," Miles threatened as he stepped in front of Mary. "You had better be gone before he returns."

The intruder pulled a long Bowie knife from his boot. "Don't try to fool me, Yank. He won't return for hours. He and every man for miles around will be chasing shadows tonight."

"I'll not let you take the colt." Miles stood his ground.

The man laughed. "How do you plan to stop me? If you had a gun it would already be pointing in my direction and you'd be no match for me with a knife even if you had one."

"Kill them and be done with it, Len." A man on horseback rode out of the blackness. "We ain't got all night." His gruff voice rattled across the damp air.

Mary recognized him as one she'd heard earlier during the dance. The planner.

"Now, wait a minute, boss. You don't know who we're dealing with. This Yank won't fight. It ain't no fun killing a man who won't fight back." Len moved a step closer and pointed with his knife. "But the woman, she screams and fights like crazy. I'll have to slit her throat, before I let the Yank die a little at a time."

"Do what you have to do," the leader said calmly as if they were of no importance to him. "The kid backed out on us. I'll need your help rounding up the colt. Get rid of the witnesses."

Chapter Thirteen

COOPER YELLED ORDERS for his men to guard the herd and let the others worry about chasing rustlers as he turned the midnight mare toward home.

"But, boss?" a ranch hand yelled over the thunder of hooves. "Don't you want in on the ride? They couldn't outrun us."

Cooper didn't bother answering. Three times the men required to round up a half dozen rustlers were riding north at full speed. The county marshal took the lead, much more at home than he'd been on the dance floor. Cooper wasn't needed in Echo Canyon. Something about the call to arms gnawed at him. Why would men try to steal a herd the night before a drive began when every able-bodied cowhand was camped out, waiting to get started, or at the dance a few miles away? And if they'd moved that many cattle, why hadn't someone heard? Cooper might have been occupied, but Duly had maintained a residence on the porch all night. The old cook could smell rain before a cloud formed.

Cooper couldn't remember the number of times he'd seen Duly start thinning the gravy before anyone else even heard riders arriving for supper.

Pushing his horse harder toward home, Cooper tried to make the pieces fit.

Mary's last words haunted him. She'd said his future was in danger. Even if the cattle he put into the drive were stolen, the ranch would stand the loss. Didn't she understand that he was solid enough to survive?

He figured the cattle, even the Steeldust colt, could disappear and they'd still make it as long as she was by his side. He had to tell her that his need for her was more than an ache deep inside. He'd built the ranch for nothing if he didn't have her to share it with. These past years he'd worked thinking he would be happy, when all he needed was to find her.

She must know that she was his future. The last few minutes they'd been together before the shouting started had left no doubt how he felt. She was his future, the only future he wanted. Why would she think she was in danger? Mary would be safe with his sisters and the other women.

Cooper didn't slow until he spotted the house. The pale moon offered him little help as he neared. He heard women's voices braided with laughter. He breathed for the first time since he'd turned the mare around.

Whatever frightened Mary had been only in her mind. He'd have to learn that about her if he planned to cherish her for the next fifty or so years. She was gentle and kind and intelligent, but not brave. He would be brave enough for them both.

Cooper grinned as he stepped onto the porch. If he'd wanted brave, bossy, and absentminded he would have looked for a woman like one of his sisters. But he wanted Mary, who needed him to take care of her and protect her and love her.

As he walked into the house his gaze searched for her. From now on he'd find her here when he got home, he thought. She'd be the one who had supper ready, who waited for him, who bore his children, who completed his life.

His house was, at present, full of every size and age of

woman. They circled in small groups, busy visiting. Mary wasn't among them.

Johanna walked by with a plate of rock-hard cookies made by one of the Williams girls. "Forget something?" she asked when he refused her offer.

"Still trying to pawn off those cookies?" Cooper barely glanced at her as he continued searching the room.

"I have to. I don't want to hurt poor Janice's feelings. Having to take a full plate home, when most of the other desserts are gone, would injure her. It is my duty as hostess."

Cooper had no time for Johanna's endless social considerations. "Have you seen Mary?"

"No," she answered as she slipped a few cookies into his jacket pocket. "Don't worry," she whispered. "They won't crumble."

"Did she leave?"

"Who?"

"Mary."

"I don't know. Winnie asked me a few minutes ago about Miles. Maybe they went home, though I'd think they would have at least said good-bye. A simple 'Thank you for the invitation' would have been appropriate."

Cooper moved through the crowd, leaving Johanna talking. When he spotted Winnie, he mouthed one word. "Mary?"

Winnie shook her head and followed as he hurried out the kitchen door.

The old buggy Miles had managed to get to the dance was still pulled up beside the barn.

Cooper moved faster. He felt it now. Something was wrong. Mary hadn't been simply frightened. She'd tried to warn him. But of what? No one would bother the women. The men were well armed. All seemed secure, but suddenly fear chewed its way through Cooper's insides.

"Something's wrong," Winnie whispered, her breathing coming out in a low whistle. "I haven't seen Miles since the other men left."

They circled the house and headed toward the barn.

At the sound of Mary's voice just beyond the corral open-ing, Cooper froze.

Winnie slammed into his back, almost knocking him to the ground. He steadied himself and motioned for her to be quiet, though he found it hard to believe those ahead of them in the blackness couldn't hear Winnie's breathing. She'd run so hard, she sounded like a teakettle at full steam.

"What . . . is . . . it?" she said as she swallowed great gulps of air.

But Cooper wasn't there to answer her question. He'd already crossed the blackness and stood by the corral, his gun drawn. He could make out three figures circled by a lantern's low glow.

Miles's voice sounded deadly earnest. "I'll not allow you to harm my sister."

"And what are you going to do?" the man with his back to Cooper asked. "Kill me?"

"If I have to. I've killed men before."

Cooper watched as Miles stepped away from Mary and toward the man holding a huge knife. Mary backed into the shadows, her dark clothes blending her from sight.

"You see," Miles sounded almost as if he were giving a lecture, "it's not all that hard to kill a man. Sometimes, in life, the true challenge is trying not to end a life." He con-tinued moving toward the knife pointed at his gut. "Some-times you have to weigh one life against another."

Still several feet away, Cooper pointed his weapon to the center of the stranger's back. If the armed man lunged toward Miles or Mary he'd be dead before he could do any damage with the knife. Cooper wished he were closer and could whisper to Mary that all was under control, but he wasn't even sure where she was in the shadows.

"Don't move," a raspy voice whispered from just be-hind him as Cooper felt the barrel of a gun press against his side. "Let's just watch this play out without interrupting Len. I've heard he's an artist of sorts at his craft."

Cooper didn't take his eyes off the man with the knife. He didn't need to see the stranger behind him. Cooper's plan hadn't changed. He would fire if the knife moved and take his chances with whoever stood behind him.

A slight whistling sound rushed across the darkness. Len turned his head, listening.

Without any hint or warning, Miles jumped toward the knife. The blade sliced across his coat sleeve before he knocked it from Len's hand with expert ease. They struggled, but Len only fought when armed and wasn't prepared for the force of Miles's attack. Len's mistake was in fighting to retrieve the knife and not defending himself. The seasoned Yank won out, pinning Len to the ground.

Winnie rushed up, yelling, "He won't hit you. Miles swore he never would, even though he had special training in the war." She leaned down, only a few inches from the stranger's face. "But I didn't promise anything." She doubled up her fist and slammed it into Len's eye. "How dare you try to hurt folks!" Another punch pounded his nose. "Don't you know better than to threaten people with a knife!" She hit him again. "You could have killed the man I'm going to marry."

Winnie paused in midstrike and turned to Miles. "Are you all right, dear?"

Miles laughed. "I'm fine. The blade only sliced my jacket."

Winnie turned back to the stranger and let another blow fly. "That's his good suit!" she yelled. "You should be more careful."

Len spit blood, struggled, and cried for help all at the same time, but Miles's good knee pinned him down.

Cooper would have joined the laughter, but a gun still dug into his side and he could sense frustration.

"Tell them to stop," the raspy voice whispered, suddenly angry. "Or you're a dead man, Adams."

Cooper didn't move. Like Miles, he'd been in enough battles to know to wait for just the right moment for action.

Mary's frightened voice came from somewhere behind Cooper. "Lower the gun, mister."

Cooper felt the man hesitate. "You won't use that knife,

little lady. Just because you may have found Len's blade don't make you killer enough to use it."

"Are you willing to bet your life on that?" Mary's voice shook.

When the stranger twisted to see Mary, he offered Cooper the chance he'd been waiting for. He swung around and flattened the man with one blow. The gun that had been digging into his ribs fired harmlessly into the night sky, bringing women and lanterns from the house.

Cooper straightened and turned in time to catch Mary flying into his arms. He held her against his heart. "It's all right, darlin'. It's over." He felt her body trembling. "You may have saved my life, you know."

He slid his hand along her arm, wanting to calm her. "That was very brave of you holding a knife on a man."

As the handle to her weapon fell into his hand, she stammered, "It wasn't a knife, it's a pie server. Johanna insisted I carry it."

Cooper laughed and held her close. His timid little Mary was far braver than he'd given her credit for being. "Don't tell Johanna what you used it for."

"Oh, no. I'm not that brave." Mary giggled in his ear.

Miles hauled Len onto the porch while Cooper half carried the other man. Within a few minutes they were tied up and waiting delivery when the county marshal returned. Winnie continued to pound on Len until Miles gently pulled her away, swearing he planned never to make her angry.

Despite all the women gathering around asking questions, Cooper managed to find Mary. He wrapped his arms around her and lifted her off the ground, kissing her soundly. When he finally straightened and faced the crowd, Miles was staring at him. For a moment, Cooper wasn't sure what might happen, for he remembered Miles's warning to stay away from Mary. Then the Yank smiled and Cooper knew there would be no more battles to fight tonight.

Johanna's voice rose above all the noise. "A thank-you would be enough, Cooper. Or of course, since she may have saved your life, a handshake might be proper."

He pulled an inch away and stared down at the face of the woman he would love for the rest of his life. "You didn't answer my question, Mary. Will you marry me?"

"More," she whispered, brushing her lips over his.

She didn't have to ask twice. He'd propose again later; right now he had a promise to keep.

Coming Home

★

PATRICIA POTTER

Chapter One

 HOME!

From the brow of the hill, Seth Sinclair looked down at the ranch nestled in the valley. A suffocating sensation in his throat took his breath away.

Four and a half years and a journey to hell since he had been there.

Anticipation replaced the deep exhaustion he felt from his six-month-long journey from a prison camp in the East. He had been ill and weakened from a fever, then had walked much of the way, stopping to work for food. He'd finally found a horse in nearly as bad shape as he'd been. The two had healed physically along the way, though he wondered whether his soul ever would.

At least the ranch was still there. So much of the South had been destroyed. Homes. Farms. Plantations. Ranches.

He continued to gaze below. He wanted to ride in. And yet . . . his heart ached as he remembered the day he'd ridden away to war with his two brothers. He was returning alone. He didn't even know whether his father and last remaining brother knew of the deaths. Or his sister. She would be nearly seven now. She'd been only a babe in arms when he'd left.

He absorbed every detail. The house looked the worse for wear. Some of the fences were broken. But the old swing under the one giant cottonwood moved with the breeze. The barn and bunkhouse appeared intact. So much the same as he had remembered, except there was little movement. No bustle of cowhands riding in to change mounts.

Instead, it seemed as if all human presence had been removed. Maybe his brother and father were out tending cattle. Marilee would be with Trini, the family's housekeeper.

He urged his horse forward. He had written a letter about the deaths of Jason and Jared, the twins, but he had no idea whether his father had received it. It would break his heart.

The twins had been the adventurous members of the family, and he knew they had been his father's favorites, although Garrett Sinclair had tried his damndest not to show it.

Seth closed his eyes for a moment: seeing the twins together again, racing the road, laughing. Always laughing and pulling tricks on one another and the other members of the family.

Neither he nor his youngest brother had ever resented the place the twins had in their father's heart. It would be impossible for anyone to resent them. They had been so full of goodwill, good cheer, good spirits.

They had died together at the Wilderness, the same battle in which he had been taken prisoner. He had refused to leave them when his own men scattered after his unit was overrun. Thank God they died quickly. He could still hear the screams of the wounded as the fires advanced.

He forced the memories away. No time to think of that, nor of the months of near-starvation that followed.

He was home.

First thing he would do was shake his father's hand, hug his little sister, and take a bath. He hadn't had a proper bath in years. It had taken every penny he could earn, steal, or borrow to get home. There had been no money for extras such as a hotel or barber or public bath.

He would probably scare the devil at the moment. He had stopped at a muddy stream to try to clean but ended up even dirtier. He had a beard and had cut his own hair. It was long and ragged, but what the hell. Trini could fix it for him.

He leaned down and ran his hand along Chance's neck. He'd named the horse Last Chance and in the last few weeks of traveling together, they had gotten to know each other.

Even now if he tried to run the gelding for long, he would probably kill him. He took it slow and easy, savored the smell of grass untainted by blood, a sky so vast and blue it made him hurt inside, and a sun that looked close enough to touch it. Damn, he had missed that bold and brassy Texas sky.

He stopped at the closed gate, leaned down from the horse and unlatched it, then rode through. He dismounted, closed it, and remounted. Something was wrong. Then he realized what it was. The Sinclair sign was gone.

Still, he could look around and see that other structures needed repair. Perhaps this was far down on the list. Worry knotted in the pit of his stomach. That should have been one of the first things fixed.

The ranch had been in Sinclair hands since before Texas was freed from Mexico. His grandfather had bought a Spanish grant from a family who'd tired of Indian raids. His grandfather had fought off Indians, Mexicans, outlaws. His father had done the same.

The land was nourished by Sinclair blood as well as the river that ran alongside its west boundary. It was the river that made the land valuable.

He reached the well and dismounted. Just then the whine of a shot echoed in the warm afternoon sun. Earth spit up just a foot away. Chance shied away and protested with a loud neigh.

Instinctively, Seth dove behind the well and drew a pistol. He had stolen it from a northern farmhouse. It was the one item he'd needed above all else. For food. For protection in a land that was lawless in the chaos following war.

He glanced around and saw a rifle protruding from a window.

"What's your business here?" came a woman's voice.

No voice he knew. "I live here."

"No, you don't. This is the McGuire spread."

He stilled.

"My name is Sinclair," he shouted. "My family has owned this place for decades."

"You alone?"

"Yes."

"Throw your gun out."

He would be damned if he would. He would never willingly give up a gun again. *Never.*

"Your gun," insisted the feminine voice again.

She must be alone.

He wondered how accurate the woman's aim was.

He knew Texas women who could shoot as well as any man. It was a necessary skill since women were often alone in their homes while their men were farming or herding cattle.

Where was his father? His brother? His sister?

What in the hell had happened?

He probably should have stopped in the nearby town but he'd been so damned eager to get home.

"Look," he said. "I don't mean you any harm. I just want to know where my family is."

"Then drop the gun."

"The hell I will."

Silence.

A standoff.

She couldn't get to him behind the brick well, but neither could he move. How long before her husband returned home?

The McGuire spread.

His stomach turned over. His father would never have relinquished this land, not as long as he had a breath in his body. Neither would Dillon, his hotheaded young brother.

"I just want some answers. Where's Major Sinclair?" His father had always been "the Major" to everyone, even his sons.

"I told you. This ranch is ours. Throw your gun out. Then you can leave."

"My horse is thirsty. So am I. And I'm not leaving until I know what happened to my family."

Chance neighed plaintively as if he understood exactly what was being said. He wandered a few more feet away.

"Get your water and leave." The woman's voice was determined.

"Where's the Major?"

The gun wavered again, moving slightly to the left. He turned around and saw the small burial ground under the huge cottonwood tree. It was protected from cattle by a fence made of iron, strong enough to discourage the largest of bulls.

He stood, careless now of the woman's rifle. He put his pistol in his holster and walked over to the cemetery.

He saw a new grave. An unfamiliar one. A simple cross stood vigil over it. He opened the gate and walked in, oblivious now of the woman in his house.

The cross held the words *Major Garrett Sinclair.*

His heart ached. So many miles to find yet another grave.

He knelt on the ground and bowed his head. Not in prayer. He no longer believed in prayer. Not after the last few years.

In respect. In love. In sorrow.

Anguish settled in the deepest part of his soul. He thought he had become immune to grief, but this . . . this was like being branded inside.

He had arrived too late. If he had traveled more quickly . . .

If . . .

He closed his eyes against the onslaught of pain. "I'm sorry, Major," he said. "I couldn't protect the twins. I couldn't bring them back to you."

Without rising, he glanced around the small fenced area. His grandfather. Two uncles were buried there. One had been a Texas Ranger who had been killed by Mexican bandits. The other had died of snakebite. His grandmother. Several babies who hadn't survived. His mother. Now his father.

No marker for Dillon. Or Marilee.

Relief flooded him, mixed with grief for his father.

Dillon and Marilee were somewhere. Alive. He had to find them. He had to bring together what was left of his family.

Damn, the woman would tell him. . . .

He rose and turned back toward the house. A woman stood on the porch, her hands clutching a rifle. She was tall, taller than most women, and her hair was caught in a long, untidy braid.

Her face was more striking than pretty, possibly because of the determination that hardened the lines. Her eyes were hazel. Cool and yet he thought he saw a momentary sympathy in them. He didn't want her sympathy. He wanted to know what in the hell had happened here.

"Don't come any closer," she warned. Her hands shook slightly. She wasn't as sure of herself as she wanted him to think.

He ignored her and walked closer. Her dress was a plain gingham that did nothing for her too-thin body. Who would leave her here alone? There should have been a cowhand or someone. Well, that was none of his business. "I want to know about my family," he said again. "I want to know what happened to my father."

She seemed to flinch but she didn't take a step back. He knew he looked frightening. Bearded. Dirty. His clothes old and torn.

"I wasn't here," she said. "They say he tried to shoot a Union soldier."

"My brother, Dillon? My sister, Marilee?"

Emotion crossed her face. "Your brother is an outlaw. He's tried to kill my father more than once."

He breathed easier. At least Dillon was alive. Marilee must be with him. Or at least with a neighbor. "Your husband?" he asked. He had assumed she was married to whoever was trying to claim this land.

"My father owns this place," she said, defiance in her voice.

"The hell he does."

"The law says he does." Bright red spots appeared on her cheeks.

He wondered whether it came from defending the indefensible. "Your father didn't pay the taxes. If my father hadn't bought it, someone else would have."

"How long ago?"

"Five months."

"Don't get comfortable. Miss . . ."

"McGuire," she replied in a tight voice.

He gave her a look of contempt. He would ride into town, find friends. He would find his brother and Marilee, then decide how best to dislodge these squatters.

"Thank you for your hospitality," he said with sarcasm.

She lowered the rifle slightly. "I'm sorry . . . about your father."

"Why? You took his land."

She started to say something, then shrugged. "Get your water and go."

He started to say to hell with the water, but stopped himself. It was Sinclair—not McGuire—water. His grandfather had built the well.

He could do without, but Chance deserved more. He lowered the bucket into the well water and drew it back out, transferring the contents into a second bucket there for that purpose.

Then he offered it to Chance, who drank thirstily.

"Easy," he said, curtailing the intake for fear the horse would get sick. He would walk the animal the several miles into town, then find a bathhouse and get cleaned up. A bath. A shave. Fresh clothes. To hell with the cost. He could get credit in town.

Then he would pay a few calls.

He would find his brother and sister.

Then he would reclaim his family's heritage.

If it was the last thing he did.

Chapter Two

ELIZABETH TOOK A deep breath as the stranger rode away.

Not a stranger. Marilee's brother.

Her hand shook as she replaced the rifle on the shelf above the fireplace.

Had she done the right thing?

The intruder had looked dangerous. Even if he was who he said he was, his father had threatened a government official. His brother was an outlaw who had been rustling their cattle. This man had looked more than capable of both.

Marilee was safe here.

Elizabeth told herself she couldn't just hand the child over to someone she didn't even know for sure was related to her young charge.

He would be back, though, if he was who he said he was. He would find out in town that she had taken the youngest Sinclair into his former home.

But she hadn't wanted to let him into the house. She and her father had been threatened repeatedly. And maybe he wasn't even telling the truth. Maybe he was a friend of the past owners, trying only to get inside. She kept telling herself that.

She had heard of the Sinclairs, knew there were three brothers missing, but when they hadn't been heard from for months and months, the town and military officials believed them dead.

Why hadn't he returned earlier if he were really Seth Sinclair? And where were the other brothers? Would they join with the one already outlawed?

If only her father had a few more men, but they'd had difficulty finding good experienced hands. Most local men were Texans to the bone, resentful of the new government and the Northerners who had come south. "Carpetbaggers," the McGuires and other newcomers had been called more than once. It was a swearword in Texas. She had been told—unkindly—what it meant, that it referred to people who got off a train or a stagecoach with nothing but a carpetbag in hand and ready to steal anything they could from hardworking farmers and ranchers.

Major Delaney had assured her and her father that the rebs had forfeited their land when they left it to fight against the Union, that they couldn't pay the taxes, and if loyal citizens like her father didn't buy it for pennies on the dollar, then someone else would.

She had never liked the idea, but her father glowed with the prospect of being a landowner, a "squire," he would say, such as those who had forced him from Ireland.

In a life marked by one failure after another, he'd finally found his pot of gold at the end of the rainbow. He had a way of ignoring the hatred in the community and enjoyed, instead, the company of others like him: men and women lured south by Major Delaney, who headed the Union forces in the Texas hill country.

Her father loved this land. As opposed to some other

areas of Texas they'd traversed, it was green, veined by streams and dotted by trees. With the land came cattle. Even horses. He had never ridden before and it had taken weeks before he could sit a horse without falling off or being thrown. Elizabeth had never seen him so determined.

Interest had always quickly died before. He was a typical Irishman, full of charm and blarney. He'd always been immensely likable. But he had never stuck to anything before. He would always turn to drink, instead. He hadn't done that here. She prayed he wouldn't.

Still, she didn't like the guilt that nibbled at her.

She reassured herself that the man who had ridden up to the ranch was a traitor to his country. He looked like a brigand, and he certainly didn't look like someone who could care for a child. Marilee was finally losing the tight, pinched look she'd had since seeing her father die, and the fierce nightmares that had kept her screaming night after night were becoming less frequent.

If he is who he claims, he has every right to her.
But what would it do to Marilee?
And to me?

Elizabeth had given up on any idea of becoming a mother. She had once wanted children more than anything else. But she moved with her father from one location to another, often searching for him in taverns, before he lost what little money she and, sometimes, he earned. He'd had to leave Boston just ahead of the law after becoming embroiled in a dubious scheme.

Then he had met a man in a Chicago tavern who had made him an offer he could not refuse. On behalf of a third party, the man said he was looking for men to go to Texas. Land was available. Good land.

Land had always been her father's dream. All his get-rich-quick schemes had been for land. When one after another failed, he drank more heavily.

Elizabeth loved him. He'd been both mother and father to her after her mother died on the voyage from Ireland. He could have abandoned her, but somehow he'd always found a woman—usually a widow—who would look after her. Some more carefully than others. All with the hope that Michael McGuire would marry them. Then one night he would leave, taking his daughter with him and often as many of the widow's possessions as he could carry.

He loved her with totality and she did the same, cooling her conscience with the knowledge that what he did he did for her.

This piece of land—McGuire land—had broken that pattern. She had seen a new clarity in his eyes, new determination. He worked harder than he'd ever worked. He had learned to ride, to mend a fence. He had hope. Real hope this time.

And she had Marilee.

No one was going to take either away.

SETH rode into Canaan, a small farming town twenty miles east of his ranch.

By God, it *was* still his ranch.

Like everything else in Texas, Canaan had changed. Union uniforms were everywhere. He took fierce pride in his own worn Confederate gray trousers. They were all that survived imprisonment and the journey that followed it. The rest of his uniform was long gone.

He wore a worn shirt and a thin coat against a wind that had grown cold. He remembered the quick change of weather in fall. One day as sweet as a day in May, the next ferocious winter.

He considered the few coins he had. Enough to buy Chance some deserved oats and himself a bath and shave. Perhaps then he wouldn't scare women and children.

Some clean clothes. Perhaps he would feel halfway human again.

His thoughts went back to the woman standing in the doorway of his house. He didn't like the way she kept intruding into his thoughts.

Still, he admired her courage.

Hell, any Texas woman would have done the same.

And yet it had been obvious to him that she'd not been born and raised to confront hostile men with a rifle.

The streets of the town were filled, but mostly with uniforms. His stomach muscles tightened. He had never believed in the war and had watched the clouds approach over four years ago with apprehension. Yet there had never been a question of not going with his brothers and his friends. He was fighting for his state, not against the Union. His family had never had slaves, but he had firmly believed that Texas had the right to write its own destiny.

It had been prison that had turned duty into hatred. He had watched men die needlessly because of sickness and starvation. Now he had only contempt for the occupying army.

There were new buildings. He thought about riding to the sheriff's office but decided his best course of action was the saloon. Abe Turling would fill him in on everything. He always knew everyone's business.

He dismounted and tied the reins to a hitch post and went inside.

In the past, he had always been surrounded by friends on entering the saloon. Now his gaze found only unfamiliar faces.

A few Union officers sat at a table with two men Seth didn't recognize. One was thin with a pale complexion and sour expression. The other was a large man with a goatee. One man stood alone at the end of the bar. With a start, Seth noticed the stranger wore a marshal's badge.

No one else.

But Abe stood in back of the bar, looking at him with narrowed eyes, obviously trying to decide whether he meant trouble or not. Abe Turling had never permitted trouble in his establishment.

Seth strode to the empty end of the bar, ignoring the curious stares directed his way.

Abe moved toward him, a frown on his face.

"Abe? Don't recognize a good customer?"

Abe stared at him for a moment, then a smile split his lips.

"Seth. Ain't you a sight for sore eyes." His gaze quickly surveyed the room, then returned to Seth. "We figured you for dead." He poured Seth a glass of whiskey. "Looks like you need this, boy."

Seth hadn't been a boy in a very long time but he took the glass and took a deep swallow.

He started to dig in his pocket, but Abe shook his head. "On the house."

Abe was uncommonly frugal and had never been known to give a drink on the house.

Seth's puzzled glance was met with a warning expression, then a gesture of his head indicated Seth should go into a back room used for private poker games.

Seth nodded, took another swallow, and Abe turned away to another customer.

Seth watched for several moments. Eyes glanced over him, then dismissed him as a saddle tramp. He gulped down the rest of the whiskey, realizing that not only had Abe donated the drink, he'd donated a glass of his good stuff.

It burned its way down his throat and warmed his stomach, then he went into the hall and opened the door to the private room.

He had played poker here many a night. It was reserved for the locals, for a handful of friends who wanted to play serious poker without onlookers. Seth had always sat in the same chair. His friends, Nathaniel, Gabe, and Quin, sat in the others. The fifth seat switched around.

Now Nat and Gabe were dead. He didn't know about Quin.

He leaned against the wall and waited.

Twenty minutes later, Abe slipped inside with a bottle and two glasses. "Hate to tell you, boy, but you smell."

"I know," Seth admitted. "I wanted to get home and didn't stop for the niceties."

"Hell, we thought you was dead."

"I almost was. Got some damn fever at Elmira Prison in

New York. It took me over a month after the war to recuperate. Took me the rest of the time to get back."

"The twins?"

"Died next to each other."

"Damn, I'm sorry to hear that. Nearly every family around here has lost sons."

"What in the hell has happened? I stopped by the ranch. Some woman accosted me with a rifle. Said her father owned it."

"McGuire," Abe said, spitting into a spittoon located near the table.

"I saw my father's grave," Seth said flatly.

"I'm sorry about that," Abe said. "Sorry as I can be. I admired the Major."

"What happened?"

"All of Texas is under military rule. This area is under a Major Delaney, crooked as they come. His men steal cattle and ride over crops, then when people can't pay taxes, he has stooges ready to buy land at practically nothing.

"Happened to the Major and he didn't take it well," Abe continued. "He and Dillon weren't ready to go. He resisted and a Union sergeant shot him. Shot your brother, too, but he was able to get away. He's wanted."

"My sister?"

"Little Marilee? McGuire's daughter took her in after Trini got sick a few months back."

"Trini? Is she all right?"

Abe shook his head. "McGuire let her stay there in return for keeping his house. She sickened about three months ago, died of some fever. I think it was just plain heartbreak. You know how much she and Luis loved your pa."

"You mean Marilee's at the ranch?"

Abe nodded. "You didn't see her?"

Anger coiled in Seth's gut. The woman said nothing about his sister being there.

"Hell no, or she would be with me now." He took a deep breath. "My brother left Marilee with squatters?"

"He had no choice. There's a thousand-dollar reward on his head. He couldn't drag a seven-year-old along with him."

"One of the neighbors . . ."

"Most of them are gone, chased out just like your father. Those still here have all they can do to hold on to their land."

Shock caused words to wedge in his throat. He couldn't imagine a neighboring family refusing to give shelter to a child in trouble. And why in the hell had the woman not admitted that his sister was in the house?

It obviously wasn't enough to be a party to murder and the theft of land. They felt they could take a child as well. He swore under his breath.

"The law? Is Nolan still sheriff?"

"Nope. He was dismissed by Delaney now that the town's under Union occupation."

"I saw a man with a badge outside."

"That's Tom Evans. U.S. marshal. This is part of his territory, though the army pretty well controls things. He stops in occasionally. Keeping up with business, he says."

Seth filed that in his mind. "What happened to the Flynns and Hopewells?"

"Ed Flynn shot himself when he heard his boy was killed. Mrs. Flynn went to stay with a sister in Missouri. Hopewell's daughter was raped by a Union soldier. The family pulled out two months ago."

He and Vince Flynn had gone to school together. So many gone.

The need to see his sister grew stronger.

"I'm going to go get her," he said, his anger becoming a fiery torch in his gut.

"You might talk to Dillon first," Abe said. "Common wisdom is that your sister is doing fine where she is. She attends church with Miss McGuire here in town, and she looks well tended."

"Do you know where I can find him?"

"No, but I think he's nearby. There's been a lot of cattle

rustling lately. Delaney swears it's your brother and some other locals."

"Is it?"

Abe shrugged. "Mebbe. Mebbe no."

"And the men in the saloon?"

"Delaney's henchmen. One is a so-called civil administrator appointed by Delaney. Does whatever he's told. I hate serving them, but I don't have any choice. They would close me down, and the Belle is all I have."

Seth nodded. "They know your sympathies?"

"They probably suspect, but I'm the only saloon in town. Right now we live and let live. Now, about Marilee . . . are you sure you can take care of her? Mebbe you should wait . . ."

Seth impaled the man with his eyes.

"I appreciate your concern, Abe, but she's my sister and I'm not waiting."

"And then?"

"I don't know. I'll find someplace we can stay."

"And Dillon?"

"I'll find him, too." But bitterness seeped deeper in his soul. All his dreams and hopes had centered around the ranch and building it with his brother and father. He'd thought about it during the long months he'd spent in prison. The ranch was not large, nor had it been particularly successful. Cattle was plentiful in Texas and getting them to market difficult if not impossible.

Yet he knew that after the war, people would flock west and with them would come an expansion of railroads.

His father could have tried to grow cotton, but the Major had hated slavery and there was no economical way to raise cotton without it.

But a father and two sons—along with a few hands— could well handle a herd of cattle. He had thought that he and other ranchers could join their herds and drive them north.

Now he had no home, no money, no cattle, no land.

But by God, he had remnants of a family left, and he intended to see them together. And on Sinclair land.

He thrust his hand out. "Thanks, Abe."

"Wish I could have done more," Abe said, taking his hand. Then he eyed Seth sadly. "Don't go out to the ranch. Delaney has an eye on the McGuire woman. He's warned off several men who wanted to court her."

"I've been officially pardoned," Seth said. "I haven't done anything wrong."

"That doesn't mean anything in Canaan. And when Delaney discovers you've returned from the dead, he'll try to use you to get to Dillon."

"Then I won't lead him to Dillon."

Abe hesitated, then shrugged. "If you're determined to get Marilee, the old Keller place is empty. I bought the land a few weeks ago. Managed to do it before Delaney got his hands on it. He particularly wanted Keller's place because a stream runs through it."

"Where's Keller?"

"Found dead. The new sheriff said it was renegades. I have different ideas. But I knew something Delaney didn't. Keller has a daughter in Dallas. I contacted her and made an offer. She accepted. Delaney's mad as hell, but I have friends, too. Anyway, you and Marilee can stay there until you find something else. There's water. Some furniture's been stolen but there's probably enough."

"I owe you."

"No, you don't. I've been here thirty years and what's going on turns my stomach."

Seth turned and left the room. He paused outside the door, grateful to Abe. The man had been afraid, that much was obvious, yet he had given his advice. A warning. And, more importantly, a place to stay.

Seth decided to leave the back way. He had no desire to see those uniforms again. Nor a marshal. He wanted no confrontations. Not until he fetched his sister.

Chapter Three

✦ ELIZABETH READ TO Marilee as she waited for her father to return from town. Elizabeth hugged Marilee closer and settled the storybook in her lap. She hoped the story would relieve some of the child's terror.

Marilee had heard the shots but she had stayed in her room as instructed by Elizabeth. It wasn't the first time threats had been made, or guns fired.

Elizabeth had found her huddled on her bed, her face pale. She had watched her father die and her brother wounded. Only Trini had kept her from running after her brother, Dillon, as he'd been dragged away by Union soldiers. Three nights later, friends had broken him out of jail.

For weeks, Union soldiers had surrounded the ranch, hoping that he would return. It wasn't until a few weeks ago that they had left, detailed instead to hunt Dillon Sinclair in the hills.

Elizabeth had worried about his return, that he would

try to take an already shaken young girl, and about what would happen to the child if he succeeded. Marilee was fragile, more than fragile, and haunted by a cough. What would happen if she accompanied a fugitive?

The newest Sinclair looked no better. He'd looked desperate and dangerous. Not only that, he wore the remnants of a uniform.

The men who had killed Marilee's father wore uniforms.

I have no right. Marilee is not mine.

In my heart, she is.

If only her father and Howie returned. Then they could ride for help.

Howie and the other four hands were out searching for cattle, though she was sure they had been rustled. Her father had gone into town to complain to the federal authorities about the latest theft and to ask for help.

It had taken more than an hour to soothe Marilee after the intrusion. "It was just a stranger who needed water," she said, hoping she wouldn't be struck dead for what she was leaving out.

"I heard shots," Marilee said.

"A stranger. I just didn't want him near the house," Elizabeth said. "He took his water and left. Everything is fine now."

"I want Dillon," Marilee said suddenly.

"He's gone, sweetpea," she said.

"I don't care. I want him."

"I don't know where he is."

"He's not dead?" Marilee sought reassurance.

"No."

"Then why doesn't he come to see me?"

"I don't think he can," Elizabeth replied. For two months after she and her father arrived, Marilee hadn't said a word. Then she gradually started to speak. The nightmares were rarer, but she still woke up screaming.

"I want my daddy." It was the first time Marilee had mentioned him since Elizabeth had first seen the little girl in Trini's small house on the ranch. Her heart had gone out to the silent child who had trembled when Elizabeth had stopped at the small foreman's house after she and her father moved in.

Trini had kept her hidden, in fact, for several weeks, afraid that she would be ordered away, and the child with her.

Then Trini had died and Marilee had suffered still another loss. How much could a child bear?

Elizabeth was determined to protect her as much as possible.

Was she doing that by keeping her away from the man who claimed he was her brother?

If only he hadn't looked like the worst of renegades.

She looked up at the grandfather clock. Afternoon. When would the man who called himself Sinclair return? Could she stay here without any help? Would he bring others when he returned?

Her father had been gone half a day, more than enough time to see to his errand and return. But she knew him too well. Once in town, he often became involved with others. He was a gregarious man who loved stories and an audience and he often forgot about time.

She reluctantly made the decision to go into town. But she didn't want to take Marilee with her. The road was too dangerous. If they were caught out alone . . .

"Let's go see Robert," she suggested to Marilee.

Robert was the son of a neighboring rancher, another newcomer. Elizabeth refused to think of either of their families as carpetbaggers, the derogatory term that had often been thrown at them.

All the other children shunned Robert. Marilee, who instinctively was for the underdog, had become his good friend.

Marilee's face brightened. "Can I?"

"Of course. I need a few things in town and I'll fetch you on the way back."

"Will you bring some peppermint candy?"

"Always," Elizabeth said.

The thought of her favorite treat, and a few hours to play with Robert, was obviously a partial cure. Marilee fetched her bonnet as Elizabeth went down to hitch the horse to their buggy. She added the shotgun at the last moment. It would be more effective than a rifle if they ran into trouble.

In minutes, they were on the road. She had been forced to use Ornery, a horse well named for his stubborn ways. But today he had been unusually cooperative, probably due to the apple she gave him.

Miriam Findley, Robert's mother, was delighted to see them and readily agreed to keep Marilee for a few hours. "Be careful," she warned. "Bud Garner was stopped and robbed last week. Rebels, he said."

"I'll be careful," Elizabeth said. "I have a shotgun with me."

"I'll send Mr. Findley after you if you aren't back by sundown."

Elizabeth nodded her thanks and got back on the buggy. Marilee had run inside to see Robert. "By the way, I had a visitor this morning. He said his name was Seth Sinclair. He looked like a saddle tramp, though."

"Another Sinclair. Oh, Elizabeth, I don't think you should go alone."

"I'll be fine, truly I will," she said. "I want to tell Major Delaney, though, and the sheriff."

Miriam Findley looked doubtful. "I hate this country. I told Mr. Findley I want to leave." She always called her husband Mr. Findley. Never just Gary.

"Oh, don't. Please. It will get better."

"It's a hellhole," Miriam said, then backed away, her face flushing as if she'd said something she shouldn't. "Be careful."

Elizabeth couldn't argue. She loved the country. She loved the streams and the hills and the wildflowers. But the hate among the Texans was an open wound, deep and festering.

She snapped the reins and Ornery stepped quickly through the gate and onto the main road. She glanced down at the shotgun at her feet. Her father and she had both learned to use both rifle and shotgun during their first weeks here. She hated the weapons but she'd learned to conquer those feelings in the past several months.

After a mile, she relaxed. The day was lovely. Light clouds shaded the sun and a breeze cooled the usually hot temperatures. Bluebonnets and Indian paintbrush colored the hills.

A sound of a gunshot shattered the silence. Its report echoed in the hills and bounced back. The horse's ears went up, then he jerked in the harness.

Elizabeth tightened her hold on the reins as another shot ripped across the hills. Then a loud ungodly yell.

Her heart thundered as she glanced behind the buggy. Four masked men approached from the east.

She snapped the reins to speed the horse, then realized she didn't have to. Ornery bolted and raced down the road. She didn't know whether to try to pull him up or to allow him his head while she just held on for dear life as she heard the riders closing in behind her.

The yell again. It sent cold shivers over her. She'd heard that cry once before when night riders had descended on the ranch. They'd been chased off by federal troops but not before they had nearly set the barn on fire.

She'd witnessed the fear of their hands, who had taken refuge in the house. They'd heard the rebel cry. It was enough to terrify anyone. She and her father lost most of the hands the next day.

The buggy lurched ahead, the horse running in blind panic. All efforts to pull back on the reins yielded nothing.

The riders caught up with the buggy, riding alongside, shooting into the air. The buggy swayed from side to side along the road and she had to grasp the side to keep from being thrown out.

The intent of the riders was obviously to cause an accident. She didn't know whether they were after her, or her father. Until now, the sides of the buggy would have shielded her from sight, but everyone knew the buggy. They used it to go to church and for trips into town.

It didn't matter who they were after.

She hung on to the reins, even as her left hand clutched the side of the buggy. She continued to pull back on them, but her slight strength was nothing compared to the power of the horse's fear.

She should have stayed at home. She knew that now. She had the protection of walls there.

But she hadn't been ready to give up Marilee, not after working so hard to scare away the demons that haunted the child.

The buggy bounced and rocked as the horse ran headlong, spurred by continuing shouts and gunfire. *Stay on the road. Stay on the road.*

She glanced at the shotgun on the floor next to her. She couldn't reach for it without letting go of the side of the buggy. Nor would she be able to use it as the buggy careened back and forth.

They could see her now. They had to know she was a woman. Two of them fired again. The buggy swerved and almost toppled and she stifled a scream.

I'm going to die.

More shots, this time from a different direction. The riders around her broke off and raced away.

But her horse didn't stop. He wouldn't stop now until he dropped. The buggy would never last that long. Her body jolted as the wheels hit a rut in the road.

She closed her eyes, uttered a prayer, then opened them again.

A horseman passed the buggy and rode close to Ornery. He leaned over and his hand caught the harness.

He was going to fall. No one could stop a horse galloping as Ornery was doing. The figure moved from his saddle onto Ornery's back, his hands pulling at the traces.

The buggy slowed and after what seemed like endless moments came to a stop.

She had seen the pinto before. The animal had been at her well just hours earlier.

Its rider looked different. He had washed, changed clothes, shaved. She wouldn't have known him if it hadn't been for the horse.

He turned, one leg resting on Ornery's back as the horse snorted and foam flew from his mouth. Sinclair soothed the hindquarters, and he whispered something soft to the animal. Ornery quieted.

Then the man looked at her. "Are you all right?"

She had to think about that for a moment. Or perhaps she was just too stunned by the change in him.

He'd been a saddle tramp before. Bearded. Unkempt. Dirty. It had been easy to dismiss him. Almost. Her conscience, which had been compromised far too often recently, assaulted her.

Something else did, too. Something just as powerful. She felt as if she had just been hit by lightning.

He was one of the most attractive men she'd ever seen. He'd lost his hat, and his hair, which had looked dark this morning, had obviously been washed. Its bronze color glittered in the sun. Dark blue eyes were piercing in a lean, almost gaunt sun-darkened face. Unlike Delaney's indulgence-swollen face, this man looked honed by pain. The renegade she'd glimpsed earlier was still in the fierce eyes, but a hero had just saved her.

He waited for her answer.

"I think so," she said, dismayed to hear the tremor in her voice. "Yes, of course I am," she added, trying to force steel into it. "Thank you," she said belatedly. "But I really could have stopped Ornery . . ."

A raised eyebrow stopped her words in midsentence. "Ornery?"

"He comes by the name honestly."

One side of his mouth twitched, though she had the impression he really didn't want her to realize it. In one easy movement, he jumped from the horse onto the ground. Without paying any attention to her, he tied his pinto to the back of the buggy. He swung up into the driver's seat, forcing her to move.

"My horse needs the rest," he said shortly. "He's not up to running like that."

His presence overpowered her. Pure raw masculinity made him appear far larger than he was.

His knee brushed hers and she felt as if she were in the way of a prairie brush fire. Her body reacted in new ways. Hot and greedy, and aching with longing.

His gaze hadn't left her. "You were saying you could have stopped the horse," he said.

Of course she wouldn't have been able to do that, and he knew it. He wanted her to say it. He wanted her to admit she would probably be dead if he had not assisted her.

Why had he stopped to help someone he obviously regarded as an enemy?

"Thank you," she said.

He shrugged. "I was coming back to your ranch to fetch my sister. You didn't tell me she was there." His voice had turned cold and accusing. Despite the heat, a chill ran through her.

There was no sense in denying the obvious. Everyone in town knew she was caring for Marilee Sinclair. "I wasn't sure you were who you said you were. She's had a very bad—"

"The people in town, or what is left of them, will vouch for me," he said. A muscle moved in his throat.

"Your friends?" she asked.

"My friends wouldn't attack ladies or children. Or old men. I can't speak for yours."

"What do you mean?"

He shrugged again. That was obviously his gesture of choice.

"Your brother has already attacked—" She stopped. "You don't look anything like him."

"You've seen him?"

"Only posters," she said.

"He has my father's dark coloring. I inherited my mother's. Marilee? Is she still a little towhead?"

She nodded. "Gold hair and light blue eyes."

"Like my brother then. You said he attacked someone? You?"

"I'm not sure who it was. It's just said . . ."

"You believe everything that's said?"

She didn't answer.

"Lady, you and your father are being used," he said wearily. "You don't belong here. You had no business riding alone out here when so many resent what you and your father represent. It was a damn fool thing to do."

Her back stiffened. "I thanked you. You can go now."

His lips curled at the edges but it wasn't a smile. "And if they come back?"

"I have a shotgun with me."

"You really think you can use it when the buggy is rocking all over the road?"

"I am a very good shot."

He shook his head in disgust.

"I don't need you," she said. Then added a bit sheepishly, "Now."

"We are going back to the ranch," he replied. "I want to see my sister. I can get Marilee, then you can do whatever in the hell you want to do. I would suggest, though, that you do not travel alone."

"I'm not going to the ranch," she said stubbornly. "I am going into town to see—"

"Some of your father's friends? Delaney, for instance?"

He was right on the mark. Not Delaney, but the judge. A friend of Delaney's. About how to keep this man's sister away from him. Her face was hot and she knew it was flooding with color. She suspected he probably knew exactly what she was thinking.

His eyes bored into her. "Lady, after I get my sister, I don't care where in the hell you go."

"Please," she said. "Wait. She—Marilee—is fragile."

"Fragile?"

"She didn't talk for months after your father was . . . after he died. Trini had stayed on the ranch and looked after her, but even she couldn't get Marilee to talk. She just sat in a chair and rocked." Elizabeth hesitated, then continued, "Then Trini died and she withdrew even more. But lately, she's been making progress. Until . . ."

He waited, his dark blue eyes wary.

"Until today when she heard the shots again. After you left, I went to her room. She was huddled in a corner, completely terrified."

Anguish crossed his face and her heartbeat accelerated, pounding harder. Maybe he *would* leave his sister with her. . . .

But he stiffened. "Any court, even a Yankee one, will give her to me," he said.

She had been going to seek help to try to stop that eventuality. She didn't want to say that. "Why did you help me?"

"I recognized the buggy. It belongs to the Sinclairs," he said. "I thought Marilee might be inside."

"You must have seen I was alone before you risked your life."

"I don't like men who pick on someone weaker," he said curtly. "The odds were all wrong."

"And if they had been more even?"

Ignoring the question, he clicked the reins and managed a smooth come-around. Ornery obeyed without so much as a protest. She had never seen the horse respond so readily. She silently thought very bad things about the horse.

She tried one last time. "I really must go into town."

"Not now. Not until I see my sister. If you hadn't been silent this morning—"

"Your sister feels safe for the first time in months," she interrupted fiercely, desperately. "Don't take her now. Let her get used to you first," she pleaded with him.

His gaze studied her for a very long moment. "Sorry, lady. I've waited almost five years to see my family. Your father and friends have taken everything else I have. You aren't going to take what's remaining of the Sinclairs as well."

"What . . . where would you take her?"

His eyes were just as cold as before. "It is none of your affair, Miss McGuire."

All the gratitude she'd felt for her rescue seeped away. She wished the attraction would, as well, but it remained strong and compelling deep inside her.

Did he feel it as well?

Of course not. She was not physically well favored. She knew that. She was taller than most men, with a body not blessed with curves. Her best feature was her eyes, and even they were a curse because they always revealed what she thought.

He, on the other hand . . .

Don't even think about it, she told herself as he guided Ornery into a trot in the direction of the ranch. He would not find Marilee there.

Should she tell him where she was? What would happen when they reached the ranch and he discovered she wasn't there? She looked at him, at the uncompromising jut of his jaw, the muscle that moved in his throat, the intensity in the line of his body as he so easily asked Ornery to do what the accursed horse wouldn't do for her.

Could she keep Marilee at the Findleys'? But he would learn his sister's location soon enough. There were no secrets in Canaan. The fact that he had already been on his way back to get his sister proved that.

If he really cared about Marilee . . .

One look at the hard, cold visage made her wonder. She could lie with her silence. But her conscience wouldn't let her. No matter his motives, he had probably just saved her life. He had seen that she was alone before he made that dangerous jump. He had risked his life for hers.

"She's not there," she said.

He turned back to her. "Then where?"

"Promise me first you will give her time to get used to you."

His right hand tightened around the reins. "What if she wants to go with me?" he asked.

"Then . . . she can go." The words hurt far more than she'd anticipated.

Only now did she fully realize the loneliness she would feel if she lost the child. "She needs a lot of attention," she said. "And patience. She saw your father killed," she said. "And your brother wounded. She's still terrified of riders." She looked up at him. "She will be terrified of you."

The muscle in his cheek flexed again. "She would get to know me soon enough."

"Where would you take her?" She held her breath for the answer.

He didn't answer. He didn't look at her. His face looked as if it were carved from granite. Control was in every movement of his body.

"Mr. Sinclair . . .?"

His head turned then and he faced her. "It is none of your concern."

"But it is. I love her and—"

"Love?" he said, arching an eyebrow. "You associate with those who killed her father and benefitted from his death. Damned strange love to my way of thinking."

The chill in his eyes changed to ice. The more she looked, the less she saw of what she felt Marilee needed: compassion, warmth, gentleness, love. Yet he was her brother.

Conscience warred with her heart and finally won. "She's at the Findley ranch."

His brows knitted together. "Findley."

"The ranch eight miles west of us."

"The Taylors'? Jack's ranch?"

She saw the sudden comprehension in his eyes. "Another profiteer," he said in his soft, biting manner.

"They are good people."

He didn't answer. Instead he made a clicking sound. Ornery immediately speeded up.

She clutched the side of the buggy. She didn't want to be bounced against him. She didn't want to feel the same

sparks she'd felt before. He was despicable. He didn't care
about his sister. He only cared about using her as part of
the war he was still fighting.

The war was over.

She suspected for him another stage was just beginning.

Chapter Four

TENSION STRETCHED BETWEEN them like tightly strung wire.

Seth wanted to race the buggy toward his sister but the woman's words echoed in his mind. *Fragile. Nightmares. Fear.*

The thought that he might hurt Marilee stabbed him deeper than any bayonet could. Did he really have the right to take her from a place where she felt safe?

One fact came hammering at him. His sister had been at the ranch when he had ridden up. Had she been hiding in fear?

Because of him.

Because of Delaney, whose men had killed her father in front of her.

And because of the McGuires, who'd had a role in Delaney's scheme.

Damn it, why hadn't the woman just said Marilee was there?

He looked away, afraid he would say something or do something he would regret.

"Tell me more about her," he demanded, still struggling to control his anger.

"She's smart and pretty. And tenderhearted. She's always bringing in wounded creatures."

"And now she's wounded herself." His voice was a whisper. He was barely aware of saying the words. They hurt too much.

His need to return home had been the only thing that had saved him after watching his brothers die. Fury replaced that need when he'd discovered his father dead, his brother gone, and his sister missing.

That coursing anger had been barely controlled as he suffered through the time it took for a bath and shave. He knew they were necessary—otherwise he'd realized he would frighten anyone, especially a young child who had no clear memory of him.

He had nursed his anger as he had traveled down the road back to the ranch. He had felt it building to a crescendo inside. And then he had heard the shots and the yells. . . .

He had immediately recognized the rebel cry. Abe had said that lawlessness was rampant. The federal authorities blamed the chaos on the Texans who were returning from the war. They were being accused of raiding ranches, stealing cattle, and even of murder. One of those being blamed was his brother Dillon.

But when he saw the woman in the buggy, he knew that Dillon was not among the masked men. Seth hadn't seen him in almost five years but he remembered his brother as the softhearted member of the family. He might attack McGuire but never a lone woman.

Nor could he imagine any of his boyhood friends doing so.

And there was the matter of the rebel cry. That would surely bring the army. Why would anyone be so foolish as to advertise a lost cause?

Unless someone was trying to shift blame.

The thought came quickly to his mind. Abe had hinted that someone else was behind the lawlessness.

He wished he had seen more of her attackers, but they had been masked in addition to wearing hats that covered the color of their hair. Their horses had included two bays, a sorrel, and a chestnut. He filed the information in his mind.

After riding in silence for a long time, he looked at his companion. "I don't know your name."

"Elizabeth. Sarah Elizabeth McGuire." The woman's shy smile transformed the plain, blunt face with the upturned nose. It came alive, as did her eyes, and an unwanted, unbidden jolt of lust rocked him.

He tried to dismiss it. It was only because he hadn't been close to a woman in years, not since the early years of the war when young officers had been eagerly sought guests in southern homes. But then came months of marching, of bitter battles, of land laid to waste. And finally imprisonment where he either froze in the winter or suffered hot humid summers, both with too little food and too much sickness.

Seth told himself she was the enemy. She and her father had taken something not theirs without a thought for those who had lived and died for the acres.

"You said she was fragile. How fragile?"

"She has nightmares. She's terrified of strangers. Especially men in uniform."

He wanted to say he wasn't a stranger, but he knew he would be to his sister. She'd just started toddling when he last saw her.

He closed his eyes for a moment, then opened them. His hands tightened around the reins. He knew the anguish he'd felt in seeing his brothers die. He couldn't even imagine how his sister had felt when her father—their father—was killed in front of her.

"Were you there?"

"No. We came . . . not long after. A . . . friend told us there was good land to be had."

"Delaney?"

She stared at him. "How . . .?"

"News travels fast. A lot of people are unhappy with your 'friend.' "

"It wasn't him," she said defensively. "And he's not my friend."

"Your father's friend, then."

"The property was going to be sold," she said. "Someone would have bought it."

He couldn't really argue with that. The ranches and farms had been sold for the taxes, a fraction of what the properties were worth. Still, he couldn't resist a comment. "He had to know what was happening, that it was little more than theft."

Her face flushed and her lips firmed into a tight line.

Only a small twinge of guilt bit at him. She was at least complicit with the theft of his family's land. "How did Marilee come to live with you?" he asked, hungry to know more.

"There didn't seem to be anyone else."

He turned and looked at her. Really looked at her.

There didn't seem to be anyone else.

The words were worse than the thrust of a sword would have been. He should have been there. God knew his family needed him more than a lost cause had.

"And my brother? Dillon?" He already knew from Abe but he wanted her to tell him.

"I have never seen him," she said. "I just know he's an outlaw."

"I understand he was trying to defend my father," he said.

She didn't say anything.

"You didn't tell Marilee about me today?"

"I wasn't sure you were who you said you were. Everyone said you were dead."

"Wishful thinking?"

She flushed. "You had not returned when the others did, and you looked . . ."

"Like I hadn't had a bath in weeks," he said. "I hadn't. I was in a Yankee prison since May of last year. I caught

some fever—I was in a hospital another month after my release. Then I had to make my way mostly on foot, stopping
occasionally to try to earn enough money for food. It didn't
matter. I was coming home."

The last words were bitter. Biting.

"And now?" she asked softly.

"I plan to claim what's mine," he said, "and find out who
killed my father. God help anyone who gets in the way."

He turned down the road leading to what used to be the
Taylor ranch, the home of his best friend, Jack. He too had
disappeared in the maelstrom of war.

Two children were playing with a puppy at the front of
the house. They looked up as the buggy approached. One
was a dark-haired boy, the other a pretty girl with golden
hair and blue eyes. She looked at the carriage, then saw
him and ran for the front door.

His heart dropped at his sister's obvious panic.

"You are a stranger to her," the McGuire woman said.

He remembered what he had told her. He wouldn't take
his sister by force. But could he really leave her with a man
who had stolen his family's land, an opportunist? A thief,
to his way of thinking.

He stopped the buggy and stepped down. It was automatic
to him that he go around to the other side and help her step
down. He grasped her fingers and heat raced through him.

The startled look on her face told him she'd experienced the same unwanted current.

Nothing could be more foolish. He intended to get her
off his land. He would take his sister and find his brother
and right all the wrongs. She had no place in that picture.

"I'll be back," she said. "Stay here." She walked rapidly
to the adobe ranch house before he could object.

He wanted to go after her, but Elizabeth's words lingered in his mind. *She is fragile.* As much as he wanted
Marilee, he couldn't bear causing her more pain.

And he had promised. Not promised exactly but agreed
to be patient.

He *would* get everything. His sister. His family's land. His brother's freedom.

No matter the cost.

ELIZABETH found Marilee in the kitchen and stooped to give her a hug.

"It's all right, sweetpea," she said. "The man with me . . . he's your brother."

She shook her head. "Not Dillon."

"Another brother. You heard your father talk about Seth?"

Marilee looked up with wide eyes. "Seth is dead. Father said so."

"He didn't die."

"Then why has he been gone?"

"He couldn't come back until now. He was hurt."

"Hurt?"

"Sick," Elizabeth said. "But now he is home and he wants to see you." She couldn't bear to say the words, *He wants to take you.* Marilee shivered in her arms. "Is he the man who came this morning?"

Elizabeth suddenly realized that Marilee must have seen more than she had relayed.

"Yes. He didn't know you were there. I should have told him but I didn't. I wasn't sure . . ."

"Did he come to get me?"

"I think he would like to meet you and maybe . . ."

"I don't want to leave you. I don't like him. He looked . . . scary."

"He looked tired and hungry. He had traveled a very long way to see you."

It was a lie. Seth Sinclair *had* looked scary. He still looked scary. Cold. Angry.

Dangerous.

But Marilee had stiffened. She looked ready to flee. Fear shone in her eyes. "I don't want to go out."

"I'll be with you."

"No! Please don't make me go away." Marilee's eyes widened and Elizabeth saw in them the ragged, dirty figure the child had seen earlier.

She also saw in her mind's eye the pain she had seen in Seth Sinclair's eyes just minutes earlier. He had lost everything. She felt at least partly responsible.

He had unquestionably saved her life. At the risk of his own. That realization had taken hold.

Despite his claim that he thought Marilee might be in the buggy, he'd been close enough to see the child was not in the buggy before he leaned over to grasp the reins.

Would he just take his sister, regardless of the harm he might cause her?

Miriam Findley walked in the room, her eyes questioning.

"Seth Sinclair is with me," Elizabeth explained. She couldn't say any more, not with Marilee listening. She couldn't let her hear about the terrifying ride and the masked outlaws. She wasn't even sure she wanted to tell Miriam.

"Sinclair?" Miriam's eyes widened.

"One of the sons who went to war," she said. Then she realized he hadn't said anything about his brothers. She knew there had been four.

"Dear God," Miriam said. "Another one."

Elizabeth gave her a warning look, then looked down at Marilee.

Miriam didn't take the hint. "I suppose he's as vicious as his brother. Why on earth did you bring him here?"

"Marilee is his sister."

"I don't want him on our property."

"He hasn't done anything."

"You know Dillon Sinclair is responsible for the rustling and murdering going on. How could you have anything to do with—"

"I don't know anything of the kind," she said, knowing Marilee was hearing every word. She found herself defending a man she'd so easily condemned just hours before.

She took Marilee's hand. "We have to go."

Marilee pulled back. "I don't—"

"I won't let him take you, sweetpea," she said, "but we have to get home. Papa will be frantic with worry."

If he was even home yet.

Seth Sinclair obviously wasn't welcome here, and she wasn't going to go out and tell him he had to leave without seeing his sister. Not after . . .

She knew she shouldn't have given the promise to Marilee. It was a promise she was physically unable to enforce. She could not keep him from taking his own flesh and blood. She could only rely on his sense of decency and love for a sister.

If she was wrong . . .

Delaney would help her if she asked him. He would make sure Marilee stayed with her. But at what price? He had been courting her in a leisurely fashion, obviously sure that his suit would be accepted. He was important, and she wasn't. She was certainly not the most attractive woman around. She had, in fact, no idea why he troubled himself, but her father had asked her to be pleasant to him, and she had.

But unlike her father, she had never trusted Delaney. Her flesh crawled when she was in his company.

Choose Delaney or the man who had just saved her life?

It wasn't that simple. Her father had realized his life's dream. And so had she. She'd always loved children but never thought she would have any of her own. Marilee had been a gift.

She brought joy and purpose to Elizabeth's life as nothing else had.

She knelt down. "He's your brother, sweetpea. I don't think he will make you do anything you don't want to do."

Marilee looked at her with trust that had been so hard to earn. And nodded.

Elizabeth took her hand and they left the house together. They walked out to the buggy where Seth Sinclair stood. When they reached him, he knelt so his eyes met Marilee's.

"Hello," he said in a voice so soft Elizabeth felt an ache

inside. He did love his sister. It was so obvious in the way he tried to dispel fear.

"Hello," Marilee said, then pressed her face against Elizabeth's skirts.

Elizabeth looked down. Seth Sinclair's face was a study in pain. He so obviously wanted to take Marilee in his arms and the struggle between doing so and exercising patience was obvious in the rigidity of his body.

"You are very pretty," he said. "You look like our mother."

Marilee turned then. "I never knew my mother."

It was one of the longest sentences Elizabeth had yet heard from her.

Seth Sinclair's hard face seemed to dissolve. She saw tears in the edges of his eyes, something she had not expected.

"I know," he said. "But I remember you. You were no larger than a tadpole when I left. And you were the prettiest little tadpole I ever saw."

Marilee screwed up her face. "Tadpoles aren't pretty."

"I think it all depends on what you consider is pretty," he said. "I like tadpoles."

Elizabeth was enchanted by the conversation, by the sincerity of his voice even through the utter nonsense of what was being said. She knew charm. Her father was charming. She had learned the shallowness of charm. Too often it masked emptiness.

This was not charm. This was a raw naked hunger to reach his sister. The ache inside her deepened.

He didn't try to force Marilee to accept him. That surprised her. He obviously respected her hesitancy, her fear. And despite her obvious fascination with him, Marilee clung to Elizabeth.

Seth held his hand out. Such a small gesture but Marilee cringed and hid behind Elizabeth's skirt.

He stood and the expression on his face drove straight into her heart. It was pure agony.

She had never known that kind of pain. She hoped she never would.

He tried again. "Would you like to know more about your mother?"

Marilee glanced up. Nodded.

"I can come tomorrow and tell you a story about her."

Marilee looked uncertain.

"Think about it," he said.

He stood and whispered in Elizabeth McGuire's ear, "I want to see her often." His voice was rough with emotion.

She nodded, too grateful to say anything more. Marilee would be hers for a few more days. Days, or weeks. Perhaps even months. She would cherish the time, however short.

She watched him look at Marilee with his heart in his eyes. Then without another word he went to the carriage, untied his horse, and in one graceful movement mounted.

He rode off without looking back.

Chapter Five

SETH TRIED TO shrug off despair as he rode away.

He wanted to look back. He wanted to capture the image of his sister in his mind. But something kept him from doing so. Pride? Pain? A bit of both.

Or was it that he feared he might change his mind? And that would be wrong for his sister. Earning her trust would take time.

He was leaving part of his heart behind. But he had to find another part of it elsewhere. His brother.

There had been a special place they'd gone as boys. If Dillon was still in the area, he would be there.

He guided his horse west toward the small valley twelve miles away. Hidden behind rugged hills, it was accessible only through a narrow opening overgrown with underbrush. He and his brother had found it years ago when riding cattle. Inside had been a cabin built against one of the surrounding hills. A human skull lay a few feet from the door. Only boys then, Seth and Dillon surmised a hunter or hermit had been killed by Comanches.

The entrance into the valley had been so overgrown that had the two boys not been searching for a lost calf whose mother was bellowing nearby, they never would have found it.

Neither would anyone else.

If Dillon was still in the area, he could well be there. And Seth was sure Dillon wouldn't leave without Marilee.

Seth had a few other places in mind, but this was his best bet.

He backtracked several times, something made easy by the hills. A man could be swallowed by them. No one was following him. Then he veered off toward the cabin. It was at least three hours away, particularly on Chance, who still wasn't at full strength.

Time to think even as his gaze continually surveyed the hills. War instilled instincts that would never leave him.

The sun was dropping rapidly. Shadows designed by clouds moved across the green hills. They were hauntingly familiar. He knew these hills; they had inhabited his dreams for more than four very long years.

Heat dissipated as the sun sank. A cool breeze ruffled his hair. He hurried the pace. He didn't have a lantern. He wanted to make the valley before last light.

If Dillon wasn't there, he could stay the night and start searching at dawn.

The last rays of sun ignited the sky with fire. He found the trail and moved cautiously. If his brother was hiding here, he would be looking out for intruders. Seth located the entrance from memory and dismounted. The brush that shielded it was easily removed and replaced.

Dillon was here. Or had been recently.

He decided to walk the horse in. Dillon and whoever was with him might be trigger-happy.

He moved cautiously. Then stopped when he heard the all too familiar sound of a rifle hammer pulled back. He had not been quiet enough.

"Strike a match," demanded a voice from the shadows.

Seth hunted for the matches in his pocket, then struck one. "Dillon?"

Silence. Then, "It can't be."

"Can't be, but is," Seth said.

Dillon stepped out of the shadows. "Seth?"

"No other," he said lightly, though emotion tugged at his heart.

"Thank God," Dillon said. "They said you were dead, but I kept hoping." He paused. "The twins?"

"Died at the Wilderness. I was taken prisoner. When the war ended, I was ill with some fever I caught in prison. I was in one of their hospitals for more than a month. Then it's a hell of a long journey from New York without money or a horse."

The flame from the match burned down to his fingers. Seth dropped it and used the heel of his boot to make sure it was snuffed. Then he reached out his hand, and Dillon grasped it tightly. Suddenly four other shadowy figures appeared as if out of nowhere.

One of them lit another match, then a torch, and he had a better view of Dillon. When Seth had left for war, Dillon had been seventeen and wanting to go as well but their pa needed him at home. Now he was only twenty-two but he looked older. His face was far harder than it should have been.

Then his gaze moved to Dillon's companions. Seth recognized all but one. They had been Dillon's friends, far younger than himself. But now they were anything but boys. They all had a dangerous look, an expression that distrusted much and feared little.

Each one shook his hand. Danny Mitchum. Micah Roberts. Sawyer McGee. The fourth man was the most dangerous looking of them all. "Colorado," he said by way of introduction. No more.

No one asked how Seth had found them. They obviously trusted Dillon and Dillon's trust made him one of them.

"Tell me about the Major—" he said.

"Come inside," Dillon said and led the way to the entrance of the cabin. The windows were covered with black blankets. Dillon quickly lit two oil lamps and sat in a chair.

Seth took the other. The other four men had disappeared back into the shadows.

"I remember all of them but Colorado," Seth said.

"He found us. He had his own battles with army authority."

"Delaney?"

Dillon nodded. "He killed Pa. Tried to kill me."

"What happened?"

"Delaney came to serve an eviction notice because Pa hadn't paid the new taxes just imposed. Pa tried to talk to him, ask for more time. We had cattle. A fair price would have paid what we owed. Pa said he would take them to San Antonio, be back in three weeks with the money. He approached Delaney, and one of Delaney's men just shot him. Said he was threatening Delaney. He wasn't. I went for the man who shot Pa. They shot me, then arrested me.

"He probably would have hanged me had it not been for Danny and Micah, who broke into the jail and freed me. Now they're wanted as well. We've been hiding out since."

Seth tried to subdue his anger. "Abe tells me he's grabbing other ranches."

"I expect him to leave the army soon. He's already starting to bankrupt the men he brought to Texas. His bank loaned them money, now it's foreclosing on them. Once out of the army, he can get their land for even less than they paid for it."

"How?"

"Rustling, for one. He's making sure no one can meet their payments."

"I thought you—"

"We're taking a few cows from Delaney's friends and giving the meat to some families," he said. "But the main rustling is being done by Delaney. At first he just offered way below market prices; the fools he lured here took them. Then they caught on, refused to sell to him. So he's rustling cattle and blaming it on us. More than a few homes and barns have been burned. Horses stolen."

"Why haven't you left?"

"Marilee. And you and the twins," he said simply. "Everyone believed you were dead when we didn't hear anything for so long. Everyone but Pa and me. I kept hoping one of you would return, and someone had to be here to tell you what happened. But I couldn't keep Marilee with me, not being hunted like I am. I wasn't ready to leave her with McGuire one day longer than necessary. The only hope I had was to expose Delaney and clear my name." He looked at Seth. "Now that you're here, you can take Marilee."

"She doesn't know me," Seth said.

"You've seen her?"

"Yes."

"She's all right? I'm told she is, but . . ." Agony was in Dillon's tight-lipped frown. "There was no one else to take her."

Seth glanced around at his brother's companions scattered around the room.

Dillon apparently saw the question in his eyes. "Their families are either dead or under attack. There's hardly a ranch that hasn't been hit. Homes and barns burned. Ranchers killed. But the McGuires are safe enough for now, safe until Delaney leaves the service and takes their land as well." He laughed bitterly. "For the moment, Marilee is safer with a carpetbagger than one of our own."

"Elizabeth McGuire was attacked on the way to town by four masked men. They gave the rebel yell."

The men looked at each other. "It wasn't us," Micah Roberts said.

Dillon's face went white. "Was Marilee with her?"

"No. I came along. The horse had bolted. I was able to stop it before she was hurt. The attackers turned and ran when they saw me. She might well have been killed."

Dillon stared at him. "You saved McGuire's daughter."

Seth shrugged. "She might have been all right on her own."

"That's Delaney's style. That and the men who work for him. They like picking on the defenseless, then run when confronted," Micah said. "You still as good with a gun as you used to be?"

Seth shrugged. "Not much practice in the past year."

"But you saw Marilee?" Dillon asked again.

"Yes—and it sent her running into the house. She was scared to death of me. I agreed to take it slow, to let her get used to me before I took her. Abe offered me the use of the old Keller place."

"How did she look?"

"Beautiful. I expected a baby. Nearly five years makes a lot of difference."

"And Miss McGuire? What did you think of her?"

"She seems kind enough. Marilee apparently trusts her." He couldn't add that his own sister didn't trust him.

"She's plain, according to talk, yet Delaney seems to have his eyes set on her for some reason."

"She's not exactly plain. Her eyes . . ." He stopped suddenly.

"Her eyes?" her brother prompted.

Seth shrugged. "They're quite pretty."

"A carbetbagger's daughter? You have been at war a long time, brother."

Unaccountably, Seth took offense. Not for himself but for the woman who was taking care of his sister. "Watch your mouth, younger brother. She's been good to our sister."

Dillon looked at him for a long time, almost like he still didn't believe he was real. He reached out and touched his shoulder. "It's just the three of us now. You and Marilee and me."

"I'm going to get us together again," Seth said.

"And our land."

"And our land," he confirmed.

Dillon held out his hand. Seth clasped it. Then pulled his brother into his arms and hugged him.

He was halfway home.

ELIZABETH cooked supper, wondering when her father would arrive home.

The big pot of stew was simmering. It was the most thrifty meal she could make, and the most tasty, with her little inside garden of herbs. She went upstairs to Marilee's room.

Marilee, holding a doll possessively, was sitting again in a corner.

"Marilee, supper's ready."

The girl looked up at her with huge blue eyes. "Did he go?"

Elizabeth stooped down. "You don't have to be afraid. The man you met is your brother, and he loves you."

Marilee shivered. "He has a gun."

"Yes, but that doesn't mean he is a bad person."

"I don't know him."

"That's because he has been gone a very long time."

"Where's Dillon?" Marilee asked plaintively.

The question again. The one that wouldn't go away. The one she'd repeated at least once a day since she had started to talk again.

"I don't know," she said honestly. She held out her hand. "Let's go down to supper, then I'll read you a story."

Marilee finally stood and took her hand, following soundlessly as she allowed Elizabeth to lead her down the steps.

What was it about Seth Sinclair that frightened his sister? He had indeed frightened even herself this morning when he appeared. But later he'd been oddly protective.

But Marilee still feared him and that was enough to convince Elizabeth to keep her close.

She would protect Marilee. With her life, if necessary.

Chapter Six

IF DILLON WAS right about Delaney's plans, then the McGuires were in trouble.

If they were in trouble, his sister was in trouble.

Seth told himself that was his only concern.

Yet the image of Miss McGuire standing in the doorway of his home with the damned rifle, then her attempts to stop a runaway horse and her coolness afterward had impressed him. She had courage, the kind that could get her killed.

He did not want her killed. Or harmed.

Her father, though, was an entirely different story.

Or was it?

Regardless, he knew he had to warn Elizabeth McGuire.

Would she believe him? Or would she feel that he was just trying to get her and her father off the land?

Even if he did, how in hell could he buy the land back?

A wave of hopelessness washed over him. He needed money. He needed it fast. He could see no way of getting it, not without breaking the law and that, he knew, would play into Delaney's hands. He hadn't left one prison to go into another.

He tried to brush away those thoughts as he used the trail he knew so well. He had stayed the night at the cabin, talking for hours with Dillon, catching up on all their old neighbors and even the newcomers.

Seth had the seeds of a plan in mind, but he didn't tell Dillon. Not until he felt at ease in his own mind that it would work. He didn't think even the Yankee army would tolerate theft on a grand scale. The question, though, was proof. Delaney would continue to blame the rustling on Dillon and his friends, on un-reconstructed rebels.

He rode by the old Keller place which Abe had said he could use. It had a sturdy ranch house, once well tended by someone who, like his family, loved Texas, loved the land. Now it looked like too many of the Southern soldiers he'd met on the long way home. It looked, in fact, probably as he had when he first met Elizabeth McGuire. Faded and dirty and most definitely having seen better times.

Would Marilee be happy there? Could she ever accept him? Perhaps if Dillon was with him.

He had to clear Dillon's name first.

And Elizabeth? Damn it, but he wished she hadn't touched a tender place somewhere deep inside. It was an emotion he thought long dead after the Wilderness.

Seth used water from the pump outside to wash, then changed into the one clean shirt he had left. He had purchased a change of clothes at the general store, a transaction that further depleted his already dismal purse.

There was an old mirror in one of the rooms and he used it to shave.

He barely recognized the man that stared back at him. His face looked gaunt, his cheeks hollow. His eyes were cold as they weighed the face.

No wonder he'd frightened his sister.

He didn't look anything like his father or brother, and his mother had died at Marilee's birth. He didn't have

Dillon's light hazel eyes and dark hair, the same features their father had.

His face had hardened; the softness of youth gone. It came of commanding men, of sending them into battle where they might—and did—die. It came from leaving too many on the battlefield and in the prison, where hunger was a constant and fever took as many lives as bullets and cannonballs had.

Given that, could he ever provide the nurturing a small child required? The nurturing and sense of safety she deserved?

Would she be better off with the McGuire woman?

The thought was unbelievably painful, but it continued to play in his mind.

And his heart.

Perhaps today his sister would open up to him, or at least acknowledge him. Until she did, he would have a huge hole in his heart.

ELIZABETH slept restlessly. She had stayed at Marilee's side until she had gone to sleep.

After leaving for her own bed, she still listened for the nightmares before drifting off into an uneasy sleep. At some time, she heard her farther come in the house. By the loud sounds, she knew he had been drinking.

She chose not to confront him tonight. When drinking, he promised the moon. He seldom kept—or even remembered—those promises.

She couldn't really blame him. Not with failure riding toward them. No cattle, no taxes. No taxes, no land. . . .

Sighing, she knew there would be no talking to him tonight.

ELIZABETH rose at daybreak. Marilee was still sleeping. Perhaps yesterday had not been as frightening to Marilee as Elizabeth feared. That would make it easier for Seth and Marilee to make their peace.

Easier for her to lose the child that had become a daughter to her. Perhaps the only one she might ever have the chance to mother. A sickening sense of loss flooded her.

But then Seth Sinclair had his losses, too.

She felt small and selfish.

She had no doubt he would return. No doubt that he cared for his sister and her welfare. His leaving her here had convinced her of that.

She tried not to consider the fact that she wanted to see him again. She only wanted him to meet quietly with his sister. It was the right thing to do. At least, she hoped it was the right thing.

She did not want him to meet her father. She knew her father's quick temper. She'd also recognized the tense emotions in Seth Sinclair. He wore a gun like a man who knew how to use it. And after killing Northerners for four years, would he have any qualms about killing one who he believed was stealing his land?

She needed to keep them apart. As long as possible.

She didn't intend to tell her father about their visitor.

As if summoned by her thoughts, he stumbled into the kitchen, his hair mussed, his face still ruddy from drinking, his eyes bloodshot.

"I waited for you last night," she said.

He looked sheepish. It was an expression she knew too well. He always thought it would cleanse his sins. It no longer did, in her eyes.

"I was talking to Major Delaney. He invited me to dinner to discuss these cattle-thieving rebels."

"Did he offer any help?"

"Well . . . not right now, but he promised he will."

"And how will we repay the loan you took out if our cattle keep disappearing?"

"He will help us," he said stubbornly. "And I asked him for supper tomorrow night. He was asking after you. He's sweet on you." He looked at her with his bloodshot eyes.

A cold chill shot through her. She had disliked and distrusted Delaney from the first moment she'd met him. For some reason, he was seeking her out. She'd found that strange, since few men had before. She knew she was no beauty, and she had never tried to improve her appearance for a man who repelled her.

"He is twice my age, and I have no interest in him. You know that."

His face fell. "Every woman wants a husband and children."

"Not without love."

He reached out and touched her cheek. "I always disappoint you, lass. I never wanted to do that." He dropped his hand. "Howie and I will go out and look for cattle. There's bound to be strays. Enough to start a new herd. Perhaps I can borrow some money. We'll make it."

"And Major Delaney?" she asked.

"It would please me if you would be pleasant to him tomorrow night," he said, "but I expect no more."

Her father rose wearily and he looked old. She'd never noticed that about him before. He was always so full of life, sober or drunk. But now he looked years older than his actual age. His face was pale, even gray looking.

"Are you ill?" she asked.

"Just the effects of last night." He reached out and touched her shoulder. "I am sorry, lass. I truly am. I just want to know you will be taken care of."

The way he said the words sent a chill through her. It was as if he knew something. . . .

"Is anything wrong?"

"Nay, Liz. I'm just getting old and I want to make sure you are safe. You would have a handsome future with the major."

He had used her before. He had used her as bait, as a shill. But he had never tried to sell her. He wouldn't do that.

Or would he?

As soon as the insidious thought came, she dismissed it.

He would never consciously hurt her. He should know that one of the Sinclairs had returned to reclaim the land her father firmly believed was his. But if she told him now, he would stay. He would try to defend this land just as Seth Sinclair's father had tried to protect what was his.

Elizabeth couldn't stand it if the two men fought and one was killed.

She watched as he gave Marilee a huge hug when the sleepy child came into the room. She remembered those hugs, and how comforting they had been.

Marilee snuggled into his embrace for a moment, then looked up.

Elizabeth prayed the child wouldn't say anything about yesterday, about her brother. Best that her father left before he knew about Sinclair.

And then . . .

She had plans.

They did not include Major Delaney. Compared to the rebel who had saved her life, he was certainly wanting in many aspects. Certainly appearance. She suspected in character as well.

She'd never thought she would—could—be attracted to a rebel, to someone who fought against his own country. And yet his devotion to his family and his courage in stopping the horse had more than impressed her. She was moved by his gentleness with his sister despite his obvious desire to grab her and take her away.

She had never been affected by a man as she was by him. His touch had been like a brand that seared through her blood. Her heart raced when she thought of him.

Elizabeth had never believed in love at first sight and of course, it hadn't been at first sight. But she suspected second sight was just as risky.

Particularly when he wanted what her father had.

She told herself such feelings were fleeting. Love, if there was such a thing, was built on trust, and knowledge of each other and common interests. She had no common interests with an angry gun-toting rebel.

And he most certainly would have no interest in the daughter of the man he believed stole his homestead. She had no attributes to attract a man like him.

Still, she barely suppressed a heady anticipation as she thought about seeing him again.

Chapter Seven

SETH ARRIVED AT his old home about noon to find only Elizabeth McGuire and his sister at home. He had expected her father to be home after the mishap yesterday. He wore his gun, though he'd hoped after the war that he would never have to use it again.

Elizabeth opened the door, her face puckered in an uncertain frown. It caught him by surprise, confusing him. His heart kicked and his stomach clenched. She had always been so certain in previous encounters, even after being attacked yesterday.

"What's wrong?" he asked as his gaze shot beyond her shoulder to the interior of the house. "Marilee?"

"She's fine. I thought . . ." She shook her head and opened the door for him.

He entered, looking around for his sister. "Thought what?" he probed, even as his gaze continued to search for Marilee. "Where is she?"

"She's . . . reluctant to see you. I thought perhaps a picnic would help. Marilee loves picnics. I . . . well . . . I prepared a few things. Not much. If you don't want . . ."

A picnic, by God. The last one was the day before he'd left for war. The church had hosted a picnic to say good-bye to those going off to fight.

They'd all thought they would be back before year's end. It wasn't nearly five years ago. It was a lifetime.

Elizabeth McGuire continued to watch him with an un-certain expression. She obviously expected him to turn her down.

A picnic with his sister—and Miss McGuire—suddenly sounded very good. "Thank you," he said simply, humbled suddenly by her attempt.

He glanced at a basket that was sitting on a table just inside.

"Where's your father?"

"He and Howie are looking for strays. We've been los-ing cattle."

"Does he know I'm back?"

"Why should he care?" The lie was in her eyes. She had not told him. She had probably even encouraged him to leave today. She had guessed far more than he'd real-ized. He had been in the mood to confront McGuire if he had tried to keep him from his sister.

Her gaze met his. Damn but her eyes were pretty. Ap-pealing in their uncertainty. He had learned she was not an uncertain woman. Something intense flared through him. A combination of desire and attraction.

Hell, she was the last woman in the world that should arouse such a reaction.

"I'll hitch the buggy," he said, tearing his gaze away from her.

Moments later, Elizabeth McGuire emerged from the house, one hand holding Marilee's, the other holding the basket and a blanket.

He took the basket and blanket from her, placed them in the buggy, and went to swing Marilee into the buggy.

Instead, she shied away. At least, he comforted himself, she didn't run from him in terror.

He steeled himself against the hurt and moved away. He'd already decided to ride Chance. Now he knew it was a good decision.

Elizabeth helped Marilee into the buggy. Then Elizabeth accepted his hand in stepping up. A pair of very shapely legs showed as her dress hitched up. Her hand felt warm in his.

Warm, hell! It was burning.

He stepped away as if burned. She looked just as startled.

He mounted Chance and followed her as she drove to a spot along the river. The water was down now, barely more than a stream, but it was shaded by cottonwoods and spotted by wildflowers.

He knew every foot of this bank. He and his brothers used to swim here when it was swollen, and fished when it carried only a trickle of water. For a moment, those scenes flashed back. He saw Dillon teasing the twins, daring them to swim across. They tried, and he had to jump in and keep them from being carried downstream. He had given them only a few more years.

He dismounted and hobbled Chance. This time he didn't try to help either Marilee or Elizabeth McGuire down. He'd realized he couldn't force himself on Marilee. He might lose her forever if he tried.

Instead, he stood aside until they were both down, then he reached in the buggy and picked up the picnic basket and blanket. He found a spot under a cottonwood and spread the blanket on the ground.

Still, Marilee looked at him suspiciously.

He knelt in front of her, so his eyes could meet hers. He did not want to be a giant. "I'm Dillon's brother, you know," he said.

Marilee looked at him with wide eyes. "Dillon went away."

He wanted to say he had seen Dillon, but he couldn't. Not in front of the woman.

"I know," he said softly. "But I'm here. I used to hold you when you were a baby. I used to sing you songs."

Marilee backed into Elizabeth McGuire but her gaze didn't leave his.

Progress.

"What songs?" she finally asked.

He hummed a lullaby he used to sing to her, then voiced the words, feeling them strangling in his throat. He had loved music. His entire family had. How many nights had they sat together, he and his father playing their guitars, his brother a harmonica. He hadn't seen that guitar in almost five years. It was something else still at the home which had been his family's.

He finished the song, a French lullaby his mother had taught him.

"Dillon used to sing that to me," Marilee said slowly. Though her body still leaned into Elizabeth's, some of the reserve had left her expression.

He looked up at Elizabeth and saw tears hovering in her eyes.

Those eyes were so clear, so damnably honest.

The tears weren't there for herself. Certainly not for him. They were there for his sister.

He sat down on the blanket. "Your mother used to sing it to Dillon and me," he said. "She died not long after you were born."

"Where are my other brothers? Papa said there were four."

"Two died. They are in . . . heaven." He didn't really believe in heaven. Not after visiting hell on earth. "But they loved you. And they are looking after you."

"Why didn't they look after Papa?"

"I don't know, sweetpea. Maybe it happened before they could do anything."

She looked at him with skepticism, even as she kept as close to Elizabeth as a shadow. "Dillon called me sweetpea," she said.

"We all did," he said gently. "We all loved you."

A rustling sound came from the trees beyond. He spun around, rising to his feet in one fast movement, his hand going automatically to the gun in its holster.

He heard a child's scream behind him.

But he couldn't holster the gun. Dillon had warned him. Delaney's men were not above an ambush. They had not been above frightening—perhaps killing—a woman by making her horse bolt.

No one was going to harm one of his again. No one!

"Mr. Sinclair?"

Elizabeth's soft voice was full of questions. He hadn't realized how soft it was.

"I heard a noise," he said as his gaze moved around the brush and trees. He heard another sound, this time more of a whimper.

He moved forward slowly, keeping the gun in his hand. Another sound. Something moving through the underbrush. He didn't think it was a man now. An animal of some kind. Perhaps a wounded one.

He moved silently ahead.

The whimpering became louder.

And then he saw it.

A small bundle of wet fur huddled and shivering near a tree.

A puppy.

He holstered his gun and leaned down and picked it up.

He wondered what had happened to its mother. Or maybe someone wanted to get rid of extra pups by throwing them in the river. He couldn't leave it here to die. It was too young to care for itself.

When he returned to the picnic site, Elizabeth McGuire was standing, her arms protectively on Marilee's shoulders. His sister's eyes went immediately to the puppy.

"Something must have happened to her mother," he said. "I think she's hungry." Seeing the sudden light in his sister's eyes, he hoped like hell the pup lived.

"Can I hold her?" Marilee asked.

He hesitated. The puppy could be sick. But the longing

in his sister's eyes made it impossible to refuse. He handed the ball of wet fluff to her.

The puppy immediately settled in her lap.

Yet he noticed that though she took the puppy, she still regarded him warily.

Because of the way he'd drawn the gun? Her cry echoed in his mind.

Violence was second nature to him, his gun an extended part of him. Could his sister accept that?

He watched as Marilee cuddled the pup. His eyes met Elizabeth's, and he saw understanding there, and . . . something else.

His chest ached almost unbearably as he saw her gaze return to his sister and the puppy. Tenderness radiated in that one glance. He felt his heart explode. He had seen too much pain and death and defeat. He had stopped believing in hope and justice. But in that moment he knew those things were still alive. Had to be alive.

She looked back up at him, and his breath caught. Her eyes glowed with an admiration that made him feel ten feet tall, like a hero.

It was just a puppy.

She seemed to feel that it was much more. But, for God's sake, what had she expected him to do? Drown the animal?

"She's going to need milk," he said.

But the puppy seemed to have wanted safety more than anything else. She huddled in Marilee's lap, the dog's small face burrowing into her arms.

"Can I keep her?" Marilee said, nuzzling the wet fur.

Elizabeth threw a questioning look his way.

"Do you think you can take care of her?" he asked. "Feed her? Brush her? Keep her safe?"

"Oh yes," Marilee said. It was the first time she hadn't regarded him with fear.

"Then if it's all right with Miss Elizabeth, I think the puppy should stay with you." He rose. "I'll look around and see if I can find the mother."

Elizabeth rose as well. He noticed how gracefully she managed the maneuver as well as the trimness of the ankle revealed as she stood.

"I'll walk with you a little way," she said.

He looked at his sister, who was happily mothering the pup.

"I won't be out of eyesight," she said.

He didn't say anything, just started walking, only too aware of her presence. A subtle scent of roses drifted over to him, and he longed to reach over and touch the copper hair caught in the long braid.

It had been a long time since he'd touched a woman's hair, since he had smelled the scent of roses.

They reached a stand of trees. She stopped, looking back at Marilee. "I shouldn't go farther," she said. "I just wanted to thank you. I should have realized she needed a pet. I never had one . . . we always moved. I didn't think . . ."

"The pup needs her as well. She looks half starved," he said.

"And if I didn't agree?"

"I would have taken the animal," he said harshly. "Do you think I would abandon it?" He started to turn away from her.

Her hand stopped him. "I . . . I don't . . . no . . ."

Her touch was warm on his arm, too warm. The air around them was charged with electricity as though a storm was gathering. But the sky was clear, the sun red and hot.

He looked down into a face that held wonder. A body that trembled slightly, lips parted as breath came more quickly than normal. He felt a peculiar intimacy, a unique sharing of the moment. And more. The awareness of exquisitely painful feelings they seemed to arouse in one another.

He told himself it was loneliness. That it had been far too long since he had been in gentle company. That Elizabeth McGuire was the last woman he needed.

Yet he stood there, enveloped by feelings he'd never thought to have again.

Remember.

Your brother. Your father. The friends and neighbors who had once made life so fine.

Their aims and needs were opposed.

He wanted what she had: his land.

She wanted what he had every right to have: his sister.

Yet he still couldn't take his eyes from hers. God, they were lovely. This was a woman who cared deeply, loved fiercely. He had seen it in the way she touched his sister, in the way she talked of her father. But now that emotion touched him. And shook him to the bottom of his soul.

Her father was his enemy.

Attraction surged between them. He could kiss her. Her eyes invited him. Lord, how he wanted to.

Marilee is yards away. The reminder was like a splash of cold water.

Instead of a bridge, Marilee was a chasm. She was a reminder of what had to be done: His brother cleared. The ranch returned to its rightful owners. Some measure of justice for the other Texans whose land was being systematically looted.

Her father was bound to be hurt in the process.

And until he had a future, he had no business courting anyone, much less the usurpers of his land. And Elizabeth McGuire was the kind of woman you courted, not used.

He stepped back and her hand fell from his arm, the warm glow in her eyes fading.

He turned away and walked into the stand of trees. He had no hope of finding the pup's mother. It wouldn't have abandoned its young. But he needed to get away from the pretty picture of Elizabeth and his sister. Of the look in Elizabeth's eyes.

And temper the need in his own body.

A walk didn't accomplish what he needed. Elizabeth's face darted in and out of his mind, the tenderness as she looked at Marilee, the yearning as she looked at him. In those moments, she was incredibly winsome. There was something about her openness, her lack of guile, that appealed to him far more than conventional beauty.

And, damn, those eyes . . .

He would see her . . . back. Not home. He refused to consider it her home.

He had done what he had wanted today. He had earned the first smile from his sister, the first piece of acceptance.

It wouldn't be long before she would willingly go with him.

He didn't want to think of the ache it would leave in Elizabeth's heart.

Chapter Eight

ELIZABETH CONTINUALLY GLANCED at Marilee and the puppy on the way home. It kept her gaze from the lean man riding beside them.

For a moment back at the creek, she'd been caught in enchantment. She had forgotten everything except Seth Sinclair's presence. His touch had been sweet, his nearness exciting.

And then he had turned away, making their differences stark and seemingly insurmountable.

Marilee chattered about the puppy. It was the first time the girl had acted like a child.

Elizabeth dreaded reaching home. *Please let Father be gone.* She did not want Seth to find him there. Nor her father to meet him.

But she realized Seth was not going to let her and Marilee drive alone. Not even on their—his—own land. Not after what had happened earlier.

As they approached the ranch, she turned to him to tell

him his presence was no longer necessary. Her words were cut off by Howie darting out of the door and running toward her.

"Your pa's been shot," he said. "Thank the Lord you come back. I was afraid to leave him."

Her stomach churned. *Dear God, no.*

She tied the reins and leapt down, then helped Marilee down. "Where is he?" she asked.

He cast a quick, wary glance at Seth.

"It's all right," she said. "He is a friend. Where is my father?" she asked.

"In his room."

"How bad?"

"Bad, Miss McGuire."

She raced for the house, only vaguely aware that Seth had dismounted and was following her. Marilee kept pace, clutching the puppy against her chest.

She went directly to her father's room. He was on the bed. Blood stained his clothes and the bed.

"I tried to stop the bleeding," Howie said.

"Fetch the doctor," she said. "Hurry."

She leaned down. Her father's eyes were closed.

"Father?" she whispered.

He didn't move. Bright red blood contrasted with the deeper color of congealed blood.

She tried to peel away his clothing. Howie had packed the wounds with cloth, trying to stanch the blood. Were the bullets still in any of the wounds?

Larger hands nudged her aside.

"Look after Marilee," Seth Sinclair said curtly. "I'll see to the wounds. God knows I've seen enough of them."

She turned and saw Marilee huddled in the corner, the terror back in her face, panic reflected in her eyes.

She couldn't leave her father. Not now. She couldn't leave him with someone who . . .

"I don't hurt injured, unarmed men," Seth said gently, as if he understood she would break at the slightest raise in his voice.

She still hesitated. "The doctor . . ."

"He might well die by the time the doctor gets here," Seth said harshly. "He's losing a lot of blood."

She saw the pallor in her father's face, heard the rapid breathing. She turned back to Marilee.

Then reached a decision. She stepped back. "What do you need?"

"Clean linen for bandaging. Needle and thread. Hot water."

She watched as he efficiently removed her father's shirt to reveal two bullet wounds. A third bullet had plowed a furrow along the side of his head. She approached Marilee and took her and the pup into her arms.

"Is he going to die?" Marilee said in a too-old voice.

"No, I think your brother will make him well," she said. "Let's get your puppy some milk," Elizabeth said.

Marilee hung back, her gaze settling on Seth. Elizabeth turned back as well. Seth was using her father's shirt to stanch the flood of blood.

"Go," she said softly to Marilee. "The puppy will get sick if he's not fed. Put some milk in a glove and make a small hole in one of the fingers. See if she will suck on it. Can you do that?"

Marilee hesitated.

Then the puppy helpfully whimpered, and Marilee turned toward the kitchen, where a little milk remained from the morning.

Elizabeth turned back to her father and the man leaning over him.

"How bad is it?"

"Two wounds are flesh wounds. The third has a bullet still inside. He's bleeding badly. We have to cauterize the wound but not until it's cleaned and the bullet's out."

"Cauterize?"

His eyes met hers. "Yes."

She leaned over the bed. "Papa. Talk to me. Papa." She willed him to talk to her, to acknowledge her presence.

His eyes fluttered open. "Princess?"

She could tell he was fighting to open them and keep them open.

"Papa. What happened?"

"Masked . . . rebel cry," he said. "Came . . . out . . . of . . . nowhere. Sinclair."

His glazed eyes moved to the man standing about him. "Who . . .?"

Elizabeth looked up at Seth. His expression didn't change, but his eyes hardened, became ice cold.

"Have you had any training?" she asked.

He laughed bitterly. "More than four years of it, Miss McGuire. We often didn't have a doctor. We did a lot of our own mending. Sometimes it worked, sometimes it didn't."

He had left it there for her to make a decision.

A low moan came from her father. His eyes opened slightly. He obviously understood a little of what was being said.

"Papa, you're losing blood. Someone has to get the bullet out and cauterize the wound. This . . . gentleman said he will try."

Her father's pain-filled face turned toward him, nodded slightly, then the eyes closed again.

"There used to be a medical box in the kitchen," Sinclair said. "Is it still there?"

She was reminded once more that this had once been his home. She nodded.

"What about alcohol?"

She shook her head. She always threw it out when she found some in the ranch house.

She heard him swear quietly before continuing in a slightly louder voice, "There should be a pair of tongs and scalpel in the box. Bring the box and heat a knife. I'll need two pans of hot water, soap, and clean cloth to bandage the wound." He paused. "I think he's unconscious again but he could wake up. It's going to hurt like hell." His eyes challenged her.

She leaned over the silent form again. "Papa?" she asked.

He didn't answer, didn't move. She hoped he would remain unconscious.

She went into the small area that served as a kitchen. She located the medical box, put kindling into the cookstove, and lit it. She found the scalpel in the medical box, and washed it with water from a pitcher. When the kindling began to flame, she shoved the steel of the knife inside, shivering as she did so. She poured water into a pan and put it on top of the stove.

It would take a few minutes for the water to heat. She had a moment to look in on Marilee. She must be frightened nearly to death and Elizabeth did not want her to wander into her father's room while Seth was digging out a bullet.

Marilee sat on the bed, holding a glove. The puppy sucked at one of the fingers of the glove.

"She's eating," Marilee said solemnly.

"I see. She's a survivor."

"How's Poppy?"

"He is very sick. But your brother thinks he can fix him."

"He found the puppy."

Finding a puppy and digging for a bullet were two different things, but she was not going to explain that at this moment. She only hoped her faith wasn't misplaced. "Stay up here, love," she said. "Take care of the puppy."

Marilee nodded, cradling the puppy in one arm and holding the glove with the other.

Elizabeth returned to the kitchen and gathered clean towels. "Please God, don't let him die. He's all I have." Her lips moved with the prayer, yet no sound escaped.

She recalled what he had said. *Masked men. A rebel cry.* The same description fit the ones who'd intentionally spooked her horse. Her father mentioned Sinclair. *Dillon Sinclair.* Could Seth be involved in some way? Was that why he had gone with her on the picnic? An alibi?

But then why was Seth trying to save her father? To claim being a good Samaritan?

Should she wait for the doctor? But she had seen how

pale her father's face had turned, how weak his voice was.

She took the medical box and towels to the room, setting them down on a table next to the bed, then hurriedly fetched the water. She planned to watch every movement Seth made.

He stood a few feet away, applying pressure to the wound on her father's shoulder.

"Keep the pressure on," he said. She moved to the side of the bed and her hands replaced his, brushing them.

Her gaze didn't leave him as he opened the box. She had seen the contents before but now they looked sinister and ugly. He removed a pair of tongs and glanced at her.

"Wipe the blood from the wound," he said. "Keep doing it." He glanced up at her, challenge still in his eyes.

She nodded, leaned over, and wiped away blood with one of the towels she'd brought in.

Seth didn't hesitate but slowly inserted the tongs into the wound. She prayed her father would remain unconscious.

Sweat ran down Seth's face as he moved the tongs with obvious expertise. And care. She saw in his face when he found the bullet, and her gaze went back to his hand as he extracted the bullet.

Blood gushed behind it and without urging she pressed a clean cloth down on the wound.

"The knife?"

"In the stove."

He left the room. In seconds, he was back, holding the handle of the knife with a towel.

"You might want to leave," he said. "This won't be pleasant."

"No."

He shrugged. "When I tell you to move your hands, do it." His voice was matter-of-fact as if he had done this a hundred times. Without waiting for an answer, he added, "Now."

She moved the towel and he pressed the blade against the wound. It sizzled and even in unconsciousness her father's body seemed to jump. She felt the impact clear through her body.

He lifted the knife and looked down at the wound. The bleeding had stopped.

She heard the release of a withheld breath. She thought it her own until she looked at Seth's face. It had been his. His lips were slightly parted, his usually cool eyes roiling with some emotion she didn't understand.

"Thank you," she said.

"Don't thank me yet. He's lost a lot of blood and there could be infection."

"You tried. You didn't have to."

"I've seen enough death in the past few years," he said curtly. "I don't want to see more." He paused. "No matter who it is."

It was a direct slap at her. At the man he had just doctored.

She was the first to avert her gaze. "What should I do now?"

"He is going to hurt. The doctor should have something to help. So would alcohol. I would leave the wound unbandaged until the doctor comes."

"You're not leaving?"

"I have other business."

"What if . . ."

"I've done everything I can do. Keep the wound clean. Make him as comfortable as possible."

She started to protest, then she heard hoofbeats approaching. She moved quickly to the window. Howie and the doctor was her first thought.

It couldn't be. Not this quickly.

She peered out the window and her heart dropped.

Major Delaney. He was looking at the buggy that was still hitched to the horses, at Seth's horse.

Why? Why now?

She turned to Seth. "You have to hide."

"Why?"

"Major Delaney is here."

"I have no reason to hide. The war is over."

"He wants your brother. He might . . ."

"Might what?"

"Try to hold you for some reason. To get to your brother."

"I am not going to run."

"Please."

"No."

"He's dangerous."

"He and your father are friends. So are you, I understand. I heard he's calling on you."

She ignored the contempt in his voice. "It could have been your brother who shot my father—"

"No," he replied with such conviction that she stepped back. "He didn't chase your buggy. Neither did any of his friends."

"How do you know?"

A knock at the door turned into pounding, and she didn't wait for an answer. "I have to go down," she said. "He knows someone is here. The horses . . ."

He took a last look at her father. The man was still unconscious. His breathing was labored.

Then Seth started out the door.

She knew she couldn't stop him.

She also knew what had happened the last time Delaney met a Sinclair.

A frisson of apprehension, of fear, darted down her spine.

He possibly had just saved her father.

Now she had to save him.

Chapter Nine

A QUICK GLIMPSE out the window had told Seth that the Yankee major was alone.

That was fortunate. More than fortunate from Seth's point of view. It handed him a chance to weigh his opponent. The major was the cause of his father's death, the loss of the Sinclair home and land, the labeling of his brother as an outlaw, and probably a great deal more. Seth relished the opportunity to meet him.

He led a reluctant Elizabeth to the door, standing beside her.

"Go into the other room," she commanded.

"No," he said again. "I've been wanting to meet him."

"Please."

"I haven't done a damn thing wrong," he said.

The pounding on the door increased. "Shouldn't you open the door?" he asked. "If you don't, I will."

Her gaze met his. Worry reflected in her eyes. Worry for him.

"It's all right," he said gently. "I've been officially pardoned. I even have the papers. There's nothing he can do."

She reluctantly opened it.

A man in Union blue stood there, his fist upraised. Hostile curiosity flicked across his face when he saw Seth. The officer's eyes weighed him, moving slowly from his face down to his Confederate uniform pants.

"You must be Sinclair," he stated. From the tone of his voice, he might as well have said "rabid dog." He took his gun from its holster and held it on Seth. "You are trespassing, Sinclair."

Seth didn't even look at the gun. "I've heard of you as well," Seth managed in a pleasant voice.

Elizabeth broke in. "He's not trespassing. I asked him in. He just saved my father's life. He was here. You were not, nor have you provided any of the protection my father requested." She paused, then demanded, "What are you doing here?"

Seth was astonished. According to Abe, she was being courted by the major. She and her father depended on his goodwill, yet she didn't back away.

"Looks like you need to be doing a better job," Seth said mildly.

Delaney's hostile eyes held Seth's. He was a bulky man with a ruddy face and a thin mouth. His uniform was impeccable, the cloth good and the fit even better. Nice goods to conceal bad sins. "I met Howie on the road," Delaney said, his gaze returning to Elizabeth. "He told me your father had been shot. He went ahead for the doctor. I thought I'd better come right away. It looks like I was right."

"As you can see, we are being well taken care of," Elizabeth said, glancing at Seth.

"He's a rebel," Delaney shot back. "He is probably in league with his brother. Drat it, Elizabeth, he probably shot your father."

"No," she said. "He was with me. We took Marilee for a picnic."

Pure rage crossed Delaney's face. "He's a traitor. If he

didn't shoot your father, then his brother did. Or his friends. You can be sure he knew about it. Anyway, he's going with me for questioning."

"Like hell I will," Seth said. "Of course, you could shoot me here. In the back. I understand that's your way of doing things. Unfortunately for you, there's a witness this time." It was a taunt. He saw Delaney's fingers tighten on the handle of his pistol.

"If McGuire dies, it's your kind who did it."

"My kind?"

"A traitor," Delaney repeated. "Just like your brother is a traitor."

"But I'm not a profiteer."

The gibe struck its mark. Delaney turned several darker shades of red, rage deepening into fury.

He visibly struggled to contain himself as he turned to Elizabeth. "I care about your father . . . and you. Thank God he is still alive. I promise you we will capture those responsible."

Seth doubted his sudden concern was very convincing to her, especially since it had been secondary to his anger at seeing him here.

"If you are so concerned, then you might ride out to hurry the doctor," she said sharply.

Neatly done, Seth thought.

"I want to see your father," Delaney persisted. "I have questions to ask."

"I don't think he can answer any now. He needs his strength."

"I'll be the judge of that," Delaney said. "He might have seen who shot him." His gaze flickered back to Seth. "In fact, I demand to see him. This man might well have done something to finish the job. You are too trusting, Elizabeth."

"I am not trusting at all," she said. "Mr. Sinclair chased off some men trying to run my buggy off the road, and Mr. Sinclair took a bullet from my father's shoulder. Where were you, Major, and the men my father has been requesting for protection?"

"I have a quarter of the state to patrol, Elizabeth," Delaney said. Seth noticed that Delaney hadn't even responded to the news that Elizabeth had been attacked—most likely because it wasn't news to him.

"You brought us here. Now you're leaving us to the mercy of outlaws. I'm beginning to wonder why."

Seth was startled by her candor. Had she also started to question what was happening?

Delaney looked equally startled. "Now, Elizabeth, you know I would do anything for you and your father. I have troops out every day looking for those outlaws. That's why I can't keep them at any one ranch." He nodded toward Seth. "This man is probably here to spy for them."

"No," Elizabeth said sharply. "He saved my life earlier, then my father's. Arrest him for no reason, and I'll go to your superiors. As far as I have to go. And you will not come any farther inside with that gun in your hand."

Delaney glared at her, then slowly put his gun in his holster. He kept his hand on it.

"I came to ask you attend our regimental ball with me on Saturday," he said with a forced smile.

"I cannot attend when my father is wounded," she said. "But thank you."

A muscle twitched in his neck. He was not, Seth thought, a man to be refused. An unexpected surge of satisfaction rushed through him. Despite what Abe had said, it was obvious by her cool reception that any feeling Delaney might have for Elizabeth was not reciprocated.

Why did he even care?

He mulled that over as Delaney glanced at him, then back at Elizabeth. Seth wondered whether he detected any of the attraction that had darted between them.

If he had, he chose to ignore it for the moment. "I still insist on seeing your father," Delaney said.

She reluctantly stepped aside. Delaney brushed by him as if he were an annoying fly and went to McGuire's bedroom as if he belonged here, had been here often. Seth didn't like the jealousy that roiled in his stomach as he followed Delaney and Elizabeth to her father's room. He had no intention of leaving her alone with the man.

Seth entered behind Delaney. Perhaps McGuire's death was exactly what Delaney wanted. Then he could claim the Sinclair land. And McGuire's daughter. She would be alone then. Vulnerable.

Or would she be? She was obviously stronger than he'd first thought.

Delaney went to McGuire's bedside.

"Michael," he said.

No answer.

He turned to Elizabeth and Seth. "I would see him alone."

"No," Elizabeth said again, and in the same flat tone he had heard earlier.

"I don't think you understand," Delaney said. "This is official business."

"Probably I am too simple to understand," she replied in a dangerous tone.

Seth knew what was coming. He wondered whether Delaney did.

"But someone who loves him should be with him," she added. "To protect him." The words could not be mistaken for anything but a warning.

Delaney's eyes narrowed. "Did he see anything?"

"No. He said his attackers wore masks."

"Sinclair's friends," Delaney said. "One brother shoots. The other saves."

Elizabeth's eyes narrowed. "Why?"

"Gratitude. Insinuating himself into your life so he can get back what he feels is his."

"Is it?"

"Is it what?"

"His land?" Elizabeth asked.

Delaney gave her a quick glance. "Of course not. Your father paid for it. It's yours."

"Is it?" she asked again. "Certainly not if we can't stop the rustling."

"Talk to your newest friend about that." Delaney's

voice was harsh. Then he looked at Michael McGuire in the bed.

Seth truly didn't know if McGuire was awake or not. He found himself caring about him, which surprised him. He shouldn't care about this carpetbagger, this usurper who had presumed to take his land.

But Elizabeth was an innocent in this, and he didn't want her to feel the kind of pain that he knew only too well.

Seth leaned against the wall while Delaney tried to arouse McGuire with his voice. Then he started to reach down.

Elizabeth stopped the movement. "Don't touch him!"

To Seth's surprise, Delaney withdrew his hand. Retreated.

Elizabeth sat down next to her father. Felt his forehead, then held his hand. She looked up at Delaney defiantly. "He was bleeding badly. If it were not for Mr. Sinclair . . ."

Delaney frowned. "Dillon Sinclair was behind the shootings," he insisted again. "Make no mistake, the Sinclairs want you gone."

"I would want me gone as well, were I in their place," Elizabeth sparred. "Yet he has twice saved me in as many days. Perhaps I've been trusting the wrong people."

Delaney stood straight and faced Elizabeth and away from Seth. "Don't be misled, Elizabeth. I've been a friend to your father. Without me—"

"Without you, the McGuires would probably have a great deal more cattle than they have now," Seth broke in. "Tell me, what kind of price did you give them for the herd my father had ready for market?"

Delaney spun around, the gun back in his hand, but Seth was just as fast. His was there a fraction of a second faster. "I wouldn't advise it," he said softly.

"Threatening an officer is an offense," Delaney said with satisfaction. "You're under arrest."

Elizabeth stood. "I didn't see anything," she said. Her eyes met Delaney's. "I want you to go. Now."

Delaney stared at her as if he couldn't believe what he

was hearing. "You're upset, Elizabeth. You don't know what you're saying. This man is dangerous. I can't leave you here alone with him."

"I *have* been 'alone' with him, and I feel perfectly safe. A lot safer, in fact, than I do with him gone."

"You heard the lady," Seth said. His finger was on the trigger. He had sworn not to kill again after the war, but he was willing to make an exception with the man responsible for murdering his father and outlawing his brother. How many others had he killed?

"I'll get you, Sinclair," Delaney said. "Just like I'll get your brother and his friends."

"I won't tell you again," Seth said. "Get the hell out of here before my finger twitches on the trigger."

Seth saw his eyes darken, his mouth clench in repressed fury.

He also realized his brother was right. Delaney was a dangerous man.

Delaney looked at Elizabeth, then back at him, at the gun pointed at him. "Get out of town, Sinclair. Next time I see you, you won't be able to hide behind a woman's skirt."

"I hardly think I'm doing that, Delaney. And believe me I won't be as unsuspecting as my father. I watch my back."

"You're a dead man."

"A threat. In front of Miss McGuire at that. I would be more cautious, Delaney."

The major looked like a coiled rattler poised to strike. His body radiated tension and fury. Both Seth's gun and Elizabeth's presence made that impossible.

Seth smiled at him. His Colt didn't waver in his hand. He was inviting a rash action, hoping for it.

Delaney didn't oblige. Instead he uttered a barely audible oath, whirled around, and left.

Elizabeth stood. "He *will* kill you. He will wait until you're alone, then strike."

"Worried about me?"

Her gaze met his. The answer was there, soft and trusting in her eyes. It didn't have to be spoken.

"I thought you two were courting," he said softly.

"He's calling only because I've rebuffed his advances. He's not a man to be thwarted."

Seth suddenly regretted what he had just done. He had wanted to bait the man, to see what he was made of. He had also wanted to prod him into making a mistake. But in doing so, he might have put the McGuires—and his sister—in the line of fire. "He's been thwarted now by a woman he wants in favor of a man he now hates," he said. "That's dangerous too."

She shivered slightly, and he realized that she knew exactly what she had done.

He reached out and took her hand, closing his big one around it.

Dammit.

He leaned down, touched her lips, and then she seemed to float into his arms. The attraction that had flickered between them from the very beginning flared, its flames licking at every nerve in his body. He reveled in the softness of her body, the slight fragrance from her hair. God, it had been a long time. Such a damned long time since he had touched anyone with gentleness.

His lips explored hers, and he had to force himself not to crush them against hers. Instead, he brushed her cheeks with kisses, feasting on the touch and feel of her, allowing her to get used to him.

There was a wistful vulnerability about her that diminished all his defenses. He wanted her. He wanted to take off her clothes and feel her body under him. Most of all, he wanted to wake up to that wondrous smile she had. . . .

"Liz?"

They both turned at the same time.

His sister stood there, an uncertain look on her face, the puppy contentedly sleeping in her arms. "I . . . I wanted to see Poppy," she said uncertainly.

Seth took a step backward. God, he hurt inside. Desire was a clawing thing inside him.

Elizabeth looked as dazed as he felt.

Nonetheless, she knelt and gave Marilee the sweetest smile he thought he'd ever seen. "He's going to be fine, love," she said softly. "Just fine."

"Promise?"

"I promise," she said.

He watched them together and felt a tightening in his heart. Love stretched between them.

He was excluded.

How could he take his sister away from Elizabeth or, for that matter, Elizabeth from Marilee?

He could marry her, but why would she want a penniless rebel who'd lost his soul during four long bloody years in the hell of war? How could he even entertain the idea when he had nothing to offer but himself?

And he had just made himself a target for the federal authorities.

Chapter Ten

STILL DAZED BY the kiss interrupted by Marilee, Elizabeth hugged the child.

As Elizabeth fought to bring sense back to her life, she looked into Seth's blue eyes. It was a mistake.

She found herself swirling in the currents there. Desire. Need. Reluctance.

She was warmed through to her toes. Every nerve ending tingled. She'd never known what the word *desire* meant before. Now she did.

An ache lodged in the core of her, a craving, a longing that was new to her. It was as if the world had caught fire and she'd been swept into its center.

She had never felt desired before. Had never considered herself desirable.

He might desire her, but he didn't want her. Or at best he didn't want to want her.

He *did* desire her. Need was in his eyes, in the tense set of his body, in the way he had touched her. Kissed her.

The sounds of a buggy rolling to a stop jerked her out of the daze.

She forced her legs to carry her to the window.

The doctor.

That snapped her out of the daze. How could she have stood here, kissing a man, while her father lay ill, possibly dying?

Because she had just realized how precious life was?

She looked toward her father. He was still. Thank God. When he woke he would be in immense pain.

"The doctor," she told Seth, who was still standing there. Watching her. She brushed by him without another word.

She greeted the doctor and led him to her father. After taking off the bandages and examining the wound, Dr. Pearson looked up from the patient. "Couldn't have done better myself," he said. "Give him some of that laudanum I gave him a few months back. If there's fever, call me."

He turned and looked at Seth. "Damn glad to see you, boy. We all thought you were dead."

"I almost was."

"Sorry to hear about your brothers. Sorry about your pa." He glanced at Elizabeth, then back at Seth. "Sorry about the land, too. Damn shame. Don't mind telling you that."

She felt the weight of his disapproval, just as she had felt it from so many other Texans. But then what he'd just said registered.

"What laudanum?"

He looked surprised. "He didn't tell you?"

"Tell me what?"

"He's had some pain in his heart. I gave him some quinine and . . ." He suddenly closed his mouth.

Anxiety churned her stomach. No wonder he hadn't been as active in the last few months.

Why hadn't he told her?

She swayed for a moment, then steadied herself. Her father's approval of the courtship of Major Delaney made sense now. At least to him. He wouldn't have wanted to leave her alone, and Delaney was the only man to ever show interest in her.

"How long?" she whispered.

"I don't know. The loss of blood didn't help. Nor will the pain he'll feel when he wakes up. Make sure he takes the laudanum."

"I will."

Seth's eyes were on her. They were curtained now. Just as they had been on their first ride in the buggy after he had rescued her. She had no idea what he was thinking.

"Thank you," she said to the doctor. "How much do I owe you?"

"A dollar."

"I'll get it for you," she said and left the room for the kitchen where she kept money in a jar. She dug out a dollar, then hurried back, only to be stopped by voices from within the room. She stepped back and listened.

"I'm surprised to see you here," Dr. Pearson said.

"It's my home."

"You are asking for trouble."

"Maybe," came Seth's low drawl. "You get around. You've always known everything that goes on. What do you know about the rustling around here?"

"I know everyone is losing cows, especially those who refused to accept Delaney's going price. His offers are so low no one can pay the taxes he imposes. Delaney says it's all the army allows, but I have a friend at headquarters who tells me the general's complaining at the cost of cattle. Apparently Delaney buys low and reports a higher price to his superiors."

"How in the hell does he get away with it?"

"Fear," the older man said. "People who cross him die. I'm ashamed to say that I haven't said anything. But I'm the only doctor in twenty-five miles. If I die, other folks will, too."

"And if people don't sell?"

"Can't prove it, but some of us believe he's responsible

for the rustling. We don't think for a moment it's your brother and young Mitchum."

"Is there any federal official who is honest?"

"There's a federal marshal in San Antonio. I hear he's pretty honest. Hearsay is he's had some run-ins with Delaney."

"Who else is still here? What other families?"

"The Knoxes. They didn't have any sons and are not tainted by Confederate service. Both daughters are back home. Widowed. One in the war, one by outlaws. Then there's Old John Carey. Gary and Morgan Simmons."

"They're still bachelors?"

"Yep. No one in their right mind would marry them. They're ornery as hell. Never did go off to war. Said it wasn't their fight, but that doesn't seem to matter to Delaney. Their horses keep disappearing as well as cattle. Then there's John and Mary Andrews. They are barely holding on to their ranch. I hear tell Delaney just raised their taxes."

"How many have lost cattle?"

"All of them, I'd say. And more."

She walked in then, letting them hear her footsteps. The voices stilled and both men looked awkward.

She held out the dollar in her hand. "Thank you for coming."

He nodded.

"I'll walk you out, Doc," Seth said with a familiarity that she had never had with the Texas doctor. He'd always been reserved, though he had come immediately when she'd called him.

She knew they weren't just exchanging pleasantries. She felt suddenly very cold as they walked out.

Frustrated at her exclusion, she sat at the edge of her father's bed. *Laudanum. Quinine.*

Why hadn't her father told her?

Her heart beat faster again, but this time it had nothing to do with the hard, lean cowboy. This time it was pure fear. Her father was all she had in the world. Her father and Howie.

There was Marilee, but she would leave soon with Seth.

She would sit here until her father woke, then she would ask her questions.

SETH stopped next to the doctor's buggy.

"Who is the marshal you mentioned?"

"Name's Evans. Talk is he's honest even if he is a Yankee. I've heard him talk about Delaney. I think he would love to arrest him."

"I think I saw him when I first came into town. He was in the saloon."

"Probably sniffing around. There's been a lot of shootings in this area."

"He would go against a senior army officer?"

"An arrogant army officer who doesn't think much of U.S. marshals and shows it? I think Evans would relish it."

"I would like to talk to him," Seth said. "How bad is McGuire?"

"His heart's failing. I don't think he will live much longer. How did you come to take that bullet out?"

"I was there when he came in."

"And what were you doing there?"

"Miss McGuire was attacked yesterday. Whoever did it is obviously trying to frame my brother and his friends."

The doctor raised an eyebrow. "That was yesterday. You aren't sweet on her, are you?"

"She's caring for my sister. I came to see Marilee."

The doctor stared at him for a long moment. "I don't like these carpetbaggers any more than you, but I don't want to see that young lady hurt."

"I don't, either," Seth said.

"You are playing a dangerous game, boy."

"I'm hardly a boy now."

"No, you take after your father. You think things through. But be careful. Delaney doesn't look it, but he's clever."

"Thanks for your help."

"These are my people, Seth. I was here when they were

born and I've mourned with them when they've buried their people. I sewed up your brother after your father was killed. Isn't right what's happening. Isn't right at all." He stepped into his buggy. "I'll go see Marshal Evans. Set up a meeting. He might trust me more than a rebel captain. I suspect you have other things to do."

"Major," Seth corrected with a small smile. "Ex-major."

"Your father hadn't heard. He was damned proud of you." He paused, then added, "I can ride over late this afternoon, stay overnight. I'll be stopping over to see Mr. McGuire tomorrow. Probably around suppertime."

"Thanks, Doc. Good seeing you again."

The doctor touched his hat in response. "Give my regards to your brother."

SETH first made a trip to the ranches of those families named by Doc Pearson.

He knew them all. They had attended church with his family.

All were faced with eviction. Most of their cattle had disappeared. When they reported it, they were told that the culprits were their former neighbors—Dillon Sinclair and several local men—who were at large.

They didn't believe it. They all knew Dillon. He'd been wild as a kid but there hadn't been a dishonest or vicious bone in his body.

He judged each one, then settled on Gary and Morgan Simmons. Neither had a wife or children. They had a few cattle but their main business had been cutting horses.

"It will be dangerous," he warned. "But I won't do it if the marshal doesn't agree."

"Our folks are buried out there in back," Morgan told him. "We didn't have no stake in this war, and we didn't go. Delaney has no cause to take our property. But now he says he's 'conscripting' our horses for next to nothing. Says he has that right, and he's threatening new taxes if we complain. We can't pay no more and he knows it. Ain't many of us left 'cept old man Carey, Tom Knox, and John down the crik. Might as well die protectin' it. Ain't gonna live forever anyhow."

Gary concurred with his brother, his answer emphasized by going over to where a shotgun hung on hooks. He took it down and fondled it like a man fondled his lover.

"Go into town," Seth said. "Talk to the banker about a loan. Tell him you're gathering cattle from area ranchers and you need the money to hire some hands to drive them to San Antonio. Explain that the army here is paying too low a price."

A smile spread over Gary's face. "Delaney can't let that happen. If army inspectors find out exactly what he's paying the ranchers for cattle, or find out they can get them one hell of a lot cheaper, they will start to wonder about the major, mebbe even ask for bills of sale."

"He will have to go lickety-split after the cattle," Morgan finished for him.

"I would think so," Seth said. "Hopefully, we will have a U.S. marshal waiting for his men. Rustling's a hanging offense. They will talk."

"But where will we get cattle?"

"Let me worry about that. It might take a few weeks, though."

"As long as we git rid of the bastard and git a fair man out here. When you want me to go to the bank?"

"A week. By then I might be able to round up some cattle."

"Should we ask where?"

"No."

"Just let us know," Morgan said.

IT was dusk when Seth reached the natural canyon. As before, he made sure he wasn't followed. He didn't think he would be. Delaney had been surprised to find him at the ranch.

He hadn't had time to get back to town and bring help before Seth had left. There was no way he would know where Seth went after their encounter.

He had no doubt that Delaney had probably sent out men to find him. His presence at his former home had obviously been disconcerting. So must have been Elizabeth's defense of him.

They would probably be waiting for him to return now.

But he had to pull together the strings of his plan.

He felt eyes on him as he neared the approach into the valley. He wasn't surprised when a rider moved in next to him and paced his horse to Seth's.

"Colorado."

"In the flesh. What in the hell are you doing here?"

"I need some help."

"Someone could be following you."

"I've been on the losing side of a war for four years, the first two as captain of scouts. I can evade the best of trackers."

Colorado didn't say more as they wound through the narrow opening into the valley and to the decrepit cabin.

His brother sat on the porch, whittling. He rose lazily, gave Seth a tight smile. "Still free, I see."

"Delaney's not happy with that situation."

"Have you seen Marilee?"

"Several times. She's safe enough for now. And happy, I think. As happy as she can be considering what she witnessed."

"I miss her."

"We will get her back. I promise."

"Do you have a plan?"

"It's forming. How many cows do you have here?"

"Not many. We have to be careful."

"Branded?"

"Some. Not all."

"What are the brands?"

Dillon named several nearby ranchers. One belonged to the Knox family.

"Where did they come from?"

"A friend of Delaney named Richmond. His herd is growing proportionately to those being depleted. He hadn't had time to change the brands. We intend to get them back to the rightful owners."

"We have another use for them now," Seth said and outlined the plan.

Colorado and Dillon listened in silence.

"I don't like it," Colorado said. "It depends on a marshal. How do we know he's not in league with Delaney?"

"Doc vouches for him. I plan to take his measure before saying anything."

"We don't have any choice," Dillon said. "Another six months and there won't be a Texan left in this area."

"And Delaney will have our ranch."

Dillon stiffened. "What do you mean?"

"McGuire was gunned down early today. I know it wasn't you, but I hear they're blaming everything else on you. They will probably add that to the list."

"Hell, it wasn't none of us. We stay hunkered down during the day."

"It was probably Delaney. He wants to marry McGuire's daughter, probably retire from the army with the best spread in Canaan. He can then scoop up other parcels at his leisure. He's draining them of all their assets. They won't have any choice but to sell or be foreclosed."

"What do you need?" Dillon said.

SETH waited until near daybreak before approaching the ranch house that once belonged to his family.

He had seen the men stationed around the house. All appeared to be peacetime soldiers. Lazy. Undisciplined. Two were asleep. Two others had laid their rifles several feet away. All were unconscious now, tied with their own belts and the severed reins of their horses. Of the four, three had seen nothing. The last had only seen a man in a mask similar to those used by Elizabeth's attackers.

Seth then moved swiftly to the back of the house, found an open window, and slid through it.

He'd seen a light in the house from a distance. Her father's room. Seth wanted to make sure he was out of danger, that Delaney had not paid another visit.

Seth moved lightly to McGuire's room, pausing at the door to listen for voices. There were none. He gently opened the door.

And came face-to-face with the wrong end of a pistol.

Chapter Eleven

HE STOOD STILL. He usually stood still when confronted by someone holding a pistol.

A sleepy-eyed Elizabeth held it.

She was still in a dress. Her hair was coming loose from the braid she usually wore and curled around her face. Long black lashes framed weary eyes.

She lowered the gun when she saw him.

"How did you get in?" she asked.

"Through a back window."

"Soldiers were here all day. They've been looking for you. They said they had an arrest warrant."

"Did they say for what?"

"No."

He shrugged. "I suspected as much. Under military occupation, it doesn't take much."

"How did you get by them?"

"I didn't. They're sleeping right now."

"Did you help them?"

"I did," he replied.

"All of them?"

"I sincerely hope so."

"You're giving them more reasons to come after you."

"I don't think they need any."

She put her pistol on the table beside the bed. "Why did you come here? Surely you knew . . ."

"I wanted to know how your father was doing. And Marilee."

"Do you really care about my father?"

"Surprisingly enough, I do," he said, realizing it was true. "I think he's a victim as much as anyone here." He went over to the man's bedside, inspected the bandages, then felt his forehead. "No fever. Has he awoken yet?"

"Yes."

"Did he tell you any more?"

"The only description was similar to those who came after me."

That puzzled him. If Delaney wanted to take Elizabeth as his wife to inherit, why would he try to kill her? Or perhaps he just wanted to frighten her enough to seek his protection. If so, he obviously didn't care if she was seriously hurt, even killed, in the effort.

She looked at him. "Could it have been your brother?"

"No."

"You've talked to him then?"

Seth didn't say anything.

Despite his efforts to save her father, Elizabeth obviously wasn't absolutely sure who was behind the attacks. The pistol that was in her hand proved that. She'd been ready to protect her father with her life.

"I told him you saved his life," she said.

"Anyone would have."

"I don't think so," she said. "I don't remember if I thanked you."

She looked so vulnerable, so tired, yet still so protective of those she loved that his heart jolted. He held out his arms and she stepped into them. He just held her for several moments, trying to lend his strength to her.

Her body pressed against his, but her eyes gazed directly into his. His breath caught at what he saw there. Trust. And another emotion. One more complicated than desire.

He felt it, too. Damn, he wanted to protect her. Her father as well because she loved him. Hell, he wanted more than to protect her. He wanted her in his life. Not just for a night. Or a week.

He lowered his head to kiss her. Gently, comfortingly at first. Lips touching lips with featherlike gentleness.

It was meant to be comforting but the moment their lips met, the kiss turned into something else altogether. Awareness flashed and thundered between them like a sudden Texas storm. His knees nearly buckled under the impact of need he suddenly felt. His hands moved along her back, touching lightly, and he marveled at the wells of tenderness that gave his hands a gentleness he'd never known before. He felt a glow of light, then a warmth that filled him so completely he realized how lonely he had been, how dark his world had become in the past years.

Her arms curled around his neck and he reveled in her embrace, the way her fingers teased and played with his hair. A barely restrained passion was evident in each touch, as it was in the hazel eyes that changed with her every emotion. They were stormy, more green and gold than brown.

He deepened the kiss, feeling her react to it. Her body moved closer into his and he felt a longing and need so strong he could barely contain it.

A groan came from the bed. Reality stabbed through the cocoon of desire that had wrapped around them.

She stepped back quickly, turned, and went to the bed. He remained where he was, his body afire.

"Liz?" McGuire's voice was barely a whisper, broken with pain.

"Papa, I'm here. I'll get you some more laudanum."

She knelt beside her father and Seth heard the love and concern and tenderness in her voice. That struck him as deeply as her passion a moment earlier.

"No," McGuire said, then his pain-filled gaze moved to Seth.

"Who . . .?" His voice broke off as if he could not manage another word.

"Seth Sinclair. He took out the bullet yesterday. The doctor said he saved your life. He also rescued me the day before."

"Sinclair?"

"Yes."

"He . . ."

"He's a good man, Papa," she said.

"Tell him . . . to come close," McGuire said.

Seth stepped closer and looked down at the man who had benefited from the theft of his land.

McGuire strained to lift his good arm and held out his hand for Seth's. "Thank you," he said simply. "For Liz, thank you."

Seth took it. Any number of emotions ran through him. And out of him. Bitterness faded. So did any desire for revenge.

McGuire loved his daughter. Elizabeth loved her father. *And I love Elizabeth.*

The thought flashed through his mind with the impact of a cannonball.

He tried to dismiss it. It was the circumstances. He'd been lonelier than he'd thought. He'd been without a woman's touch too long.

It's been too short a time. Love doesn't happen like that.

He had to get out of here before he made any more of a fool of himself.

He nodded his acknowledgment of McGuire's thanks and stepped back. "I have to go before someone wakes up. Do you have any protection here? Besides that?" he asked, glancing over at the gun.

"Howie is here. He's in the barn."

"I won't be back for a while. There are some things I need to do. If you need anything send Howie to Abe at the saloon in town. He'll know where to find me."

"You're going to try to stop what's happening?" she asked on a shuddering sigh. "To the other ranchers. To you."

He said nothing as he stared at her, taking one last look . . . for a while. Just a while.

"I want to see Marilee for a moment," he said.

She nodded and led the way to the small bedroom at the end of the hall. She opened the door, and he looked inside.

His sister was curled up in a ball, a light covering over half her body. Her arm was around a sleeping puppy.

He went over to the bed and pulled the sheet up over her thin body. He hesitated, wanting to lean down and touch his lips to her forehead. To hug her. But that might wake and frighten her. Instead, he locked the picture of her into his mind.

Elizabeth was standing just outside the room. "I will take good care of her."

"I know that."

"Be careful," she said softly.

"I'm hard to kill. And find."

"I'll still worry."

"Doc or Abe will keep you informed."

"The doctor doesn't like me."

"He's just a cautious man, Elizabeth."

"Liz," she corrected.

His heart tugged again. He sensed that no one called her that but her father and Marilee. She'd just torn down a barrier.

He wondered whether he could tear down his as well. He wondered whether he could ever be whole again. He hadn't told Elizabeth that, like Marilee, he had nightmares. His were about the killing fields, about the boys he had killed, the friends he had lost in a nightmare called war.

He touched her cheek. "Be wary of Delaney."

She nodded, her eyes fearful but not, he knew, for herself. For him.

He left.

The guards were still trussed when he checked on them, though two were awake and struggling. He tapped them on their heads again. He didn't want anyone following him.

Then he retrieved Chance, mounted, and rode toward their canyon.

ELIZABETH'S father was better the afternoon after Seth's predawn visit, though still in a great deal of pain. He refused to talk about his heart condition, closing his eyes in pretended sleep when she tried to broach the subject.

A sense of loss had filled her the moment Seth had left. It would be there until he returned again. It was made more difficult by the fear she had for her father.

Howie appeared at the door of the bedroom. "The major is here," he announced flatly.

He didn't like Delaney either. Delaney had always treated Howie dismissively, even with contempt. Elizabeth had never understood how her father tolerated it.

She and her father exchanged a glance. He knew her suspicions now. He hadn't agreed, but neither had he argued about it.

Howie had barely made his announcement when Delaney shouldered his way inside.

"What happened last night?" he said angrily.

"Other than more of our cows being rustled?" she said tartly.

"My men were attacked and tied up."

"Where?"

"Here, dammit. I want to know what happened."

"I didn't even know they were here," she said. "You should have informed me you were finally taking our requests for protection seriously. They must not have been the most competent of men, though, if they allowed themselves to be taken while what's left of our cattle was being rustled."

His face mottled in anger. "*He* was here yesterday."

"He?"

"Sinclair. I want to know where he is now."

"I have no idea. He did not confide in me. In truth, he doesn't care much for us. Claims we stole this land. Still, he did help Papa."

His face got redder. "My men were watching for him. He must have returned last night."

"I thought your men were here to protect our cattle," she said with surprise in her voice. "And why on earth would Mr. Sinclair visit us last night?"

Delaney shoved past her to her father's bed. "Michael, where is he?"

Her father shook his head. "I don't know what you mean. I have been sleeping. Laudanum, you know. And if my daughter says he wasn't here, then he wasn't. She doesn't lie."

Delaney eyed both of them with disgust. "You aid him and you're as much a criminal as he is."

"A criminal?" she asked. "What did he do?"

"He attacked my men."

"Oh, they saw him then?"

He stomped to the door. "If you see him . . ."

"I'll send Howie immediately," she said. She very consciously did not add the two words, *for you.*

He slammed the door behind him.

She turned back to her father, who looked stunned. Delaney had always been smooth and charming around him.

"That's the real Delaney," she said.

Chapter Twelve

SETH STAYED AT the hideout, going out at dusk with his brother and the other three men who rode with him. Each night they gathered a few more animals, herding them back into the valley.

Information was coming from newly hopeful ranchers. They spied on the army details and reported to Abe. Abe's son reported to someone else who, in turn, met Colorado at a specified place. If cattle were sold or rustled, Seth knew about it nearly immediately, and the cattle were quickly liberated before anyone could change the brands.

Five days after McGuire's shooting, Doc arranged for Seth to meet with the marshal he'd mentioned. They met at the home—the old Keller place—Abe had offered him. As far as either Doc or Abe knew, Delaney was unaware that Seth used it.

Dillon accompanied him partway, then veered off to a position where he could watch the road. If more than one rider approached, he would fire two warning shots.

Seth hid Chance in a clump of trees half a mile from the ranch house, then found a tree about an eighth of a mile from the house and climbed up into it, found a comfortable perch, and waited.

An hour later, a lone horseman wandered in, dismounted, and sat on the porch of the house. Seth recognized him as the man in the saloon but still he waited thirty more minutes. He had learned to be cautious.

He finally lowered himself through the branches and dropped to the ground, taking his pistol from its holster as he landed.

Aiming it at the lawman, he approached.

The man watched him without blinking. He didn't stand. He didn't go for his gun, or the rifle lying on the steps beside him.

"Use your foot to push the rifle off the step," Seth said.

The lawman obliged and started to stand.

"Don't!" Seth said.

The lawman settled back down. "Sinclair?"

"Yes."

"You've stirred up a hornet's nest."

Seth ignored the comment. "Doc says you're honest."

"I try to be."

"Did he tell you what's going on around here?"

"Enough to bring me here."

"The army has authority over civil authorities."

"That's true. However, if I bring malfeasance to the army's attention, they have to acknowledge it. I know who to take it to. If you have proof."

"I want you to help me get it. Doc says you have your own doubts about Major Delaney."

"I've heard rumors," the lawman said. He held out his hand. "Tom Evans."

Seth hesitated. It could be a trick. He would have to switch his pistol from his right hand to the left. There would be a split second . . .

"If I didn't want to hear you out, I would have men crawling all over here," Evans said.

"And I wouldn't be here."

Evans gave him a thin smile. "I didn't expect you would. Now, can I stand so we can go inside?"

"I would rather stay out here where I can see."

"Have it your way. Doc told me some of what he thinks is happening. I want to hear your side."

Thirty minutes later, Evans rose. "I have about six deputies I trust completely, as well as an officer from headquarters. He doesn't care for Delaney either. But we have to catch him actually rustling the cattle. He has important friends."

"When?"

"Four nights from now. Tell me where, and I'll be there."

Seth nodded his head in acknowledgment. "It could go wrong, you know. Why are you willing to risk your badge for this?"

"I fought in the war too. Other side. But it's over, dammit, and I don't like anyone misusing power for their own gain. That's not what I fought for. That good enough for you?"

"Good enough," Seth said.

He watched as Evans mounted and rode out.

He had taken measure of the man and knew Doc had been right.

BEFORE he could leave, Abe rode in.

Gary Simmons had been ambushed while returning from the trip to the bank. He was at Doc's, badly injured.

Seth knew immediately it was his fault. He had baited Delaney, and Delaney had responded faster than he'd thought.

It was too late to go after the marshal.

"Something else," Abe said. "Miss McGuire sent a note by Howie." He held a crumpled envelope in his hand.

Seth took it and read it quickly.

Father improving. He understands what D is doing. He wants to speak to you. Howie says the ranch is still guarded, but he can take care of it tonight.

Seth held it for a moment, inhaled the faint scent of roses. Her scent.

Then he took a match from his pocket, struck it, and burned the note. He did not want anyone to find it on him.

THEY were asleep. Different guards, but just as obviously careless.

Whatever Howie had given them, or done to them, he had done it well.

Seth had waited until dark, then approached his former home. After finding the soldiers asleep, he moved around to the back and went in the window as he had before.

He checked Michael McGuire's room first, found him asleep and alone, and then checked the other rooms. He found her reading. She was fully dressed, but her hair hung down free, tendrils curling around her face. She was uncommonly appealing.

She looked pleased to see him. "Hello," she said shyly.

"Hello." He felt like an awkward schoolboy.

Her smile was blinding.

His heart jumped. His throat constricted.

"How's your father?" he said after a moment's pause.

"He is walking now. He still hurts but there's no infection."

"His heart?"

"It's bad. He finally told me about it. It's why he kept trying to force Delaney on me. A bad husband in his view was better than my being alone. I don't believe he thinks that now." She paused. "I heard about Mr. Simmons from Howie."

He nodded.

"I know you have some kind of plan. My father wants to help. I do, too."

He sat down then. He had been thinking about canceling the whole plan.

And now she was offering a new opportunity.

He didn't want to endanger her. Yet both her and her father were in very grave danger already. The last few weeks had shown how much. The McGuires would be perfect to implement the plan. They'd been brought here by Delaney. They had been loyal to the Union. Their motives could not be questioned.

"You and your father could leave Canaan," he said. "That would be the safest thing for you."

"I don't want safe. I want to belong here." Her chin lifted and her eyes blazed. "Someone tried to kill me and my father. We both want to know who, and why."

"What about Marilee?" he asked.

"What if she had been with me the day I rode into town? She could have been thrown out of the buggy," Elizabeth countered. "And you're not safe until Delaney is gone. Neither you nor Dillon."

He sat down and took her hand. She was like his mother. Strong and resilient and determined.

"We are putting together a small herd of cattle," he said. "We put out the word that some local ranchers will take them to San Antonio to sell directly to the army instead of going through Delaney. According to some folks, the army has been paying top dollar for cows Delaney purchased for practically nothing, or that he rustled. He must have forged bills of sale and probably bribed the purchase agent as well. He can't afford to let the army know what he paid for them. Nor can he afford to let a herd of cattle be offered for half of what he's been charging the army."

Her hand tightened in his. "But how—"

"A U.S. marshal is aware of the rumors but hasn't been able to catch him. We want to offer Delaney an opportunity to rustle cattle. Right in front of the law."

"Where will you get the cattle?"

"Better you don't know. No one will be hurt. They will be repaid for their cattle."

"What can we do?"

"I think I'd better talk to your father."

* * *

EVANS and his men waited in Seth's former home, in the stand of cottonwoods along the river, and in the barn. Some two hundred cattle lowed and complained in the pasture between the house and the river.

Dillon and Colorado had brought them halfway from the hidden canyon. Morgan Simmons, Knox, John Andrews, and Seth had met them there and drove them on to the ranch. Most had been rustled by Delaney and his men from local ranchers and still wore those brands.

But Seth didn't want Dillon and his friends involved. They were already wanted for other charges. They had done their part.

After bringing in the cattle, Seth waited with Michael McGuire who sat up in a chair, his arm in a sling. Both of them had pistols at their side. Elizabeth had a shotgun nearby.

Elizabeth had taken Marilee to the Findley home earlier and asked if Marilee could stay the night. It was the one place away from home where she didn't feel threatened. Elizabeth had told the Findleys that she couldn't take care of Marilee and her father as well.

Miriam Findley had readily agreed.

Evans and three fellow marshals sat at a window watching. A man in Union blue, a captain, was with them. Their horses were already saddled in the barn.

Seth paced restlessly. Abe had been charged with spreading the news that McGuire had joined the effort to take cattle to San Antonio and they would leave at dawn.

The lights were quenched.

One man, another deputy marshal, leaned against a fence and lit a match. It would appear strange to rustlers if the herd were not guarded.

One hour passed, then another. Elizabeth made coffee and offered the waiting men fresh bread. Seth's gaze continued to wander back to her.

She was so damnably pretty. And had so much grit. He

became giddy every time he watched her. If there had not been so many in the house, he would repeat their kiss, want more, so much more. If they weren't caught in this conflict, he'd ask for more.

But they were not alone . . . and they were fighting for their lives.

And after this . . .

After this he didn't know.

He still had to clear his brother. He had to earn a living. . . .

"Someone's coming," one of the marshals said in a low voice.

Both Evans and Seth went to the window and peered out. Figures on horseback began to move toward the cattle.

"You stay out of it now," Evans told Seth. "Take care of these folks and let the law deal with Delaney."

Evans and his men slipped through the same back window Seth had used. Just then the barn door opened, and three more marshals emerged on horseback, each holding the reins of two saddled horses. Seth watched from the house as the marshals mounted the horses just as a gunshot started the cattle running.

He wanted to be with them. But the marshal was right. Better to let the law take care of Delaney so that no false charges could be made later.

More shots rang out. Seth saw one horse go down with its rider, and another rider fall. Cattle stampeded. Minutes went by, then more. Shots grew more distant.

Then he heard a noise behind him and he swung around, his pistol in his hand. A man in a mask stood at the back, near the same window the deputy marshals had used. Blood stained his trousers. It must have been his horse that went down.

The man grabbed Elizabeth and held his pistol close to her head.

He wasn't wearing a uniform but Seth recognized Delaney from his build, the arrogant way he moved, even with a bullet hole in his thigh.

"You did this," he said to Seth.

Seth stood still, waiting. Watching for an opening. His heart pounded as anger and despair swept through him.

"Miss McGuire will see me safely away," Delaney said, reaching out and taking her arm.

She stood calmly, staring at Seth. With trust.

Fear dried his mouth as he watched Delaney threatening Elizabeth, the gun at her temple. He had to think. He swallowed down everything but resolve.

"You're right, Delaney. I did do this. All myself. You are not nearly as smart as you thought you were. Arrogant men are foolish men." He shifted subtly, balancing himself to move fast if need be. "There are a number of deputy marshals out there as well as one of your own army friends. They know a lot, and they will know more when they capture your men."

"You are also a coward," Michael McGuire said suddenly from behind him. "A yellow coward. Hiding behind a woman. A snake isn't any lower."

Delaney's eyes flickered from one man to the other, then dismissed McGuire and focused on Sinclair.

"Put your gun down, Sinclair, or I'll shoot her. Now."

There was something insane in his voice that made Seth believe him. The marshals should be back soon. Very slowly he leaned down and put his pistol on the floor.

Delaney watched him so intently, he seemed to forget McGuire, or perhaps he didn't consider the older man a threat. Once Seth's gun was lowered, Delaney swung his pistol toward him, his finger on the trigger.

Two shots rang out simultaneously.

Fire lanced through Seth's side as he fell to his knees, reaching for his gun. He knew where the other shot had come from. Delaney would turn on McGuire now.

He saw Delaney swing his gun toward McGuire, saw Elizabeth hit his arm to spoil his aim.

Seth swept up his gun from the floor and started firing.

Delaney went down.

Elizabeth staggered away from him, her eyes wide and stunned.

Ignoring the pain in his side, Seth strode over to Delaney. He leaned down and checked the pulse in his neck, then pulled the mask from him.

He was dead.

He took Elizabeth in his arms, cradling her. She was safe. That was all he needed at the moment.

And the man he thought he hated had saved his life, and he had saved McGuire's.

TWO hours later, Evans appeared. He saw the body on the floor and raised one eyebrow.

Seth stood with him in the main room, bandaged and shirtless. It was amazing, he thought, how Elizabeth's doctoring could soothe the pain.

She had offered him some laudanum, which he had refused, and then taken her father to his room. She had not emerged yet.

"He apparently was shot in the first few minutes of the ambush," Seth explained. "He tried to take Elizabeth hostage."

"I imagine the army won't be too upset," Evans said. "Better than a messy court-martial."

"I want my brother cleared."

"I doubt that will be too difficult, especially if you swear to be . . . discreet about what happened here."

"Some people are owed their land back. And cattle."

"I'll see what I can do."

"Thanks."

"I've been wanting that bastard for a long time," Evans said. "You ever need a job . . ."

"I might take you up on that," Seth said. He still didn't have anything. No money, no land, no cattle.

"Anytime. All right to leave the cattle here and let people come pick up what's theirs?"

"I don't think the McGuires will object."

"Then good night, or is it good morning to you? Don't forget that job."

Seth nodded and Evans left.

Weary, he sat down in a chair. When Elizabeth was finished with her father, he would say good night. He would return to the valley and tell Dillon what had happened. He and his friends would have to remain hidden for a bit longer, then . . .

Elizabeth suddenly emerged from her father's room. She looked oddly uncertain and held something in her hand. She offered it to him.

He took it and glanced at the text. "The deed to the ranch," he said, a lump lodging in the base of his throat.

"Papa and I want you to have it. It's yours."

"And you and your father?"

"We will find a place."

He had learned in the past few days how much this land meant to McGuire as well as to Elizabeth.

He reached out and touched her cheek. "I thought I wanted it more than anything. I was wrong."

She watched him with those wide hazel eyes. Waiting.

"I want *you* more than anything. Perhaps we can . . . share."

She still waited, eyes questioning.

"A partnership," he struggled. "Oh hell, what I mean is, well, I want you to marry me."

She looked stunned. He realized then how much she had been willing to give up for him. Her home, her livelihood. She had never expected . . .

But then neither had he.

Where had he heard that once you saved a life, you were responsible for it forever?

He smiled. The devil had a very strange sense of humor. Or was it the angels?

"Will you?" he asked her, realizing that he hadn't quite managed the question very well.

She reached up and touched his mouth with her hand as if still disbelieving the words, then stood on her tiptoes to kiss him.

It was all the answer he needed.

Epilogue

"HE'S COMING! HOWIE just rode in and said he saw dust in the distance."

Marilee barely paused for breath as she skidded in front of Elizabeth. Marilee had been haunting the front porch for the last two weeks, at times worrying herself to tears.

Elizabeth dropped the cloth she was using to dry the supper dishes. Her heart jounced with joy and anticipation.

Six months. Her husband had left six months earlier on a cattle drive to Kansas City. She had wanted to go, but she had just discovered she was carrying a child.

She had not told him. She had not wanted him to feel as if he had to stay. This drive was too important to him. To her. To the community. He had been the one person who could bring together all the ranchers—Texans and newcomers alike—to combine the herds. It meant top price—and survival—for many of them.

What would he think when she told him the news—that he had a newborn son?

Would he feel the same joy she did? Or would he be angry she had kept that secret from him? She glanced down at the cradle. Her wee gift was two weeks old and waiting for a name.

She wished she had time to brush her hair. She had none. She ran from the kitchen out to the porch where Marilee waited while jumping on one foot, then another in anticipation. Howie had one foot on the corral fence, looking out toward the setting sun, a hand shading his eyes as he watched for Seth.

Marilee had come to love her brother with all her heart. He had been patient, and heartbreakingly tender and, bit by bit, had won his sister's adoration. She was nearly wild with anticipation of showing the baby to her brother.

Out of the dust individuals emerged, and her heart pounded. Elizabeth saw Seth first and he filled her eyes. Then Dillon, who had been cleared of all charges and now worked the ranch with his brother.

Thank God they had returned safely. She knew how treacherous the drive could be: indians, rustlers, drought, stampedes.

His clothes were as dirty and dusty as he had been that first day she had seen him but now he raced his horse toward her and tumbled off to fold her in his arms. He had obviously shaved in the morning, but bristle tickled her face as he leaned down and kissed her. A very long, a very heartfelt, a very needy kiss.

She cherished every second of it.

Then he straightened as if aware of the eyes on him. "Tonight," he whispered, then he leaned down and hugged Marilee. "Hello, sweetpea. Have you been taking care of my girl?" he asked.

"Oh yes, I helped birth—"

"She was a great help," Elizabeth broke in. This was something she wanted to tell on her own.

He looked at her curiously and took her hand.

"It was everything you hoped?" she asked.

"We were one of the first herds there," he said. "We got good prices. Enough to buy a bull and build a new barn."

She led him inside, pulling him toward the kitchen where the baby lay in the cradle.

He stood still, stunned, as his gaze went to the cradle, and then to the infant lying in it.

His eyes were full of questions as he raised his head to meet her gaze.

"Your son," she said, presenting him.

He looked disbelieving for a moment, then he leaned down and picked up the sleeping child and cradled him. "You didn't tell me."

"I wasn't sure until just before you left. I didn't want to keep you from going."

"You didn't want me to go," he reminded her. "Why didn't you—"

"I never want you to be gone that long," she interrupted, her fingers touching his lips. "I never want you to be gone at all. But I knew how important it was to you. To us."

"You think it was more important than my child?" His voice had a dangerous edge.

"There was nothing you could do for me, love. Howie and Marilee were wonderful. So were the neighbors."

"I could have been here for you."

"You *were* here. In my heart," she said softly.

She watched as he tenderly whispered something to their child.

"What did you say?" she asked.

"I told him you were a stubborn, independent woman," he said but he had a twinkle in his eyes. "It's a good thing I like stubborn, independent women."

She relaxed. "He needs a name."

Their eyes met. "I think it should be Michael," he said immediately.

Emotion flooded her. Seth and her father had grown close in the first year of their marriage, perhaps because they both cared for her. He had mourned with her when her father died.

"I was thinking perhaps Garrett for your father."

"Then Michael Garrett Sinclair?"

Tears burned behind her eyes. She still missed her father. His stories. His capacity to love. She nodded.

Reluctantly, Seth handed young Michael to Dillon, who had followed them inside and was watching with great interest. He looked startled at first, as if he were being handed a box of dynamite, but then a wide smile creased his hard face.

Seth took her in his arms again and showered her face with tender kisses. "Thank you," he said. "Thank you for my son."

Her heart trembled as her gaze went from his face to her son's. Her cowboy. Her two cowboys.

"Welcome home," she murmured just before his lips sealed hers and the enchantment began all over again.

Tombstone Tess

EMILY CARMICHAEL

Chapter One

TESS ANN MCCABE brushed the trail dust from her jeans and slapped her weather-beaten hat against the hitching post before stepping into the Bird Cage Saloon. The warm, dusky interior washed over her with comforting familiarity, but the scowl on her face didn't ease. She had to do what she had to do, Tess told herself. But dadgummit, she didn't have to like it. Life could sometimes be downright unreasonable.

Heads turned when the clunk of her boots on the plank floor announced her presence, but the men enjoying their liquor, cards, and the attentions of the saloon girls didn't pay her much mind. The newcomer was just Tess from the Diamond T. Nothing to get stirred up about.

But when she brought down her fist upon the polished top of the long bar, eyes turned her way.

"I need a man!" Tess announced. A shameful confession, but there it was. "Now. Today. I need a goddamned man."

All activity in the bar ceased. Silence as heavy as the pall of cigar smoke answered her. She stood rigid and proudly upright under the curious regard, refusing to lower her eyes, refusing to give in to cowardice and run from the saloon.

Then a throaty feminine chuckle broke the silence. "Honey girl, don't we all! Join the line."

Tension broke in a wave of laughter. Tess didn't smile.

"Hey, Tessie," came a hoarse shout from Joe Daniel, who sat at a poker table near the back of the room. "I'm your man, sweetie! I could use me a nice little ranch down on the river and a sweet little gal to go with it."

Laughter greeted his offer.

"Gettin' mighty brave, Joe," a man at the bar said.

Another shouted. "You take some sweet little gal onto Tessie's ranch and Tess'll likely hog-tie her, brand her, and sell her to the Injuns like a side of beef. Ain't it so, Tess?"

Tess felt her face heat. True, she had threatened her brother, Sean, with such a fate once, but that had been in fun. Besides, he had deserved it. Her father had never tired of jawing and guffawing about the incident to anyone who would listen. And of course nobody believed that she, Colin McCabe's "wild" daughter, might be the one Joe meant by "a sweet little gal."

Glory Gilda, one of the Bird Cage's most popular whores, strolled up to stand by Tess's side. "You jackasses shut your yaps. Ain't a one of you in here such a catch that you can make fun of Tess. Besides, she could whup every one of you in a brawl."

"That ain't exactly true," Tess admitted to Glory. "But I could outlast any one of them in the saddle."

"Course you could." Glory guided her toward an empty table. "Given half a chance, a woman can outlast a man at just about anything you can think of. Whiskey?"

"You know I don't hold with strong drink."

"You look like you could use a strong drink, though. The stronger, the better." The woman plunked herself down at the table with a sigh. "So you're finally up against it, are you?"

"Between a rock and you know what." Tess heaved a disconsolate sigh and pulled up a chair to straddle.

Everyone in the bar knew her problem. Hell, everyone in Tombstone knew that Colin McCabe had reached up from the grave to twist his daughter's tail. Many a man laughed out loud to think that Tess Ann McCabe, one of Arizona's most ineligible females, had to find a husband or lose her ranch to her runty little brother, as worthless a piece of flesh and bone that ever God allowed to breathe the world's air.

Okay, maybe Sean wasn't totally worthless. He was her brother, after all, and he probably did have good qualities somewhere, if a person looked hard enough.

Gilda commiserated. "That was a bum thing your daddy did to you, Tess, honey. Have you talked to a lawyer?"

"Hell yes. But the only lawyer in town is Harvey Bartlett, the skunk who wrote up Daddy's will. Fat lot of help he is. Maybe I will have a whiskey. What's it taste like?"

"Damned good, most times."

When Tess took her first sip of the amber liquid Glory set in front of her, she disagreed with a grimace. "Uck!"

"It grows on you," Glory assured her.

It would have to, Tess mused. The whiskey burned all the way down her gullet into her stomach. Fine comfort that was! But she took another sip, just to be sure that she hadn't missed something.

"So how long has it been since the old man bit the dirt?" Glory asked.

"Five months, two weeks."

"And he gave you six months to find yourself a husband?"

"Six months," Tess confirmed. "The rat. All my life I was my daddy's right-hand man. Hell, when I was five years old he had me driving cattle and riding half-broke horses. I'm the best damned cowboy on the Diamond T, probably the best damned cowboy in all of Arizona, but that crazy old man kept expecting me to bring home a husband along with the cows."

Glory nodded sympathetically.

"A husband is harder to rope than an ornery bull," Tess said with a morose sigh.

"That's a fact. But, honey, it's not like you ain't got nothing to offer a man. The Diamond T is a nice little ranch, with plenty of water and a good crew."

Tess took another sip of whiskey, which began to send warm streamers into her veins. "That's the rub, Glory. No husband is going to move in on my territory, boss my crew, or run my ranch. Hell, he might even expect me to cook and mend and all that nonsense." She brought a fist down on the table with force enough to make her shot glass jump. "What I need is a lazy, worthless sonuvabitch who'll run out on me after a few days' time. Me and Miguel and Rosie have it all figured out."

Glory laughed her throaty laugh. "Well, honey, the world is crawling with worthless men. It's the good ones that are hard to come by. I might even be able to help you out."

A twinkle of mischief lit Glory's eye as the amiable whore surveyed the room. "How about old Jack Campbell? He hasn't done a lick of work in the last two years as far as anybody can tell. Feed him a meal or two and he'd most likely do anything you say."

"Too old. Yellow teeth. Smells bad."

"You said you wanted someone worthless."

"Yeah, but if I've gotta actually marry the fella, he'd better be at least a couple of steps above a goat, or no one's going to believe it."

Glory screwed up her face in concentration, creasing her thick makeup. Then she smiled. "I have it!"

"You have it?"

"I have it!"

Hope rose in Tess's chest. Or was that the liquor?

"Tess, honey, look at the fellow drowning in his glass at that corner table. He's been drinking for two days, that one has, too wed to his whiskey to even take me up on the offer of a tumble. He might clean up right nice if you took a scrub brush to him and poured strong coffee down his gullet."

Tess looked at the cowboy in the corner. He looked worthless enough. Hell. She might as well give him a try.

JOSHUA Ransom looked drunkenness straight in its ugly face, and he welcomed it. The drunker he got, the more chance he could forget his goddamned brother, David, forget the Double R Ranch—once the finest ranch north of the Mexican border—and forget that a rancher with no cattle was a rancher with no future. If Josh got falling-down, blind, drooling swacked, maybe he could forget that two days ago he had sat at this very table, in this same saloon, and listened to his last hope in the world tell him the bank wouldn't loan him the money he needed.

So what the hell could he do now? Where does a man turn when his best and last chance rears up and smacks him in the head? How does a man deal with a brother who squanders a family business, a family home, a family tradition, on a bad poker hand?

Josh didn't want to think about it. He wanted another drink, another shot of liquid fire to numb his brain. If he could only manage to lift his hand to summon one of the bar girls.

Magically, one of them appeared without a summons, a yellow-haired angel in pink lace and fishnet.

" 'Nother drink," he slurred.

"Sweetie pie, you don't need no more whiskey. But I brought you something better."

Josh focused blurrily upon what she offered. It was a girl, he thought. But he wasn't sure. Yeah. A girl. Her jeans and denim shirt could have belonged to a man, but no man ever filled out clothes in quite that way.

Strange way for a whore to dress, but there was no accounting for taste.

"No, thanks," he mumbled. "No woman. Drink."

Hell, right now he wouldn't be any use to a woman. Not

in his state—which state he really needed to help along with at least one more shot of whiskey.

The yellow-haired vixen in pink chuckled throatily and turned to her associate. "He's all yours, honey, if you can hook him."

THE man smelled of sour whiskey and other things Tess didn't really want to think about. The notion of hitching herself to this slug, even for a short time, made her stomach turn. She looked to Glory for help, but Glory's attention had turned elsewhere, namely, to a poker player who looked as if he might donate all his winnings for a chance to peer down her corset.

Tess sighed and sat down, trying not to scowl at her prospective suitor. The man was old enough to be her father. Silver hair hung in his face, reddened eyes sunk into shadows, and his mouth sagged. He might start drooling at any minute. All in all, the bum looked like something you might find beneath a rock.

Even if she scrubbed him up, would anyone believe that Tess McCabe would hitch herself to this piece of dog shit? Well, maybe they would. She had a certain reputation in these parts. Most folks would shake their heads and say something like "That's what comes of a woman wearing pants."

The man seemed to have forgotten Tess was there, so she woke him up with a kick beneath the table. "Hey, you."

He jumped. "Huh?"

"You look like you could use some help."

His laugh sounded something like a burp. Maybe it was. "I've got a deal to offer. Maybe it would help you out."

The man simply looked into his empty shot glass. "You wanna go get me a drink?"

Tess wrinkled her lip. She didn't much approve of boozing, at least not on this scale. Plainly she'd better work fast before the poor slob passed out.

"You don't need another drink, looks like to me, mister."

Maybe she should try to put on some feminine airs, Tess mused, then decided that ploy didn't have a snowball's chance in hell. Less, maybe. She decided to come right to the point of her offer. "You married?"

He snorted. She took that as a no.

"You need money?"

That put a spark into his eyes. A dull spark, but there it was.

"How does three hundred dollars easy money sound to you, mister?" Tess pitched her voice low so it wouldn't carry to the other tables.

The man choked. "Three . . . three . . ."

Glory abandoned her poker player and came to Tess's aid. "Shush now, you. Tess, honey, you don't want the whole saloon listening in on your private business, so why don't we take this up to my room?" She nudged their reluctant Romeo. "What do you say, sweetie pie?"

He crossed his eyes and nearly fell from the chair. They took that as a yes.

Glory's "room" was one of the upstairs gilded "cages" that gave the Bird Cage its name and fame. Getting the poor slob up the stairs posed a challenge, because he was bigger than Tess expected. When she took his arm and braced it across her shoulders, the hard muscle beneath his shirt surprised her. Apparently the fellow had only recently turned to liquor. Jerking him off of his downward path could be a good deed.

Or not. This could be the biggest mistake of her life. Still, a woman had to do what a woman had to do.

"Let's sit him on the bed," she told Glory. "I don't like him towering over me like that."

The stair climb had brought the fellow around a bit. His eyes now looked more wary than dull.

"What are you gals up to?"

"Saving your sorry ass from boozing yourself to death," Glory answered primly. "And setting you on the road to riches."

"That's right. We're doing you a good deed, is what."

Tess nearly strained a muscle helping Glory sit the fellow on the bed. He didn't carry much fat on him to lighten things up. Finally, she straightened up and looked him narrowly in the eye. "I'll put it to you honest, cowboy. If you aren't already hitched to a wife, you can earn yourself three hundred easy dollars in one afternoon's work. Just stand up with me before a preacher and say 'I do.' Then you can be on your way to whatever hell you're headed for."

The poor man nearly toppled over. Glory and Tess both took an arm and hauled him upright again.

"You see . . . ," Tess continued, hoping to make her proposal sound reasonable, "my father left me the ranch when he died. It's not much of a ranch," she added hastily. It wouldn't do to set the fellow's thoughts running along lines of greed. "But it's home, you know? But my no-account brother gets the whole thing unless I get myself hitched by March fifteenth. And today is March first."

In truth, her father had been buried on a hot day back in September. He had given her six months to find a husband, but she had kept putting things off, hoping a miracle would happen. A miracle hadn't happened, and so now she found herself facing this sorry excuse for a man in Glory's gilded cage.

He made a choking sound that might have been a laugh. "You . . . you want me to marry you?"

Tess bristled. "You don't have to make it sound like I asked you to go to hell and back."

He laughed again. This time it was definitely a laugh. "You want *me* to marry *you?*"

"A few minutes with a preacher," Tess continued through gritted teeth, "then, when the deed is in my name, you can collect your money and be on your way. I don't need a husband, and if I did, I sure wouldn't choose a drunken bum like you."

Glory lifted a cautioning finger at her. "Now, Tess, honey. You're wanting this man to do you a favor. Mind your temper."

The prospective groom heaved an alcoholic sigh and shook his head. "I'm not much for lovin' and leavin'."

Tess hastened to squelch that notion. "You won't be doing no loving in this deal, mister! You can be sure of that!"

"You wouldn't be married long," Glory hastened to assure him. "Once things have settled down and people have forgotten about Colin's stupid will, you'll get an annulment, won't you, Tessie? It'll be like the marriage never existed."

"Right!" Tess confirmed. Then she narrowed her eyes suspiciously. "You aren't already hitched, are you?"

The man chuckled a little too cynically. "Hell no."

"And you could use the money, couldn't you?" Tess took an envelope from her shirt pocket, extracted a sheaf of bills, and dangled the money before his eyes. "Couldn't you?"

The poor sot's eyes crossed as he tried to focus on the greenbacks. "Three hundred dollars," he said slowly.

"Three hundred dollars," she echoed temptingly. Good old money, the bait that would hook almost any fish. "And you'll be a free man to use the money however you want."

He reached out to take the money, but she pulled it away. "When the deed is in my hand, cowboy. Not before."

He squinted suspiciously. "No strings?"

"I'll cut the strings while the ink is still drying on that deed." Her heart jumped. The fish had taken the hook.

"Nobody gets hurt."

"Not a soul."

"Nothing ill . . . illegal," he slurred.

"Of course not. Say a few words and sign a piece of paper. Then you leave, and a while later, I send word that you're legally free. Simple."

Simple. Right. Anything but, a voice in her head warned. But she had no choice.

Her groom-to-be looked a bit queasy. "You got yourself a deal."

TESS wasn't about to let her fish squirm off the hook while she dilly-dallied about. Glory stood guard over the groom on the excuse of letting him sleep off his liquor in her room, while Tess dispatched the bartender's son to the Diamond T to fetch Rosie and Miguel for the wedding. The ranch was an hour's ride on a fast horse, and longer for her foreman and stepmother to hitch the buckboard (Rosie flat refused to climb up on any horse) and drive back to town, so Tess had time to talk Preacher Malone into a hurry-up wedding and also drop by lawyer Bartlett's office to inform him that she was about to head up the matrimonial trail. She didn't bother to tell him what a short trail it would be.

Tess left the attorney's office with a chuckle bubbling in her chest. The look on Harvey's face had told her that he didn't think she had what it took to lasso herself a man, not if her daddy had given her six years instead of six months.

Arrangements made, Tess had time on her hands, something she didn't want. So far the morning had moved fast—the ride into town, meeting Glory in the Bird Cage, putting her persuasive powers to the test with—what was the damned fellow's name? She hadn't even asked. Oh well. His name didn't really matter.

Tess walked over to the hotel for lunch, even though her stomach didn't much welcome the idea of food. Through the steam swirls rising from her coffee she saw her father's face. She had labored so hard to please that hard-edged, obstinate man. His rare words of praise were hoarded treasures. His impatience, hot temper, and above all, his razor strap, had inspired her to labor even harder to please him.

Her brother, Sean, on the other hand, had fought the bit like a sour mustang. He had hated the ranch, hated the work, hated the livestock, the dust, the summer heat, and the winter cold. On his fifteenth birthday he'd up and left. Colin had been both furious and embarrassed that his only son "had a limp noodle spine." And he'd leaned even harder on Tess, who had tried her best to be better than a son to him.

But in one thing she had never pleased him. Colin couldn't understand why his daughter couldn't lasso herself a husband and bring him home to help run the Diamond T. Her mother could have told him that no man wanted a woman who could handle a branding iron but not a clothes iron, who could butcher a hog but didn't know the first thing about fixing a fancy pork roast. By the time Tess had reached marrying age, however, her mother wasn't telling Colin anything. She had died in childbirth, trying to deliver a third child, when Tess was ten.

Tess dropped another lump of sugar into her cup and stirred. *I've got myself that husband now,* she told her daddy silently. *But things aren't going to be the way you wanted, you stubborn old jackass. You're gone now, and I have to live life the best I know how. And I'm not taking up with some man who wants the Diamond T, not me, and who thinks he can step in and run things better than some silly woman.*

So now she was stuck with a pickled bum. But not for long. Everything would work out, Tess assured herself. She would make it work out.

By three o'clock, Tess had rebraided the long black hair that hung to her waist, washed her face at the OK Corral watering trough, and readied herself to meet her bridegroom on the steps of the white frame church on Allen Street. Just as she arrived at the church, Glory turned the corner, headed her way, and the man beside her walked on his own two feet, though his boots didn't exactly track a straight line. From the other direction, a familiar wagon rattled toward her with Rosie and Miguel perched up on the box. Perfect timing. It was a sign, Tess told herself. A good sign.

Rosie and Miguel arrived first, and her plump, brown-haired stepmother jumped down from the wagon to give Tess a hug. "You found someone so fast!"

"Glory helped."

Glory and Rosie were good friends from the days when Rosie also had earned her living at the Bird Cage. The two women sometimes banded together to give Tess annoying lectures on how she ought to wear frills and curls to catch a man, but Tess loved them anyway.

Miguel, dark, lean, and wiry, climbed down from the wagon more slowly, favoring a stiff knee that had been stomped by a cranky steer two years before. He gave Tess a smile, but his attention swung quickly to the pair coming up the street. "That him?"

"Yup."

"Big fella. And that don't look like fat filling him out. You sure about him?"

"Seems pretty no-account to me. I found him drunk in the Bird Cage. He jumped on the money fast enough."

Miguel's eyes narrowed. "You sure he won't jump on more than the money?"

Rosie batted the foreman with her reticule. "Don't talk like that in front of Tess."

"Woman, I'm just looking out for the girl's interests. She ain't no lily-livered little miss who ain't ever heard a cow turd called a cow turd."

Tess put her hands on her hips. "Call a truce, you two. And don't worry about my bridegroom. I made it pretty clear the money is all he gets."

Miguel scowled, first at Rosie, then at Tess. He had been foreman at the Diamond T for the last thirteen years, and in many ways, he had been more of a father to her than Colin McCabe. He had a father's protective instincts.

Tess grimaced at him. "Don't look like you're going to hog-tie the poor sot and carve a brand into his hide, Miguel. You'll scare him away. After all, this was your idea."

"It was Rosie's idea. Only a woman could think up a plan like this one."

"Well, you agreed."

"Two against one. I didn't have much choice."

"Yeah, damn." Tess sighed. "Neither do I."

Tess's soon-to-be husband looked a bit dazed when Glory hauled him by the arm up the church steps. "Here he is," the saloon girl declared proudly.

He shrugged off her arm and nearly toppled with the effort. The bum must have really tied one on to still be soused after sleeping for a couple of hours.

"Well, now," she said with false heartiness. "Here we all are. Time to get this thing done."

Rosie eyed the groom with growing doubt. "If there were another way—"

"There's not." Tess wished there were.

"Well, then." Rosie pasted a smile on her face. "Let's do this up right. Come inside. We'll just clean you up a bit."

"Aw, Rosie!"

"You will not be married looking like you've just ridden in from the range."

"He looks worse than I do!"

"Him I don't care about. You, I do. Come."

Miguel chuckled. "You better not argue with Rosie, *chica*. You know how she gets."

Rosie gave the foreman an arch look.

"I know how she gets," Tess grumbled.

But she followed Rosie into the preacher's office, where Rosie had enough privacy to fill a basin with water, make Tess scrub her face—in Rosie's mind the watering trough of the OK Corral didn't make for proper washing—and then sat Tess down to brush and braid her hair once again.

Rosie never gave up trying to make Tess look like a proper woman. Such persistence had to be admired, even if it was annoying as hell.

"The man you found is big," Rosie noted. "And he looks like he knows how to work. No fat. All muscle."

"He's a drunk. He'll be off to drink his way through my three hundred dollars without a thought to how he earned it."

Rosie shook her head dubiously. "I don't know. You be careful, Tessie. I wish I'd thought to bring a dress."

"Forget that! This isn't a real wedding."

Rosie humphed. "It would have been nice if you could have found a real husband. Every woman needs a man, and men are lost without a woman to keep them in line."

Tess snickered. "Miguel, for instance?"

Rosie yanked at the braid. "That one? Ha! It would take an angel from heaven to put up with that mule of a man."

They met Glory, Miguel, and—what was his name?—in the back of the church, and Tess noticed that Glory had spruced up the groom a bit as well. But even with his hair slicked back and his face washed, he still looked like a bum.

"I guess I'd better know your name for when the preacher gets here. Preacher Malone can get picky about marrying folks who don't really know each other. He's funny that way."

The man gave her a fuzzy look. "Ransom."

"Ransom what?"

"Joshua Ransom."

"Josh Ransom," Tess repeated. A good strong name to be wasted on the likes of this fellow. "I'm Tess McCabe. Diamond T Ranch."

He had the nerve to look uninterested.

"But don't get any ideas about the ranch, just because you're standing up with me."

So why had she even mentioned the Diamond T? Tess wondered. Maybe because Tess McCabe wasn't anybody without it. She always attached it to herself. Tess McCabe of the Diamond T. That was who she was. One without the other just wasn't worth much of anything.

Before she could pursue that unhappy thought, Preacher Malone walked in. Tess warned her groom with a subtle elbow to the ribs. "Just say the right words to earn your money."

The wedding ceremony was mercifully short. Preacher Malone delivered long, windy sermons in Sunday service, but this being a Tuesday, the preacher seemed to have his mind more on getting back to his carpentry business than running off at the mouth about the sanctity and responsibilities of marriage. Good thing, Tess reflected, because the longer she stood in that church with what's-his-name, the more the man swayed beside her. The groom had taken on a tinge of green, and the church had begun to smell like a still. If the preacher hadn't been in such a hurry, he might have noticed such things.

But more important, if the ceremony had dragged on

much more than five minutes, Tess herself might have showed a yellow streak and run. Her stomach began to turn somersaults, and the palms of her hands broke out in sweat. Should she back out before the words were spoken? Could she back out?

"I now pronounce you man and wife," Preacher Malone declared.

Too late. The deed was done, for better or worse.

Slow, insolent clapping from the rear of the church made Tess's heart jump. In unison with Rosie, Glory, and Miguel, she turned.

"Congratulations, Tessie girl."

Looking like a greenhorn in a fancy suit and slicked-back hair, her brother leaned against the frame of the open church doorway, applauding sarcastically.

"You finally caught yourself a husband, did you? How lucky for you."

His grin told Tess her luck had just stepped in a cow pie.

Chapter Two

JOSH RANSOM COULDN'T remember a time when he'd felt quite so lousy. Of course, right at the moment, his memory didn't work all that well. Neither did his stomach, his legs, or his tongue; and his eyes still slipped in and out of focus. A pounding headache hammered his brain, and every muscle in his body screamed for mercy.

Liquor and he didn't get along. Never had. Never would. Why hadn't he remembered that when he'd tried to drown his sorrows in a bottle? Liquor could numb the brain for a while, but when those nerves woke up again, there was hell to pay. Except that hell couldn't be anywhere near as bad as this. He lay back in the tub of hot water and contemplated drowning himself—until a cheerful voice walked in on the legs of a short, plump woman with clear blue eyes and a sympathetic smile.

"Soaked some of the whiskey out, have you?"

A blush heated his face hotter than the bathwater as he

sank lower beneath concealing suds. At least he hoped the suds concealed.

The woman laughed. "Don't worry, *muchacho*. You've got nothing I haven't seen so often I'm plumb bored." But her eyes twinkled. "Though I've got to say, you're less boring than most."

"You aren't . . . you aren't—"

"I'm Rosie." She laughed. "You thought maybe I was the one standing beside you in front of Preacher Malone? Ha! You really were in a fog, weren't you?" She took a scrub brush from a nail above the sink and advanced toward the tub. Josh, not a man accustomed to feeling helpless, felt mighty helpless right then.

"Wait. What're you—"

"You need a good scrub, my friend. Tess—that's your wife, by the way—she don't allow liquor in the house, and you're just about as potent as a bottle of pure whiskey. Some of that stink has to come off."

"Wait a minute, lady!" As Rosie applied the stiff brush to his back, Josh flailed, sending water sloshing onto the kitchen floor. Rosie didn't seem to mind the soaking. "Hey! Ouch! Give me that!" He managed to grab the bristled weapon from her hand. "I can scrub myself, missus. Could I have some privacy here?"

"A touchy one, ain't ya?" But she chuckled good-naturedly. "Just see that you scrub good. I'll just put a few more sticks of wood in the stove before I leave and then you can have your precious privacy."

Josh did make good use of the scrub brush once the woman had left. He wished he could scrub away the last few days—hell, the last few weeks!—along with the dirt and clinging smell of whiskey. Maybe if he'd had those weeks to live over again, he could have kept David away from that poker game, or managed to lay hands on the entire six hundred dollars to settle David's marker, or at least not gotten tanked in the Bird Cage. His memory at this moment struggled with a whiskey-induced fog, but to Josh's best recollection he'd up and married some woman—not the lady with the scrub brush, he gathered—for a sum that would put him over the top for David's debt. That sort of lamebrain stunt just about put him on a level with his idiot brother, or maybe even below. He had already had one foot in a mule pile, and now had the other foot in as well. Smart of him. Josh thought upon David's foolishness with a bit more sympathy. Blockheadedness apparently ran in the Ransom blood.

He looked around him, his brain clearing a bit as some of the fogginess dissolved into the warm water. A wood stove pumped out heat against the March chill. Pots hung from a rack—nothing fancy, strictly utilitarian. A chipped metal worktable doubled as a dining table, with benches pushed beneath on either side. A colorful rag rug—the only touch of decoration he could see—covered part of the smooth clay floor.

The curtain between the kitchen and the rest of the house brushed aside to admit another visitor, this one walking on four legs. A rough-coated gray dog about the size of a good-sized coyote regarded him with confident, measuring eyes. One ear stood up, the other flopped down, but the dog didn't lose any dignity to his lopsided looks.

"You're not the one I married, are you?" Josh asked miserably.

The dog's look changed to sympathy, and it padded over to give Josh's wet arm a lick.

"Friendly, aren't you? Want to answer a few questions? Like what the hell am I doing here?" Josh wrinkled his brow in a frown, then grimaced with the pain such an effort caused. Thinking hurt. Frowning hurt. Everything hurt. He dimly remembered the ride from town in a poorly sprung wagon. At the time, climbing into the wagon and heading for somewhere seemed a reasonable thing to do, but wasn't he supposed to hightail it out of town, money in hand, after the ceremony? So why was he sitting in an unfamiliar kitchen in a tin washtub scrubbing himself raw and talking to a dog?

*   *   *

TESS wore a path on the clay floor in front of the fireplace with her pacing. "Dadgummit! Everything was just hunky-dory until Sean showed up. I hate that grin of his. It's his gotcha grin. He knows exactly what I'm up to."

Rosie rocked in the chair next to the fireplace, her hands full of mending. "I'm not surprised, Tessie. He's your brother. You two think alike."

"We're nothing alike!"

But they were, in a way. They had grown up together, helped each other, ratted on each other, made trouble with each other—until Sean got fed up with the Diamond T, and with their father, and took off for California to find his fortune.

"Maybe you're right," Tess admitted with a sigh. "Sean was as stubborn about getting away from the ranch as I was about staying. He knows damned well that I'd hitch myself up with a rattlesnake if it would let me keep the Diamond T. The question is, can he do anything about it other than complain?"

Rosie shook her head. "You've done what Colin wanted you to do, Tessie. I still don't know if it's what you should have done, but it's done."

"Yeah, but Bartlett—that braying mule—he might side with Sean no matter what. After all, when has the law ever favored a woman over a man? Bartlett said right to my face he thought the will was stupid—not because I had to get married, but because I'd get the Diamond T at all. Never mind that Sean took off. Never mind that he gave our daddy nothing but grief. To a man's way of thinking, having *cojones* automatically makes a person stronger, smarter, and just plain better than anyone burdened with breasts."

"Tess! A lady doesn't talk that way."

"I'm not a lady, I'm a cowboy. And I'm the best dadgummed cowboy for miles around."

Rosie's lips tightened in disapproval, but Tess didn't care. She could almost feel the steam coming out of her ears.

"Damn it all, anyway!" she growled to herself. She could think of only one solution to the problem of Sean, and she didn't like it. Didn't like it at all. "Why doesn't that sorry sot I married climb out of the tub and come out where a person can talk to him?"

"I don't think he feels so good," Rosie opined.

"I don't care how he feels. I need to tell him the way things stand before he makes any plans to spend my money."

Tess's patience, never her long suit, wore out in a few more minutes of pacing. What's-his-name had been lounging in the washtub long enough to drown a whale, and she didn't intend to cool her heels waiting for his lazy butt to get out of the bath.

"You about through in there, cowboy? 'Cause we need to talk."

The reply sounded grumpy and mostly unintelligible.

"Okay then, fella. I'll come to you."

Ignoring Rosie's squeak of a warning, Tess pushed through the curtain, ripe with indignation. Her groom sat in the tin washtub surrounded by dirty gray water that covered him from midchest down, except for his bare knees, which stuck up like two bald islands rising from a sea of soap scum. He appeared to be carrying on a conversation with Rojo, the best damned cattle dog west of the Rockies. Rojo regularly got above himself, though, trying to run the ranch and everyone on it. Typical male.

"Rojo, git!" Tess tapped the dog with a toe. "Get outside and do something useful, you mangy cur."

Rojo got, and the man in the tub sank deeper into the water. "Hellfire! Can't a man have a shred of privacy from you women?"

"Not in this house. But don't worry about it. You won't be here long enough for it to matter."

Queer that the sot didn't look like a man who poisoned himself with liquor. Broad shoulders stretched from one side of the washtub to the other, and below the shoulders, hard muscle slabbed his chest. Silver hair shot with black plastered his skull, and dark eyes, clear now of alcohol's haze, regarded her suspiciously.

Sitting in that tub all scrubbed and bright-eyed, he didn't look as old as Tess had figured, even with the silver hair.

His mustache, and an admirable mustache it was, showed darker than the thick thatch on his head. Maybe the fellow was middle age. Maybe even a sliver younger than middle age. He boasted prime muscle, hardened by work. How had he slipped far enough down to climb into a whiskey bottle?

At her interested perusal, the man reached for his hat on the table beside the tub and clapped it between his thighs.

The man had nothing to hide that interested Tess in the least. "You've been washing long enough to shrivel up like a pea," she complained.

"That woman took my clothes."

"That woman? Rosie? You could'a yelled."

"Okay. I'm yelling."

"Okay." She measured him with her eyes. He would fit well enough into Colin McCabe's clothes. "I'll get you something," she promised, "as soon as we talk."

"How about you get me something now?"

"Don't get pushy." She grinned, not about to give up an advantage. "You're in no position."

He glared, but she just let the glare bounce off her. A man sitting in scummy water with bony knees sticking up like pink pimples had to work harder than that to be intimidating.

He gave up with a sigh, closed his eyes, and sank deeper into the water. "Okay, then talk."

"You and I made a deal."

"Yeah. I seem to remember it included something about me riding out of town three hundred dollars richer."

"You'll get your money."

"Good. You know, lady, you ought to be ashamed of yourself for taking advantage of a man who's stumble-down drunk."

She folded her arms across her chest and chided, "You ought to be ashamed of yourself for getting stumble-down drunk."

"Yeah." He grimaced. "Well, I'm paying the price. And speaking of prices, if you get me my clothes and my money, I'll be out of your hair quicker than you can blink. When you get your annulment, or divorce, or whatever, just let me know."

"That's what we need to talk about." Here Tess felt less certain of her ground, and he seemed to sense it, because his eyes narrowed suspiciously. The eyes changed color with his mood, Tess noted. When he was drunk, the eyes had been muddy green. Now they looked almost gray—steel, knife-edged gray, and so sharp they managed to stab clear through to her conscience.

Tess liked to deal straight up and honest with people. If Colin McCabe hadn't been such a sneaky old coot . . . but no. She wasn't stiffing the guy, Tess told herself. Adding a few conditions after the fact, out of dire necessity, simply made good sense in this case.

"Okay, cowboy, here's the deal. I had to get married or this ranch"—she gestured grandly to indicate the house, barns, grassy range, and the San Pedro River that flowed through it and made the pasture so rich—"goes to my lazy jackass brother. I told you this."

The eyes didn't get any less sharp.

"But, you see, I don't need some man coming in here and unpacking his bags like the place belonged to him, so I found someone willing to make a deal. Marry me, and leave. You."

"You're crazy, you know that?"

"I'm a hell of a long way from being crazy."

"If my brain hadn't been pickled, I would've hightailed it out of that saloon so fast all you would have seen is my dust."

"Well, your brain *was* pickled. And don't worry about your money. I'm keeping the bargain. A McCabe always keeps a bargain."

"Glad to hear it. So just bring me some clothes and my money, and I'll go. And I could use the loan of a horse, too."

The fool just wasn't getting this. Tess sighed. "That squinty-eyed fellow who showed up in the church with the half-baked grin on his face was my brother, Sean. And he knows something isn't straight here. If he gets wind that we're not hitched for real and proper, he'll go squealing to lawyer Bartlett like the pig he is, and Bartlett will take his side, because he's a pig too."

Her groom's eyes narrowed. "And why should I be concerned about this?"

She threw up her hands. Could it be more obvious? "Because I married you to keep this ranch! What good is wasting three hundred good dollars and going through this nonsense if I lose the ranch anyway? You've gotta stick around a few days and make this look real, just until Sean goes back to his hole in California. How hard could that be?"

A muscle in his jaw twitched as he gritted his teeth. "Listen, lady, I don't have a lot of time to hang around here playing house. You have a problem with your brother? Well, I have problems of my own. And three hundred dollars will help solve them. So keep your bargain, give me what you owe me, and I'll be on my way. Now."

She tried to be patient. "You're not being reasonable."

"I'm being reasonable for the first time in two days, because I'm sober for the first time in two days." He exhaled a frustrated sigh, which deflated him enough to make his shoulders sink below the water. "I can't believe I actually married you."

That stung. "Hey. Lots of guys would be glad to marry me!"

"Then why didn't you get one of them?"

"Because I don't want a permanent husband. Don't you ever listen?" Her patience threatened to wear thin. "I don't see that asking you to park yourself here for a few days is expecting so much. After all, you *are* getting three hundred dollars."

"So you keep promising."

He lifted one arm from the water and draped it along the rim of the tub. His fingers had crinkled from the water, but other than that little detail, that arm was remarkably muscled, sprinkled with black hair plastered against sun-bronzed skin. Tess felt a flush turn her own skin warm. She'd seen her daddy in the tub often enough, and Sean too before he left. But the sight of them in the wet altogether had never made her feel hot and dizzy. Tess wondered if Rosie had stoked up the stove too hot.

"Listen, *wife*." The emphasis he put on the word made it a mockery. "I'm going to get out of this tub and find some clothes if I have to parade naked in front of everyone on this godforsaken ranch. Then I'm going to walk back into town, if I have to, to catch a stage out of here. So if you don't want your maidenly modesty outraged, I suggest you get the hell out of here and get my money. Because I'm going to be one unhappy cowboy if you welsh. And you don't want to see me unhappy."

His voice had risen in volume, but Tess knew a bluff when she saw one, so she just chuckled smugly, confident that she held all the cards. Then he rose up. Water cascaded from slabs of muscle and ran in streams that outlined every sinew. And everything else. Her eyes widened and an involuntary gasp escaped her mouth.

Her face more fiery than Rosie's stove, Tess whirled around and squinched her eyes shut, as if she could erase the sight imprinted on her unwilling brain. "I'll get you some clothes," she choked out, struggling to regain at least one finger of the upper hand. "But you can wait for your money until I have the deed to this ranch in my hand. So I'd just think about sticking around for a few days, cowboy, because you don't want to see me unhappy either. Trust me on that."

With a flourish she didn't quite feel, she marched out of the kitchen, sweeping the curtain closed behind her. The cussing that followed her out made her almost smile.

JOSH furiously rubbed himself dry with the towel that had been draped across one of the kitchen benches. Damned but that woman had more *cojones* than most men he knew. What kind of creature was she, anyway? She dressed like a man, talked like a man, swaggered like a man—and apparently had no trouble in outsmarting this particular man. This sorry state of affairs could convince him to never touch liquor again. He couldn't believe he'd been drunk enough and downright stupid enough to do this to himself.

Before he had toweled away the last of the water on his skin, men's clothes flew like missiles through the curtain that separated the kitchen from the rest of the house. The jeans were big, but he cinched them in with a worn leather belt. The gray flannel shirt pulled across the shoulders, but otherwise fit. Josh wondered if some other unsuspecting male had stumbled into this nest of women and left so fast he plumb left his clothes behind. He could understand it.

"Are you dressed?" Rosie's voice asked from the other side of the curtain.

"Yeah. Come on in."

Rosie flung the curtain aside and stood for a moment to regard him appreciatively. "You don't look so bad when you're not swaying like a drunken mule."

"Uh . . . thanks. Where should I empty the water?"

"Oh, I'll do that."

Josh couldn't imagine letting a woman carry the heavy tub of water while he stood around and watched. "No, ma'am. Just tell me where to dump it."

A slow smile softened her face. She had a pretty face that had seen a lot of wear. The smile called up remnants of a fresh girl, though.

"Take it out back. This way."

He picked up the tub and followed her out.

"Colin's clothes fit you fine. Though I could let out the shoulders of that shirt."

"I won't be around long enough for you to bother, ma'am."

"Tess said you'd be staying a few days."

"That's yet to be settled."

"You can't leave while Sean is still sniffing around. He'd be on to Tess for sure. He doesn't deserve this ranch. Not any part of it."

"I'll take your word for it, ma'am."

"You don't have to. Ask Miguel. Ask any of the hands who've worked here since before Sean left. It wasn't that he was a bad boy, just lazy. That boy spent more energy dodging work than anybody I've ever known."

"Yes, ma'am."

Josh emptied the tub and hung it on a nail on the back wall. Everything here had its place, he noted. No clutter messed up the yard. What Rosie called the "back" was actually a courtyard, where a five-foot adobe wall connected the main house with a smaller building constructed in the same style—single-story adobe with few windows that could be quickly shuttered in case of foul weather or Indian attack. Though the Apaches hadn't given anyone much trouble for the better part of two decades, Arizonans had long memories.

In the courtyard was a hearth for outdoor cooking, a couple of worktables, a scattering of stools for those who wished, maybe, to sit outside on a mild evening and whittle or swap tales. The hard ground was swept clean of dust and debris.

Beyond the courtyard wall Josh could see two corrals, a barn, bunkhouse, chicken house, toolshed, and smokehouse, all in good repair. Grass already sprouted green between the mesquite, piñon, and cedar, and in the near distance wound the San Pedro, which carried precious water to give life to a land that would otherwise be parched. Fat, healthy-looking cattle grazed the river bottom, and on the crest of a nearby hill, a herd of horses stood in silhouette against the setting sun.

The people here had good reason to value this ranch. Many a man's dream centered on having a place like this. A woman's dream could rest here as well, Josh figured.

Rosie had noted his visual survey. "The Diamond T isn't like the grand rich places that run thousands of head, but it's a good ranch. Colin McCabe, God rest him, was a hardworking man. He knew cattle, and he knew horses."

He heard words left unsaid, maybe that Colin McCabe should have known his children as well. But this wasn't his problem, Josh reminded himself.

Miguel came out of the barn, spied them in the courtyard,

and wandered over. "Woman," he said to Rosie, "haven't you got nothing to do but stand around and talk?"

Rosie snorted, but her eye had softened, Josh noted, when the man walked up. "Old man, you should keep your nose to your own work and not bother about mine. Have you seen Tess?"

"Chopping wood for the stove."

"Tell her dinner is in half an hour. Luis and Henry too."

With that, she turned up her nose and marched inside. Miguel's eyes followed her, and a wry smile pulled at his mouth, but all he said was, "You'll like Rosie's cooking. But if you know what's good for you, don't ever eat anything that Tess fixes. That girl can shoe a horse and ride a herd, but she sure can't cook."

"I won't be here long enough for her to poison me," Josh reminded him.

Miguel's weather-lined face turned to granite. "You'll stay until Tessie tells you to leave, and then leave when she tells you. And you show proper respect, hombre, with Tess and Rosie too. Likely Tess could whup you if you got uppity, but if she don't, I will. You hear? That girl has a lot of friends, and you're right in the middle of 'em."

Josh raised one brow. "It's a right friendly place, then."

Rosie's cooking proved to be all Miguel had boasted. Supper was fried chicken, corn, and apple pie. Everyone ate at the big table in the kitchen, including Luis and Henry. Luis, a rangy Papago Indian, was Miguel's half brother, Josh discovered from the conversation. They shared a mother. Luis spoke little English, apparently, because both Miguel and Tess addressed him in Spanish. Henry, with ragged blond hair, pale blue eyes, and skin like leather, talked as much as he ate, and he ate a lot.

As they tucked into their supper, Tess waved toward Josh with a fork. "This here's my new husband."

Luis grunted something inarticulate. Henry eyed him curiously but said nothing. Apparently the men here attached as much importance to Tess's marriage as she did.

Josh thought of the Double R, waiting in limbo until he

could get back to settle David's debt. A foreman and six hands depended on him coming back with six hundred dollars in his hand, and here he was, piddling away time on a second-rate ranch under the thumb of a crazy woman and her "friends." What did he have to do to get her to give him his money and kick his butt off her property?

An idea occurred to him when Tess yawned and said good night, Luis and Henry ambled off to the bunkhouse, and Miguel cut half a loaf of Rosie's bread to take with him to his bunk in the "little house" across the courtyard. "You can bunk with me," Miguel told Josh. "Get some blankets from Rosie."

"Nope."

Miguel stopped halfway through cutting the bread. "Nope? What nope?"

"Nope means I'm not bunking on your floor with only a couple of thin blankets between me and the cold. I married the lady of the house. Seems I have a right to sleep wherever I want."

"Like hell."

But Josh had already reached the door of the room into which his "wife" had disappeared. He knocked. "You decent, *sweetheart?*"

The door instantly flung open. Regrettably, Tess still wore her jeans and shirt, though the shirt had been untucked and now hung loosely past her hips. Her unbraided hair cascaded in a dark, shining fall down to those same hips, and she gripped a hairbrush as if it were a club. Her eyes narrowed when Josh grinned.

"What?" she demanded.

"It's been a full day, *wife*. I figure I'll turn in."

"Go right ahead. And you can forget the sweetheart and wifey talk."

Miguel and Rosie regarded them uneasily from the kitchen doorway, Rosie wringing her hands and Miguel wearing an incredulous expression that was almost comical. Josh began to enjoy himself.

"Is that any way for a new bride to talk?" He pushed

into the room. "Good thing the bed is big enough for two."

"You're crazy." Tess tried to block the way, but had about as much chance as a reed standing against a rolling boulder. His chest collided with hers, and she retreated as if she'd been burned. Josh felt a bit singed himself. Tess McCabe, for all her mannish dress and habits, definitely boasted a woman's charms.

Miguel clumped toward their little confrontation. "I'll tear him apart, Tessie."

"I can fight my own fights." Her tone stopped the man in his tracks.

"But—"

"Git, Miguel. When have I ever not been able to take care of myself?" She made the claim proudly, though her cheeks had turned pink. Josh's grin grew wider. He would be out of here in no time.

While Tess watched Miguel and Rosie retreat, Josh sat himself on the bed and patted it. "Nice mattress," he noted.

Tess whirled around in a one-woman tornado. "You are insane," she hissed, low and dangerous.

He grinned nonchalantly. "I don't know about that. I think I'm a fairly good judge of beds."

She pointed toward the door. "Get out! Get out now!"

"A case of newlywed nerves, sweetheart?"

"Get. Out. Now!"

"It's my understanding that married folks sleep together."

"We are not *that* kind of married. And if you think that you are sleeping in this room, then you're dumber than I first took you for. Out!"

And Tess McCabe was a good deal prettier than he'd first taken her for. Not to mention more interesting. With every furious movement her hair shimmered in the lamplight. Her face came alight with passion—cheeks aflame, eyes on fire. Not exactly the kind of passion a man likes to see in a woman, but still damned distracting.

He didn't remove himself from the bed. "Not that kind of married, eh? I got the idea that wasn't what you wanted the world to think."

Those fiery eyes narrowed. She backed up a step. "That's a threat, isn't it?"

He just smiled. "I'm not such a bum to threaten a lady."

"And I'm not enough of a lady to believe that load of horseshit." But her tone became more cautious. "All right. You can sleep on the floor. In the corner."

With deliberate insolence, he stretched out on the bed, hands behind his head. "Nope. I've had a hard couple of days. I fancy a night spent in a nice, soft, clean bed."

He could almost hear her teeth grind.

"All right, rat bastard. You win. I can put up with almost anything for a few days." She grabbed the quilt folded at the foot of the bed and jerked it from beneath his legs. Then she headed for the door.

"Where are you going?"

"It won't be the first time I've slept in front of the fireplace."

"That might look passing strange if one of the hands happens in."

"I care how it looks?"

"Isn't that what your whole scheme is all about? Looking married? Aren't you the one willing to go to any lengths, cheating or otherwise, to get the family ranch?"

She stopped in her tracks and turned slowly and deliberately back toward him. "I do not cheat. McCabes are straight as an arrow and twice as honest."

Those green eyes of hers could turn remarkably hard, Josh noted happily. He gave her his most infuriating smile. He knew it was infuriating because his sister had told him so at least a dozen times.

"And I am not letting some two-bit sot turn me out of my own place."

That stung a bit, but Josh figured he might have had it coming.

Still glaring at him, she settled huffily in the room's one chair and wrapped herself in the quilt. "Enjoy the bed," she invited sourly. "Just don't infest it with fleas."

Chapter Three

TESS UNCURLED FROM her chair in the predawn, the smell of rain tickling her nostrils. Before she left the bedroom, she took a moment to observe her roommate, who snored quietly on the bed—her bed. She made a face. Beneath the covers—her covers—her "husband" looked warm and comfy, while Tess had spent an uncomfortable, almost sleepless night clutching the quilt around her, trying unsuccessfully to ward off the cold. Obviously the fellow was a slugabed, for the cock had already crowed. A lazy smile touched his mouth as he dreamed. The mouth, Tess couldn't help but notice, was the sort of mouth a sculptor might carve on a statue, and its smile gentled the rugged face. His cheek with its morning shadow of coarse, dark beard, bore a crease from the pillow. Her pillow.

With broad shoulders, tousled hair, and that seductive mouth, the sot wasn't all that hard on the eyes, Tess decided. Not that it mattered. The fellow could look like a billy goat for all she cared. Sean had better hightail it back to California soon, so she could boot her "husband" down the road. She couldn't put up with this nonsense much longer.

Cautiously, Tess took her boots from the floor where she had dropped them the night before and tiptoed toward the door. She hoped the fool slept through breakfast. Going hungry would serve him right.

He didn't sleep through breakfast. Ten minutes after Tess had grabbed a biscuit and a cup of strong coffee, her thorn-in-the-side husband strolled out of the house and over to where she talked with Miguel, Luis, and Henry at the corrals. He looked annoyingly fresh and chipper from a good night's sleep.

"Good morning," he said, cradling a steaming mug in his hands. "Nice morning."

Tess nodded curtly. The men mumbled a greeting. Rojo quit giving the eye to the horses in the corral and bounded over to the newcomer with a friendly greeting. He scratched the cattle dog's ears, and the dog melted in ecstasy.

Tess watched in disgust. Rojo didn't show much taste when it came to people.

"Be careful of Rojo," Tess warned curtly. "He's a good cattle dog, but he doesn't take to strangers."

The bed-stealer gave her a lazy smile. "Most dogs know who deserves a show of teeth and who doesn't."

Tess almost showed her own teeth. This fellow had a way of eating at the edges of her temper. What had happened to the woozy, boozy cowboy she had practically poured into Glory's crib the day before? Or the self-conscious, confused fellow who had looked so ridiculous sitting bare and hairy in her washtub?

Now the man looked almost clean-cut. He had taken time to trim the steel and silver mustache, and his silver-shot-with-black hair shone in the bright sunlight. Her father's old shirt stretched tight across axe-handle shoulders which whittled down to slim hips and long legs. The man stood at least a head taller than Tess, who looked eye to eye with Miguel.

"Nice-looking bunch of horses." He pointed his freshly

shaven chin toward the green broncs in the corral—two bays, a chestnut, a gray, and two blacks.

Miguel nodded. "We throw a saddle on these for the first time this morning. They are mustangs brought up from Mexico."

"Sell them once they're saddle broke?"

"Sí. Señora Bermudez at the Circle T has already said she will take the chestnut, and she likes the gray as well. She likes mustangs, because they are smart, strong horses that can work all day. And the army always buys from us. Some of the other ranches too."

Tess scowled at Miguel. The stranger didn't need to know their business. But Miguel didn't notice. Once he got to talking about horses, there was no shutting him up. Her husband seemed to have a similar interest.

"You buck them out?"

Miguel shrugged. "If they have spirit, they will buck."

The bum grinned. "Kinda like women, eh?"

Miguel looked cautiously from the newcomer to Tess, whose fists had clenched, and back again to her husband. When Tess had first walked out of the house, the foreman had given her a swift perusal, then nodded when he found her in one piece after spending the night in a room with her new husband. Now a small smile twisted the mouth beneath his mustache. "A man must know his horses, señor. Some will buck until they drop dead. Some will roll to crush the rider beneath them. There are some who should never be mounted, because they will never be gentled."

"Have you known many to be that ornery?"

Miguel's smile grew broader. "Not many."

The stranger nodded. "On my place, we don't break a horse, we gentle it. The process takes more time, but it results in a more dependable mount."

Tess immediately bristled. "The horses we turn out are the best in the area. They're loyal, smart, and still have plenty of spirit. Hell, they'll go places even a mule won't go."

The uppity fellow just shrugged.

"What's the matter," Tess taunted, "are you afraid to buck out a horse? Afraid you'll land on your tail?"

Luis and Henry leaned against the fence and grinned. Miguel tried to hide a smile.

The stranger met her eyes with an unruffled gaze. "I can stick a saddle as good as most others." He crossed his arms on that broad chest. His eyes, almost green in the morning sunlight, twinkled with something that might be amusement, and that twinkle was the last straw for Tess.

"You can, can you?"

"Usually."

"You want to put your bony backside where your mouth is, cowboy?"

He smiled. "You think you can stick a horse better than I can?"

"It's likely."

"That would be a surprise."

"Then get ready to be surprised."

Rojo whined, gave his new friend a sympathetic look, then trotted over to join the men, who looked on, grinning hugely. Even Miguel, usually more cautious, didn't bother to hide his anticipation of a good time coming up. There was nothing a cowboy loved better than a good bronc-riding contest.

Well, they wouldn't get to see much of a contest, Tess told herself smugly. There wasn't a man on this place she couldn't outride, and she expected to laugh long and hard when this uppity jackass left his butt print in the dust.

"Okay—what was your name, cowboy?"

That got his goat just a bit. Tess could tell.

"Joshua Ransom."

"Okay, Joshua Ransom. I'll let you prove how well you ride, and then we'll let the men decide who's got the upper hand when it come to horses. You game?"

His smile shone with confidence. "I'm game."

"Good enough." She grinned wickedly. "Henry, bring out Nitro."

Miguel's brows shot up. "Nitro?"

"We want to give our friend here a challenge, don't we?"

Miguel just shook his head as a grinning Henry sprinted toward the barn. "Nitro's a stallion we haven't been able to ride," he told Josh. "We keep him for breeding, but he's a wild one under saddle."

Tess smirked. "Even my daddy couldn't sit Nitro for long, and there's more than one cowboy who owes this horse a broken bone or two. Nitro likes to be creative and see how far and how high he can toss anything that climbs on his back. Want to back out?"

Now he looked a little concerned. "Which one of us is going to ride him?"

"We both are. We'll take turns and see who stays on longest. I'll cut you a break and go first. Maybe he'll be tired by the time you get on him."

Luis chuckled. "Or angry."

Tess just chuckled. She was about to get revenge for a cold night spent in a chair, and if she got some bumps and bruises in the process, seeing this fellow flat in the dust would be worth the price.

Nitro came out of the barn snorting steam into the early morning air. He was a horse who enjoyed a good romp—a romp in his mind being a chance to break someone's bones and then stomp him into the dirt.

They snubbed the stallion to a post to get the saddle onto his back, but he stood in docile patience. Nitro knew the drill, and he looked forward to wreaking a little havoc.

"I'll go first," Tess said cheerfully. "Miguel, ear him down while I get on."

When Miguel let go of Nitro's ear, the horse exploded. Tess knew she couldn't stick for long, but she figured her performance would be better than anyone else attempting to ride the demon. He bucked, twisted, sunfished, and did everything but turn himself inside out to send her flying. When he connected with the earth, the stiff-legged jolt nearly snapped Tess's spine, or so it felt.

As always, Nitro won. Tess connected hard and painfully with the ground, then scrambled out of the way while Rojo ducked into the corral to keep the horse occupied.

"Ten seconds," Miguel said, checking his pocket watch. "Not bad, Miss Tess."

She grinned at what's-his-name. "I tired him out for you."

Nitro did not appear to be tired, though. When Josh climbed aboard, the bronc took off like a bad-tempered tornado that had just happened to touch down in the McCabe corral.

"Fifteen seconds," Miguel noted approvingly when the intrepid rider bit dirt. "Damned good."

"What? Fifteen seconds?"

"Sí."

Tess's jaw tightened. "We'll see about that!"

As Tess got ready to mount again, her grinning adversary spit out a mouthful of dirt and taunted, "I tired him out for you, sweetheart."

Tess was too busy to retort.

And so the morning went. None of the three parties involved—the man, the woman, or the horse—came close to giving in. Foam flecked Nitro's damp hide. Tess wore dirt and sweat head to toe. Her stubborn husband looked little better. Finally, when Tess went flying for the fifth time, her adversary looked at her, looked at Nitro, and shook his head.

"The horse has had enough," he said.

Instantly, Tess's back—what small part of it wasn't bruised, battered, and scraped—went up, but before she could reply, Miguel butted in.

"He's right. Nitro will keep going until he falls over."

Sitting in the dirt, every inch of her aching, Tess still wanted to object. She hadn't yet won. But she looked at Nitro and knew that Miguel was right. Nitro was blowing hard, too tired even to come after her for a few good stomps.

And oh, all right, her uppity husband was right, too. She sighed.

"Okay. Luis, walk him out, would you? And make sure he's good and cool before you put him away."

"It's a draw," Miguel announced, looking relieved.

Tess had to admire a man who could stick a horse like this fellow could. He hadn't learned to ride like that with his head stuck in a whiskey bottle. Josh Ransom. This time she would remember his name.

"If I had a week," Josh boasted, "I could be up on that horse without him batting an eyelash."

"You have a week," Tess growled.

"I don't think so."

"You do if you want your money." She fixed him with a challenging glare. "Another hundred dollars if you can break Nitro to saddle and rider."

He looked thoughtful.

She hated to part with any more money, but Nitro was worth it. So was convincing Sean that she was good and married. "That's a lot of money, Ransom."

She could see the calculation in his eyes. "I'll think about it."

He limped over and offered her a hand up. She thought about slapping his hand away, but then her real problem rode around the corner of the barn, and she grabbed Josh's hand and forced a smile. "Thank you."

"Well, now," Sean said as Josh pulled her to her feet. "Isn't that sweet. What've you two been doing? Wrestling in the mud?"

Josh turned to give Sean a dark look, and at the same time he slipped his arm around Tess's shoulders.

"They were working," Miguel told him. "Work. Ever heard of it?"

"Excuse us," Josh said. "Rosie's got a good dinner on the stove, and we need to get cleaned up. Join us if you want, Sean."

Tess tried to object, but acquiesced to Josh's subtle pressure on her shoulder as he guided her toward the house. Then, on the porch, he did the unthinkable. In full view of everyone, he kissed her. Not a civilized peck, but a cheek-sucking, air-stealing lip lock that sent a bolt of surprise from her nose to her toes. Surprise, and a shivery,

strength-stealing strangeness that threatened to turn her
knees to water. Dadgummed but she got so flustered that
she almost forgot that Sean stood there staring at them.
Sean and everyone else.

Of course that was the reason behind the kiss. Josh staged
the passion, the enveloping arms, the warm, delicious close-
ness all for the benefit of her weaselly brother. He put on a
show, and what a show it was. She'd have to thank him later,
Tess mused dizzily, when she got her brain back in order.

A perverse part of her almost hoped that Sean stayed
awhile.

UNFORTUNATELY, Sean did stay awhile. He moved into the
bunkhouse with the declaration that he missed the "old
days" and wanted to get reacquainted with the ranch—a
load of horseshit as far as Tess was concerned.

Josh Ransom also stayed. Leaving would have been
hard, Tess figured, after he'd boasted that he could gentle
Nitro in a week. When the man said he would do something, Tess discovered, he followed through on his word,
something she admired in a man. He wasn't quite the bum
she had first thought.

She and her new roommate reached a compromise in
sleeping arrangements. For newlyweds to sleep anywhere
but in the same room would make Sean's ears prick up for
sure, but Tess didn't intend to spend more than one night in
that chair. She settled for guarding her virtue with a rolled-
up quilt placed between them on the bed. The arrangement
didn't leave either of them much room, but then, how much
room did a body need just for sleeping? Tess wasn't about
to crawl unguarded into a bed with any man, especially a
man she had dragged out of a saloon.

Not that she had much worry that Ransom would get
fresh. He looked like a man who could have a host of females fawning over him if he wanted—all of them with
silky hair, rosy lips, plump breasts, and soft skin. What
would he want with a whipcord-lean, sun-browned female

who wore trail dust instead of perfume? Not that Tess cared. Why would she?

Yet a strange, tingly feeling crept through her at night as she lay tense and sleepless on her half of the mattress, listening to her husband's breathing, feeling the male body heat that somehow managed to seep through the barrier between them. She would certainly be glad when she was rid of the man. Glad, glad, glad. No more worrying about keeping him out of her business. No more sharing a room and a bed. No more looking at his face over the table at meals, hearing him swap tales with the men, worrying about the hands starting to like him too much. No more getting distracted by the way he sat a horse, the way his hair turned to spun silver in the sunlight, or the way his eyes crinkled when he smiled. No more worrying about when and if he might try to kiss her again.

Ah yes. There *had* been that kiss. . . .

During the waking hours, Sean watched them like an eagle, forcing Tess to play the role of a lovesick bride, or at least a halfway interested bride. Her groom took delight in making her uncomfortable. Tess just knew the man enjoyed himself hugely whenever he put an arm around her shoulders or gave her a peck on the cheek, just because the skunk liked to see her squirm—his bit of revenge for her making him stick around.

By the time Saturday rolled around, Tess's nerves were wearing thin, and so was Josh's patience. Tess sat in the barn tack room cleaning her saddle when Josh walked in, his boots thudding heavily on the packed dirt floor, his face looking like he had just eaten nails.

"Do you know what day it is?" he demanded.

"Yup." Here it came again. Every day he strained harder at the leash. Soon that tether was plumb going to break.

"Just how long until—"

"Well, howdy, you two." Sean strolled up with his gotcha smile. "Nice day, isn't it?"

Josh regarded him narrowly, then his face brightened. "Tess and I were just about to ride out and look for that buckskin mustang who tried to run off some of the mares. Weren't we, sweetheart?"

"Uh . . . sure." *Sweetheart. Sheesh!* "We were." They hadn't planned any such thing, but Josh was matching Sean gotcha grin for gotcha grin, so she played along to see what he was up to.

"Want to come?" Josh asked Sean.

"Well, I—"

"You did say you were lonesome for the old days," Josh said amiably.

"Yes, Sean. You did." Tess tried to ignore Josh's hand, which rested with apparent affection on the back of her neck. Queer how a warm hand could send such tingly shivers down a person's spine.

"It would help," Josh said innocently, "to have an extra man along."

The hand kneaded gently. Tess didn't know whether to grit her teeth or melt into a little puddle.

Sean gave them a sour look, then surrendered sullenly. "I guess I could use the exercise."

When Josh led out Amigo for Sean to ride, Tess began to understand. Amigo, a rangy gray with huge hooves, had the most bone-jarring gait of any horse that lived at the Diamond T. Josh knew it well, because just two days before, Tess had put him on Amigo when he insisted she give him a tour of the ranch. After two hours in the saddle, he had sat gingerly the rest of the day.

They set off at a good pace, assuring that Sean endured the greatest possible pain. Rojo trotted along with them, dashing off now and again to flush a rabbit or investigate a scent trail, then returning to play a game he and Josh had invented, where the dog grabbed a stick, leapt into the air high enough for Josh to grab it from his mouth, then ran full speed to retrieve the treasure when Josh threw it.

"You're going to wear him out so he won't be any use to us," Tess complained.

"He's got energy to spare," Josh assured her.

In truth, Tess's complaint came from a twinge of jealousy.

Rojo only tolerated most people other than Tess. Tess he adored. His taking up with Josh was a betrayal. She wouldn't have wanted the dog to threaten Josh, of course. But a little standoffishness would have been nice.

"This horse feels like a broken rocking chair," Sean complained before thirty minutes had passed.

"You've gotten soft," Tess told him from her comfortable perch on Ranger, who floated over the rough ground. "Didn't your ambitions for the Diamond T include doing any work here?"

"Didn't you even read the letter I sent you after our father died?" Sean asked through jarring teeth.

"I read it, and I couldn't believe you wanted me to sell the ranch and divvy up the money."

"At least you wouldn't have had to get married." Sean gave Josh a cynical look. Ransom just smiled.

"Had to get married? Ha! I wanted to get married," Tess lied. "The man just swept me off my feet."

"Who do you think you're fooling?" Sean scoffed.

Josh took offense. "Why do you have such trouble believing your sister is happily married?"

"I think a man with any sense would rather be staked out on an anthill than marry my sister. And you seem like a man with sense."

The look on Ransom's face took Tess by surprise, and it made Sean back into a lame apology. "Uh . . . that came out wrong. Tess is a great girl. After all, she is my sister. But you've got to admit that she doesn't go out of her way to please a man. I mean, just look at her. Or listen to her."

"Since I sleep with her every night," Ransom said coldly, "I might know a bit more than you do about how Tess pleases a man."

Tess hoped the shadow of her hat hid the flush that crawled up her neck. A rush of gratitude for his defense almost made her glad Rojo was being nice to him.

Lucky for her, before she could go totally mushy, something else demanded her attention.

"Looks like a mired cow over there." Josh pointed to the

brushy bank of an unnamed creek—unnamed because it seldom carried water. The uncommonly regular rains during the last month had turned more than one dry creek to quicksand and mud.

The cow was there, big as life. If Tess hadn't been so distracted, she would have seen it without Josh's help.

"She's a mama," Tess said.

Indeed, a spindly legged calf fled at their approach, but Rojo circled behind it to block its retreat. It halted uncertainly, bawling distress. Mama bawled back, more angry at the separation from her calf than the mud sucking at her legs.

When Tess started to dismount, Ransom told her to stay put. "No reason for all three of us to get mucked up," he said cheerfully. "Sean here can back me up. Can't you, Sean?"

Ordinarily, Tess would have bristled at Josh taking charge, but the prospect of seeing Sean make closer acquaintance with the slobbering, foam-flecked, mud-encrusted cow made her gladly settle for the role of spectator.

With impressive skill, Josh dropped a rope around the cow's horns, wrapped the rope around his saddle horn, and drew the rope taut. Sean got the job of pushing from behind.

Predictably, he objected. "You expect me to wade out in that slime? These are new boots!"

Ransom grinned. "We could ask your sister to do it."

Sean shot him a filthy look, but the challenge to his manhood was clear. Minutes later he stood knee deep in mud with a shoulder propped against the cow's dung-coated rear end.

"Heave ho," Ransom said as his horse put tension on the rope. "Push, Sean. Lean into her."

"Go to hell." But Sean pushed. The cow bawled her distress, raised her tail, and treated Sean to a stream of greenish brown cow plop.

Tess howled with laughter. She couldn't help it. Her brother covered with steaming dung was a sight to treasure in her memory. Her sides nearly split.

Sean didn't see the humor. Between moans and curses,

he vainly searched for water to wash off the stuff, which spattered his chest and dotted his face. The creek offered no water, though. Only mud.

Tess took mercy on him. "Take my canteen," she offered. "It will rinse some of it off."

He waved it angrily away, still cursing the cow, Josh, Tess, the ranch, the mud, and the whole bovine population in general, which made Tess laugh yet again. In the meantime, the cow, with Josh's horse steadily pulling, managed to struggle free of the mud. She shook herself and bawled as Josh flipped the rope from her horns. In response, her calf trotted in their direction. Still muttering and waving his arms in disgust, Sean started for his horse. Like some greenhorn, he made the mistake of getting between the distraught mama cow and her calf. Mama, already on edge from her ordeal, saw the man in her line of vision and did what any cranky range cow would do. She charged. Sean looked up to see a thousand pounds of beef bearing down upon him with tossing horns and distended nostrils.

Tess reacted in midlaugh, digging heels into Ranger and leaping forward to head off the charge even as Rojo rushed forward, barking frantically. But Josh got there ahead of both of them. He careened his horse into the angry cow's beefy shoulder, making her stumble and go down on her knees. The move was both gutsy and dangerous—and probably the only one that could have saved Sean from becoming part of the soil layer.

Sean made a dash for his horse. The bewildered cow got to her feet, shook her head, and with Rojo's loud encouragement, ambled off toward her calf.

"And you ask why I want to sell the ranch!" Sean growled. Less than an hour after they got back to the ranch, he packed his gear, saddled his horse, and rode off without so much as a huffy good-bye.

The story of Sean's rescue got passed around the ranch faster than Rosie's hot biscuits. Josh became the hero of the day. He had won the men's admiration when he'd stuck with Nitro alongside Tess, but saving a fellow cowboy (even though Sean hardly qualified as a cowboy, in Tess's opinion) sent him right up the ladder to a pedestal. The next morning, he just about elevated himself to sainthood when he led Nitro out of the barn with a saddle on his back, mounted, and in full view of everyone, rode the stallion one circuit of the corral and dismounted, still in one piece. The stallion tossed his head and regarded the man disdainfully—just to keep his dignity intact—but otherwise, he behaved like a well-broke mount. Among the onlookers, jaws dropped, eyes widened.

"Whoo-hoo!" Henry shouted, once Josh had both feet safely back on the ground. "Ride that sucker, Josh!"

Miguel tapped Tess's shoulder with a fist. "We found you a good one, eh, Miss Tess?"

Could the day get more annoying? Tess wondered. "You didn't find him, and he's not a 'good one,' okay? And he'll be leaving soon."

As she stalked into the house, Miguel grinned at Rosie. "If I hooked a mighty fine fish, I wouldn't be so anxious to throw him back."

Rosie shook her head in disgust. "What men don't know about women is pathetic."

As soon as they finished the midday meal, Tess saddled two horses—one for her and one for Josh—and announced that they would ride into town for a talk with lawyer Bartlett. She was good and married, and had been for a week. The time had come for Bartlett to cough up the deed to her ranch.

"Look convincing," she advised her husband. "When I get that deed in my hand, you get your three hundred dollars."

"Four hundred," he reminded her. "Remember Nitro."

Oh yes. That foolish offer she'd made. Who would have thought the man would make good on his boast? "It's a good thing you're not staying longer," she grumbled. "I can't afford you."

Still, riding beside him on the way to town felt strangely

pleasant. Tess had gotten used to his presence beside her in bed, and after the strangeness had worn off, his warm bulk on the other side of the rolled-up quilt had made the nights less lonely. Before this last week, Tess hadn't realized her nights were lonely. She did now.

And the men liked having him around. After just this short time, they trusted him. Even Miguel liked him. Rosie had hinted that Tess having a husband might not be such a bad thing after all, as long as that husband was a "damned solid cowboy" like Josh.

The very fact that Tess entertained such a thought just pointed up the dire need to have the fellow gone. Some built-in weakness in the female constitution must turn a girl's brain to mush the minute she started keeping company with a half-decent man. Yes, Josh Ransom—she wouldn't be forgetting that name again—did qualify as a half-decent sort of fellow. He had guts. He had a way with horses. He knew cattle almost as well as she did. Okay, just as well as she did. He had all his teeth, didn't stink more than any other man who worked hard and wore the sweat to prove it, and he knew enough to take off his mucky boots before coming into the house. Someone had brought him up to manners. What's more, in spite of Tess finding him in such a sorry state at the Bird Cage, he hadn't touched a drop of liquor since coming to the Diamond T.

Quite a catch, all in all, if a girl were fishing for a husband. Which Tess wasn't. Definitely wasn't. Didn't need one, didn't want one, and for sure she would get used to sleeping alone in the blink of an eye. The sooner she sent Josh Ransom on his way, the happier she would be.

Therefore, Tess got very unhappy when lawyer Bartlett refused to cough up her deed.

"Now, then, Tess. Don't be so impatient," he advised. "You know your daddy wanted to see you settled like a woman should be settled. That's why he wrote his will the way he did."

"I *am* settled," Tess gritted from between her teeth. She

took Josh by the arm and pulled him forward for inspection. "I'm married, dadgummit. A whole week. Just ask Preacher Malone."

Bartlett gave Josh a passing glance, as if he were an offering that failed to measure up. "I believe the will's exact words were 'settled into marriage.' Your brother, Sean, came by my office earlier this morning and expressed grave doubts as to the nature and commitment of your marriage, Tess."

"What do you mean nature and commitment?" she cried. Only a lawyer would use words such as those. Her fists balled at her sides, nails digging into her palms.

Then Josh took one of those hands, uncurled it, and interweaved their fingers, just as a real husband might have done. In a reasonable, man-to-man voice, he brought the conversation back to a civilized level. "Mr. Bartlett, I think Sean McCabe's motive is pretty obvious, and I'm surprised you're lending him an ear."

The warmth of that masculine hand supporting hers eased the knot in Tess's stomach. In fact, she felt amazingly light, as if she could have floated toward the pressed-tin ceiling of Bartlett's office.

"The way I understand it," Josh said calmly, "Tess has fulfilled the terms of her father's will, and now she wants the deed to the Diamond T in her name and in her safekeeping. That seems both legal and reasonable to me."

Bless the man. Bless him, bless him, bless him.

Bartlett looked him up and down, as if just now recognizing he was part of this. "Mr. . . . . uh . . ."

"Ransom."

"Mr. Ransom. Do you have a sister?"

"Yes sir, I do."

"Then you should understand that a brother's instinct is to take care of his sister. I don't know if Tess told you this, but Scan McCabe proposed shortly after their father's death that the ranch be sold and the proceeds split between them, because he knew that Tess wasn't inclined to marry, and half the proceeds from the Diamond T would set her up in modest circumstances where she could live securely without having to waste her life on backbreaking ranch work that is difficult even for a man. That is not the proposal of a greedy, unprincipled man, as you seem to imply Sean is."

The idea of selling the ranch that had been in her family three generations made Tess want to spit, but Josh tightened his hand around hers.

"Mr. Bartlett," Josh said in that reasonable voice of his, "do you have a legal right to withhold the deed?"

"I believe the wording of the will demands it."

Tess thought the lawyer's smile looked like a rattlesnake's snide grin.

"Don't worry, Tess." Bartlett gave her arm a condescending pat. If Josh hadn't been restraining her, the lawyer might have lost a hand. "What difference does it make whether the deed is in my desk for a bit more? As you say, you're married. Soon it will be obvious to everyone that your marriage wasn't an impulsive act meant only to secure the Diamond T."

Tess couldn't think of a reply that didn't involve cussing. Fortunately, Ransom had more presence of mind. He said something stiff about retaining their own lawyer while tugging Tess toward the door. She scarcely heard what he said, distracted as she was picturing her daddy, his lawyer, and her brother all staked out on an anthill.

"I'll see you at the barn dance tomorrow tonight, won't I?" Bartlett said as they went out the door.

Tess got out the "Fat" of "Fat chance!" before Josh firmly shushed her.

"Maybe," he replied.

"Dadgummit!" Tess growled once they reached the safety of the street. "That snake! He's never liked me. Always told my daddy that he'd raised me to be a heathen. He can't do this!"

Josh put a finger to her lips to shut her up. "Tess, you need to get a lawyer to handle this for you."

"Bartlett's the only lawyer in town."

"There are other towns."

"Lawyers and their fancy words and sneaky ways. If it

hadn't been for a lawyer, my daddy would never have thought of that stupid will. Just give me a few days. I'll think of something. I will."

The twitch of muscle at the hinge of Josh's jaw told Tess he had run out of patience.

"Ransom, honest! Just a few more days."

His mouth a tight line, he held up two fingers. "Two days. Then I'm leaving, Tess. You can make up any story you want to explain why I'm gone, and you can honor your deal or not. Two days, and I'm gone."

Chapter Four

TESS LOOKED AT herself in Rosie's full-length mirror and made a face. "Two days," she said in a mockery of Josh's voice. "Two days and I'm gone. You can take that news and stick it up your—"

"Tess!" Rosie scolded. "When you're dressed like a lady, you should talk like a lady."

Tess snorted. "These sleeves are cutting off my arms."

"I can let out the seams," Rosie offered. "Most ladies don't have so much muscle in their shoulders and arms."

"Well, pardon me for working every day to make a living."

Tess couldn't believe the woman who looked from the mirror was her. She felt like a little girl playing dress-up in her mother's clothes. Actually, this dress had never belonged to her mother. Her mother had been an aristocrat from Mexico—small, refined, and delicate. Whenever Tess looked at her mother's wedding portrait, she felt like a gorilla. No, this dress was one of Rosie's best, decked out with flounces, lace, and ribbon. It was tight in the waist, loose in the bust, and inches too short.

Tess thought she looked dadgummed silly dressed in bows and flounces with her hair not sensibly braided, but tortured into curls that kept falling in her face. But Rosie surveyed her with warm, approving eyes. "I haven't worn that dress since I was your age and just married. That was before my bones got the padding they have today. It may be out of style, but it makes you look like a princess. I'll just add a flounce to the hem, let out the waist. . . ." She gave Tess's chest a dubious frown. "Maybe we can stuff a couple of kerchiefs up there. We don't want you to look like you're lacking."

"Dadgummit, Rosie! You aren't getting anywhere near me with any kerchiefs. Not unless they're going around my neck or on my head!"

"Don't be so testy, dear. I know this feels strange to you, but we agreed, you, me, and Miguel, that the best way to make your husband stick around longer is for you to get him a little bit interested. It's nothing to be ashamed of, sweetie. Women have been doing this since Eve. It's tradition."

"Not with me, it isn't." Tess extricated herself from the dress and managed to escape with only two pricks from Rosie's pins.

"Do you want the man to stay or not?"

Tess sighed. "Just long enough to convince Sean and Bartlett."

"Then you have to put some work into it. Besides . . ." Rosie's eye warmed in a way that made Tess nervous. "Maybe it's not such a good idea to toss the man out. Maybe you should try to make this a real marriage, Tessie."

"Hell no!"

"Why not?" Rosie sat on her bed—formerly the bed she had shared with Colin McCabe—and started ripping the seam of the dress's waist. "At first I thought this Josh Ransom was bad news. But from what I've seen, he has more good points than bad ones. A woman is always better off with a man by her side, if he's a good man."

Tess knew Rosie spoke from her own experience. Married young, abandoned only two years after her marriage, Rosie had been left on her own to sink or swim. With no money and few skills, she had sunk—at least in the eyes of the world—and ended up plying womankind's oldest trade along with Glory at the Bird Cage. Glory thrived in such a place. Rosie had not.

When Colin McCabe had come along and taken a fancy to her, Rosie hadn't hesitated to move out to the Diamond T, put up with Colin's two motherless children, and cope with the hard life on an isolated ranch. They had never married, because Rosie still had a husband wandering the country somewhere, but she had given Tess's father all of her devotion and loyalty.

"Did you love my father, Rosie?"

Rosie smiled. "There are as many kinds of love as there are men and women on this earth, Tessie. Your father was a good man, a strong man. He was kind to me, and I loved him for that, even though he had some peculiar ways about him. But now that he's gone, I could love another man, with a different kind of love." She glanced toward her bedroom's closed door, her lips pursing. "If the man wasn't such a rock-headed idiot."

Tess smiled, wondering if Miguel would ever catch on that Rosie's sharp tongue hid a willing heart.

By midafternoon, the dress fit—sort of. Tess sported more frills and bows than a porcupine had quills.

"Won't Josh be surprised?" Rosie gushed cheerfully.

Surprised might not quite be the word for it. Seeing Tess gussied up like some fancy porcelain figurine might just make the man laugh himself silly. Not that she would blame him.

WHEN Josh drove the McCabe buckboard around to the front of the adobe house, he found Miguel lounging in the shade of the covered front porch. The foreman grinned at him.

"The women are inside, fussin' with clothes or something."

"Figures."

Josh had gotten a new shirt and jeans in town. Rosie had burned the ones he'd worn on that day-long, or was it a two-day-long, binge in the Bird Cage. She'd said with a smirk that the fumes had near lit themselves. During the last week he had worn Colin McCabe's duds. But McCabe's clothes, too tight in the shoulders, too loose around the middle, weren't exactly fit for social calling. Though Josh didn't look forward to the prospect of sashaying around the Hoffsteaders' new barn showing off his "bride," he'd be damned if he would go to this hoopla looking like someone who couldn't dress himself.

Besides, Tess wanted them to look like a respectable married couple, and Tess, in spite of her unwomanly ways and touchy independence, didn't deserve to be shamed by the man on her arm. She was an honest woman with a good soul, and over the past week, Josh had come to respect her. How could he not respect someone, man or woman, who feared neither hard work, wild cattle, ill-natured horses, or equally ill-natured men.

Since the women were taking their own sweet time, Josh set the wagon brake and climbed down to sit in the shade of the porch. The foreman gave him an appraising look. After a moment of silence, he nodded. "Tonight will be a good time. Rosie can dance a barn down, and Tess . . ." He hesitated and gave Josh a meaningful look. "It's time Tess learned that she's a woman."

Josh snorted. "Don't look at me for that, amigo. I'm temporary here."

"A man could do worse than to settle on the Diamond T."

"A man could get killed settling on the Diamond T unless Tess McCabe wanted him here."

Miguel smiled. "Tess Ransom, now. She is Tess Ransom."

Josh chuckled, trying to picture Tess as any man's wife. Tess Ransom indeed!

"How come a man like you don't have a real wife?" Miguel asked. "There are more women here now that the Apaches are not trying to kill everyone."

"I could ask you the same question," Josh replied gruffly.

Miguel snorted. "My mother was Papago, my father was Mexican. The respectable women of both my mother's people and my father's people look at me like I have a disease."

Josh nodded. Every kind of people hereabouts looked down their noses at every other kind of people. The Mexicans hated the Indians. The Indians hated the Mexicans. And most whites despised them both. "Well, for my part, I think that no respectable woman belongs on a ranch in this country. It withers them up, wears them down. Pulls all the life out of them just like sap. I watched it happen to my mother and sister. No need to watch it happen to a wife."

Miguel shrugged. "Rosie is respectable, though she didn't used to be. She likes it here. And Tess blooms like a flower in the desert." The foreman slid a meaningful look in Josh's direction.

Josh chuckled. "Tess a flower?"

The image inspired an upward quirk of Miguel's mouth. "Maybe she blooms like a weed. But nothing will suck the sap out of our Tess."

That made Josh laugh. "I wouldn't exactly call Tess a weed. But she isn't a run-of-the-mill woman. She's more like a—"

At that moment, out Tess walked, knocking all thoughts of flowers or weeds right out of Josh's head. She looked like . . . well, certainly not like any man's wife, but miles from being herself, either. He didn't know what he had expected her to wear to a barn dance—a cleaned-up version of her usual work garb, maybe. He certainly hadn't expected this!

Rosie presented her creation like an artist unveiling a master painting, and Miguel grinned from ear to ear.

"Isn't she beautiful?" Rosie asked.

Tess squirmed uncomfortably in her frills. Josh tried to

think of something creative to say that would be complimentary and not an out-and-out lie. Hell, he decided. This called for a lie.

"You do look beautiful, Tess. And so do you, Rosie."

Clearly Rosie had learned women's fashions from her time at the Bird Cage. Miguel had told Josh all about Rosie's transformation from saloon girl to "respectable lady," relating the story with shining pride and noticeable fondness. But the "respectable lady" still saw beauty through the eyes of the saloon girl. Rosie herself wore a dress that displayed an interesting expanse of chest, but otherwise seemed plain beside the getup she had hung on Tess.

"You don't think I look...uh..." Tess obviously searched for words that wouldn't hurt Rosie's feelings. Uncertainty brimmed in her eyes like tears. Josh wouldn't have suspected that Tess McCabe could be uncertain about anything, and the revelation inspired an odd protectiveness inside him.

"You look stunning," Josh supplied. It wasn't exactly a lie. The first sight of her had certainly just about knocked him over.

Miguel liked Josh's choice of words. "*Sí*. Stunning. You both look stunning."

The mild day made the drive to the Hoffsteaders' place a pleasure. Birds fluttered among the mesquite and juniper, scolding the travelers for disturbing the day's peace. A bright sun ducked in and out of gathering clouds, painting the valley and surrounding mountains with constantly changing purple shadows. Tess stayed silent during the ride, but seated together with legs dangling from the rear of the wagon, Rosie and Miguel volleyed insults in the afternoon sunshine. The jibes flew with practiced ease. He complained that she made biscuits like rocks. She accused him of having the manners of an Indian. Since Miguel's mother had been an Indian, he might have taken offense, but no. He just laughed and said that his Papago mother knew how to cook better than any American or Mexican woman he'd met.

Listening to them snipe at each other, Josh wondered why everyone on the Diamond T snickered behind their backs and took bets on how many months would pass before they set up housekeeping. God himself couldn't explain the ways of women with men and men with women, Josh decided. So why should Josh Ransom understand?

Wagons and people crowded the Hoffsteaders' place, which was situated in the foothills of the Dragoon Mountains among the piñon and juniper. The timber house was certainly bigger than the Diamond T's little adobe compound, and the huge new barn made a perfect site for a neighborly get-together. Rosie hurried to greet friends and bring their offering of food to a heavily laden table. Miguel ambled off to join a knot of men gathered around a keg.

But Tess held back.

"Come on," Josh urged. "We're here. We might as well go in and act like a married couple."

She backed up a step, very unlike the Tess he knew.

"What's wrong?"

"I can't go in there," she admitted from between clenched teeth. "I . . . just can't."

"You wanted to look married."

"It's not . . . that. I . . . I don't feel like myself. All gussied up like . . . you know. Everyone will stare. Everyone will laugh."

He sighed, then held out his hand. "Come on."

She frowned.

"Come with me. Show some guts, woman."

That brought her chin up, as he knew it would. She put her hand in his, and for the first time he noticed the graceful, tapered fingers that looked almost delicate. "This way," he told her and led her around behind the barn, where prying eyes couldn't find them. There he took out the knife he always carried on his belt.

"We'll just make a few changes." A half dozen big silk bows fell victim to his knife before she could object. Several gaudy flounces shared the bows' fate. The resulting dress had simpler lines and showed off Tess's womanly shape. And Tess did have a womanly shape, Josh noted—a slender waist, trim hips, and, well, other attributes that a decent fellow wasn't supposed to stare at.

"There now," he said, clearing his throat and forcing himself to behave. "You look fine. You don't need all those gewgaws hanging on you. They just distract people from noticing how pretty you are."

Tess looked down at herself with a dubious frown.

"You can't get the picture from where you're standing," Josh told her. "You'll just have to take my word for it. You're prettier than a flower in spring."

At that, she snorted. "Save it, cowboy. You don't need to tell me lies."

"I don't lie. You're damned pretty! Haven't you ever looked in a mirror, woman? You've got—well, hell!—you've got everything a pretty woman should have. A nice smile. Shiny hair, great eyes, good . . . well, a gentleman isn't supposed to talk about the details, you know. Just take my word on it. The men in that barn are going to think you're downright beautiful."

She was, Josh suddenly realized. Maybe her man's dress and mean-dog attitude had blinded him up until this moment, but seeing Tess in a dress—now that he'd chopped away some of the excess—served as a revelation. Or maybe she was a woman who took time to grow on a man. She possessed the finest pair of eyes Josh had ever seen—deep green, like a quiet shady pool. Lush black hair and smooth olive skin—bronze even beyond the touch of the sun—hinted that her Irish father had taken a Mexican wife. And from the looks of Tess, her mother must have been a beauty.

She still looked doubtful. Strange to see uncertainty reflected upon that usually confident face.

"Tess, in the one week I've known you, I've seen you climb on top of ornery broncs, face down your obnoxious brother, and push around range cattle who wouldn't mind stomping you into the dust. You can't possibly turn chicken because a few folks have gotten together for a barn dance."

Her jaw stiffened. "Who's chicken? I'm not chicken."

He held out a hand. "Then let's go. It's starting to rain."

Teeth clenched, but head held high, she took the offered hand.

TESS had never felt so out of place in her life as in that barn with the fiddlers sawing out lively tunes, the couples doing jigs or polkas or whatever foolishness they wanted to do, and the other folks eating, drinking, talking, and smiling. Children ran wild through the crowd, getting in the way, tripping the dancers, making off with food from the heavily laden planks laid across bales of hay, but no one scolded them. This was a time for kicking up heels and having a good time. Everyone looked as if they just naturally knew how to have fun. Tess didn't. Colin McCabe hadn't been much for socializing. Work had always gotten in the way.

As Josh guided Tess toward the food, lawyer Bartlett spotted them and waved, a sly smile on his face. Or at least the smile looked sly to Tess, but she might have been just a little bit cranky when it came to Tombstone's one lawyer. And dancing with Meg Riley, the blacksmith's pretty daughter, was none other than Sean. Tess hoped Meg knew what a skunk her brother was.

The thought depressed her, because she hadn't always thought her brother was a skunk. When they had been kids, Tess had been right fond of him. After he left, the two of them had occasionally written letters. Their daddy had refused to hear of Sean, but Tess had loved to read of the places he'd been and the things he had done. Maybe he really did think selling the ranch would fix them both up right. But he didn't have the feeling for the Diamond T that Tess did.

Josh nudged her. "Smile, and stop looking daggers at Sean. You're married and happy. So look it."

Looking married and happy proved tough. Eyes pressed in from all sides, staring at her as she nibbled on chicken and roasted corn, then following every awkward step when

Ransom made her dance. He insisted, despite her telling him flat out that she didn't know how.

"Learn," he told her. Just like a man, always wanting to be the boss, but after a few minutes of stepping on toes and stumbling about, looking like a fool, dancing became almost fun. Tess liked the feel of Josh's arm around her. It was a strong arm. And from close up, the man looked even better than he did from farther away. She liked his face, Tess decided. His eyes crinkled when he smiled, and when they danced, he smiled a lot. What's more, he smelled good, like soap and leather.

Too bad she wasn't some pretty thing like Meg Riley who had been brought up liking the idea of having a husband run her life. Tess was beginning to suspect that Josh Ransom would make a dadgummed fine catch as a husband—for a girl who wanted one.

And he'd said Tess was pretty. Imagine that. Even if it was a bald-faced lie, it was a nice lie, and mighty kind of him to say.

They waltzed by Bartlett and his wife. "You two having fun?" the legal eagle inquired.

Tess gave him a smug look. "Of course we are. Being newlyweds is very romantic."

As the crowd of dancers swept Bartlett away, Tess felt rather than heard a chuckle deep in Josh's chest. "Tess, I don't think you know the meaning of romantic."

She looked up, jaw squared pugnaciously. "I do so."

He shook his head. "Someday, some fellow is going to have the guts to teach you, and I'm not sure I don't envy him."

She would have shown her contempt by sticking out her tongue, but Sean was looking their way, so she settled for a quiet snort. "Some folks don't have time for that sort of nonsense, Ransom."

"It doesn't take time," he replied. "Just heart. Or so I'm told."

"Sounds to me like you don't know that much about it either."

He laughed amiably. "Maybe I don't, now that you mention it."

The conversation got Tess's mind churning about how romance, real romance, would feel like. Dancing with this man, absorbing his warmth, moving to the guidance of his body, feeling his breath trickle through her hair—it all made her feel flustered and achy inside, with her heart jumping around and a couple of unmentionable parts of herself tingling very strangely. Was that romance, or did the flutter in her belly mean only that the chicken had been a little off?

When Miguel brought the wagon around, Tess discovered with some surprise that, once started, the evening had flown past. She didn't really want to leave, but that was pure silliness, because her father had always said that wasting time jawing with the neighbors never brought the beef home or broke a green horse. Still, she wanted to try this again next month, when the Hernandez family had their annual spring get-together. Then she remembered: next month her life would be back in its normal rut, and she would have no reason to get gussied up. Josh Ransom wouldn't be around to make her dance, or to tell her she was pretty.

Unless . . .

Maybe you should try to make this a real marriage, Rosie had told her.

That was just about the worst idea Tess had ever heard. But still, it stuck in her mind like a burr.

By the time the four of them piled into the wagon for the ride home, the pleasant sprinkle of rain that had fallen all evening had changed to a pelting downpour. Luckily, Rosie had packed two canvas tarps for just this happenstance. Tess and Josh huddled under one on the driver's box. Miguel and Rosie shared the other.

The night closed in, dark as a cave, as the horses ploddingly pulled the wagon through the storm. Under the tarp with Josh, Tess felt isolated from the whole world, acutely aware of the man next to her. Their shoulders, arms, hips, and thighs touched, pressed together both for heat and to make use of the sheltered space beneath the tarp.

The contact produced some interesting sensations in Tess. Warm, tingly, heart-racing feelings, even stronger than when they had danced. She wondered, suddenly, what kissing Josh Ransom, really kissing him, would feel like. He had kissed her once, that time that Sean had shown up after their contest on Nitro, but that kiss had been a spur-of-the-moment taunt, a take-this-and-choke-on-it sort of thing. But even that unexpected, annoying kiss had made her toes tingle. What would a real kiss, a thought-out, planned, full-cooperation sort of kiss feel like?

The speculation sent of bolt of wet heat from the top of her head to the ends of her toes. Enough of that! Tess decided. Such thoughts were downright dangerous. They led to thoughts even more wild, like what might happen between a man and a woman who were truly married—not just the stuff in the bedroom, which Tess regarded as something a woman just had to put up with, but the good stuff, like sharing work and worries during the long days, sitting side by side in front of the fire in wintertime, or in the hot summer drinking Rosie's lemonade out in the courtyard, listening to the men tell tall tales.

Damn but these were dangerous thoughts. When a woman dressed in lace and bows, she stopped thinking with anything like common sense. Likely the corset Rosie had laced so tightly had cut the blood flow to her brain.

When they arrived at the ranch, lamps burned in the bunkhouse and barn. Rosie and Miguel promptly jumped off the back of the wagon and headed into the dark house, still holding the tarp over their heads. But something anchored Tess to the hard wooden seat, there under that tarp with Josh sitting so close beside her. He didn't move either. Tess didn't know what his excuse was. She was the one losing brainpower to a corset, not him.

But he stayed, while the horses stood patiently in the rain and the wind tried to snatch the tarp from their hands. He stayed, and she stayed, and the tension that had been building between them all night shimmered like heat. If he tried to kiss her, Tess decided, she would let him. A girl should have a real, no-holds-barred kiss once in her life. He moved closer, and her heart jumped clear up into her throat. Without actually telling herself to present her face, kisser foremost, she did. In the dim light that spilled from the barn, his eyes looked smoky, his focus single-minded. Closer, closer, until she could almost feel the burn of his lips on hers. Then . . .

"It's about time you got home, boss-lady. We got us a problem!"

They sprang apart like guilty children caught with hands in the cookie jar. The wind grabbed the tarp, snapping it smartly and sending a cascade of cold rainwater into their warm, cozy world.

"Henry!" Tess snapped, exasperated. "What the hell?"

"We got about a hundred head of stupid, blockheaded goddamned beeves stranded on a sandbank down in the river, and the river's rising like hell itself opened the floodgates. Luis and me and the dogs have been trying to move 'em, but we need help."

The spell of the night broke as the ranch laid its heavy hand upon her, drawing her back to the real world. "Saddle Ranger for me," she told Henry. "I'll get into some real clothes."

When she got to the barn minutes later, a dripping wet Henry, looking cold to the bone, stood with a blanket over his shoulders while Josh adjusted the saddle cinches of both Ranger and Jughead.

"You don't have to help," Tess told Josh. After all, this wasn't his ranch, and she'd paid him to marry her, not risk his neck trying to move ornery cattle through a rising river before they got their silly selves drowned.

He didn't say anything, just swung aboard Jughead. Tess wasn't about to argue. If the man wanted to help, she wouldn't turn him down.

They rode for twenty minutes alongside the churning San Pedro before Luis's cussing, the dogs' barking, and the bawling of frightened cattle carried to their ears. Tess cursed the darkness. All she could see were black-on-black shadows. She could make out Luis only because his shadow rose taller than the cattle's. Frantic barking pierced the night above the pandemonium. Bold cattle dog Rojo must have crossed when the water was lower. Tess doubted he would be able to fight the current now. Rojo's son Chief, not as bold as his father, barked in frustration from the near bank.

Without saying a word, they all three headed straight for the water. Ranger was Tess's favorite mount. The big buckskin gelding would go anywhere or do anything she asked, which didn't say much for his brains but spoke volumes for his heart. He didn't hesitate, but plunged into the flood. Josh, mounted on the somewhat smarter Jughead, had a fight on his hands, but he finally goaded the horse into the swirling water. Henry's mare, already tired from a night's work and having already swum the river a time or two, absolutely balked. No amount of spurring would send her down that path again.

Ranger swam steadily while Tess tried not to think of unseen dangers the swirling current might send careening toward them. Whole trees torn from the bank could ride the flood and spell death for an unlucky rider. Whirlpools and eddies could suck horse and rider beneath the churning water. Floating mats of vegetation could sweep them downstream like a lethal broom. Crossing such a flood during the day was dangerous. At night it was just damned foolhardy.

But the fool cattle would simply stand there and drown while the river ate at their sandbar.

Both Ranger and Jughead climbed onto the sandbar at the same time, carrying rain and river-drenched riders. Luis raised his arm in the darkness and Rojo barked a greeting.

"Take the rear," Tess told Josh.

He didn't argue.

Luis already had the left flank in hand, and Rojo read the situation as any good cattle dog would and harried the beeves on the right. After squinting through the darkness for a few minutes, Tess spotted the lead cow, the animal whose loud bawling drove the others to greater panic, the animal they would follow if she could be persuaded to reason.

Tess urged Ranger through the churning mass of cattle and tried to cut her out. The cow wanted none of it. Tess cursed, but the cow didn't care. The wind snatched away Luis and Josh's shouting. Even Rojo's hoarse barking whipped away into the night.

"Well, damn it all, anyway!" Tess maneuvered upwind of old bossy and let her lasso fly. Three tries later, it hooked around the lead cow's horns. "I don't care if you want to go or not, flea-brain. You're going."

At a touch of Tess's heels, Ranger tightened the rope and pulled the struggling cow toward the water. She bawled and bucked, went to her knees, and struggled like a fish on the end of a line until the current snatched her feet from beneath her. Then she followed instinct and swam, striking out for the opposite bank, where Henry and Chief waited to welcome her. Tess snubbed up the rope and swam beside the cow on Ranger to keep her headed in the right direction.

Under the goading of the two men and dog, the beeves began to move, mindlessly following the lead cow. Josh and Luis kept the animals in a tight knot in the current. When the last one climbed onto dry land, Josh turned Jughead back into the current. Tess's heart caught in her throat as he lunged up onto the rapidly shrinking sandbar and scooped a dripping Rojo onto the saddle in front of him.

Tess would have gone back for the dog, who—forty pounds dripping wet—didn't have the bulk to fight the still-rising current. A cowboy didn't leave a good cattle dog, or even a bad cattle dog, behind. The dogs were part of the family. But for Josh to do it, without even being asked—well, there she went turning to mush again, and she couldn't blame a corset this time.

She didn't have anything to blame at all, except herself, when she met him at the river's edge, leaned over Rojo's wet body, and gave Josh Ransom that full-cooperation kiss she'd thought about all evening. And suddenly the rain, the wind, her drenched hair and soggy clothes no longer were cold.

NEXT morning, Tess slept long past her usual predawn rising time. Perhaps her slothfulness resulted from stumbling to bed in the wee hours of the morning after hours spent cold, drenched, and in danger of losing both her cattle and her life. Or perhaps she snuggled more deeply into her bed because of the dreams entertaining her sleep. The dreams featured Josh Ransom in a prominent role. Josh smiling, Josh shaving in front of the little mirror hung outside the kitchen door, Josh riding Nitro and giving her that smug look that he did so well, Josh hauling poor Rojo onto his saddle and letting the dog kiss his face. Then Tess was kissing his face.

Josh kissing. Yes indeed, that was the meat of the dream, complete with heart-thumping, blood-boiling bolts of sensation that shot through her like lightning.

Periodically she woke, soft and warm with remembered sensations, and in those brief conscious minutes, having a real-life husband didn't seem like such a bad idea, as long as that husband was Josh. In fact, in those otherworldly moments between one dream and the next, having the man here day and night seemed a hell of an idea. Why had she ever thought that it wasn't?

Sun streamed through the bedroom window and made square patterns on the bed when Rosie marched in and put an end to Tess's dreams.

"Aren't we the lazy one this morning!" Rosie punctuated her comment with a sharp slap to the lump beneath the covers that was Tess's rear end.

"Ow! Don't! I'm getting up!"

"Well, you'd better, because you've got business to attend to in the kitchen."

Tess stuck her head out from beneath the blankets. "What business?"

"Just you get up and find out. And don't be too long about it."

Tess grumbled as she rolled out of bed, pulled on clean jeans and a cotton shirt, and quickly plaited her hair into one long braid. She couldn't think of a thing she needed to take care of in the kitchen, except maybe grabbing some breakfast. What had Rosie all stirred up this morning?

She found out when she walked into the kitchen to find Josh sitting at the table. At the sight of him, her dreams hit her smack in the chest and nearly stopped her breath.

She greeted him normally, even though heat climbed into her face. "Ransom."

"Tess."

His expression looked a bit grim. And at his feet lay a small carpetbag that belonged to Miguel. What was this? After last night, he couldn't still be . . . still be—

"I'm leaving this morning, Tess."

Her heart nearly stopped. "Leaving?"

"I told you I would go at the end of two more days. Two days is up."

Right. But he would change his mind if Tess told him she wanted him to be a real husband, that he could be master—well, assistant master—of the Diamond T. Any man's head would turn at a precious gift like the Diamond T.

Rosie stood by the stove, plump arms crossed over her chest, regarding Tess with a "what are you going to do now?" expression.

"Rosie, git!" Tess didn't intend to make this bargain in front of witnesses.

Rosie got, but not without sending Tess a look over her shoulder. She pulled the curtain closed behind her, leaving Tess and Josh alone. Tess started talking before she lost her nerve.

"I know you said two days, but things have changed. I don't think it would be a bad idea for you to stay. I mean, at first I thought you were a sot and a bum, but you're not. You're steady, and you're good with horses, and you know cattle. And . . . and I don't mind your company. Not at all.

I figure we're already married, so that's out of the way. You might as well stay."

He replied with an awkward silence, and the muscle at the hinge of his jaw twitched. Tess tried to tell herself that he was overwhelmed by his good fortune, but her heart sank.

"You could run things right along with me," she said. "This is a fine ranch, with good people. It's a better life than, well, whatever . . ."

Tess stared at the toe of her boot, wanting to take back her babbling. She sounded stupid, saying all the wrong things. But what did a girl say to a man to get him to stay?

The crease between his brows deepened. "Tess—"

"Last night . . ." She couldn't let him start. Somehow, he had to understand. "Last night you did great. And we . . . we . . ." Did she actually need to mention the kiss? The kiss she had started and he had finished, that had turned into two kisses, then three, and then a silence that had seemed heavy with affection, or maybe something more urgent than mere affection.

"Tess . . ." He sighed. "Last night . . . I took advantage of you. I apologize."

He took advantage of *her*?

"I can't stay, Tess. I have a place of my own, over by Arrivaca, and I sure as hell need to get back to it. I'll come back and make sure you get that deed of yours, and then we can talk about this. And if you want, you can just forget the money. I'll get what I need somewhere else."

A lead weight descended on Tess's stomach. She thought she might actually throw up. The money. He cared about the money, not the Diamond T. Not her. Of course. How could she have forgotten about their bargain? Josh Ransom had married her for money, had stayed at the ranch day after day, because of the money.

The lead weight started to heat, to bubble, to boil, firing her blood and sending color racing into her cheeks.

"I'll get your goddamned money."

He followed her to the jar where she kept her cash, and when she turned around, he stood so close that she nearly slammed into him. With a forceful push, she knocked him backwards. "Go ahead and leave." She stuffed a roll of bills into his shirt pocket. "And don't do me any favors by coming back. I can take care of myself. I can take care of my ranch, and my own business. And I don't the hell need you!"

Then she fled the room before he could see the tears gathering in her eyes.

Chapter Five

JOSH SAT BACK hard onto the stony ground, his clothes as well as his hands—and one long smear on his cheek—grimy with blood and muck. He exhaled a deep sigh, every bit as exhausted as the cow that had just given birth, but also content in the day, the blue sky, the warm spring air, and the satisfaction of being where he wanted to be and doing what he wanted to do.

Only one thing wasn't quite right in his life, and that was something he didn't want to think about right then. He was too tired, and his mind wasn't up to the task of Tess McCabe.

No, he wouldn't think about her.

The cow lumbered to her feet, and Josh did the same. The bull calf, eyes blinking at the world he had just been launched into, uttered a wondering bleat.

"Okay, kid." Josh rubbed the newborn's slimy neck with rough affection. "Let's get you on your feet."

He gave the wobbly little creature a hand at getting all

four feet beneath him, then nodded in satisfaction as the little fellow instinctively went for the chow wagon. Birth never failed to leave him in awe. It was a wondrous thing to behold.

Some men, a bothersome inner voice nagged, got to watch their own babies open eyes to their first view of the world. Men with wives. Men with families. Men who didn't have to face an empty house at the end of each day.

But the Double R ranch house wasn't empty, even though David had hightailed off to look for gold in Colorado. Marguerita, chubby and amiable, cooked, cleaned, and tried to ride herd on every part of his life. Eight hired hands lived in the bunkhouse only a hundred feet from the house, and more often than not, they tromped through the Double R kitchen, begging an extra roll or piece of pie from Rita or stopping in the main room to talk about this cow or that horse or the rustlers who liked to heist a few beeves and then hop over the border to Mexico.

No, Josh didn't lack for people in his life. He had plenty of people.

But not the right person, the annoying voice insisted. Josh did his best to ignore it.

He left the cow and her new son to themselves and led his horse the short distance to a tank just over the rise. The little man-made depression trapped rainwater for the cattle—when the weather blessed them with rain. Today the tank stood full. The storm two weeks ago that had trapped the Diamond T cows had been followed by smaller rains that filled the depression and turned the landscape spring green.

The green of Tess McCabe's eyes.

Damn! He wasn't going to think about her. Josh stripped off his filthy shirt and dunked himself into the water, head, shoulders, and chest. The cold, clean shock felt good. This was probably the same cold rainwater that had fallen from the sky two weeks ago when they had struggled to save those blockheaded beeves. Images crowded his mind. Tess with her hair drenched and hanging in her face. Tess plunging into the water, fearless of danger. Tess leaning over and kissing him, a wet, aromatic dog in between them.

Kissing him . . . What a kiss that had been. It had inspired him to throw away all gentlemanly instinct and take full advantage of her momentary weakness. What a kiss indeed. It had heated his blood all through the night and convinced him that he had to leave then, right then, or get so deeply entangled with that astonishing, surprising, engaging woman that he would never break free.

Had he truly broken free? Did he really want to break free?

Josh groaned and dunked himself again. Surely enough cold water would bring him back to his senses.

But later that night Tess crept back into his thoughts as he sat in front of the fireplace mending a shirt by the light of a kerosene lamp. Rita came in from the kitchen, where she had been washing the supper dishes. Even with his eyes on the torn seam of the shirt he felt her disapproving frown.

"If you would get yourself a wife like most men you wouldn't have to do that, Señor Ransom."

He had a wife. Sort of. But not really.

"What do I need with a wife when you're the best cook north of the Mexican border, Rita?"

"Ha! Excuses! You are just like your father, may he rest in peace! The Ransom men don't grow from boys to men. You, and Señor David, and your father. When a boy grows to a man, he takes a good wife, raises a family."

Josh gave up and put the shirt aside. "Rita, my father had a wife, in case you didn't notice. She's living in Tucson with my sister."

"You see!" She waved a chubby finger in his direction. "What woman did he choose? A boy's dream, your mother is, not a man's. Soft and beautiful, fit only for decorating some rich man's arm. It is no wonder that she wilted like a flower here. A ranching man must choose wisely—a real woman, not a flower."

"Marguerita . . ." He always called her by her full name

when she annoyed him. Not that annoying him bothered her a bit. She seemed to think of it as her duty. "Why the lecture?"

She shrugged. "The place is very lonely right now. Señor David is gone."

"He'll be back when he gets tired of looking for gold."

"But not to stay. And you, señor, have had your face dragging on the ground since you came home."

"I have not."

"You should be happy. You have the cattle back, don't you? My man Carlos says the calving has started, and everything is well. So I think to myself, why does Señor Joshua frown all the time and bark at his people like an angry dog?"

"I do not frown all the time, and I only bark when barking is needed."

She answered with an indignant "Hmph! You live an unnatural life, señor. Man was not meant by the Almighty to live without a wife."

"Only women think that," he shot back.

She dismissed that with a wave. "Boy, that's what you are. A boy. You Ransoms never grow up." On that sour observation, she donned her shawl, grabbed up the shirt he had been mending, and marched out to join her husband, Carlos, the foreman, in the little house they shared. "I will take care of the shirt," she groused, "because you do not have a wife as you should. So the rest of us must suffer. Hmph."

Josh had to smile as Rita banged the door behind her. The lecture rang familiar, because he got one at least once a month. Rita wanted children to fuss over. Hers were grown and gone, so now she wanted his.

If Marguerita knew he was legally hitched, she would dance with glee—until she met Tess, that is. Tess McCabe sure as hell wouldn't be caught dead mending any man's shirt. Josh would be willing to bet on it. And he doubted Tess could bake a pie or make fluffy biscuits.

But she could ride as if she were born on a horse. She could throw a rope over a set of horns or snag a steer's foot

in a single toss. Flooding rivers didn't faze her. Cold and
wet didn't stop her. She feared nothing—except losing her
home and her way of life, and maybe being laughed at by
people who didn't understand her worth.

No one who really knew Tess McCabe would laugh at
her, Josh reflected. She marched to a different drum, perhaps, but along that march she had become a special sort
of woman. Strong, proud, undaunted by things that sent
most women into a tizzy. But when she took off those work
clothes and got dressed up like a woman, run for cover, because Tess could knock a man's socks right off his feet.

Or kiss his lips right off his face. Tess McCabe kissed
like an angel. No, not an angel, she kissed like a woman.
A hell of a woman.

A woman who would likely shoot him if she saw him
again, considering the way he had left. By now she would
have remembered why she didn't want a man messing up
her life. And she sure as hell wouldn't want to leave her
precious Diamond T to be his wife for real, even if he
asked her.

But then, there had been that kiss. . . .

MIGUEL scraped the mud from his boots before he came
into the house, where Tess was helping Rosie put dinner on
the table. The aroma of Rosie's beef stew mingled with the
warm scent of freshly baked bread, and Miguel inhaled
appreciatively.

"You look like a drowned rat," Tess commented.

"You didn't look much better an hour ago," Rosie reminded Tess.

Tess, Miguel, and Luis had spent most of the day beating the brush looking for mired cattle. Tess had come in
early to look over the accounts. Her freshly braided hair
still dripped water down the back of her shirt.

"Can't complain about the rain," Miguel said. "The way
the cows are dropping calves, we'll need the good pasture
this summer."

"You'll never hear me complain about rain," Tess agreed. "Not in this country. Even if it does make more work." She smiled. "Even if it does make you—and me too—look like something that the high water swept in."

She put a tureen of stew on the table as Miguel sat in his accustomed spot. "Where's the others?"

"In the bunkhouse, cleaning up. Henry's been cleaning the barn all day, and he smells worse than a cow. And you can't see Luis for the mud. Compared to those hombres, I look dressed for company. And speaking of company, Don Sebastian de Moros will be along any day now, I'm thinking. I heard in town yesterday that he's bringing another herd of those long-legged Spanish horses he breeds. I was thinking we could pick up a few from him this year. Improve the mustang blood in what we're turning out."

"He always wants a lot of money," Tess said, tucking into her plate of stew.

"Worth it," Miguel replied.

"Maybe. We can think about it when he shows up." Normally, Tess loved an evening of talk about horseflesh, cattle, and plans for the future of the Diamond T, but lately she couldn't maintain much interest. She still loved the land, loved the ranch, but her former single-minded concentration had disappeared. Her mood had been gloomy as the gray spring skies.

A week later, the sun shone brightly from a clear blue sky and wildflowers perfumed the warm spring air, but Tess's mood hadn't improved. It dropped yet another notch as the familiar figure of her brother, Sean, rode down the road toward the house.

"Just what I need," she muttered to Rosie. They were busy hanging wash on a line strung between the main house and the little house on the other side of the courtyard.

"Have patience, Tessie girl. He is family."

"Which means we're stuck with him for life," Tess grumbled. "Joy."

Sean rode up to the courtyard wall and grinned at Tess. "Howdy, Sis. How's life treating you?"

"Thought you'd be headed back to California by now," Tess grumbled. "Heard that old Maisie at the hotel threatened to take a broom to you unless you paid your bill."

"A minor misunderstanding," Sean said. "We worked it out."

Tess knew that Sean had been hanging around town talking to lawyer Bartlett. She'd had reports from the men that her brother spied on the ranch as well, probably trying to see if her so-called husband was still here. Tess had grown so weary of this deception she could spit, preferably hitting both Sean and lawyer Bartlett with the same effort.

"You're looking good, Tess. Marriage must agree with you."

"Right," Tess snapped. "I'm sure you mean that."

"Mind if I stay and chat awhile?"

"I could stop you?"

He just smiled.

While Sean put his horse in the barn, Tess thought furiously about what she would do. If he had been slinking around as the men said, he probably knew that Josh was gone.

With more violence than necessary, she snapped a wet shirt into the breeze with a sharp cracking sound. Had it connected with someone's backside, the wet material would have delivered an attention-getting sting. She could think of several backsides that would be good targets.

"Miguel is waving from the casita," Rosie told her. "He wants you to come."

"Later," Tess groused. "First I have to send Sean packing. Somehow."

Sean ambled through the courtyard gate, picked up a bedsheet, and helped Tess pin it on the clothesline. "I don't see your husband about. What's his name?"

"Joshua." Joshua Ransom. She wouldn't forget the name again. Not ever, as much as she might try.

"Haven't seen him in town, either."

Tess kept her mouth shut. Lying made a person tired, and she didn't have the energy for it.

"I found out a thing or two about your husband. Want to hear?"

"I doubt you know anything I don't," Tess said through clenched teeth. "After all, we *are* married."

They picked up another wet sheet. "Did you know he has a big spread over by Arrivaca?"

"So?"

"And his brother, the fool, gambled away their entire herd of beeves? Ransom came to town because he had a friend at the bank. Tried to hit him up for a loan to get his cattle back."

So that was why he had wanted her three hundred dollars. That was why he had been desperate enough to marry her. Tess could understand a man—or a woman—going to any lengths to save a ranch. Look at what she had done. Too bad her scheme seemed doomed to fail, thanks to Sean and that lizard Bartlett.

She hoped Josh Ransom had gotten his beeves back.

"Tess!" This from Miguel, impatiently beckoning from the doorway of the little house. Tess ignored him. Whatever it was, she could take care of it later.

"Are you two gonna pin up that sheet or stand there staring at each other like two bad-ass dogs?" Rosie complained.

Stiff-jawed, Tess draped the sheet over the line. Sean sighed unhappily. "Tess, listen, will you?"

"I got ears."

"This isn't anywhere near a real marriage you got with this Ransom fellow. You know it. I know it. And it won't be hard to prove to Bartlett, who's got the judge wrapped around his finger, anyway, if it comes to that. But hell, I don't want this ranch. To me it's just a hunk of dirt and sand that's full of bad memories."

She gave up any pretense of hanging the wash and focused a level green stare on her brother. "Sean, if you don't want the Diamond T, then go away. Just go away."

"No. I won't. Because it's not fair that our rat of a father didn't leave me anything. Not a blessed thing. Do you think that's fair?"

"You left."

"I lived here fifteen stinking years." He kicked at the dirt with the toe of his boot. "The only fair thing is to sell the place and divide the money. We should get enough so that I could go back east and go to college. That's what I've always wanted to do. And you wouldn't have to work yourself to death on this stinking ranch. You could get married for real, maybe. Hell, Tessie, when you're not covered in dust and cow muck, you're not half bad to look at. I'll bet you could find someone to settle down with you."

Tess wondered if strangling him would be worth getting strung up.

"Tess, you're just as stubborn as the old man was. I put up with just as much as you did."

Not nearly as much. Still, if she were to be entirely fair about it . . .

But Sean continued and took all inclination to charity right out of her mind. "I just wasn't good enough to shine beside the princess of cow pies," he said bitterly, "the queen of dust and dirt and horse sweat."

"You piece of—!"

An unexpected voice interrupted. "That's my wife you're talking about, you horse's ass. I suggest you apologize to the lady."

Both Tess and Sean gaped at Josh Ransom, while Rosie folded her arms and looked on with a satisfied smile. "Where did you come from?" Tess demanded.

He strolled over, casual as you please, and laid an arm across her shoulders. "Sweetheart, I told you I'd be back sooner than an eye can blink. Didn't I?"

Too astounded to answer, Tess just stared.

Leaning on the door frame of the little house, Miguel said, "I tried to tell you." He shook his head and muttered something that sounded like *Idiota,* but Tess couldn't be sure.

Sean looked skeptical. "Give it up, you two. Everyone knows you're faking it."

"Really?" Josh sounded as if he were enjoying himself. "Is this faking it?"

Before Tess could pull away, Josh's mouth came down upon hers. Then she decided that she didn't want to pull away. She should have been embarrassed with such an audience looking on, but embarrassment didn't even occur to her. This kiss felt too right, too much like fate, and just too dadgummed good. Her arms wound around him, pulling him closer—that wonderfully wide, wonderfully hard chest. The broad, sturdy shoulders. The narrow hips that pressed so close to hers. Oh my! She had missed him!

Finally, he pulled back just a bit, and softly against her mouth posed a question only he and she could hear. "Marry me for real, you incredible woman? I don't want the Diamond T. I just want you."

Then while Tess tried to keep her knees from buckling, he grinned at Sean. "Did that look fake to you, college boy?"

ROSIE wept against Tess's shoulder, turning her shirt into a soggy mess. Smiling, Tess patted the older woman's back. She had smiled a lot these past two days, more than she had smiled in her entire life, it seemed.

"I'll miss you so much," Rosie sobbed, pulling back a bit.

"What could I do?" Tess spread her hands helplessly. "He needs me, poor man."

"Ha. You don't fool me for a minute, my girl. You love the man, and he loves you." Then she broke down in tears from the sheer sentiment of it all, collapsing once again on Tess's shoulder.

Tess gave her a solid hug. "Rosie, Rosie. I'll be a day's ride away. That isn't so much. Besides, you'll be too busy to do much missing. This place doesn't run itself, you know."

Rosie swiped at her tears with the back of her hand. "It's true. Oh, look what I did to your shirt."

"It doesn't matter."

"Now that you're a married woman for real, you should be wearing a dress."

There Tess went smiling again, even when she should be taking Rosie down a peg. "I have a full day in the saddle ahead of me, and Josh would think I'd gone loco if I put on something as silly as a dress."

Who knew a man could be so sensible? Who knew a man, a terrific, good-looking, strong, competent fellow like Josh Ransom, would want Tess McCabe—no, Tess Ransom—just as she was? Miracles never ceased.

"And now that you're a married woman for real, Mrs. Miguel Cabo, you should be paying attention to your new husband instead of bothering me while I'm trying to pack."

Packing consisted only of stuffing a carpetbag with two pair of jeans, three shirts, a hairbrush, and the hand mirror that used to belong to her mother. There was nothing else in the house Tess wanted to take with her. Her future promised to be far different than her past, and while that frightened her a bit (not that she would ever admit to being frightened), the prospect excited her as well. Josh would be there, and Josh loved her. After the night before, she knew that for a fact. No man could be so sweet, so gentle, and so dadgummed, downright wonderful to a woman without loving the hell out of her. And nothing less than real, no-doubt-about-it love could have convinced her to pull up stakes at the Diamond T and move herself to Josh's place over the mountain.

She wadded up the last shirt and stuffed it in her bag. Rosie still looked at her as if she might disappear forever any minute.

"We up and lassoed me a good one, Rosie. I'm going to be happy as a hen in a barrel of chicken feed."

Rosie nodded, smiling through tears.

"And we caught you a good one too. And don't you go feeling guilty about hitching yourself to Miguel when that jackass you married all those years ago might still be above ground. He's no husband to you, and God knows that. Miguel's your real husband. He's the one who counts.

I always knew when you two were going back and forth like a couple of feisty jaybirds that you belonged together."

Rosie ventured a small smile. "That man needs a woman to keep him in line."

"Well, you kept me in line all these years. Ah-ah! Don't turn into a water pump again. Let's go on out."

Miguel and Josh waited for them on the porch. At the sight of Josh, Tess's stomach fluttered. She grew warm thinking about the night before, when they'd become man and wife for real. She understood now why mares switched their tails at stallions and cows bawled out their invitations to the bull.

Tess grew warmer when Josh greeted her with a brush of his lips—just enough to tantalize, but not enough to be publicly indecent. "Well, Mrs. Ransom, ready to ride?"

Ranger stood patiently under saddle, along with the stocky chestnut that Josh had ridden in on—a gorgeous animal. Josh obviously knew what he was doing with his horses, at least. But he might need her advice when it came to cattle.

Tess smiled a smug little smile at the thought of the Double R, a huge new ranch just waiting for her to start running things right. Along with her husband, of course. A partnership. They would make it work.

"I'm ready."

She kissed Miguel on the cheek. Being a man, he certainly wouldn't cry, but his eyes glistened with suspicious moisture.

"You are my angel," Miguel said. "I will take care of this place like it was my own."

"It practically is, as long as you pay the rent." Tess tried hard to keep a stern tone in her voice. Otherwise she might melt down as mushy as Rosie.

"You sure you want the rent to go to Sean?"

Miguel had insisted upon paying rent when Tess asked him to take over the Diamond T. Rent would make him feel like a rancher, not a caretaker, he said. So Tess had named a small amount and told him to send it to Sean. The money wouldn't send her brother to a college back east, but it would be a start. Sean had been right. The Diamond T belonged to him as well as her.

They rode out to a chorus of good-byes and accompanying barks from Chief, who had been promoted to cattle dog in charge. Rojo trotted by Ranger's side. Where Tess went, he went also.

"I got a dog in the deal along with a wife?" Josh asked when he noticed Rojo.

"Hell yes," Tess replied. "A woman can buy a husband in any saloon in the West, if she has the cash. But a good cattle dog is hard to find."

Finding Home

✫

MAUREEN MCKADE

Chapter One

WINSTON TAYLOR EASED back on his horse's reins, bringing the animal to a halt. He rested his crossed wrists on the saddle horn as the gelding blew noisily and swished his tail at the ever-present flies. Ahead of him, orange, red, and coral rays streaked out from behind deep purple mountain peaks and violet clouds. However, it wasn't the spectacular sunset that captured Win's attention.

Instead, it was the small cluster of corrals and buildings set against the breathtaking backdrop that made his heart slide into his throat. A barn with a pole corral disappearing around its side had been added since he'd been here with his pa, but little else had changed in the ensuing ten years.

Ten years since he'd felt a sense of home and belonging.

Ten years since he'd seen Caitlin Brice.

Unease shot through him, making him question his good sense in responding to the telegram. He'd stayed away all these years, even when his father had made his annual visits to his old friend Tremayne Brice. Win had hoped to protect Cait by his absence.

With his pa dead, the Brices were the closest thing to kin Win had, and he'd broken his self-imposed exile because they needed his help. Seeing Cait again would be difficult, and he was thankful her father would be there to act as a buffer between them.

Suddenly impatient, Win clucked his horse into motion. The sooner he found out why they sought his help, the sooner he could accomplish his task and disappear from Cait's life. Again.

As he drew nearer, the cabin door swung open. A shadowed figure stepped onto the porch and froze, obviously seeing him. He tipped his low-crowned hat off his forehead, affecting a reckless nonchalance.

He drank in her appearance, from the practical trousers that enhanced her long slender legs and slightly rounded hips, to the loose shirt that camouflaged the gentle curves beneath it. Despite the men's clothing and rifle gripped in her hands, there was no doubt Cait had blossomed into a beautiful woman.

The ten years evaporated as Win recalled with startling clarity the smoothness of her bare skin, and the way she'd arched against him, giving herself freely without regard to the repercussions of being with *him*. He'd been fifteen-year-old Cait's first man, and he'd been little more than a boy himself at seventeen.

He sucked in a deep breath and willed his body to ignore the insistent rush of lust that bolted through him. Even after all these years, Cait made him feel like a rutting stallion.

Her lush lips curved downward and her backbone stiffened. Although he couldn't see her eyes clearly, he knew their blue depths would be snapping with that fierce Brice temper—full of fire and passion.

God, he'd missed her. Not just the woman, but the childhood friend he'd known since they'd been knee-high. She was the only friend he'd had while growing up, despite the fact they'd only seen one another two months out of each year. His shoulders slumped as he realized his abrupt leave-taking ten years ago had destroyed whatever affection she'd harbored for him.

Isn't that what I intended, to ensure she wouldn't pine for me?

He dismounted gingerly, ignoring the twinges in his legs and back from long days in the saddle. After wrapping the leather reins around the hitching post, he faced the woman once more. "Hello, Cait," he said in a voice husky with disuse.

"Win." Her voice was cool but she set the rifle down, leaning it against the porch rail.

"I got the telegram."

She crossed her arms, unintentionally drawing his attention to her modest bosom. "I reckoned."

He dragged his gaze back to her face and frowned at her terseness. Where had the talkative girl gone? "The message said you needed me."

Cait flinched, then her lips settled into a grim line. "I need your *help*."

He shrugged. "Same thing."

She glared at him and opened her mouth, then abruptly closed it. She looked beyond him, anger radiating from her ramrod-straight figure.

For a moment, Win was tempted to tell her why he had left so abruptly all those years ago, but the impulse passed. She might understand his reasons, but it wouldn't make her hate him any less. "You and your pa sent for me. Why?"

She continued to stare over his shoulder, then finally relented and motioned with her chin toward the new circular enclosure. Win turned his head and spotted a magnificent black horse prancing around in the corral. His breath caught and held as he watched the stallion shake its regal head, its mane flowing like an ebony river. The animal must have been concealed by the barn when Win had arrived because he surely would have noticed him.

"He's our hope to breed and sell more than the run-of-the-mill cattle horses," Cait continued, her voice not quite steady. "He's got champion blood running through his veins."

"Wild?"

She nodded and slid her hands into her pockets. "Me and Pa caught him in the foothills about a month ago. We got half his mares, too." Her voice possessed a hint of pride.

Win whistled low. "You did good."

Cait's lips curled downward. "Except he won't let anyone near him." She cleared her throat. "Deil can't be tamed."

"Deil?"

"The stallion. It means 'devil' in Scottish."

Win turned back to the stallion, surprised to see it watching them, as if knowing he was the subject of their conversation. "If he can't be tamed, why did your father send for me?"

"Because Pa figured you were the only man who had a chance."

Win smiled. Tremayne had always respected the abilities of both Win and his father, Adam, to gentle even the most savage horse. He glanced around. "Where is Tremayne?" He grinned wryly. "In town drinking his supper like he and Pa used to do?"

There was a long moment of silence. "He's dead," she said without emotion, her arms crossed tightly.

Win reeled with shock, his mind unwilling to accept the flat pronouncement. "When?"

She shrugged. "Two weeks ago."

"I'm sorry," he managed to say past the godawful lump in his throat. Tremayne had been more like an uncle than a friend.

"Me, too." Cait's reticence slipped and Win glimpsed the pain beneath her tough-as-gristle exterior. Suddenly, Win saw a little girl in the woman's place. Young Cait had caught a butterfly, and ran to him, eager and excited to share her treasure. But when she opened her hand to let it fly away home, the green and blue butterfly was dead. Tears had dribbled down her rosy cheeks and Win, two years older, had comforted her with an awkward hug and a gentle punch to her arm.

Win wanted to do the same now, but suspected Cait would thump *him* this time, and it wouldn't be a friendly cuff.

Cait cleared her throat and the brief vulnerability vanished. "I'm sorry about your father, too."

"Thanks, but it's been two years." He paused, and couldn't help adding with more than a hint of accusation, "You didn't come to the funeral."

Her slender fingers curled into her palms and her lips thinned. "Pa was there."

Win took a deep breath, knowing he would only stir up the past more than he had already if he told her he'd missed her. "I wish you'd wired me about Tremayne. I would've liked to pay my respects." His words came out harsher than he'd intended.

"It only would've made things harder." She stared past him again. "I didn't need you."

Win studied her proud carriage and sighed. "No, you never did, did you?" he said too softly for her to hear. Fighting both annoyance and guilty acknowledgment, he fished around for a less-painful subject. "When did you build the barn and second busting pen?"

Her defensiveness eased, but her taut shoulders revealed continuing wariness. "Six years ago for the barn. The corral was put up last month, right before we rounded up the wild horses." She motioned to the barn and the network of corrals beyond the copse of trees. "This was Pa's dream."

Win nodded. "I remember. It was all he talked about—building a horse ranch where folks would come to buy the best horses." He studied the pale oval of her face through the growing dusk. "It was your dream, too."

Cait gazed into the fading brilliance of the sunset. Her skin reflected the orange tint of the western horizon. "It still is." She motioned toward the stallion again. "On his deathbed, Pa asked me to bring you here to tame Deil."

She faced him, then, and met his gaze. "If it were up to me, I wouldn't have sent you that telegram." She paused, and confessed hoarsely, "I never wanted to see you again."

After all the years of believing what he'd done was the right thing, her confession shouldn't have hurt, but it did. Yet he'd brought it on himself. He'd wronged her and her father, and had tried to make it right by disappearing from their lives. But he owed them, and Tremayne's last wish would be his penance. He'd tame the stallion so Cait could attain the dream for both her and her father.

"I understand," Win finally said. "I'll leave as soon as the stallion's ready."

All emotion seeped from Cait's features. "I'll pay you a dollar a day plus room and board."

"You don't have to—"

"Yes, I do. This is strictly business." Steel glinted in her eyes.

"I ain't likely to forget," Win said dryly.

"See that you don't. You can sleep in the barn. Breakfast is at six."

"Fine."

Cait grabbed her rifle, spun around, and marched back into the cabin. She paused in the doorway and called over her shoulder, "I'm a light sleeper and I keep the rifle next to the bed." With that not-so-subtle warning, Cait entered the cabin.

A light flickered and swelled from within, dappling pale light onto the porch. Win remained rooted in place, watching her shadowy figure against the thin curtains until a cool breeze smelling of rain blew across his face.

Win unwrapped his gelding's reins and led his horse toward the barn. He paused by the corral where Deil stood motionless, neck arched imperiously as he stared down at Win.

"So, Deil, are you really the devil?" he asked, meeting the stallion's haughty gaze.

The devil reared up on its hind legs and trumpeted a shrill whinny.

Win instinctively stepped back, even though Deil had no chance of touching him. The first raindrops began to patter against the hard ground, giving Win an excuse to retreat.

Deil would definitely be a challenge, but taming the stallion would be a cakewalk compared to trying to tame his mistress.

AFTER lighting the kerosene lamp, Cait lowered herself to the rocking chair, which had been her father's favorite place in the evenings. Ever since his death, she'd felt comforted by the rhythmic motion of the chair. Sometimes she closed her eyes and remembered how she used to clamber into his lap when she was small and demand he tell her a story.

Sitting there now, Cait could almost hear the faint Scottish burr in his low, rumbly voice. A tear rolled down her cheek, surprising her. She didn't think she had any left, but informing Win of her pa's death brought back the razor-sharp sorrow.

Ever since she'd walked into the telegraph office nine days ago to carry out her father's last wish, she'd been preparing herself to see Win again. She thought she was ready; after all, ten years was nearly half a lifetime ago. However, the brittle reality of seeing him in the flesh released a flood of memories—some sad, some happy, but mostly painful.

For nearly ten years, she'd immersed herself in her and her father's dream. Now twenty-five, Cait was a spinster, but she'd made that choice herself. Her father hadn't understood, but he hadn't pressed either. She was glad he hadn't. How could she have told him how stupid and naïve she'd been? Not one to shirk responsibility even back then, Cait knew she was as much to blame for what happened that night as Win. But when Win had ridden away the next morning without even saying good-bye, Cait's love for her long-time friend gradually turned to hatred.

Unable to remain sitting, Cait stood and paced the length of the two-room cabin. She paused by a window and eased the curtain back to gaze at Deil. Her free hand clenched into a fist as the knot in her stomach tightened. If it were up to her, the stallion would've been put down on the day he murdered her pa.

Instead, Cait had been forced by her dying father to send for the man she despised to tame the horse she hated.

If it weren't so tragic, Cait would've found the irony laughable.

Chapter Two

WIN CUPPED HIS hands and splashed night-cooled water from the tin pan across his face. He gasped, but repeated the action again and again, hoping to rid his mind of the cobwebs from a restless night. Using the bar of soap sitting on the porch bench beside the pan, Win washed and shaved.

He drew the straight razor across his whiskered cheek and jaw, then gave a wry chuckle at his reflection in the small square mirror. Of all that he'd inherited from his mother's half Indian blood—high cheekbones, straight dark hair, and perpetually tanned complexion—he hadn't inherited the lack of facial hair, which would've come in handy. Finishing the routine task, he rinsed with more cool water and plucked a rough towel off a wooden peg and wiped dry, then finger-combed his thick damp hair back from his forehead.

The front door opened and Cait stepped out into the dawn's rosy glow.

"Mornin'," he said.

"Morning," she echoed, not meeting his gaze.

Win wasn't surprised to see her in trousers again. The only time she'd worn a dress was that evening ten years ago. He could see the gown clearly in his mind—pale blue with white lace bordering the low neckline, accenting the soft swell of her breasts. She hadn't resembled the girl he'd known for so many years, but had been transformed into a desirable woman who'd sparked his hot young blood. He'd never forgotten that dress or that night.

"Was the barn comfortable?" she asked.

Win blinked in surprise at her attempt at a civil conversation. "I've slept in worse."

"At least it doesn't leak."

"Good thing, since it rained buckets last night."

She nodded, a slight smile quirking her lips. "Breakfast is ready."

He followed her into the cabin, enjoying the gentle sway of her backside and the long blond braid that fell to her waist. He recalled the smell of honeysuckle, and how her silky hair had slid across his chest and caressed his fingers.

He hung his hat on the rack by the door just as he'd done so often as a boy. A wave of nostalgia startled him. He'd been drifting for so long, he'd forgotten what it was like to think of some place as home.

He waited until Cait sat down before taking his chair, and hid a smile at her faint blush when she realized what he'd done.

"You don't have to act so polite, Win. We've known each other since we were kids," she said irritably.

He smiled, using the charm that had never failed him with the ladies. "But we aren't kids anymore."

She raised her deceptively dainty chin. "That's right. I grew up fast, thanks to you."

Win flinched at the bitterness in her tone. "Seems to me you weren't complaining too much at the time." In fact, they'd spent much of the night together and their youthful passions had kept them awake for most of it.

Cait's cheeks reddened, but she didn't argue. Instead, she picked up her fork and began to eat.

Win swallowed back a smile and dug into a hefty pile of fried potatoes, scrambled eggs, sausage, and biscuits and gravy. Cait rose halfway through the quiet meal to fill their cups with fresh coffee.

"Do you have any hired help, besides me?" Win asked after pushing aside his empty plate.

Cait shook her head as she idly traced the rim of her cup with a fingertip. "I haven't had time to look for a hired hand since Pa died." Abruptly, she stood and carried their plates to the tin wash pan.

"You'd best start looking. You can't do everything that needs doing yourself."

"I manage just fine." If she were a cat, she would've arched her back and hissed.

Win leaned forward, resting his forearms on the table. "You'll work yourself into an early grave."

She gripped the back of her chair and stared down at him. Her eyes blazed with stubborn pride. "This was our dream, me and Pa's, and I'm not going to let it go now that it's so close."

There was nothing of the laughing, innocent girl Win had known in the plucky woman before him. "I'm not asking you to, just that you hire someone to give you a hand."

"No. As long as you can tame Deil, I can take care of the mares and the foals they'll soon drop."

Win dragged a hand through his unruly hair. "Damn it, Cait, don't be so stubborn. I couldn't handle that many horses myself and I'm not afraid to admit it."

"Well, it's a good thing I can, then, isn't it?" She marched to the door. "Daylight's wasting and I've got work to do." Cait donned her wide-brimmed hat and snugged the horsehair string beneath her chin. She strode out, leaving Win alone in the cabin.

He threw himself back in his chair and let loose a string of Cheyenne curses. What the hell had happened to the sweet girl he'd known? Granted, he'd taken her virginity and ridden out the next morning without so much as a good-bye, but dammit, he'd had his reasons. She'd had ten years to get over it, yet she clung to her resentment.

She was twenty-five now, an old maid, even though she hardly looked like some dried-up spinster. Why hadn't she married? Girls got over boys and moved on, but it seemed Cait hadn't.

Why not?

He finished his coffee, hardly tasting the strong bitterness that he favored. After sliding his cup into the warm water, he donned his hat and followed in Cait's wake.

He paused on the porch and noticed the barn door was open. He'd closed it behind him that morning. Knowing it was better to leave Cait alone until she got over her tantrum, Win strode toward the corral where Deil pawed at the ground. As he approached, the stallion tossed his head and snorted, and Win felt the familiar thrill of pitting himself against a strong-willed horse.

Win had been an itinerant bronc buster most of his life, following his father from one ranch to another after his ma died. They were normally paid five dollars a head for every horse they saddle-broke. But unlike some of their fellow busters, Win and his pa never used a whip or quirt on a horse. Neither of them could abide such cruelty to an animal.

Win's mother's people had taught Adam Taylor how to break horses their way. Combining the best methods of both the white and Cheyenne worlds, he and his son had established a reputation as busters who could saddle-break a horse without destroying its spirit.

"How will you do it?"

Win whirled around, startled to see Cait standing beside him, her hands in her back trouser pockets. She was staring at Deil impassively.

Win forced himself to relax and leaned against the top corral pole. "Depends. Do you plan on riding him or will you just use him for breeding?"

Cait narrowed her eyes. "Both. I have to be able to trust him."

"He's a wild horse, Cait. You'll never be able to totally trust him."

"If I can't trust him, I'll put him down."

Win scowled. "You don't have to—"

She faced him squarely. "Yes, I do."

"It'll take some time."

Cait's attention returned to the stallion that stared at them with intelligent and cunning eyes. "Use whatever means you have to. I want him broke."

"I won't whip an animal," Win stated, hoping that wasn't what she meant.

"He's an outlaw." Cait clasped her hands and rested them atop the corral rail. Her knuckles were white. "But he's the best chance for this ranch to succeed, so do what you have to in order to break him."

"You've changed, Cait," Win said softly after a few moments of stunned silence.

"What the hell did you expect?"

Win flinched inwardly at the unexpected cuss word and her venomous tone, but kept his voice even. "The Cait I knew used to cry over dead butterflies."

"The Cait *you* knew is long gone."

The statement was delivered in a flat monotone that both frustrated and angered Win. He'd ridden away to protect her, yet he was beginning to suspect he'd done the opposite.

"Are you going to forefoot him?" Cait asked, the anger replaced by bland curiosity.

Win eyed the spirited stallion, gauging how difficult it would be to lasso the animal's two front legs. If he did, he'd have to take Deil down and tie his hind foot up as well. "Probably," he finally replied. "If he's as tough as you say, I'll have to bust him, too. I'll need your help if I do that."

"Pa tried to do it himself."

Win scowled. "That's a good way to get hurt."

"Or killed," Cait murmured and turned toward the barn. "Let's get started," she said over her shoulder.

Puzzled by her words, Win retrieved his lariat from the barn, while Cait brought another out from the tack room.

She'd donned gloves and was checking the rope with the assurance of someone who'd done it numerous times.

Win had never known a woman bronc buster other than Cait. They'd both been taught by their fathers, with some of their training overlapping while Win and his father visited the Brices. Cait had forefooted her first mustang when she was thirteen years old. Win had been in the corral with her, ready to help if the horse needed to be taken down. He'd been impressed by her skill, but instead of praising her, he'd teased her.

"I'll rope him," Win said, unlooping his reata.

Cait stopped by the corral, her gaze never leaving the stallion. Her breath rasped in and out with rapid puffs.

"Are you all right?" he asked, concerned by her pallor.

"Fine."

Although she sounded anything but fine, Win mentally shrugged and opened the post corral's gate to slip inside. He latched the gate behind him when it was obvious she wasn't going to follow. Instead, she climbed onto the corral's top rail and sat there, her loop in hand and ready.

Deil pawed the ground, his hooves tossing dirt behind him. His nostrils flared widely and he snorted. Not once did the stallion take his eyes off Win, which sent a shiver of unease down the buster's spine as he continued to hold the horse's gaze. To look away would give Deil the victory, and Win had yet to be defeated by a wild horse. He increased the rope's loop as he began to twirl it over his head.

Most horses fled when they saw the rope, and in a round enclosure, it was fairly easy to forefoot a running mustang. However, rather than flee, Deil reared up on his powerful hind legs, forcing Win to retreat, away from the flailing hooves.

"Look out," Cait shouted, an oddly frantic note in her voice.

Win didn't dare spare her a glance as Deil came down onto all fours, and instead of distancing himself from the man as most wild animals would do, the stallion charged. Instinctively, Win hit the ground and rolled toward the rail fence. Deil's left hoof grazed Win's forearm a moment before he cleared the pen and he gasped at the unexpected pain, sucking in a lungful of dirt and dust. Wracked by a coughing fit, Win curled up on the ground, cradling his injured arm against his belly.

Cait stumbled to her knees beside him and rested her hand on his shoulder. "Are you hurt?"

The coughing eased and Win spat out gritty sand. He nodded with a jerky motion, still rattled by the close call. "Just bruised."

He began to push himself to a sitting position, and Cait helped him with a steady pressure on his back.

"You're bleeding," Cait suddenly said. "Let me take a look."

Win glanced down at his throbbing arm and blinked at the red stain across his sleeve. "It's nothing."

Cait glared at him. Knowing he wouldn't win this argument, he carefully held out his arm and was relieved to find it didn't feel broken. He'd earned enough broken bones through the years to know what it felt like. "I've been cut worse shaving."

Cait rolled her eyes at the phrase they'd both heard for years. "You, Pa, and Uncle Adam—one of you could be dying, and it'd be, 'I've been cut worse shaving.'"

Win grinned. "You're one to talk. You said it yourself one time."

"My one and only time." Cait unbuttoned Win's cuff and rolled up the bloody sleeve. Her fingertips brushed his skin, leaving pockets of warmth, and she leaned so close that her flowery soap scent rose above the sour scent of sweat and fear. "When Pa told me I'd never have to shave, I cried."

Win remembered the scene vividly. "You cried more over that than your broken collarbone."

Cait huffed a soft laugh. "I don't think Pa knew what to do with me."

"Good thing I was around."

Cait lifted her head and her eyes were almost warm. "I guess it was." Her attention returned to his injury and her tone turned businesslike. "Let's go to the porch and I'll clean this up and bandage it for you."

Although Win figured a tied bandanna around the wound would suffice, he didn't argue. He didn't want to disturb the fragile harmony between them.

Leaning on her more than necessary, Win relished the feel of her arm around his waist and her unique scent that reminded him of a field of wildflowers. He'd doubted he'd ever touch her again, even in friendship, after her chilly reception last evening. Exaggerating the seriousness of a minor wound was a small sin to have her so close.

She settled him on the rickety rocker on the porch and he wished he dared pull her onto his lap. As children they argued over who would get the rocker. Sometimes they decided by playing a marble game where they would take turns trying to hit each other's marble with their own. The first to miss lost. But more often than not, they ended up scrunching together on the chair.

"Do you still have your topaz cat's-eye?" Win asked curiously.

Cait paused before entering the cabin and studied him blankly, then comprehension filled her face. She dug into her pocket, drew her fist out, and opened her hand. In the center of her palm lay a golden brown marble. She shrugged and shoved it back into her pocket. "It got to be habit carrying it around."

Amazed that she still had it, much less kept it with her all the time, Win realized maybe *his* Cait wasn't long gone. That maybe the spirited but gentle-hearted Cait he'd known most of his life was hiding behind this woman's cool reserve.

"Do you still have yours?" she asked, still standing in the doorway and gazing at him intently.

For a moment, Win would've traded everything to have his lucky marble in his pocket, but he'd lost it long ago. "No."

Disappointment flickered across her face, but all she said was "Oh." Then she went into the cabin without another glance.

Chapter Three

ONCE INSIDE THE cabin, Cait leaned against the door and forced herself to breathe deeply. Between Win's close encounter with Deil and the unearthing of long-ago feelings, she felt shaky and uncertain. Her heart gradually slowed its rapid gallop.

Memories she shared with Win unsettled her, and they jumbled with images of Deil trampling her father. She recalled with horrifying clarity the moment she believed Win would be struck down in the same manner as her father. Terror and helplessness slashed through her, leaving her weak and nauseous. If Deil had killed Win, too . . .

In two long strides, she crossed the room and seized the cool metal rifle in her trembling hands. Damn her father's last words—a man's life was worth far more than a broken promise.

She jerked open the cabin door and stormed out.

Win glanced up from the rocking chair, his injured arm resting in his lap. "Cait?"

She ignored him, intent on her mission. Reaching the corral that held Deil, she lifted the rifle stock to her shoulder and sighted down the barrel at the center of the stallion's forehead.

"What the hell are you doing?" Win demanded.

His appearance so close startled her, ruining her perfect aim. "Stay back." She hardly recognized the growl as her voice.

Deil stared at her, motionless, his head held high as if daring her to squeeze the trigger. Cait was more than ready to take that dare.

Suddenly, Win jerked the rifle from her grip and she made a wild grab for it. Stepping back, he kept it out of her reach.

"Give it back!"

"Not until you tell me why you were going to shoot him."

She made a final attempt to retrieve the weapon, but Win evaded her again. Fury thrummed through her as she breathed heavily. "He's a killer!"

"I'm not dead." Impatience made Win's words curt.

"Pa is!" The truth burst out before she could stop herself. "Deil attacked Pa, trampled him. I dragged him out of the corral before Deil could finish him, but he'd been hurt so badly . . . so badly." Her breath hitched and she dropped her chin to her chest, unable to bear the sympathy in Win's eyes.

"The doc did what he could but Pa was bleeding inside and it was only a matter of time. I was going to put down the stallion then, but Pa wouldn't let me. He said—" Her voice broke and she cleared her throat noisily. "He said Deil was my only hope of holding on to the ranch. He made me promise to send for you to tame Deil." She finally lifted her chin and met his stunned gaze. "And now Deil almost killed you. He *is* the devil. He has to be put down before he kills anyone else."

Win's jaw muscle flexed. "Why didn't you tell me?"

Cait turned away, incapable of facing him as she spoke the words that condemned her. "*I* was the one who talked Pa into going after the wild horses. *I* was the one hell-bent on capturing Deil. *I* was the one who insisted on taming the stallion. If I hadn't been so stubborn, Pa would still be alive."

She felt his solid presence at her back. "If your pa didn't want to go after them, he wouldn't have. And if he thought Deil couldn't be tamed, he wouldn't have tried."

Cait whirled around to find his face inches from hers. "We *shouldn't* have tried, but we did, and now he's dead." She glared over his shoulder at the stallion. "And *he's* still alive."

Deil tossed his head and pranced around the corral, muscles rippling beneath his shiny black coat. As much as Cait loathed him, she admired him just as passionately. He was the most magnificent stallion she'd ever seen. How could such a beautiful creature be so evil?

"I wish you would've told me this before I started," Win said wearily, rubbing his brow.

She pursed her lips, unwilling to confess that she'd been shamed by her guilt.

"Very few horses are actually killers," Win continued, eyeing the stallion. "Even though he trampled your father, I don't believe Deil is a killer. I'm just going to have to take things slower."

"You're crazy." How could he continue to work with Deil now that he knew the horse's true nature? "He nearly trampled you, too."

"I got cocky," Win admitted. "I figured he was just like all the others. Now I know better. I'll be more careful. Besides, your pa thought I could break him."

"Pa was out of his head with pain and fever."

"Then why did you send me that telegram?"

Cait's mouth lost all moisture. "I made a promise."

"And I'm going to keep my end of that promise." Win glanced at the rifle, then held it out to her. "Can I trust you not to do anything foolish?"

Cait's desire to shoot the stallion had faded along with her rage and she took the weapon from his hand with a small nod. Her gaze fell to the drying blood on his forearm. "That wound needs to be tended."

"I'll take care of it. It's just a cut." He smiled and cupped her cheek, brushing her skin with his callused thumb. "Honest."

Cait studied his hazel eyes, seeing an echo of the sincerity and tenderness that had been there so many years ago. She nodded, afraid if she touched him—even to treat a wound—she'd be forced to confront feelings she'd laid to rest a long time ago. "I have to clean out the barn, then I plan to work with the mustangs."

"Deil's mine," Win said firmly.

"All right." Cait swallowed her apprehension and stated her conditions. "But if he attacks you again, I won't be stopped a second time."

Win nodded somberly. "Fair enough. But I don't plan on giving Deil another chance to get that close."

"Pa didn't either."

"I'm not your pa."

Cait recognized the stubbornness in Win's eyes and knew there'd be no way to talk him out of working with the killer stallion. She only hoped her pa had been right in placing his faith in him.

Because she'd lost her faith in Win a long time ago.

CAIT concentrated on threading the leather traces through the worn harness. Ever since her father's death, she'd let things go around the ranch, including cleaning and repairing the tack, which had been his job since he had been more patient and skilled. However, she couldn't tempt fate any longer. Shabby equipment led to serious injuries, sometimes death, if it broke at an inopportune moment. Cait understood the necessity but that didn't mean she liked the task.

A sweat droplet trailed down her cheek and, using the back of her wrist, she swiped away the irritation and stifled a hiss of pain. She'd started working with the wild mares again two days ago, after Win's close brush with Deil, and had earned muscle aches and bruises for her labor.

Although she'd told Win she could handle the work, she was beginning to wonder if she really could keep up with the chores. There were a dozen wild mares, two of which were heavy with foals and three that had already foaled in the last month that had yet to be handled. The eight she'd managed to set a saddle on still had hours of training before she'd be able to sell them.

Glancing up from her task, she spotted Win through the crack in the barn doors. She could see him in profile and his lips were moving, but she couldn't hear his voice. He was probably talking to Deil again.

Ever since Deil had nearly trampled him, Win had done nothing but remain in the stallion's presence. Sometimes he sat on the top rail; other times he rested his crossed arms on the rail and leaned into it. And every time she'd walked by the corral, Cait could hear Win talking to Deil in his soothing timbre. She usually hurried past, hating how her body responded to the seductive resonance of his low voice.

That hypnotic voice was what made him so different from other bronc busters. He didn't just slap a blanket and saddle on a horse, then jump on and claw leather. Nor did he whip the animal until it flinched like a beaten dog every time a person came near. No, Win first gained the horses's trust, ensuring the spirit remained and only its body was tamed.

He'd worked the same magic on her, and his presence here now was a constant reminder of her naiveté and lost innocence. When he'd gone, he'd left a fifteen-year-old to face the consequences of their actions alone. She could never forgive him for that.

Suddenly feeling tetchy, Cait laid aside the harness and stood, stretching her back and shoulders. The popping joints sounded ominously loud in the barn's silence. She strode outside, determined not to look in Win's direction. However, her traitorous gaze defied her intentions and fastened onto his denim-clad backside, framed by brown form-fitting chaps. A plaid shirt spanned his broad shoulders and was tucked into his narrow waist. His body had filled out in the intervening years, transforming a wiry boy's body into a man's lean, rock-hard one.

Cait never could recall the moment when she'd stopped thinking of Win as a bothersome big brother to deciding he was the handsomest boy she'd ever seen. She remembered how she'd sought his attention, showing off her roping and riding abilities, but he'd only teased her. He'd finally noticed her when she donned one of her ma's dresses she'd found in an old steamer trunk.

"Where are you going, Cait?"

She blinked the memories aside and focused on Win, who'd turned to face her. Where *was* she going? "I thought I'd get lunch started."

Win squinted up at the sun. "It's only midmorning."

Was it that early?

"I'm hungry."

He chuckled and his eyes twinkled, as if knowing exactly what had been on her mind. Although he'd been able to read her like a well-worn book years ago, she hoped she wasn't as transparent anymore.

Deil's whinny startled her, and Cait turned to see a rattletrap buckboard rolling into the yard. A familiar frumpy figure hauled back on the reins, and Cait smiled warmly at the old woman.

"Whoa, you worthless sack of spit," the woman cussed at her swaybacked mule.

"Good morning to you, too, Beulah." Cait grinned as she strolled toward the wagon.

Beulah Grisman shook a gnarled finger down at her. "Don't you be sassin' your elders, young lady."

Beulah slapped at her patched and faded skirt, and sent a small column of dust rising from her lap, inciting a raspy cough. She waved a blue-veined hand in front of her face, and her fit subsided. She adjusted her floppy hat, held by a scarf tied beneath her chin, then glanced around and spotted Win approaching from the corral.

Beulah grabbed the double-barreled shotgun in the

wagon's box and aimed it at Win before Cait could explain his presence. "Who's this varmint?" the old woman demanded.

Although the shotgun barrel didn't waver, Win didn't seem to notice. He swept off his hat and met Beulah's suspicious gaze. "Win Taylor, ma'am."

Beulah's lips pursed and her eyebrows beetled. "This Injun a friend of yours, Cait?"

Cait's mouth gaped. Although she knew Win was part Indian, she'd known him for so long that she didn't even notice the characteristics he'd inherited from his mother's half-Cheyenne side. It was just part of who he was. But the way Beulah said *Injun* told Cait the older woman didn't see Win the same way. "He's the one Pa said could gentle Deil," she replied, then added firmly, "He's only a quarter Indian."

From her lofty perch on the buckboard, Beulah spat a stream of tobacco toward Win, narrowly missing his boot. "Ain't nobody, not even someone like him, can break that stallion."

"I'm betting I can," Win said. "My pa was the best and he taught me all he knew."

"He's right," Cait said. Although she didn't owe Win anything, past loyalties were hard to break.

The white-haired woman studied Win from head to toe, then lowered her shotgun. "He's got nice teeth, I'll give him that, and he ain't too hard on the eyes neither."

Cait had to admit Beulah was right on both counts.

"Thank you, ma'am," Win said drolly.

"But that don't mean I trust you. My ma always said you can trust a purty man as far as you can trust a sidewindin' rattlesnake." Beulah continued to eye Win suspiciously.

His eyes twinkled with amusement.

"What're you doing here, Beulah?" Cait asked, hoping to sidetrack her.

Beulah raised her eyebrows. "We was goin' into town to pick up supplies, remember?"

Since Cait lived along the route Beulah took into town, they often went in together. "I'm sorry. I forgot today was town day. Why don't you come in for some coffee while I clean up?"

"Don't mind if I do." The older woman stood and gripped the edge of the seat to climb down from the wagon.

"Let me help, ma'am." Win took hold of Beulah's elbow.

"I'm old, not crippled," Beulah muttered, but accepted Win's help.

Accustomed to Beulah's cussed independence, Cait was surprised she didn't shake off Win's hand. Although Beulah had to be seventy years old or more, her spryness belied her age. Cait had always taken for granted that Beulah would never change, but the years weren't slowing down for either of them.

"Thanks," Beulah said grudgingly.

He merely touched the brim of his hat, then turned to Cait. "I'm going back to work with Deil."

"Be careful." The words were out before Cait could stop her tongue.

Win smiled warmly and creases appeared at the corners of his eyes. "Yes, ma'am."

He sauntered toward the corral, and Cait couldn't help but admire his animal-like grace.

"Pull them calf eyes back into your head, girl," Beulah scolded.

Cait's cheeks heated with embarrassment, although her body's uncomfortable warmth was triggered by something she thought she'd never feel again. Especially for him. "He's an old friend of Pa's," she murmured.

Beulah cackled with laughter. "Iffen you think he's old, you'd best get some spectacles, girl." She sobered and wistfulness eased the weathered lines in her face. "My husband was as handsome as the day was long, too, but he didn't have no backbone like that Taylor feller."

They entered the cabin and Cait poured Beulah a cup of coffee from the pot on the stove. Beulah had never talked about a husband, so Cait was fascinated by the glimpse into her friend's past.

"What happened to him?"

Beulah shrugged. "Got up one morning and he was gone. Skedaddled like some skunk in a chicken coop. Left me alone, without even a young'un."

No wonder Beulah had understood all those years ago—she'd been left high and dry by a man, too.

"You gonna flap your mouth all morning or you gonna change so we can get goin' before the sun gets too hot?" Beulah's characteristic grumpiness returned.

Cait entered the only other room of the cabin and quickly slipped off her everyday shirt, replacing it with a clean blue gingham one. As she buttoned it, she wondered what Beulah would do if she discovered Win was the one who'd driven Cait to accept Beulah's help all those years ago. Beulah would more than likely give him a piece of her mind, and maybe some buckshot in that fine-looking ass. While tucking in her shirttails, Cait laughed silently at the image that thought conjured. Win deserved that and more for what he'd done to her. Maybe it wouldn't have been so bad if . . . She curved her arms around her waist as the humor faded.

Cait glanced up and caught sight of herself in the rectangular mirror hung on a nail on the wall. Dark smudges beneath her eyes made her appear haggard. She'd long ago given up on trying to gain the attention of a man, yet the thought of Win seeing her look so worn out made her wonder if he was now glad he'd ridden away that spring morning so long ago.

Loneliness—a constant companion since her father died and, if she was honest with herself, for years previous— ached like a sore tooth. She'd lost her best friend as well as her first lover when Win had left her. Surprisingly, it wasn't the physical loving, but the companionship she'd missed the most. Not that she didn't have a woman's needs, but she could deal better with those than the loss of Win's friendship. How could she not hate the person who'd made her suffer through hell alone?

"The past is gone. You've made your bed and now you have to lie in it," she said to her reflection. She reached out to touch the mirror's surface. "Even if it's a cold, lonely one."

"What're you doin'—dressin' for a ball?" Beulah asked from the other room.

"I'll be ready in a minute."

After a careless sweep of her hairbrush, Cait joined Beulah.

"In all the years I knowed you, I never seen you gussy up for a feller," Beulah commented with a knowing smirk.

Heat filled Cait's cheeks. Beulah was right. If Win hadn't been there, she wouldn't have changed just to ride into town to buy supplies. People were accustomed to her unfeminine clothing and wouldn't have looked twice.

"My shirt was dirty," Cait said, not meeting Beulah's gaze.

Beulah's snort echoed in the cabin as Cait grabbed her shopping list.

Outside, Cait found Win standing inside a corner of the corral. It was the first time there was no barrier between Win and Deil since the stallion had tried to kill him. Her heart collided with her throat. "Get out of there," she whispered hoarsely.

Beulah wrapped her bony fingers around Cait's elbow. "He ain't your pa," the older woman said in a low voice.

"No, but Deil's already tried to kill him once."

"I've heard tell of Injuns who can talk to horses. That Taylor looks like he may be one of 'em."

"Maybe, but I'm not leaving while he's in the corral with that devil." Cait crossed to the pen and stood there, the block of fear growing in her throat. She forced herself to watch Win, and thought Beulah might be right. Deil's ears were pricked forward, as if listening intently to Win's voice, and there didn't seem to be any murderous intent in the stallion's stance. Could those previous days when Win had talked until he lost his voice finally be making an impression on the stallion?

Win, keeping close to the rails, neared Cait. "I thought you were going into town."

"Not while you're in there with him."

Win shot her an annoyed glance. "I'll be fine."

His words chilled her to the bone—those were the exact ones her father had used. She folded her arms over her chest to hide her trembling hands. She didn't plan on moving until Win came to his senses.

He muttered an oath and ducked between two rails to join her. "I'm out."

Relief made Cait light-headed. "And you won't go in there again until I get back?"

Win's eyes were shaded by his hat brim, but she could feel his exasperation. "If it'll make you feel better."

She swallowed her abating terror. "It will."

Cait turned and clambered aboard Beulah's wagon. The older woman took up the reins, and as they drove past the corral, Win gave them a barely perceptible nod.

"He won't do anything foolhardy," Beulah reassured her once they were clattering down the road, away from the corral, the stallion, and Win.

"I hope not." Cait sighed, releasing some of the tension that bunched her shoulders. "Seeing him in there, where I found Pa . . ."

"Your pa was too old to be breakin' mustangs," Beulah said in her no-nonsense tone. "He tol' me so himself 'bout four months back."

"He never told me."

"He didn't want you worryin'. You know how he was, always wantin' to protect you."

Cait threaded her fingers together and squeezed tightly. "I know and I hated that he treated me like a child. If he'd worried more about himself, maybe he'd still be alive."

Beulah slapped the leather lightly against the mule's rear end, urging it into more than a plodding walk. "He knew somethin' was wrong with you, too, but he never pushed. But I think it hurt him to know you was hidin' something from him."

Cait stared off to the side, barely noticing the summer green or the colorful spill of wildflowers around them. "I couldn't tell him. It would've killed him."

"*You* was the one who damned near died back then."

Cait smiled bitterly. "I made the mistake. It was my price to pay."

"Lots of girls make mistakes."

Cait turned to the only person in the world who knew what had been stolen from her, although Beulah didn't know the identity of the thief. "Pa wouldn't have understood."

Beulah sent her a sidelong glance, but didn't comment. The remainder of the trip into town was thankfully silent.

Chapter Four

WHEN CAIT AND Beulah returned from town with their wagonload of supplies, Deil was alone in the corral, and there was no sign of Win. His horse, however, was in the other pen along with Cait's own saddle mount, so Win hadn't gone far.

Beulah halted the wagon in front of the house and Cait hopped down to unload the dry goods onto the porch. She'd carry them inside later, after lugging the sacks of grain into the barn. Cait walked ahead of the wagon, while Beulah drove the mule. She reached out to open the wide barn door, but jumped back when it was pushed out from the inside.

Wiping his damp torso with a towel, Win smiled at her. "I thought I heard someone drive in."

Frozen, Cait stared at him, her gaze following a single water droplet that rolled down the middle of his smooth, glistening chest. Muscles flowed beneath the bronze-tanned skin, tantalizing her and giving her an odd fluttery feeling deep in her belly.

"Cait, the man's askin' you a question."

Cait dragged her gaze away from the tempting expanse of skin and sinew. "Uh, what?"

"Do you want some help?" Win asked, a hint of amusement in his voice.

"I can do it," she snapped. "Besides, you've got a hurt arm."

He held out his injured arm, which no longer had a bandage wrapped around it. "Good as new."

The gash had closed, and a faded blue, purple, and yellow bruise surrounded the scab. The wound wouldn't be bothered by carrying a sack or two of grain, but she didn't want him near, especially after she'd made such a fool of herself staring at his bare chest. As if she'd never seen a chest before. Hell, she'd seen her pa's chest hundreds of times while he'd washed up on the porch. One man's chest was just like another.

Liar.

"No, I—" Cait began.

"Let 'im help, girl," Beulah interrupted in exasperation. "It 'pears he's used to heavy liftin'."

Not appreciating Beulah's interference or her deliberate look at Win's muscled arms and torso, Cait pretended not to hear. She reached for a sack of oats from the wagon bed.

Big, work-roughened hands brushed hers. "I'll take that," Win said.

For a moment, Cait wasn't going to release it, but her common sense overcame her stubborn pride. She allowed him to take the bag, then reached for the next one.

Carrying the forty-pound sack, Cait entered the well-lit barn and fought to keep her attention from straying to Win's broad, naked back and shoulders. But his body lured her, just as it had so long ago.

"Why didn't you let me get that?" Win asked with a scowl.

"I've been doing it for years." She dropped it onto the sack Win had just laid down.

"Why?"

Startled by the question, Cait stared at him through the barn's shadows. "Why wouldn't I?"

"Your pa—"

"Was getting old. He couldn't do it all himself."

"He should've hired some help."

"How? We were barely scraping by before he died. Capturing the wild herd was going to take care of all our problems. Now my only chance is that stallion." Cait had leaned closer and closer to Win, until her nose was almost touching his chin. His scent—musky sweat and maleness—suddenly filled her, making her heart pound and her palms dampen.

"And you need me to tame that stallion."

His matter-of-fact words and warm breath fanning across her cheek made Cait reel back. "Yes, dammit. I need you. Does that make you feel better, to hear me admit it?" Despite her anger, her voice was subdued.

He stared at her, his eyes softening with regret and apology. "I'm sorry, Cait."

They both knew he wasn't only apologizing for his blunt remark. Cait's insides clenched and she felt the humiliating sting of tears but fought them back. She lifted her chin. "Don't be. I wanted to find out what it was like and you obliged me. I'm glad you left. It would've been uncomfortable with you hanging around like a lost puppy."

Win's nostrils flared and his lips became a grim line. "So it didn't mean anything to you?"

Cait shrugged, while her insides cramped with agony. "It meant as much to me as it did to you, which obviously was nothing."

Win's eyes blazed and he grabbed Cait's shoulders, yanking her against him. Cait felt her breasts crushed to his bare chest and her nipples hardened. He swooped down and kissed her, his lips at first unyielding, then moving like a summer breeze across a smooth pond.

He teased her lips open and swept his tongue into her mouth. Her hands, trapped between their bodies, flattened against his bare, silky-smooth chest. She could feel his heart thundering against her palms and her fingertips pressed into his warm skin. Cait groaned and surrendered, brushing her tongue against his and savoring his unique, masculine taste.

Suddenly, he thrust her back. "I wouldn't call that 'nothing.'"

Hot shame poured through her veins. She'd hated him for ten years. How could one kiss make her forget so easily?

"What're you two doin' in there?" Beulah called from outside the barn.

"Nothing," Cait hollered back immediately, then realized she'd echoed Win's word.

Her face heated, she stalked out of the barn. Beulah had jumped down from the buckboard and was attempting to lift a sack of grain. As Cait approached her, a coughing fit stopped the older woman and she grabbed a crumpled hanky from her sleeve and held it against her mouth and nose.

"It sounds like you're getting croupy," Cait said in concern. "Would you like to come into the house for some tea?"

Beulah shook her head. "I'd best get going." Her voice was muffled by the handkerchief she held to her face.

There were only two sacks left in the wagon, and Cait tossed one over her shoulder. Win, who must've come out of the barn soon after she had, grabbed the other one. Cait ignored him as she carried the grain sack into the barn. She hurriedly dropped it beside the other two and rejoined Beulah, who was stuffing her handkerchief back up her sleeve with trembling hands.

"I can saddle Pepper and ride back to your place with you," Cait offered.

Beulah snorted. "Why in the world you wanna do that, girl? There ain't nothin' wrong with me but some dust gettin' up my nose." Shaking her head and muttering, the cantankerous woman climbed into the buckboard. She picked up the reins and eyed Cait closely. "Now, you best behave yourself, girl. I got to run back into town in a few days so I'll stop by to see how you and Taylor's doin'." Beulah raised her head and gave Win, who lounged against the barn door, a warning look.

"I'll be good," Win said with a wink.

Beulah leaned down toward Cait and said in a loud whisper, "Don't you let him be talkin' you into anythin' you don't want."

Surprised by the oddly phrased warning, Cait only nodded.

Without so much as a wave, Beulah hiyahed her patient mule into a lazy walk. Cait, feeling a frisson of worry for her friend, watched until the buckboard disappeared from view.

Win, buttoning his shirt, joined her. "Now I remember her. She's that crazy lady from down near Otters Gulch."

As children, Cait and Win had only known Beulah as that crazy lady from Otters Gulch. It wasn't until after Win had disappeared that Cait had come to know Beulah Grisman as an eccentric, independent woman with a heart the size of a saddle blanket.

"That's what we used to call her," Cait admitted, then added, "She may be a little strange, but she's not crazy. We became friends after you left."

Win's brows furrowed, probably wondering how they came to know each other, but Cait wasn't about to enlighten him. That chapter of her life was closed.

Cait knew she should shelve the box of goods she'd picked up at the mercantile, but standing in the shade with Win was oddly comforting in spite of the shocking kiss they'd shared earlier.

"How is Deil coming along?" she asked.

Win slid his thumbs into his front pants pockets and stood hipshot, with one knee bent. "I'm going to try to forefoot him again tomorrow morning." He paused and his gaze felt like a caress, sending a shiver down her spine. "I could use your help."

Cait's muscles tightened, hoping she had the strength to face the demon again. "I'll be here."

With the predatory grace of a wolf, Win stepped in front of her. "Can I count on you?"

Her heartbeat climbed a notch or two, but she met his intense gaze squarely. "Seems to me I should be asking *you* that question. I wasn't the one who ran off like some horse thief in the night."

"I guess I deserved that." He lifted his shoulders in a shrug. "I had my reasons, Cait."

"You could at least tell me what they were."

He tipped his head back and stared at the hot blue sky. "It was nothing you did, Cait." He chuckled softly. "You did everything right. Too damned right." Win's steady gaze settled on her. "You were so young. Hell, we were both kids. But I was older and knew better. I shouldn't have taken advantage of you."

Even after all the heartache he'd caused her, she believed his remorse. He was older than her and had often taken the blame for the mischief they'd gotten into together. She laid her hand on his forearm. The light hairs tickled her palm and his skin's warmth brought a burst of heat with it. "What happened that night was as much my fault as yours, maybe even more so. I was the one who had to tempt you with that stupid dress."

"It wasn't a stupid dress, and it sure as hell more than tempted me." He chuckled, and creases appeared at the corners of his eyes. "Where did you get it?"

Cait stared at his laugh lines, suddenly faced with the tangible evidence that they were no longer fifteen and seventeen. They'd both grown up, but scars remained.

"It was in my mother's trunk. Pa never could throw any of her things away." Cait remembered the one and only time he'd tried to sort through her mother's belongings. After opening the trunk, he'd quickly closed it and hurried outside. Cait had followed him and stood in the doorway, shocked to hear her big, strong father sobbing in the deepest shadows of the porch.

"Do you still have it?"

Win's question startled Cait out of the past. "Yes, but that was the only time I wore it."

"I figured you'd wear it to the town dances and all the boys would line up to dance with you."

Cait peered into Win's face, trying to determine if

he was teasing or serious. "I never went to any dances."

"Why?" Win asked, genuinely puzzled.

She shrugged. "I didn't plan on marrying, so it didn't make any sense to go."

"Why?" he repeated.

Becoming annoyed, Cait snapped, "Because."

Win held up his hands, palms out. "Whoa. Don't be getting all riled up again. I didn't mean anything. I'm just trying to figure out why someone as beautiful as you isn't married yet."

Beautiful. Cait would've given the moon to hear him call her beautiful years ago, but now it brought a strange lump to her throat. She forced a nonchalant shrug. "The ranch kept me so busy I never had time to think about it." She glanced at the angle of the sun. "I'd best make us something to eat. It's long past noon."

She felt Win's burning gaze on her back as she walked to the cabin, but there was nothing more she owed him. She picked up the box containing flour, sugar, and coffee she'd left on the porch and carried it inside.

As she put away the goods, she allowed her memories free rein. She remembered how she'd had to lie to her father for the first time in her life to hide her humiliation. How she'd cried every night for nearly a year before the pain became tolerable. How the love she'd had for Win had burned away, leaving ashes of hate.

But their kiss in the barn showed that beneath the hate, love's embers still smoldered.

Cait couldn't afford to fan those embers back to life. Even if Win still held some affection for her, he would undoubtedly ride away again. And this time, even the embers would become extinguished, leaving nothing but the empty shell of a bitter woman with no hope of a family.

Chapter Five

FOUR NIGHTS LATER, Cait bolted upright in bed. She sat there in the darkness, disoriented, trying to determine what had awakened her. A horse's scream split the night's silence and Cait scrambled out from under the muslin sheet and wool blanket. She jerked on her boots and trousers, but didn't take the time to don a shirt over her gown.

She grabbed the rifle propped beside the bed and dashed out of the cabin. Pausing on the porch, she searched for Deil in his pen and found him looking toward the trees. The shrill cry sounded again. It came from the mares' corral, the direction Deil faced.

Cait bounded across the moonlit yard, almost colliding with Win when he hopped out of the barn, tugging on a boot.

"What is it?" he demanded.

Cait slowed her pace slightly to answer. "Something's spooked the mares." She turned and ran, her heart thrumming wildly.

Cait was barely aware of Win following her, his long legs devouring the distance between them. She angled through the trees, not wasting time by going through the wide opening she normally used. Branches slapped her face and arms.

She stumbled to a halt at the edge of the clearing. Before her lay a network of three corrals that Win and his father had helped build. The first pen housed three mares and their foals. The biggest corral held the rest of the wild horses, and the smallest enclosure was where Cait worked with one mustang at a time. The herd milled about nervously, nickering and kicking at one another. Something had obviously frightened them.

"Do you have trouble with cats around here?" Win's close voice startled her.

"Not lately," she replied. "A few years ago two came down from the mountains, but that had been a bad winter. The Duncans and Crowleys lost a few head of livestock, but the mountain lions never came this far south."

Win grunted and she glanced at him. He was surveying the area, his eyes narrowed and body tense. She noticed he wore his gunbelt around his trim hips, obviously expecting trouble, too.

"What is it?" she asked quietly.

He took a deep breath and his nostrils flared, as if sniffing the air, searching for something that didn't belong. Instead of answering her, he prowled around the corral, his gaze aimed at the ground.

Cait remained in place, narrowing her eyes as she watched him through the silvery glow of the nearly full moon. He circled the outer perimeter of the pen, his fluid motions and cautious steps giving her an even more powerful impression of a stalking wolf.

He hunkered down, examining something on the ground. "Come here," he called to Cait.

She hurried over to his side and leaned over him. "What is it?"

Win pointed to a barely discernible indentation in the

loose dirt. "It was a mountain lion. Only one, but enough to get the horses riled up," he announced grimly.

An icy chill swept through Cait and she glanced around nervously, her mind conjuring wild cats out of fuzzy shadows. "But they never come this close to humans unless they're starving. After the mild winter, they shouldn't have any trouble finding food."

Win shrugged. "Maybe it's a rogue. I've heard tell of mountain lions coming into ranch yards and taking a dog or foal."

Cait's grip on the rifle tightened. She couldn't afford to lose a single horse.

"He's long gone," Win said quietly. "At least he's still afraid of people."

"What about the horses?"

"They warned you this time. They'll do it again."

"But what—"

Her question was interrupted by a mare's distressed whinny. With her eyes adjusted to the moonlight, Cait spotted the horse immediately and recognized the mare as one whose milk had dropped into her teats only two days earlier. Usually that meant a foal would be born about six days later, but it appeared this mare was going into labor early.

"She's ready to foal," she said tersely.

Win nodded. "The scare probably triggered it."

Cait's gaze remained on the restless mare that pawed at the ground in between pacing a small area of the corral. "I need to get her moved into the smaller pen so the others don't bother her. I'll get my horse."

"I'll help," Win offered.

"You can do that by keeping an eye on her, then opening the gates for me."

For a moment, Cait thought he'd argue, but Win nodded shortly.

She ran back to the barn and caught Pepper, her pinto mare. Pepper snapped at her, obviously not liking to be bothered in the middle of the night. Cait slapped the mare's nose lightly. "Behave yourself."

Pepper curled back her lips, but didn't try any more tricks.

It took only a few minutes to ready her, and Cait vaulted into the saddle. As she rode out of the yard, Deil neighed piercingly and reared up on his hind legs, probably upset that he was being left behind.

Two minutes later, Cait drew Pepper to a halt by the wild horses' corral.

Win stood by the gate, his hand on the latch. "Ready?"

"Yep."

Win pressed back the bolt and opened the gate just far enough that Cait and Pepper could ride through. He secured the gate behind them.

Cait picked out the foaling mare and used her knees to guide Pepper closer to her. The expectant mare snorted and pranced nervously. "Easy, girl," Cait crooned.

The wild horses separated into two groups as Cait drew near, allowing her a path to ride through. The mare tried to follow one of the clusters, but a shift of Pepper's reins and the well-trained pinto cut the mare off from the others. Cait gave Pepper her head and leaned into the sharp turns as the pinto herded the sweating mare toward the gate leading into the smaller pen. Just as Cait was about to yell at Win to open up, the gate swung outward and the foaling mare ran through it. Cait and Pepper followed, then Win latched the gate.

In a corner of the smallest pen, the mare trembled visibly and her flanks were sweat-soaked. Concerned, Cait dismounted, intent on examining her.

"She's all right," Win called out in a low voice. "Leave her be."

"I want to see if she'll let me near her in case she has problems," Cait said impatiently.

"You'll only upset her more. Get out of there."

Cait wavered between her instincts and Win's order, a rebellious part of her eager to disobey Win, even if he was right. Finally, Cait relented and led Pepper out of the enclosure. With Pepper's reins wrapped around her hand, Cait stopped beside Win.

"We should go back to the house," Win said, his gaze moving from her face down to her breasts and quickly back up. He shifted his weight from one foot to the other. "Most horses don't like an audience when they foal. Wild ones are even more that way."

"What if she has trouble? What if the foal is turned? What if she's too tired to push?"

Impatience flickered in his face. "She's more likely to have trouble if she's nervous, and with us around she's going to be twitchier than a spinster on her wedding night." Again, his attention fell to her chest.

Cait pressed her lips together, irritated that his eyes kept dropping below her neck. She finally glanced down, and saw that her thin gown was pressed against her bosom and the cool air had made her nipples harden. It was obvious she wore nothing beneath the gauzy material. Fighting her instinct to cross her arms over her breasts, she tried not to wonder what Win might be thinking. But the more she tried, the more she couldn't help but imagine what was racing through his mind. Probably the same thing she was thinking when she stared at his bare chest the other day.

Stop thinking!

Shoving the wanton thoughts aside, she forced herself to concentrate on the mare. She didn't like leaving her, but Win had a point. Her father had said the same thing. *Horses been havin' babies a long time afore people was around to get in the way.*

"I'll go, but I'm going to come back and check on her every fifteen minutes," Cait said.

Win shrugged. "Suit yourself."

"I will."

He chuckled, which only made Cait more annoyed. Maybe she was being overprotective, but she had a big stake in ensuring each and every foal survived. She couldn't let her pa's sacrifice be in vain.

Leading Pepper, Cait walked to the yard beside Win, much too conscious of her unbound breasts and the sensuous feel of the cool air against them. Delicious shivers streaked through her, and they intensified when she caught Win glancing at her. A devilish imp made her bump into him and her breast nudged his arm. He jerked away, as if a hot coal had burned him.

She should've thought it was funny, but she was reeling from the wonderful sensations of the "accidental" contact. It brought back vivid memories of the night they'd made love, when he'd done sinfully delicious things to her breasts until she was almost out of her mind with pleasure. No man had ever touched her before or since Win Taylor. Cait had thought about such intimacies with another man, but nobody she imagined could come close to her memories of that night's bliss.

"You did a good job, Cait," Win said as he watched her unsaddle Pepper.

"I learned how to cut out a horse not long after I started walking," she said with a shrug, then faced him. "You were never impressed before."

"I never realized how special you were before."

"Don't!" Her face flaming, Cait stomped into the barn to get some oats for Pepper.

Damn him! Years ago she'd tried everything she could think of to get Win to call her special. The only thing special about her now was being a spinster without her virtue.

She remained in the barn until her emotions were back under lock and key. Returning with her composure intact, she climbed onto the lowest rail and held out the bucket containing a handful of grain for her mare. Pepper crunched noisily.

"You can go back to bed. No need for both of us to lose more sleep," she said with forced lightness. Win's silent watchfulness increased her awareness of him, making her vibrate like a taut wire.

He didn't move. "I kind of like how the moon makes you all silvery-like. Reminds me of that night."

Cait's eyes widened as her heart jumped into her throat.

She clamped down on her emotions and kept her voice bland. "You must be thinking of someone else. It was a new moon that night. No silver moonlight."

"No, it was you, Cait. I'd never seen anything as pretty as you that night."

"I'm not that young girl anymore, Win, and I'm not going to throw myself at you like I was stupid enough to do back then. I learned my lesson the hard way."

She scrambled down from the rail with the empty bucket and strode toward the barn. Win caught her arm, swinging her around. Cait trembled, half-hoping he would kiss her again, then hating herself for being so weak.

"No, you're not a girl anymore," he began softly. He cupped her face in his palms. "You're a beautiful, independent woman who should be married with a passel of kids tugging at her apron strings."

Cait forced a laugh. "Have you ever seen me in an apron?"

Win dropped his hands to her hips and spanned her waist with his fingers. "I can imagine, just as I can imagine you with beautiful blond, blue-eyed children."

Cait propped a hand on her hip, then realized she'd only made her nightgown tighten against her breasts. She quickly lowered her arms. "That's funny. When I was younger I used to dream of dark-haired children with hazel eyes."

Win's hands fell away and he stepped back. "I rode away so that wouldn't happen."

Cait's smile felt more like a tortured grimace. "Don't worry. It worked." She spun around, set the pail by the barn, and grabbed her rifle. "I'm going to check on the mare. Good night."

She was fearful that Win would follow her, but he must've taken her not-so-subtle hint and returned to his bed in the barn. The night was still, broken only by the familiar sounds of the horses, an occasional owl's hoot, and a nighthawk's screel. She shivered from the cool air and wished she had gone to the cabin to put on a heavy shirt before returning to the foaling mare.

Tiptoeing, she neared the pen where the mare lay on her side with a damp puddle behind her. The water bag had already broken. It would be a quick birth.

Cait laid the rifle on the ground and stood motionless, watching as the foal's front feet appeared out of the birth canal. She caught her breath even though she'd lost count of the number of times she'd seen a new foal come into the world.

Over the past years, the significance of each birth had grown for Cait. Ten years ago, she'd felt the beginning of life fluttering within her. Although she'd been ashamed of her condition and terrified of the day her father would learn her secret, the awe of a baby growing within her would make her cry at the oddest times. Sometimes she even imagined herself holding her child as it suckled her breast. There were even moments when she'd remember with joy, instead of regret, the night the child was conceived.

However, four months later she'd lost her baby and the ability to bear more. Now she would give anything, even the ranch, to be able to have a child. Instead, she brought foals into the world, tasting her bitter loss anew every time she did.

The foal's nose peeked out and Cait found herself breathing with the panting mare.

C'mon, girl, you can do it.

More of the head emerged, then the knees, followed by the neck and flanks. Cait gripped the wood rail tight, but she hardly noticed the splinters biting into her palms. Her attention remained focused on the drama in the corral.

The mare pushed again and all but the back legs and hips of the baby were outside the birthing canal.

Cait brought a fist to her lips and gnawed at her knuckles anxiously. She'd seen this happen before and most of the time the back end of the foal was expelled some minutes later. The few times the foal remained locked in this position Cait's pa would help the baby get free of its mother.

Long, fretful minutes passed and Cait considered getting Win, but discarded the idea almost immediately. This was her ranch now, and her responsibility. Win wouldn't be here much longer and she'd have to know how to care for the horses on her own.

The mare tried a few more times to free the hindquarters of its offspring, but finally gave up, her side heaving up and down with her exertions.

Cait's stomach fluttered, but she resolutely slipped between the rails and very deliberately neared the mare. She could see the whites of the mare's eyes, but there was little strength remaining to continue the struggle.

"It's okay, girl. It looks like you might have a small problem here," Cait crooned softly, her voice trembling. "I can help, girl. It's okay. Easy now."

The mare's gaze tracked Cait and she tried to rise once, but was too weak.

"Shhhh. Relax, Mama. You've got a beautiful foal here, but you both need a hand."

Cait slowly squatted beside the mare and laid her hand lightly on her hindquarters. The mare's skin rippled, but she didn't seem overly fearful, only nervous.

"That's right, Mama, I'm going to help you." Cait concentrated on what her father had done and gently took hold of the foal's slime-covered front legs.

"It's okay, little one." With slow steady pressure, Cait pulled downward, toward the mare's heels. Her hands slipped once and she regained her slick hold on the foal. Again she strained carefully, tugging the foal until the hips popped out of the birth canal, along with the hind legs. Cait fell onto her backside with the foal's head in her lap. She remained sitting on the damp earth, eyeing the tiny filly with wonder and joy.

She eased away from the foal and scuttled backward, away from the mother and its newborn. Slipping out of the corral, she tried not to disturb them. The longer the mother lay there, the more blood would be given to its baby through the cord connecting mother to daughter. The mare instinctively would know when it was time to struggle to her feet and break the cord.

Cait observed the new family, drinking in the healthy baby's appearance. The filly's long legs lay tangled beneath her, and it would be a challenge for the little girl when she got around to standing.

It wasn't long before the mare rolled, getting her hooves beneath her to rise. The cord between her and her offspring broke and only a small bit of blood was shed. Mama sniffed every inch of the filly, then began to lick the infant clean.

Cait smiled as her eyes misted. Another healthy foal. There was only one expectant mare left now and she hoped that birthing went as well as the previous four.

"She's a beauty."

Cait whirled around and collided with Win. He grabbed her arms to steady her.

"You shouldn't go around sneaking up on folks," she said, pulling away from him.

"I wasn't sneaking. You just didn't hear me."

She'd been so enthralled by the newborn that she wouldn't have noticed a train barreling out of the trees.

"The foal's hips got locked inside the mare so I had to give her a hand," Cait said.

"I know." He motioned toward her. "You could use a bath."

For the first time, Cait noticed her arms and gown were covered by drying mucus and blood. She wrinkled her nose at the coppery scent that filled her nostrils. "I didn't even notice."

Win smiled crookedly. "I didn't think you did." He reached out and scrubbed her cheek with his thumb. "Here, too."

Although, looking like she did, Cait knew Win couldn't possibly have any type of indecent thoughts of her, she enjoyed his gentle touch. After hating him for so long, she couldn't figure out how she could have tender feelings for him again. Was she that starved for intimate contact that she could be swayed so easily by a simple deed? Even from a man she had considered hunting down and putting out of *her* misery?

"You're right. I'd best go clean up and get some sleep," Cait said, suddenly not liking where her thoughts were headed. She glanced at the mare. "Everything's gone well so I don't think she'll have any trouble with the afterbirth."

"Do you want me to stand guard?" Win asked.

Normally, she wouldn't have worried, but knowing there was a mountain lion nearby and that he'd surely smell the blood . . . "It's not what you signed on for."

His lips quirked upward. "I didn't sign on for a lot of things, but that doesn't mean I mind doing them."

Even as a boy Win had been generous. While most little boys stuck girls' pigtails in inkwells, Win rescued butterflies and bruised hearts. She blinked at the sudden sting of moisture in her eyes. Why had that kind-hearted, compassionate boy left her without so much as a good-bye ten years ago?

"Are you all right?" The concern in Win's voice only made her more teary. "What's wrong, Caity?"

He hadn't called her Caity since . . .

She picked up her rifle and thrust it at him. "You might need this." She whirled around and dashed away, her mind aswirl and her emotions seesawing like an uneven teeter-totter.

Chapter Six

WIN SHIFTED HIS backside on the cold, unforgiving ground. Even with a blanket wrapped around him, the night's chill had seeped into his bones. The predawn glow illuminated the eastern horizon and gave the surrounding mountain peaks a coral blush.

A butterfly flitted past and Win followed its erratic flight from one resting place to another. Win could almost envision Cait in her pigtails and overalls scampering after it. He'd asked her one time why she tried catching them and she'd told him, in her little grown-up voice, that she wanted to give them a home. He'd told her each butterfly already had a home and if she caught it, it'd never find its way back. She'd thought about that for a full day before she started chasing them again.

Win had spent most of the night thinking about Cait, trying to figure out why she was so prickly one minute and soft and sweet the next. Despite his vow to keep his distance from her, he found himself looking for reasons to get nearer.

And that damned kiss. He tried to tell himself it was to prove her wrong, that there was still something between them. But the honest-to-God truth was he'd wanted to kiss her. He'd wanted to do a hell of a lot more, too, but his napping conscience had finally awakened and kicked him in the ass.

Last night had been a test of his resolve, and he'd nearly failed. But how could any man ignore what lay beneath the filmy gown she'd worn? Intimate memories of her had only made it more difficult. He'd managed to hold on to his sanity by a thin thread and had escaped into the barn while she'd gone to watch over the mare.

However, when he'd watched Cait pull the foal from its mother and her brilliant smile afterward, he'd felt something fracture within him. Something he'd fought against ever since he'd ridden out of her life was slowly eroding his determination.

He pressed himself upright and stretched, groaning at the stiffness in his muscles. The mountain lion hadn't returned, but Win didn't know if it was because the cat was long gone, or because it had smelled a human near the horses. Either way, the mare and her newborn filly, which was now sucking greedily on her mother's teat, were doing well.

He caught a movement out of the corner of his eye and turned to see Cait walking toward him. She wore clean tan trousers, a brown and green plaid shirt, and no hat. Her long blond braid swayed with her stride that was both purposeful and feminine. The picture was marred, however, by her somber expression, which was absent of vulnerability and softness.

"No problems," Win said before she could ask.

She didn't meet his gaze, but studied the mare and foal. "The afterbirth?"

"No problems there either. I took care of it about an hour ago."

"Thanks."

Silence surrounded them and Win didn't feel the need to

disturb it. He was tired, not only from the sleepless night, but from Cait's mercurial moods.

She finally turned toward him. "Breakfast is about ready."

He merely nodded and they walked quietly back to the cabin, where he washed up and shaved before coming to the table. The meal was eaten in silence.

"When will you need my help with Deil?" Cait asked as she cleared the table.

Win noticed the barely perceptible shudder that passed through her. "Are you certain you want to help?"

She met his gaze steadily. "No, but I'll do it anyhow."

Startled by her honesty, Win leaned forward, his hands wrapped around his coffee cup. "He's only a horse, Cait, not Satan himself. He didn't kill your father out of mean-ness or hatred, but because of his nature. By putting him in a pen you took everything away from him and he's fighting back the only way he knows how."

"You make him sound human."

Win shook his head. "No, you're the one who's making him human. Hating him for killing your father is like"—he struggled to find the right comparison—"like blaming a gopher for your horse tripping in a hole."

Cait stared at him, her features blank, but he knew she was considering his words. She pursed her lips and shook her head. "I don't like gophers much either."

Win spotted the barest twinkle in her eyes and couldn't help but smile. "Me neither, but I don't blame them for do-ing what they were born to do."

Cait took a deep breath and let it out slowly. "I under-stand what you're saying, Win, but Deil is different. When I look in his eyes, I get the feeling he knows exactly what I'm thinking." She shivered and rubbed her arms where goosebumps rose. "He scares me."

"I suppose if I'd seen him trample my father, I'd feel the same way."

"I don't know if I'll ever stop hating him," Cait con-fessed, her voice husky.

"You will. Someday."

The sound of a horse's hooves interrupted them, and Win stepped over to the window. A man dismounted by the hitching post and strode toward the house, raising a cloud of dust as he slapped his hat against his thigh. Although ten years had passed since he'd seen him last and the man had gained a few pounds, Win recognized him. His breakfast settled like a cannonball in his belly.

"It's Frank Duffy," he said to Cait.

She frowned. "What's he doing here?"

"He used to work for your pa now and again, didn't he?"

"Until he signed on full-time with Crowley's outfit five years ago."

"Miz Brice, you in there?" Duffy called out, pounding on the door.

Cait swung open the door. "Morning, Frank. What brings you here so early?"

The big man's gaze shifted past Cait to Win, who stood with his arms folded over his chest. Duffy's eyes widened then narrowed. "Taylor?"

"Hello, Duffy."

"Never thought I'd see you back here."

Win could feel the tension in the cabin rise, and saw Cait's puzzled frown as she noticed it, too. "Tremayne wanted me to tame a horse for Cait."

"That black devil?"

Win nodded.

"He killed Brice. The murderin' son-of-a-bitch oughta be shot."

"What do you want, Frank?" Cait interrupted, her tone sharp.

Duffy swung his attention back to Cait. "Beulah Grisman's at Doc's place. It don't look good."

Cait's face paled. "What happened?"

"Doc didn't say. Just asked me to let you know on my way back to the ranch. He said the old lady's askin' for you."

"How long has she been there?"

"Guess she come into town yesterday and went straight

to Doc's." Duffy shrugged his meaty shoulders. "That's all I know."

Cait's frightened eyes met Win's. "I've got to go."

"I'll go with you," Win offered immediately.

"No. Someone has to stay around in case the cat comes back."

"Cat?" Duffy interjected. "You got problems with a mountain lion?"

"There was one hanging around the mares last night," Win answered. "One of the mares foaled overnight so there's a good chance the lion will come back."

"I'd best let my boss know. He'll want to put out some extra guards." Duffy eyed Win. "You plannin' on stickin' around?"

"I'm only staying until I break the stallion."

"Glad to hear it."

What Duffy didn't say was just as loud as his words. Frank Duffy was one of those men who didn't like Indians, and always made a point to badger Win when they were alone.

"I'd best get back to work. Spring's a busy time," Duffy said.

"Thank you for letting me know," Cait said.

"Yes, ma'am. I hope everything works out. Beulah ain't the most likable, but she's been around these parts for longer'n most of us." Duffy backed out of the cabin. "Bye, Miz Brice." He glanced at Win and said with less warmth, "Taylor."

Cait closed the door behind him and leaned against it. She looked like she was on the verge of collapsing.

"Are you all right?" Win asked, concerned by her pallor.

She nodded, then grabbed her hat from the rack and opened the door, but paused before running out. "I don't know when I'll be back."

Win squeezed her shoulder gently. "Don't worry. I'll take care of the chores around here."

Cait closed her eyes and swallowed. When her eyelids

flickered open, her blue eyes glistened with unshed tears. "She means a lot to me, Win. I owe her my life."

"Your life?"

She shook her head. "I'll be back when I can." She turned and fled.

Win clapped his hat on his dark head and stepped onto the porch. He braced his right shoulder against the post and watched Cait saddle her pinto mare. What was she hiding? What secret did she and the old lady share?

Cait mounted her mare and trotted down the road. She looked back and waved. Win lifted a hand in return, but she'd already turned away.

Win tipped his hat back and rubbed his pounding forehead. He hadn't expected to see Duffy again. It was men like Duffy who had convinced Win his pa was right. Folks didn't take kindly to an Indian carrying on with a white woman, and oftentimes it was the woman who suffered the shame. It didn't matter that Win was only one-fourth Indian. He'd protected Cait the best way he knew how.

CAIT recognized most of the people on the boardwalk and absently greeted them. She only wanted to see Beulah and find out what had happened.

She stepped into the doctor's office and blinked at the relative darkness after the bright sunlight. After slipping her hat off to let it hang down her back, she rang the little bell on the desk.

Ann Mercer, dressed in a black dress with a starched white apron and hat came out from the back room. "Cait. I'm so glad you're here." The nurse clasped Cait's hands. "Beulah's been asking for you."

Cait's heart was pounding so loudly she was surprised Ann couldn't hear it. "What happened? Is she all right?"

Ann's expression grew somber. "I'll let the doctor talk to you."

The room spun and Cait gasped. "What's wrong with her?"

But Ann only led Cait up the stairs to the rooms Doc used for seriously ill or injured patients. Cait's memories of this place were anything but good. Her father's broken and bloody body. The bitter smell of medicine and alcohol. The cloying scent of death.

Cait forced herself to breathe steadily, to shut out the horrific images that returned to haunt her.

"Wait here. I'll get the doctor," Ann said. She left Cait standing in the hallway while she entered the same room where Tremayne Brice had died.

Cait tilted her head back against the wall and stared at a crack in the white ceiling. A tear trickled down her cheek and she brushed it away impatiently. She'd had a bad feeling about Beulah the day they went into town. Why hadn't Cait checked on her the next day? Beulah wasn't a spring chicken anymore and she lived all alone. She could've died there and nobody would've found her for days.

Another tear escaped. If she hadn't been so caught up in Win and the past, she would've noticed Beulah hadn't shown up when she said she would.

The door opened and Ann emerged, followed by Dr. McKay. Four inches over six feet and weighing over two hundred pounds, Dr. McKay looked more like a logger than a doctor.

"What happened? How is she?" Cait asked immediately.

Dr. McKay's brown eyes filled with compassion. "Beulah doesn't have much time left. I'm sorry."

Cait's vision faded in and out and she felt someone steady her.

"Cait? Can you hear me?" the doctor asked.

She blinked and found Dr. McKay's concerned face directly in front of her. "What—"

"She's known about it for some time, but didn't want to tell anyone, especially you. She wanted to spare you."

Cait's heart tightened with fear. "What's wrong with her?"

"She was having pains in her chest and stomach, but

didn't come see me until she started coughing up blood."
Dr. McKay licked his dry lips. "She knew it was only a matter of time then."

"She should've told me!" Anger sharpened Cait's voice and she glared at the doctor. "Why didn't she tell me?"

Ann rubbed Cait's arm. "You know Beulah better than any of us. Would she have wanted someone fussing around her?"

Riddled with guilt and pain, Cait could only shake her head. "I didn't even notice," she whispered hoarsely.

"Beulah was a master at hiding her pain." Dr. McKay smiled slightly. "She's also a stubborn old woman."

Cait released a watery laugh. "That she is." She took a deep breath and locked her gaze on the door hiding Beulah from her. "Can I see her?"

"Of course." Dr. McKay opened the door for her. "Try not to tire her."

Her mouth suddenly bone dry, Cait nodded. She forced herself to walk into the dim room, her knees trembling. At first she couldn't even see Beulah buried within the bedclothes. Then she spotted her withered face, which was the same color as the milky white pillow. Cait curled her fingers into her sweating palms and the ball of dread that had dropped into her stomach grew.

"Beulah?" she called out softly.

The wizened woman, who appeared years older than she had four days earlier, opened her eyes. She seemed to have trouble focusing and Cait moved closer, leaning down to clasp her cool, bony hand.

"I'm right here, Beulah," Cait said, sinking into a chair close to the bed.

Beulah turned her head and her rheumy eyes settled on Cait. The barest of smiles touched her dry, blue-tinged lips. "What's with the . . . the sad face?" she asked in a weak voice.

Cait attempted a smile, but knew it fell flat. "Why didn't you tell me?"

Beulah's thin eyelids flickered. "Because I . . . I didn't

want you . . . carryin' on. I've made . . . my peace with my
Maker. D-don't know where I'll . . . end up, but I done the
best I could." She wheezed and began to cough with a
deep, harsh sound that made Cait's chest ache in sympathy.

Cait leaned over Beulah and touched her leathery
cheek. "Shhhh. Take it easy. No need to rush."

Beulah's hacking finally subsided but it took a few more
minutes for her to regain her breath. "I only got . . . one
last thing to do." She paused and her eyes filled with moisture. A tear rolled down the side of her face into her thin
gray hair. "You was like . . . a daughter to me, Cait. I . . .
know I never showed it, but . . . I love you like you was . . .
my own."

Cait's throat constricted and for a moment she couldn't
breathe. "You were like a mother to me, Beulah. I don't
know what I would've done without you." Her voice broke.

"You'da survived. You're . . . a strong one. Like me."
Again Beulah stopped to catch her breath. Her lungs rattled. "That fellah . . . Taylor . . . he's the one . . . ain't he?"

Cait nodded, not surprised by her perceptiveness. "He
doesn't know."

"Tell him!"

Cait flinched at the forceful words. "I-I can't."

"Why?" For a moment, Cait saw Beulah's former strength
of will in her eyes.

"He ran out on me. I hated him."

"You love him." Beulah closed her eyes as her breath
rasped noisily.

Cait bowed her head, thoughts and feelings skittering
around like water on a hot griddle. She'd spent ten long
years hating him. He'd abandoned her, left her to face
bearing their child alone. Then she'd miscarried and lost
her ability to have more children. She'd blamed Win all
these years, yet wasn't she equally at fault? If anyone had
forced anyone, it was Cait who'd forced herself on Win.
He'd tried to resist, but she'd continued to tease him, and
she'd been so smug when he'd succumbed to her. So who
was truly at fault?

"You were . . . only a girl," Beulah said, as if reading Cait's thoughts. "But you're . . . a woman now. Don't let . . . him get away again."

"I don't know if I can."

"You . . . c-can do anything you . . . put your mind to." Beulah gazed at her with affection, pride, and love.

"I'll try."

Beulah stared at her a long moment. "I ain't . . . gonna ask you to promise." The rasping grew louder. "Your decision. Your life." Beulah's eyes closed and Cait could sense her spirit leaving.

"No, Beulah. Please." Cait perched on the edge of her chair, grasping Beulah's thin hand between both of hers.

Beulah took a deep, shuddering breath, then lay still.

Cait fell to her knees beside the bed and buried her face in the colorful quilt.

Now she was completely alone.

Chapter Seven

WIN ROCKED RHYTHMICALLY in the chair he and Cait used to squabble over, remembering the past with bittersweet nostalgia. The deepening twilight added to the melancholy that had plagued him all day. Earlier he'd managed to keep busy feeding the horses, as well as green-breaking one of the mustangs. The horse needed more work to make a decent cattle horse, but he knew Cait could handle that part of the training. He'd seen her do it enough when they were younger. He'd also spent a couple of hours talking to Deil and managed to lure the stallion close enough to eat a thick carrot Win had tossed on the ground only three feet from where he stood. He knew he'd only won a single skirmish. He still had the main battle ahead of him.

Now more than ever, Win was anxious to tame the stallion and put as many miles between himself and Cait as possible. There was no doubt she was drawn to him, just as he was tempted by her. But now that Duffy knew Win was staying with Cait, Win couldn't spend a minute longer here than he had to. When he arrived, he'd thought Tremayne would be there to act as a chaperone, but alone with Cait, he knew the gossip was only a whisper away.

A movement down the road caught his attention and he stood to see the figure more clearly in the disappearing light. He recognized the black and white pony first. As Cait approached, he noticed the slump in her shoulders. Apprehension slithered down his spine.

Cait drew her pinto up by the corral and Win strode out to meet her.

"How is she?" Win asked.

Cait's spine stiffened but he couldn't see her face as she concentrated on removing her mare's tack.

"She's—" Cait cleared her throat. "She's gone."

Win silently damned fate for taking Cait's friend so soon after her father's death.

Cait carried her saddle into the barn and Win followed. She stacked the saddle in its proper place but remained standing there, her back to him as she fingered the latigo laces. "She'd been wasting away for months and I didn't even notice."

Win wasn't certain which was worse—her grief over Beulah or her self-loathing. "I'm sorry, Cait," he said awkwardly.

"First Pa, now Beulah." She turned slowly and raised her gaze to Win. The hollow sadness in her eyes was like a spear through his chest. "Are you going to leave me, too, Win?"

He ignored his own warnings to keep his distance and hugged her. "Awww, Caity."

She stiffened, then slowly relaxed into his embrace, her weight resting more fully against him. She wrapped her arms around his waist and laid her cheek in the center of his chest. The same protectiveness he'd felt for her when they were children swamped him. He'd never felt this fierce emotion with any other woman.

He rubbed her back with a soothing up-and-down motion

and rested his chin on her crown, whispering gentle, calming words. He didn't realize she was crying until her tears soaked through his shirt, dampening his skin. Tightening his embrace, he kissed the top of her head.

"Let it all out, Cait. It's okay," Win murmured.

Dust motes swirled around them and the horses' quiet whickers wafted in with the cool evening air. Insects buzzed and an owl hooted.

Win had lived the past ten years riding from one ranch to the next, spending his money in every saloon he could find, and never leaving more than a soon-forgotten memory behind. He'd never been tempted to stay in one place longer than it took to do what he was hired to do. There was always another job, another saloon, and another woman down the road.

None of those things were what he wanted. Not anymore. Cait had stolen his heart all those years ago and he hadn't even realized it was missing until this moment. But what could he do about it?

"Are you hungry?" he asked when she shifted in his hold.

"Not really."

"Did you eat something in town?"

He felt her shake her head against his chest.

"Why don't we go inside and I'll see what I can throw together?"

Cait eased back and lifted her head. "Last time you did the cooking, we ended up gnawing on burnt beef and nearly raw potatoes."

He chuckled, remembering his attempt long ago at making supper when he'd complained about Cait's cooking one night while he and his pa'd been visiting. "I've never criticized a woman's cooking since."

He expected a chuckle or maybe a smile, but Cait merely looked at him somberly. "Were there a lot of women, Win?"

Surprised by the question, his amusement bled away. He shrugged and looked past her. "A few."

"Why didn't you get hitched to one of them?" There was only curiosity in her voice.

He forced a laugh. "One or two tried to harness me, but I'm not the marrying kind, Cait. I always wanted to follow the wind, see what lay down the next road."

"Sounds more like a tumbleweed than a person."

This time his amusement was genuine. "I suppose it does to someone who's lived in one place most of her life. After my ma died, Pa just didn't have the heart to settle down with another woman. The closest I had to a home was this place."

She stepped back and he dropped his arms. She eyed him shrewdly. "So why'd you stay away for ten years?"

The fading light was his ally as he lied through his teeth. "After what I did to you, I figured your pa would be holding a shotgun next time I stopped by."

"I never told him, and he never mentioned it so I figured he didn't know. What about your pa? Didn't he think it was strange that you wanted to leave so early that morning?"

"I got my drifting ways from Pa. He figured I just got a powerful itch to move on and followed." The blatant lie burned like acid. It was his father who had insisted they leave immediately. He'd known what Win and Cait had been up to, and he hadn't approved. Adam Taylor had been married to a half Indian woman for six years. He knew about folks' narrow-mindedness firsthand, and had informed his son that unless he wanted to make Cait's life miserable, he'd leave her alone. There was no choice to be made. Win rode away.

"Did your pa know?"

When did she start reading my mind?

Cait's point-blank questions gnawed at Win's conscience. He'd never liked lying or people who did it, yet here he was spinning tales like some crazy old mountain man. "Why all the questions now, Cait? That was ten years ago."

"We've danced around it ever since you got here. I'm getting tired of not knowing why you left the way you did." She glared at him. "I have a right to know."

"Why?" he asked, hoping to keep her off-balance enough that she would drop the question-and-answer.

She stared past him. "You took my virginity then rode off like it meant nothing."

Although her reason made sense, Win knew she was hiding something from him. "What did it mean to you?" he asked quietly.

Cait hadn't expected him to turn the question around on her, but she should have been prepared to give him an answer. She'd thought about Beulah's words during the long afternoon after she met with the undertaker to discuss the funeral. She'd argued with herself while riding a circuitous route back to the ranch, delaying seeing Win for as long as possible.

Beulah had given her a choice, unlike her father, who'd taken it away when he'd made her promise not to kill the murdering stallion and to have Win break it. It would've been so easy without that promise. One well-placed bullet and her father's death would be avenged and Win wouldn't have disrupted her life.

Isn't that what she wished?

"Cait." Win's voice brought her out of her dark thoughts. "What did that night mean to you?" he repeated.

You were ... only a girl, but you're ... a woman now. Don't let ... him get away again.

You ... c-can do anything you ... put your mind to.

I ain't ... gonna ask you to promise. Your decision. Your life.

Beulah's last words echoed in Cait's mind. How had she known Cait had crossed that fine line from love to hatred and back to love?

"It meant everything," Cait whispered, her throat full and tight. "I loved you, Win. When we were children, you always understood me. I didn't even have to speak and you knew. Why didn't you understand that night?"

His Adam's apple dove up and down, and his eyes glittered brightly. "I knew, Cait."

Shock and dismay filled her and she stepped away, putting more space between them. "Then why?" The truth hit her and she nearly doubled over with pain. "You never loved me, did you?" Her voice quavered.

Win crossed the distance between them and grabbed her arms. "I did, Cait. I loved you. I *love* you." His eyes widened and his breathing paused. "I never meant to hurt you. I only wanted to protect you."

Frustration made Cait clench her hands at her sides. "Protect me from what? *You* were the one who hurt me!"

"I'm part Indian, Cait."

She stared at him, even more confused. "So?"

"Pa said if you and I got married, you'd be treated like trash. I couldn't do that to you."

Her mind sifted through his confession and one fact jumped out. "Your pa made you leave that morning."

Win jerked back. "He didn't make me. He just explained to me why I couldn't stay."

Cait closed her eyes as she tried to readjust her thinking after having her memories clouded by ten years of hatred and pain. Maybe it was time to clear the air once and for all. Her heart hammered against her ribs as she struggled to find the words she needed. "After you left, I was hurt and angry, but I kept hoping you'd come back. One week led to a month, to two months. And that's when I knew something was wrong."

Win frowned. "What do you mean?"

She felt the heat of embarrassment, but said, "I'd . . . I'd missed my monthly."

It took only a moment or two for him to grasp the meaning. "Cait," he said hoarsely, "I didn't even think about—"

"Neither did I until I was faced with it." She took a moment to gather her composure. "Beulah found me crying by the pond where we used to go swimming. I couldn't tell Pa and there was no one else I trusted enough to confess my shame."

"I'm sor—"

Cait held up her hand. "Don't. It's in the past. Just let me get it out before I lose my nerve." She forced a weak smile. "Beulah promised to help me. She also gave me a kick in the butt whenever I was feeling sorry for myself. She reminded me that I was carrying a child, the most precious gift a woman can receive.

"My trousers were starting to get tight and I was wondering how much longer I could hide my condition from Pa, when it happened." She wrapped her arms around herself and began to pace. "It started with cramps in the morning and by the afternoon, I knew something was wrong. I'd started bleeding."

Win's face was silvery white in the moonlight coming through the open door. Cait turned away, unable to bear his agonized expression.

"I wasn't thinking very clearly, but I knew I couldn't let Pa see me that way. I rode over to Beulah's. By the time I got there, I—" The remembered fear and helplessness made her voice break. "The saddle had blood all over it and I would've fallen off my horse if Beulah hadn't helped me. I stayed at her place for a week until I was well enough to leave. We told Pa I was taking care of Beulah."

"The baby?" Win asked in a hoarse whisper.

"I lost it," she said bluntly. "Beulah told me there was nothing I could've done, but I still blamed myself. I kept thinking that maybe if I hadn't ridden over to Beulah's, the baby would've lived. Then Beulah told me that I'd never be able to bear a child again." She hardly noticed the tear that rolled down her cheek. "That's when I started to hate you. I blamed you for the loss of our baby, and I blamed you for turning me into something less than a woman, a person who could never marry and have a family. Everything was your fault."

"It was," Win said in a raspy voice. "If I hadn't ridden away . . ."

Without thought, Cait went to him and placed her hand over his mouth. His whiskers rasped her palm and a sensuous shiver skated down her spine. "It wasn't anybody's fault. Not yours. Not mine. Beulah kept telling me that and I never believed her until today."

Win grasped her wrist and lowered her hand from his mouth, but he didn't release her as he brushed his thumb across her knuckles. "Why today?"

"She knew it was you," Cait said, ignoring his question. "How?"

"I don't know. She just did. She told me to stop acting like a child and start behaving like a woman. She was right. I've been hiding from it for so long." She reached up and cupped his cheek in her palm. "Even when I hated you, I loved you. I never stopped, Win. Beulah made me face the truth."

Win groaned and swept her into his arms. He hugged her close and Cait accepted his strength and warmth. Maybe she'd used the excuse that she couldn't have children to keep her distance from men, but the truth was she'd only wanted one man.

Win Taylor.

He kissed her hard, almost savagely, and Cait welcomed his possessiveness. She returned his kiss equally as passionately, determined to show him what she'd kept inside, hidden beneath hurt and bitterness.

Deil's frantic whinny startled them apart, and Cait jolted out of the circle of his arms. The timing couldn't have been worse and she barely managed to stifle a groan of disappointment. "Do you think the mountain lion's back?"

Win nodded grimly and Cait noticed his lips were slightly swollen from their kiss. "Stay here," he ordered.

"No. This is *my* ranch and you're not going to leave me behind."

Win's eyes glittered and a crooked smile claimed his lips. "All right, but stay behind me."

She didn't argue, but would do what she had to. She pulled her rifle from her saddle boot, glad she'd carried it in with the saddle instead of leaving it outside by the corral. Win retrieved his revolver from his bedroll in a corner stall and stalked to the wide doorway. Cait followed closely. He stood there, peering into the twilight and sniffing the air like a predator scenting his prey.

Deil paced back and forth in the corral, his attention focused on something only five or ten yards from his position.

Fortunately the moon was full, and Cait spotted a slowly moving shadow not far from Deil's corral, on the far side near a stand of bushes. She'd never known a wild animal, especially a cat, to come so close to buildings.

"It's over there." Cait raised the rifle to her shoulder.

Win slid his Colt out of its holster. "Dammit, I'm too far away for a decent shot."

"I'm not," Cait said evenly, although her heart was threatening to make a break from her chest. She could see the faint outline of the cat and centered her sight on what appeared to be its head.

Deil reared up repeatedly, slamming his front hooves on the ground. He grew more frantic as the lion crept closer.

Cait's finger wavered on the trigger. All she had to do was delay firing and the cat would take care of the hated stallion for her. Either the lion would kill Deil or the horse would be injured so badly he'd have to be put down. And Cait wouldn't even have to break her promise to her father.

"He's only a horse, Cait," Win whispered close to her ear. "He didn't murder your father. He doesn't deserve to die."

"You didn't see him." An unexpected sob rose in her throat. "Deil kept rearing up and Pa kept rolling, trying to get away."

"Deil was terrified, Cait, and just like when people are scared, they lash out at what they fear most. He was afraid of your father, and he reacted the only way he knew."

The cat stalked closer to the corral and Cait followed him with her rifle.

"It might seem that Deil hated your father, but he was reacting the only way he knew how." Win paused and said quietly, "Just like when you were scared, Caity."

The cat rose up and launched itself upward. Cait squeezed the trigger and the rifle kicked her shoulder. The mountain lion dropped like a rock and lay motionless just outside the corral.

Cait closed her eyes and slumped. She felt Win take

the rifle from her numb hands, and his arm encircled her shoulders.

"You did it, Cait," he said. His chest rumbled against her arm.

She gazed up at him. "Why didn't you just take the rifle and do it yourself?"

"Because it was your decision, Cait. You had to make the choice."

"What if I made the wrong one?"

Win smiled gently. "You wouldn't have."

"How could you be so certain?"

"Because I know you, Cait."

She thought about that for a minute, then smiled. "Yes, you do."

"Go on inside and I'll take care of the cat," Win suggested.

She clung to his arm. "Will you come to me when you're done?"

"Do you want me to?"

She released him, suddenly uncertain if he wanted what she did. Or even if she had the right to ask. "I love you, Win, and I don't give a damn what people say. But I can't give you children." Her throat choked off the rest of her words.

Win's expression filled with grief. "If I'd have known, I would've been here for you, Caity. I swear it. I wouldn't have let you go through that alone."

"I know." She could barely squeak out the words and quickly looked down.

Win raised her face with a gentle grip on her chin. "Since I couldn't have the woman I loved, I never planned to get married, which meant I'd never have children. But if you're able to put up with what people will say about us, then I'd be honored to become your husband."

Cait's eyes burned with unshed tears. "I'll be expecting you in the cabin."

He grinned and Cait was struck by how much he

resembled the boy she'd fallen in love with so many years ago. "Yes, ma'am."

She watched him leave but turned away before he began his grisly task. Turning her attention toward Deil, she couldn't help but feel that something between them had changed. When the stallion met her gaze, his eyes no longer appeared to mock her. Instead, she saw his pride and something akin to gratitude. She shook her head, laughing silently at her imagination.

Then Deil deliberately approached the end of the corral closest to her and tossed his head. Cait held her breath and forced herself to walk slowly toward him. She held out her hand as she neared him but only got within a yard before Deil backed away nervously. He gazed at her and seemed to nod, then turned away and pranced around the corral.

Cait watched him, allowing her admiration and hopes to rise. Her heart swelled with joy and contentment until it seemed to fill her chest.

She nodded to Deil, then turned to walk to her cabin to await Win's arrival. This time she'd give him a true homecoming.

Epilogue

WIN HELD A carrot out to the frolicking stallion, and Deil trotted over to take it almost daintily from his hand. Win smiled and scratched the horse's forehead.

"You think you're so tough, but you're just a pussycat," Win teased the stud.

The ebony horse whinnied in indignation and trotted away.

Win laughed at the stallion's antics. After he and Cait had finally managed to tame him, Deil acted more like a spoiled child than the prize stud of the Brice-Taylor Ranch.

Win turned away from the corral and spotted his wife strolling toward him with a radiant smile that made her eyes glow with happiness. Love and contentment made his own lips turn upward.

When she drew close enough, he wrapped an arm around her waist and tugged her close to his side. "What're you looking so secretive about?"

Her eyes danced with affection and mischief, a combination that never failed to ignite the passion that always smoldered close to the surface.

She sniffed. "As if I could keep any secret from you."

"You managed to keep my birthday present secret for a full five hours," he teased.

She stuck her tongue out at him. He laughed and dropped a kiss on her impertinent nose.

Comfortable silence surrounded them as they watched Deil trot around the pen.

"Do you think he knew?" Cait asked softly, burrowing closer into Win's side.

"Who?"

"My father. Do you think he knew why you left that morning, and he tried to make it right when he made me promise to send for you?"

"I don't know. Maybe." Win had thought the same thing a time or two but never voiced it.

"I think he knew, and I think he used Deil to bring us back together."

Win thought about that a moment. "If that's so, I owe him."

"We both do." Cait took a deep breath. "I went to see Doc this morning while I was in town."

"What's wrong? Are you sick?" Win demanded, fear making his voice curt.

"No, everything's fine." She smiled and he was shocked to see moisture glimmering in her eyes. "We're going to have a baby."

Win's vision narrowed and wavered, and he was aware of Cait steadying him.

"But I thought—" He broke off, uncertain what to say.

"Beulah wasn't a doctor," Cait said quietly. "I told Doc what happened with the first child. Doc wants to see me every month, just to make sure everything's going all right with this one."

Win stared at Cait's calm, composed features. He had

a million questions, but now didn't seem the time to ask. Instead he wrapped his arms around her and swung her around. "We're going to have a baby!" Suddenly he set her down, terrified he'd inadvertently hurt her. "Are you all right? Did I—"

"No, you didn't hurt me." Cait laughed. "And I don't expect to be treated like glass for the next six months."

"But you will be careful. And no more breaking horses. I'll take care of that. I can do the chores, too. And you should take at least one nap a day to make sure you don't get too tired."

Cait jabbed him in the ribs with her elbow, effectively silencing him. "Doc said definitely no breaking horses and I agree with him. However, doing my chores won't hurt the baby or myself unless I try to lift something too heavy." She placed her palms over her still-flat abdomen. "I want this baby as much as you do, Win. I'll be careful." With her forefinger, she drew an X over her left breast. "I promise."

Win captured her hand and held it against his chest as he hugged her close. His throat felt clogged and he struggled to breathe past the lump there. "I love you, Cait."

"I love you, too," she whispered.

A black and white butterfly landed on the corral pole less than two feet away. Win turned Cait in his arms so her back was against his chest and she could see the striking butterfly.

"Aren't you going to catch it?" Win teased.

Cait sank into him and laid her hands over his, which were clasped at her waist. "I don't catch butterflies anymore."

"Why's that?"

She leaned her head back against his shoulder and tilted her face up to meet his gaze. Her eyes sparkled with love. "If I caught them, they'd never find their way home . . . like you did."

The butterfly fluttered away and Win smiled, silently wishing it luck in finding home.

TURN THE PAGE FOR A PREVIEW OF

JODI THOMAS'S

NEXT HISTORICAL ROMANCE TELLING
LACY'S STORY

A Texan's Luck

COMING IN NOVEMBER FROM JOVE BOOKS

LACY FOLDED A few dollar bills into the last pay envelope and stuffed it in the bottom drawer of her desk. She leaned back, breathing in the familiar smells of the print shop. Ink, sawdust, paper, poverty. Home.

In the two years since she had taken over the shop, she managed to make the payroll every month but one. Once she'd taken all the money from the cashbox and traveled halfway across Texas to meet her husband. She shrugged. Once she'd been eighteen and a fool.

As the wind howled outside, Lacy closed her eyes, remembering how excited she'd been when she learned that Frank Walker Larson was stationed little more than a day's ride by train and then stage from her. Finally, her husband would be more than just a name on the marriage license.

She'd dreamed of how it would be when they met. He would be young and handsome in his uniform. She'd run into his arms and he'd tell her everything was going to be all right. After the year of taking care of his father and keeping the shop running, Lacy would cuddle into his embrace and forget all her worries.

She opened her eyes to the shadowy world of her small print shop. The real world. Her husband had been handsome, she admitted. So tall and important he took her breath away. But he hadn't welcomed her. His arms had folded around her in duty, nothing more. The Frank Larson she ran to was only a cold captain who preferred to be called Walker.

Lacy pushed away a tear as she remembered riding back on the dusty stagecoach that day. Now twenty, she was old enough to realize what a fool she had made of herself with Larson. The ride home had only prolonged her agony. Her body hurt from being used, but the dreams he killed scarred. The coach had been crowded with women wearing too much perfume and men smoking cheap cigars. When Lacy threw up in her handkerchief, the passengers decided that she would benefit from more air.

At the first stop, she was encouraged to take the seat on top of the stage. She'd pulled on her bonnet and gladly crawled into the chair tied among the luggage. As she watched the sunset that day, Lacy took the letters from her bag that Walker had written to his father years ago. She fell in love with her husband through reading his letters of adventure, memorizing every line as if it were written to her.

One by one, she watched them blow out of her hands, drifting in the wind behind the stage like dead leaves. That day she put away childhood. That day she'd given up on dreams.

Lacy stood in the dimly lit shop and pulled her shawl around her as if the wool could hug her frame. She stretched tired muscles. It was late and tomorrow would be a busy day. Every Saturday after all the papers were sold and the flyers nailed, Lacy rode out to her friends' farm. There, she could relax for a few hours. She'd play with Bailee and Carter's children and remember how years ago, when Sarah, Bailee, and she had been kicked off of a wagon train, they'd talked about what life would be like in Texas. Bailee had sworn she'd never marry and Sarah had thought she wouldn't live to see another winter. But Lacy, then fifteen, had boasted that she would marry and have so many children she would have to start numbering them because she'd run out of names.

"Five years ago," Lacy whispered to herself as she climbed the stairs. Five years since they came to Texas half-starved, out of money, and out of luck. Bailee found her man and had three sons with another baby on the way. Sarah wrote often about her twins.

"And then there is me." Lacy walked into her small apartment above the shop. "I had a husband for fifteen minutes, once."

Her rooms welcomed her with colorful quilts she'd made and tattered books she'd collected. When she first moved in and began to learn the newspaper business, she could barely read, but Lacy studied hard. Her father-in-law never tired of helping her learn those first few years. He'd treated her like a treasure even though she'd been little more than a rag-a-muffin when he'd paid her bail and married her to his son by proxy. From the first he talked of what a grand jewel she'd be to his son when the boy finally came home from serving in the army.

On evenings like this, she missed the old man dearly. She longed for the way he always talked about Walker as if his son were still a boy, and the way he could quote every article he'd ever written as though it were only yesterday and not material from twenty years in the business.

Before Lacy could heat water for tea, someone tapped on the back door.

She lifted the old Navy Colt from the pie safe drawer and went to answer. No one ever climbed the stairs to her back door except Bailee and she wouldn't be calling so late.

The minute she saw Sheriff Riley's stooped outline through the glass, she relaxed and set the gun aside.

"Evening." She opened the door to a cold blast of air that almost took her breath away. "Want to come in for a cup of coffee, Sheriff? It's cold enough to snow." The little porch area at the top of a narrow flight of stairs held no protection from the night and lately, the sheriff was thin as bone.

Riley shook his head. "Now you know I can't do that. What would folks say, a lady like yourself having a male guest after dark?"

She grinned, knowing no one would think a thing about the old man coming in from the winter night to sit a spell, but she wouldn't spoil his fun. "You know you're the only gentleman I ask inside. I'd shoot any other man who came knocking after dark."

Riley nodded. "I'd hope so. You being a respectable lady and all. I wouldn't even bother with a trial if I found a body on this porch." Though he'd listened to their confessions of killing a robber on the road to Cedar Point five years ago, the sheriff had always treated Lacy, Sarah, and Bailee more like daughters than outlaws.

The sheriff, like everyone else in town, regarded her as if her husband had simply left for the day and would be back anytime. Here, she was Mrs. Larson and there was a solidness about it even if there was no substance to the man she married.

Riley shifted into his coat like an aging turtle. "I just came to tell you that I got a telegram a few minutes ago saying Zeb Whitaker will be getting out of jail next week. I promised you I'd let you know the minute I heard."

Lacy fought to keep from reaching for the Colt. Big Zeb Whitaker was an old nightmare she laid aside years ago when he'd finally gone to prison. She could still feel his hands on her when he'd grabbed her and ripped the front of her dress open to see if she were woman enough to kidnap. She thought she killed him once. She would kill him for real if she had to. He was the first man Bailee, Sarah, and she met when they came to Texas and if Zeb had his way he would have taken their wagon and left them for dead.

"Lacy?" Riley said as though he didn't think she listened.

"Yes." She balled her fist to keep her hands from trembling.

"Rumor is he still thinks one of you three women has his stash of gold. I wouldn't be surprised if he showed up around here. I'm not too worried about Bailee way out on the farm with Carter watching after her, and Sarah tucked away where Zeb will never find her." Riley's face wrinkled. "But you . . . with your man gone and all."

He didn't need to say more. She knew she was alone. Her man wasn't gone, Walker had never been here. Except for the one brief meeting he was no more than a name on a piece of paper.

"I think you should leave town, Lacy." When Riley met her stare, he added quickly. "Just for a few weeks. Go see Sarah. Or maybe you have family back East you could visit."

Lacy wanted to scream, 'with what!' There were times over the past few years when she didn't have enough money left to buy food. Once she survived on a basket of apples Bailee brought in from their farm. The two friends never discussed how Lacy was doing, but Bailee always brought apples and eggs and more from the farm, claiming she wanted to trade them for a newspaper. More often than not, Lacy swapped a ten cent paper for a week's worth of food.

Lacy didn't want the sheriff, or anyone else in town, to know how little she had. They all seemed to think her invisible husband sent her money regularly. "I'll be fine here, Sheriff, don't worry about me."

Riley shook his head. "I don't know, Lacy. I'm not as spry as I used to be. I'm not sure I can face a man like Zeb Whitaker."

"He's aged too, you know. He's probably barely getting around. Who knows, he might come back to say he's sorry for causing us so much trouble five years ago."

"Mean don't age well." The sheriff frowned. "I'd feel a lot better if your man were here."

"Walker's down on the border fighting cattle rustlers,"

Lacy lied. She'd been using that excuse for months now; it was time she made up another reason. "I'll be all right. I have the gun you gave me."

Mumbling to himself, Riley turned and headed down the steep stairs. Lacy knew he wasn't happy about her staying, but this was her home, her only home, and she needed to run the shop. None of the three men who worked for her could take over her job.

Duncan was almost deaf. Folks coming in to place an ad had to stand next to his good ear and yell their order. Eli's bones bothered him so much in winter that he stayed on his feet most of the day. If he sat for more than a few minutes he seemed to rust. And, of course, Jay Boy was just a kid Lacy paid a man's wages because he supported his mother and little sister. He might be learning the business between errands, but he couldn't take over.

Lacy closed the back door and locked it. She had to stay. If Whitaker came, she'd fight. Maybe even die, but she wouldn't run.

TURN THE PAGE FOR A SNEAK LOOK AT

MAUREEN MCKADE'S

NEW HISTORICAL ROMANCE

To Find You Again

COMING IN JULY FROM BERKLEY BOOKS

Chapter One

"AMAZING GRACE, how sweet the sound . . ."

The voices of the Sunset Methodist Church members blended with wheezy organ notes to circle Emma Louise Hartwell. Emma's lips moved with the remembered words, but no sound came forth. Although she held her head high and aimed at the front of the church, her gaze followed dust motes, which drifted aimlessly through sunlight slanting in between boards covering a window. Next week the shutters would be removed, heralding the church's official recognition of spring.

Emma shuddered as the four walls closed in on her, and her heart pounded like a war drum. She should've waited until next Sunday to make her first public appearance. At least then she would have the illusion of freedom through the glass panes. Now there was only warped wood and shadowed corners, so unlike . . .

No! She didn't dare think about that, not while surrounded by those who had judged and sentenced her even though they didn't know the truth. Of course, if they knew everything, her total condemnation would be assured.

A hushed scuffle between the Morrison children caught Emma's attention. The boy and girl were tugging and punching at one another as their parents ignored them.

A Lakota child would never be so disobedient during a religious ceremony. They were taught from infancy to remain quiet and honor their elders, as well as revere their traditions and rituals. But then, the Lakota children wouldn't have had to sit on hard benches surrounded by four walls for two hours either. Emma, who'd grown up attending Sunday service, found herself anxious to escape the confinement. However, the intervening years had taught her to remain still and silent, like a mouse when a hawk passed overhead.

The final hymn ended with a concluding groan of the organ, and Emma herself nearly groaned in relief. She wished she could forego decorum and run outside like the children, but this was the first time she'd attended service with her family since her return five months ago. Her mother said they had wanted to spare her the pitying looks. Emma believed her parents wanted to spare *themselves* the town's censure.

Familiar townsfolk greeted John and Martha Hartwell, as well as their fair-haired daughter Sarah, but only a few acknowledged Emma's presence. Even Sally and George, whom she'd known for years, didn't stop to visit with her, but only sent her guarded nods, as if she had a catching disease. Still, Emma could understand their wariness. They had all grown up with the same stories she had heard about the "red devils."

But they hadn't lived in a Lakota village for almost seven years.

Emma followed her family to the doorway where the minister stood, shaking hands with the members of his flock.

"Fine job, Reverend," Emma's father said. He'd spoken those same words to the minister every Sunday that Emma could remember. It was another one of those oddly disconcerting reminders that some things hadn't changed.

"How is Emma doing?" the reverend asked.

Emma bristled inwardly, but kept her outward expression composed and her eyes downcast. They talked about her as if she wasn't standing right beside them. She hated that, but had promised her parents to remain as inconspicuous as possible.

"She's fine, Reverend," Martha Hartwell replied.

Emma risked sneaking a look at her mother and recognized the strain in her forced smile.

"We're thinking of sending her to visit her aunt back in St. Paul," her father interjected.

Emma gasped and opened her mouth to protest, but his warning look silenced her. Her cheeks burned with humiliation and anger. Her parents were going to rid themselves of their embarrassment one way or another. And they hadn't even deemed her important enough to discuss their plans for *her* future. Bitterness filled her and the air suddenly seemed too heavy.

"Excuse me," Emma whispered and stumbled past her sister, her parents, and the minister.

Her face burned from all the looks—pitying, accusing, and morbidly curious—directed toward her, as if she were a wolf caught in barbed wire. Her eyes stung, but she lifted her head high and held the tears at bay with the same stubbornness that didn't let her despair overcome her. She had lived a life that few white women could even imagine. Nobody had a right to judge her.

Nobody.

She rounded a bend and her gaze blurred as the tears finally defeated her control. Now that she was out of sight, she surrendered to the anguish twisting in her belly, making her gasp for air. But she didn't slow her pace. She prayed to God and Wakan Tanka, the Great Mystery, that she would escape the suffocating life that was now hers.

Nobody knew what she had left behind when she was returned—not even her family.

Pain arrowed through her breast and Emma stumbled. A firm hand caught her arm, steadying and shocking her.

"Easy, ma'am."

She whirled around and the stranger released her. The man hastily removed his hat and worried the brim between callused fingers. He wore brown trousers with a tan buckskin jacket and a red scarf around his neck. Thick, wavy, brown hair hung to his shoulders and his dark blue eyes were steady, but guarded. The man's black and white pony stood patiently on the road, its reins hanging to the ground.

"I'm sorry if I startled you, ma'am. It's just that I saw you stumbling-like and thought you might be sick."

The man's voice was quiet and husky, as if he didn't use it very often.

Emma's cheeks warmed and she dashed a hand across them to erase the telltale tear tracks. "No, that's all right. I didn't hear you."

A cool spring breeze soughed through the tree's bare branches and Emma shuddered from the chill beneath the too-light cape.

The man removed his jacket, revealing tan suspenders over a deep blue shirt, and awkwardly placed the coat over her shoulders. "You shouldn't be out here, ma'am. You'll catch your death dressed like that."

Emma's fingers curled into the soft material and the scent of cured deerhide tickled her nose with memories of another life. She caught herself and tried to hand the jacket back to him. "No. I can't—"

"I'm fine. You're the one who's shivering like a plucked sage hen."

She almost missed his shy, hesitant smile.

"Thank you," she said softly. Besides the leather, she could smell woodsmoke, horses, and the faint scent of male sweat in the well-worn jacket. "You're right. It was stupid of me to run off like that."

The man dipped his head in acknowledgment, and his long hair brushed across his shoulders.

"Are you from around here?" Emma asked.

"Yes'm. About four miles northwest."

That would make him a neighbor.

The steady clop clop of hooves directed Emma's gaze to the road. A man dressed in a cavalry hat and pants and a sheepskin coat rode into view. He drew his black horse to a halt beside the other man's mare.

"I was wondering what happened to you, Ridge," the man said, eyeing Emma like she was a piece of prime rib.

She shivered anew, but this time it wasn't from the cool wind.

"Ease off, Colt," the man called Ridge said without force. "The lady needed some help is all."

"She all right?" the man asked.

"The lady is fine," Emma replied curtly. She'd had enough of people talking about her like she was invisible to last a lifetime.

The clatter of an approaching buckboard put an end to their stilted conversation and Emma's heart plummeted into her stomach when she spotted her father's stormy expression.

Colt backed his horse off the road as the wagon slowed to a stop beside them.

"Get in, Emma," her father ordered in a steely voice.

Words of refusal climbed up her throat and she swallowed them back. She wouldn't humiliate herself or her family in front of two strangers. With tense muscles, she returned her Good Samaritan's jacket. "Thank you."

She kept her chin raised and her backbone straight as she climbed into the wagon's back seat. Ridge's hand on her arm aided and steadied her until she sat beside her sister.

"Stay the hell away from my daughter, Madoc. She doesn't need the likes of you," her father ordered.

Shocked, Emma only had a moment to give Ridge a nod of thanks before her father whipped the team of horses into motion.

Her mother, too, was pale. There would be little mercy from her father for embarrassing the family with her abrupt departure from church, and for her improper actions with the man called Madoc.

A man her father thought wasn't good enough even for her.

EMMA endured the awful silence all the way home by thinking about the man who'd been so kind to her. Madoc. The name sounded vaguely familiar, but she couldn't place it.

The wagon rattled into the yard and her father halted the horses in front of the house. He hopped down and helped Emma's mother, then her sister. Emma didn't wait, but clambered down herself, earning a disapproving scowl from him.

"Wait in the study, Emma," he ordered. Then he exchanged a brusque look with her mother.

Emmna settled into a wingback chair in front of the desk, sitting with her feet flat on the floor and her hands resting in her lap like a proper young lady. She would've preferred to sit with her legs folded beneath her, but she figured she'd provoked her father enough for one day.

Her mother perched on the twin of Emma's chair, her face pinched with worry. Her father, however, didn't appear the least bit anxious. No, he was spitting mad.

"What do you have to say for yourself, young lady?" he demanded.

She met his glowering eyes without flinching. "You and Mother have no right making decisions that affect my life without talking to me first."

Her father blinked, apparently startled by her forthrightness. "You're our daughter and you live under our roof. That gives us the right."

"Would you ship Sarah off without talking to her about it?"

"Sarah is not you."

Boiling anger and hurt engulfed Emma as she gripped the armrests. "What you mean is Sarah is still clean and pure, but poor Emma is used and soiled." Her nostrils flared and her fingernails dug into the armrests. Long-held silence exploded in defiance. "I am not a *thing* you can cast aside and forget about. I have a life. I have hopes and dreams."

"Which will never be realized around here," Emma's mother interjected almost gently. "No respectable man will have you."

Emma's stomach caved and she stared down at her fisted hands, which had somehow ended up in her lap again. She raised her head and turned to the older version of herself. "Thank you for sharing that with me, Mother."

Her mother flinched at the sarcasm, and even Emma was shocked by the depth of her own bitterness.

"That's enough, Emma Louise," her father ordered. He stood and paced behind the desk, his body silhouetted against the windows.

The regulator clock ticked loudly in the muffled silence. Emma concentrated on its steady rhythm—tick-tock, tick-tock—to block out the other sounds swirling through her head, but the memories were too powerful to be denied any longer.

Pounding hooves.
Gunshots.
Screams.
Blood.

Her heart hammering, Emma stared at her hands, almost surprised to find they weren't scarlet-stained. Instead, she noticed how they'd finally lost their dried parchment texture, but weren't nearly as smooth as they'd been seven years ago.

Her father stopped pacing, but remained standing behind his desk. "Maybe it was wrong of your mother and I to make plans behind your back, but we were only thinking of your best interests. As you know, your aunt Alice is a widow with no children. Your uncle left her very comfortable financially, and we doubt she'll ever marry again. She's willing to let you move in with her and begin a new life."

Emma took a deep, steadying breath. "I'm fond of Aunt Alice, but I want to stay here. This is my home, where I was raised. I don't want to leave."